EXILE'S GATE

C.J. CHERRYH

DAW BOOKS, INC.

DONALD A. WOLLHEIM, PUBLISHER

1633 Broadway, New York, NY 10019

DAW Book Collectors No. 731.

First Printing, January 1988

1 2 3 4 5 6 7 8 9

PRINTED IN THE U.S.A.

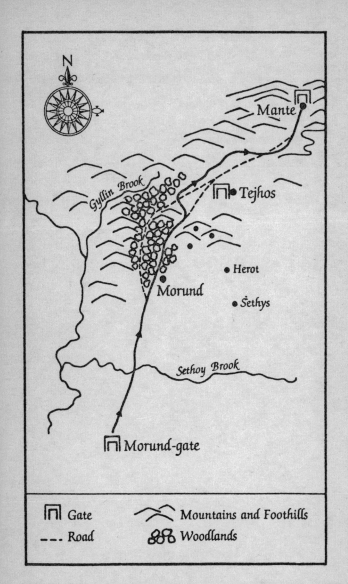

N

Mante

Gyllin Brook

Tejhos

Herot

Morund

Sethys

Sethoy Brook

Morund-gate

Gate Mountains and Foothills
Road Woodlands

Prologue

The qhal found the first Gate on a dead world of their own sun.

Who made it, or what befell those makers, the qhal of that age never learned. Their interest was in the dazzling prospect it offered them, a means to limitless power and freedom, a means to shortcut space and leap from world to world and star to star—instantaneous travel, once qhalur ships had crossed space at real-time, to carry to each new site the technology of the Gates and establish the link. Gates were built on every qhalur world, a web of eyeblink transport, binding together a vast empire in space.

That was their undoing . . . for Gates led not alone where but when, both forward and backward along the course of worlds and suns.

The qhal gained power beyond their wildest imaginings; they were freed of time. They seeded worlds with gatherings from the far reaches of Gate-spanned space . . . beasts, and plants, even qhal-like species. They created beauty, and whimsy, and leaped ahead in time to see the flowerings of civilizations they had planned— while their subjects lived real years and died in normal span, barred from the freedom of the Gates.

Real-time for qhal became too tedious. The familiar present, the mundane and ordinary, assumed the shape of a confinement no qhal had to bear . . . the future promised infinite escape. Yet once a qhal made that first forward journey, there could be no return. It was too dangerous, too fraught with dire possibilities, to *open up backtime. There was the deadly risk of chang-ing what Was. Only the future was accessible; and qhal went.*

Some went further than certainty, pursuing the hope of Gates which might or might not exist where they were predicted to be built. More lost their courage completely and ceased to believe in further futures, lingering until horror overwhelmed them, in a present crowded with living ancestors in greater and greater numbers. Reality began to ripple with unstable possibil-ities.

Perhaps some desperate soul fled to backtime, seek-ing origins or a lost life or a memory; or perhaps at last the very weight of extended time and energies grew too much. Might-have-been and Was were confounded. Qhal went mad, perceiving things no longer true, remember-ing what had never been true in the worlds which now existed.

Time was ripping loose about them—from ripplings to vast disturbances, the overstrained fabric of space and time undone, convulsed, imploded, hurling all their reality asunder.

Then all the qhalur worlds lay ruined. There re-mained only fragments of their past glory . . . stones strangely immune to time in some places, and in others suddenly and unnaturally victim to it . . . lands where civilization rebuilt itself, and others where all life failed, and only ruins remained.

The Gates themselves, which were outside all time and space . . . they endured.

A few qhal survived, remembering a past which had been/might have been true.

Last came humans, exploring that dark desert of worlds the qhal had touched . . . and found the Gates.

Men had been there before . . . having been victims of the qhal and therefore involved in the ruin; Men looked into the Gates, and feared what they saw, the power and the desolation. A hundred went out those Gates, both male and female, a mission with no return. There could only be forward for them; they must seal the Gates from the far side of time, one and the next and the next, destroying them, unweaving the deadly web the qhal had woven . . . to the very Ultimate Gate or the end of time.

World after world they sealed . . . but their numbers declined, and their lives grew strange, stretched over millennia of real-time. Few of them survived of the second and third generations, and some of those went mad.

Then they began to despair, for all their struggle seemed hopeless: one Gate omitted anywhere across the web would begin it all again; one Gate, anywhen mis-used, could bring down on them the ruin of all they had ever done and make meaningless all their sacrifice.

In their fear they created a weapon, indestructible save by the Gates which powered it: a thing for their own protection, and containing all the knowledge they had ever gained of the Gates—a doomsday force against that paradoxical Ultimate Gate, beyond which was no passage at all—or a truth worse than all their nightmares.

They were five when that dreadful Weapon was made.

There was one who survived to carry it.

Chapter One

Vision of horses, one gray and shadow, one star-white, both shod for war . . . one dark rider, one pale, across void and night—

*

In gray lines, horses and riders appear along the river-ridge, concealed in mist and the uncertainties of dawn. Weapons bristle up, lower, all in one nightmare movement of the charge. It is ambush, and below them, humans ride along the sedge-rimmed river, Ichandren's men, their weapons laid across saddle-bows. Ichandren looks up aghast at the first thin shout, the thunder that comes down on them in morning mist, the hedge of weapons that materializes out of the fog. The promised truce is broken, the valley has become a trap into which shadowy riders pour off either slope.

"Back!" Ichandren yells, wheeling his horse about.

The hindmost of his men shriek and die, pierced by lances, and the riderless horses splash along the reed-edged banks. The mist is full of shadows, shadows of enemies, of human riders fleeing in confusion, small bands battling in isolation. Even sound is distorted, echo mingling with present orders, screams and the clash of weapons ringing off the hills.

Some attempt retreat; but other shadows come pouring out of the mist behind, and horns sound in wild confusion. Ichandren shouts orders, but there is no relief, the enemy is too numerous, and his voice is lost in the confusion.

In despair he rallies such of his guard as he can, and turns and drives back the way he has come, in a world of shades and ghosts.

*

Vision of horses, the gray and the white, hooves descending, slowly, all of time and existence suspended upon that single motion—

*

In the opal dawn, in the mist, arrows fall like black sleet on flesh and steel, and thunder on wooden shields, finding chinks in the failing defense. Hammer and hammer again, blow after blow. Horses are down, threshing and screaming, crushing the wounded and the dead. Men flee afoot, cut down by the sweep of riders on the perimeters.

There is no more hope. Ichandren has met ambush. The fox has been out-foxed, and the enemy riders circle, cutting down those few who evade that last sweep.

But most rally around Ichandren, as horses go down, as men fall.

No arrows now. At the last it is swords and a battle afoot, humans against humans, Ichandren's men against those who have sold their souls to Morund.

"Bron!" Chei ep Kantory cries, seeing his brother fall, his place suddenly vacant in the defensive circle and Morund crests surging against it. He tries to gain those few feet, in that desperate knot about Ichandren, to die shielding his brother, for it is only a question of place now: weight of numbers bows their slight defense and breaks their shield-ring.

But thunder breaks behind him. Chei turns and lifts his sword, but there are two of them, helmed and masked, who come thundering toward him across the brook, throwing a fine spray in the first breaking of the sunlight.

*

Third stride, the gray horse and the white, stately slow, inexorable as fate—

*

The solemn procession reaches the killing-ground, the place of execution. They have walked this far, these last survivors of Gyllin-brook. Ichandren is not among them. The fox's head stands on a pike outside Morund-gate, his countenance strangely tranquil after so much he has suffered; and by now the crows will have claimed the eyes, as the crows and the kites have claimed so many, many others.

Carrion crows rise up here, at this end of all roads, black shapes against a pale, sickly sun, dull clap of startled wings that recalls the thunder of hooves on sand—

But that day is done, Ichandren is dead, his men have seen him die, and seen the things done to him, which made his death a mercy.

Now is their own turn. And disturbed birds settle back to the field, one solitary raven pacing on the roadside in the important way of his kind.

"Halt," lord Gault calls out, Gault ep Mesyrun, but this is not the Gault Ichandren knew, the brother in arms he once trusted. This is a different creature, who now holds lordship over Morund Keep. Qhal serve him, though his hair is human-dark and his body heavy and of no remarkable stature; the humans in his command fear him greatly. That is the kind of man he has become. And Gault has brought the prisoners here, to this place where crows gather, where the woods grow strange and twisted. He has cause to know this vicinity. In a place not far hence the woods grow strange indeed: no beast will go there, and no bird will fly above the heart of it. By that place Gault holds power over the south.

But they will go no further than this, for this purpose, for the disposal of enemies, here on the boundaries of law and reason. Horses shy and snort at the carrion smell of the place. White bits of bone, scattered by animals, litter the dust of the roadway, beside a bald hill—and on that hill stakes and frames stand against the sky, some vacant, some holding scraps of flesh and bone.

Blows and curses drive the prisoners staggering toward their fate, blows more cruel than the others they have suffered on this march, for even the guards fear this place and are anxious to be away. The prisoners go, bewildered; they climb most of the way up that hill before something, be it courage, be it only the breaking of a fragment of skull under a man's foot, or the regard of one black, beadlike raven eye lifting from its fixation on carrion—breaks the spell, breaks the line, and a man attempts escape. Then horses cut him off, two riders gather him up by the arms and haul him screaming to the hilltop. Other riders, humans with staffs and pikes, rain blows on the rebellion that follows, and drive the remainder to the stakes.

"I shall not leave you destitute," lord Gault follows them to say, riding his red roan horse to the crest, bones breaking under its hooves. "I leave you food. And an abundance of water. Can I do more?"

Chei ep Kantory is one who hears him, but dimly, as a voice among other voices, for the executioners have laid hands on him, as already they have taken Eranel, ep Cnary, Desynd, and red-haired Falwyn who is Ichandren's youngest cousin. He resists, does Chei, as he has been trouble on the march; but repeated blows of a pikestaff bring him down, at the last without a struggle, stunned and waiting only for whatever the enemy will do. The carrion stench is everywhere, his groping hand feels the brittle shards of bone among the silky dust on which he lies, the sky is a white, burning fire and the shadows of devils move across it, press at his body, drag at his booted ankle and clamp a grip about it which does not relax when they let him go.

A man curses. Chei recognizes it for Desynd's voice, distant and strained. Gault's laughter follows it. And because breath has come back to him and the shadows have gone he rolls over onto his hands, flinching from the bones, and tries the chain. Finally, because it is a solidity in so much that is flux, and a protection should the riders have some sport in mind, he huddles against the stake to which he is chained.

By each of them is set a water-skin. By each a parcel of food. And the lord Gault wishes them well, before he and his servants ride away.

Each of the condemned is secured alike, by the ankle to separate weathered posts; and at the fullest stretch of each chain a man is within reach of the man next at the fullest stretch of his. Their hands are not bound and they have their armor, but that is only to prolong matters.

In the evening the wolves come, dilatory, to a prey they have learned to expect when the riders are about. There is no haste. They are a bastard breed, and much of the dog is in them. It is in their eyes, in that way they creep forward, like hounds at hearth seeking some tidbit, with a kind of cunning and bravado neither breed alone would have. They retreat from such missiles as bone-chips and even handfuls of dust, they slink from shouts and threats, but in the long hours of the night they come closer, and rest, tongues lolling, one of them rising now and again to pace the line and to try the temper of this offering, whether any of them has yet weakened or determined to surrender.

By the second evening patience is rewarded. And at full stretch of the chain, in the night, the wolves and the survivors can reach truce, of sorts, while the terrible sounds proceed, of quarrels and the tearing of flesh and the crack of bone.

For the remaining nights, the wolves have leisure.

*

The horses stride into the world, the dapple gray

and the white, in an opal shimmering, stride for stride. Their hooves touch the leafy mold of a forested hillside and their legs stretch, take their weight—like the riders, they are bemazed by the gulf, and chilled by the bitter winds.

The riders let them run. They have no knowledge where they are . . . but they have taken such strides before.

*

The sun came mottled through a grove of twisted shapes, saplings, trees, blighted as by some perpetual wind . . . such places as this, they had seen before, and they had passed gates before the one which hove up on the hill above them, still powerful, still baneful and flinging power into the heavy air.

The horses ran out their terror, slowed as the trees grew thicker, and walked a gentler course in a forest where, among the trees, stood stones half again taller than horse and rider together. They snorted their acquaintance with a foreign wind and the smell of this world, while the riders went in silence.

But in time they stopped of their own accord, and the riders only listened to the world, the whispering of wind and branch, and looked about them at this strangely twisted place.

"I do not like this," Vanye said, and gave a twitch of his shoulders as he leaned forward against his saddle.

Horses dapple-gray and white, male and female, like the riders: Morgaine in black and silver, Vanye in forester's gray and green, her hair qhal-silver and his hair human-hued, pale brown beneath a peaked steel helm, wrapped round the rim with a white scarf . . . that was the look of them. They were lost, except for the road which led them—which they trusted they would find again: for qhal whenever they had built, had built much of the same pattern; and to leave the Gate and its confusion was the only thing that mattered, across such a gulf as that void at their backs, that cold nightmare which lay between them and a yesterday—Heaven knew how long lost.

They went armored and armed. Morgaine was liege and Vanye was liegeman; she was—what she was, and he was Man; that was the way of things between them.

"Nor do I care for it," said Morgaine, and started the gray stud moving, a gentle, careful pace.

There was no retreat for them. That, they neither one mentioned. Vanye cast a quick look back, where the thin, spiral-twisted trees hid all view of that great span which was a qhalur Gate—little different than other gates they had seen, very like one he had known, in a land like this one—but this was not that land: he knew that well enough, knew it in the patterns of the rare leaves which grew in dispirited clumps at the end of limbs, lit by a wan and (he thought, and time proved) westering sun.

Although the gate behind them stood still powerful, and disturbed the air and worked at the nerves, it could not carry them back, and it could not carry them where they had now to go, or tell them their direction. For now, it was only downslope, from standing stone to standing stone, in a woods as unwholesome as the feeling in the air.

Life here—struggled. What had feet to flee, fled; what rooted, grew twisted and strange, from the trees to the brush, the shoots of which were tormented and knotted, the leaves of which were deformed and often curled upon themselves. And the horses laid back their ears and shook themselves from time to time, likeliest with that same feeling that made the fine hair stand up on the body and made the ears think that there was sound where no sound existed, until they had put more and more of the hill between them and the gate.

They rode in amid a jumble of stones and trees, finally, a leaning conspiracy of broken stone walls and twisted saplings none of which attained great age, but many of which lay rotten or broken by winds.

Vanye looked about him as his white mare danced and fretted beneath him, hooves ringing on half-buried paving in quick, nervous steps, echoing out of time to the pace of the iron-shod dapple gray. "This was a keep of some sort," he murmured, and crossed himself anxiously, forgetting as he forgot in such moments, that his soul was damned.

"A great one," Morgaine answered him, whether that was surmise or sure knowledge; and Vanye blinked and stared round him a second time as the horses moved and the ruin of walls unfolded. "We have found our road again."

Hooves on stone. Buried pavings. Vanye conceived of the Road as a thing of all places, all gates, all skies: it was one Road, and the gates inevitably led to it.

"No sign of men," he murmured.

"Perhaps there are none," Morgaine answered him. "Or perhaps there are."

He took nothing for granted. He gazed about him with a warrior's practiced eye, looking for recognizable points, things by which he could make order out of this jumbled buff and white stone. These flat stretches, these narrower places were the foundations of houses, craftshops, warehouses. People—uncountable numbers of people would have dwelt in such a place, and plied their crafts; but how much land must they till, how feed so great a number in so rough a land, except they take their provender from war and tribute? It did not suggest peace.

He tried to imagine these ruins near him as they might have stood, bare foundations rising into forms which (he could not help it) very greatly resembled the keep and the barracks and the guesting-house of Ra-morij of his birth, in distant Andur-Kursh, a courtyard cobbled and usually having a standing puddle down the middle of it, where the scullery dumped its dirty water. It was gray cobbles in his vision, not the buff stone under the mare's hooves—was an aching touch of home, however cruel it had been in his living there.

He remembered other crossings of that gulf they had just passed, the night he had looked up to see two moons, and constellations strangely warped; that night he had first looked on a sea of black water, among drowning hills; a dawn that had risen and showed him a land unwalled by mountains for the first time in his life, horizons that went on forever and a sky which crushed him beneath its weight. He blinked this ruin about him clear again, in its desolation; and the cries of birds brought back keen memory, a presentiment of danger in the sea and the omen of the gray gulls, and the threat of moons unnaturally large.

A third blink, and it was forest, and they were black ravens that cried, and the stones held no present threat.

Behind them was dust, friends were long dead, and all they had known was changed and beyond recall, although the pain of parting was for them as recent as this morning and keen as a knife. He tried to be wise as his liege and not to think on it.

But when they rode over the shoulder of that hill, the ruin and the forest gave way to barren plains on their right hand, and sunset on their left. A wolf cried, somewhere beyond the hills.

Morgaine let slip the ring of her sword-belt, letting the dragon-hilted weapon which rode between her shoulders slide down to her side.

It had a name, that sword: *Changeling*. His own nameless blade was plain arrhendur steel. Besides his sword he had a bow of arrhendur make, and a quiver of good arrows, and a stone next his heart, in a small gray pyx, as a great lord had given it to him—as memory went, it had been very recent. But the worlds shifted, the dead went to dust; and they were in a place which made that small box no comfort to him, no more than that ill-omened blade his liege handled, on the hilt of which her hand rested.

Birds rose up from that horizon, black specks against the setting sun at that hour when birds would flock and quit the field; but not birds of the field, nothing so wholesome, gathered in hills so barren.

"Death," Morgaine murmured at his side. "Carrion birds."

A wolf howled, and another answered it.

They were there again in the twilight, yellow-eyed

and slope-shouldered, and Chei ep Kantory gathered himself on his knees and gathered up the weapons he had, which were a human bone in one hand and a length of rusty chain in the other; he gathered himself to his feet and braced his back against the pole which his efforts and the abrasion of the chain had cut deeply but not enough. The iron held. The food was gone, the water-skin wrung out to its last drops of moisture.

It would end tonight, he thought, for he could not face another day, could not lie there racked with thirst and fever, listening to the dry rustle of wings, the flutter and flap and the wafts of carrion-stench as a questing beak would delve into some cranny where flesh remained. Tonight he would not be quick enough, the jaws that scored his armor, the quick, darting advances that had circled him last night, would find his throat and end it. Falwyn was gone, last but himself. The pack had dragged Falwyn's body to the length of the chain and fed and quarreled and battled while Chei sank against the post that was the pivot and the center of all his existence. They had worried the armor to rags among the bones; the ravens helped by day, till now there was nothing but the bones and shreds of flesh, too little, perhaps, to content them.

"Bastards," he taunted them, but his voice was a croak like the birds', no more distinct. His legs shot pain through the tendons, his sight came and went. He did not know why he went on fighting. But he would not let them have his life unscathed, not do what ep Cnary had done, passing his food and water to Falwyn, to sit waiting for his death. Ep Cnary had lost a son at Gyllin-brook. It had been grief that killed him as much as the wolves. Chei grieved for a brother. But he was not disposed to quit. He worried at the chain hour by hour of his days, rubbing it back and forth on the post; he had strained himself against that limit to lay hands on the rusty links which wolfish quarrels over Desynd's body had pushed a hand's-breadth nearer: with his belt he had snagged it, some relic of a previous victim which was now his defense and his hope of freedom. He battered at the post now with all the force his legs and his failing strength could muster, and hoped that his weight could avail to snap it where he had worn it part way through; but it stood firm as the rock in which it was set: it was weathered oak, and it would not break.

The black-maned wolf moved closer, jaws agape, a distraction. It was always the notch-eared one that darted to the flank. He had seen this before, and knew her tricks. He spun and swung the chain, and Notch-ear dodged: Black-mane then, and the gray one—he gave them names. He taunted them with a voice that rasped like the ravens'. "Here, bitch, try again. Try closer—"

They came in twos and threes this time. He turned with his back against the pole, his right foot failing him, swollen in the boot and the chain, a lifeless thing at the end of his leg. It was that which the wolf caught, driving in with serpent-quickness, and he swung the chain at it, jabbed down onto its shoulders with the jagged bone and felt it snap on tough hide and bone. Jaws closed on his armor at knee and elbow, teeth snapping in front of his face and a wolf dodging with a yelp as he swung the chain in the limited range he had. The pack closed about him in a snarling maelstrom, out of which the flap of wings, the thunder of riders—he saw them in a whirling confusion, the pale horses, the gleam of metal, the pale banner of hair a-flutter in the wind—

—back, then, to that moment. The wolves shied away, their grip leaving him, all but the gray bitch, and a sword flashed, the rider of the white horse leaning from the saddle to strike—

He cried out then, falling against the post, which did not belong on that river-bank. It began again. He fell, and the riders, afoot, walking their horses across the debris of bones, came to take him to torment. That was the worst cruelty, that he was lost in a dream wherein the end began it all again.

The man fought him. Well he might, though there was little strength left in him. "Have care!" Morgaine cried as the chain swung, but Vanye jerked his head out of the way, guarded himself against a knee-thrust, and with the press of his weight and a twist at the arm, disarmed the wild-haired, armored man of the chain he wielded. It did not end the fight, but he had the man, then, beyond any dispute, gripped in both arms and carried struggling to the ground.

"Be still," he said in his own language, for the man was human. "Be still. We are not your enemies."

That did no good. "We are not here to harm you," Morgaine said in the qhalur tongue. And in the human: "Hold him still."

Vanye saw what she was about and edged further from the post, dragging the struggling man with him and drawing the ankle chain taut between the man and the post, as Morgaine took that small black weapon of hers and burned it. A smell of heated metal went up. One link reddened and bent under the pull, and the man writhed and fought his hold, but Vanye freed a hand and laid it on his cheek, shielding his vision from what a man of simple beliefs might not want to see, while iron sparked and sputtered and parted.

"There, man, there. You are free of that."

"Tie him," Morgaine said, being the crueler and the more practical of them both.

"I must," Vanye said, and patted the man's face and shared a look with him, one glance into blue and desperate eyes that sought—perhaps—some hope of him, before he took the man in both his arms, wrestled him over face down and sat on him till he could work loose one of the leather thongs from his belt and tie his hands behind him.

After that, the man seemed sane, for he stopped fighting and lay inert, only turning his face out of the unwholesome dirt, his cheek against the ground, his eyes open and staring elsewhere as if nothing that proceeded could interest him further.

He was thin, beneath the armor. There was filth all about, a stench of death and human waste and wolf. Vanye got up and brushed himself off, and bent to drag the man up to his feet with him.

The man kicked, a futile effort, easily turned. Vanye shrugged it off and hauled him up to his feet with a shake at the scruff, grabbed him up in a tight embrace from behind and held him there against his struggles. "Enough," he said, and when he had gotten his breath: *"Liyo,* a drink of water might improve his opinion of us."

Morgaine fetched the water flask from her saddle, unstopped it, filled the little cup that was its cap. "Careful," Vanye said, anxious, but careful she was, standing to the side, offering it for a moment until the man turned his head and committed himself to their charity.

Rapid sips, then, a trembling throughout the man's body then and after Morgaine drew the cup away. "We will not harm you," she said. "Do you understand?"

The man nodded then, a single movement of his head. And shivered in Vanye's grip—a young man, his beard and hair sunbleached blond and matted with every manner of filth. He stank, like all the air about this hill; dirt and gall-marks were about his neck where the edge of his armor had rubbed him raw, and the chained ankle would not bear his full weight.

"Who put you here?" Vanye asked him in the qhalur language, as Morgaine had spoken.

"Lord Gault," he thought the answer was. Or some name like that, which told him nothing.

"We will put you on my horse," Vanye said. "We will take you somewhere safe. We will not harm you. Do you understand me?"

Again a nod. The trembling did not cease.

"Easy," Vanye said, and supported him gently, the grip become an embrace of his left arm. He slowly led him to the slope where their horses stood—well-trained and waiting, but skittish near so much wolf-smell and decay. He sought after Arrhan's reins, but Morgaine took them up and held the mare steady for him. He did not offer the man the stirrup, considering his hands were bound. He only steadied the prisoner against

Arrhan's side and offered his hands for a stirrup: "Left foot. Come."

The man did as he was told. Vanye heaved him upward, pressing close with his body while Arrhan shifted and fretted, and the man landed belly down on the saddle, struggling then to right himself. Vanye set his own foot in the stirrup, stepped up and rested his leg across the low cantle and blanket roll till he could get hold of the man and haul him upright enough. Then he slid down behind him, occupying most of the saddle, all the while Morgaine held Arrhan to an uneasy standstill; and the prisoner rested against him, his leg hooked round the horn, for he had no strength to bring it over.

"I have him," Vanye said, and took the reins Morgaine handed up to him.

She had a worried look. So, he reckoned, had he; and he wanted clear of this place, wanted them on lower ground and less conspicuous, wanted the stink of death out of his nostrils—but he held it against him in human shape, inhaled it through his mouth much as he could, and thought that even his armor and his gear would hold the smell for days.

In front of him, leaning against him, the man gave a racking cough. *Disease and plague,* Vanye thought. It went with such places. He reined about carefully, following Morgaine as she mounted up on the gray. The stud was fractious too, snorting and working at the reins, but she did not let Siptah have his head. They rode carefully over the bone-littered ground.

"Are they near," Vanye asked the prisoner, "the men who did this to you?"

Perhaps the man understood. Perhaps he did not. He did not answer. Intermittently he underwent spasms of coughing, racking and harsh, then, exhausted, slumped against him, his body rolling more and more to the motion of the horse.

"He is fainting," Vanye said to Morgaine. "I think all his strength is going."

In a little time more, the man's head fell forward, and it was loose weight leaning against him. But when

Vanye pressed his hand over the man's heart he felt it beating steadily. It was a strong heart, he thought, of a man stubborn beyond all reason, and such a man might touch his sympathy—might, except such a man might be fair or foul, and he had known more than one enemy and more than one madman on this Road.

Morgaine led them back to the road again, and across it, to a place where a small river ran at woodsedge. In the last light, they rode a pathless track among the trees, in a land where they already knew that there were wolves, and men who had done the like of this. It was enough to know.

They gave him water, they brought him a long dazed ride deep within the twisted forest, laid him on a streamside and there freed his hands, the man of the pair giving him a little way-bread soaked in cordial so strong it stung Chei's throat.

After which they let him lie, busy at the making of their camp, and through his slitted, aching eyes, Chei saw them moving here and there in the light of a tiny fire, illusory and ominous. Chei's heart beat in panic when they would come near; it eased whenever they would seem occupied about their own business. Then he knew that he was safe for a while, as he had known that he was safe when the wolves were feeding: and in such intervals, as then, he drifted only scantly waking.

A shadow fell between him and the fire. He came awake, saw the reach toward him, and feigned unconsciousness as a hand rested on his brow. "There is tea," a man's voice said, in the qhalur tongue, "here, drink."

He did not intend to break his pretense. He was still even when a hand slipped beneath his neck, though his heart was hammering in fright; he stayed quite limp as the man lifted his head and slid support under his shoulders.

But the cup which touched his lips smelled of herbs and honey. A little of it trickled between his lips, warm and wholesome, and he swallowed, risking the harm in it—a sip which touched off a spate of cough-

ing and destroyed his pretense of unconsciousness.
The cup retreated, came back to his lips. He drank
again, eyes shut, tears leaking from between his lids as
he fought the rawness in his throat; and drank a third
sip, after which his head rested on the man's knee and
a gentle hand soothed his brow.

He ventured to open his eyes, and met a face human as his own—but he had learned to doubt appear-
ances.

All about them were twisted trees, the night, the
fire. He knew that he had come to Hell, and that this
qhalur woman from beyond the gate had laid claim to
what the qhal-lord this side of the gate had flung
away. These strangers had no use for revenge: there
was nothing he personally had done to them save be
born. There was nothing he knew that would be valuable to them. There was no cause at all for their mercy
to him save that they had use for him, and what use
the tall, lordly qhal had for a young and fair-haired
human man he knew all too well.

They would take him through the gate with them.
He would come back again, but with such a guest in
him as Gault had, an old thing, a living hell which
spoke with Gault's mouth and looked out through
Gault's eyes, and which was a sojourner there. Qhal
did not use qhal in that way, or it was rare. A healthy
human body would serve, when a qhal outlived the
one he was born with.

So they touched him gently, this qhalur woman and
this maybe-qhal who did her bidding. So they gave
him drink, delicate drink, perhaps because the great
qhal-lords gave him what they themselves drank, because it did not occur to them that it was too precious
to waste. So the man let his head down to the soft
grass and spoke to him reassuringly, looking to the
iron that banded his swollen ankle: "This is a simple
lock; I can strike it off, have no fear of me, I will take
good care." And he fetched a hand-axe and one flat
stone and another, to Chei's misgiving—but the axe-
blade was for a wedge, the one rock for a brace, the
other for striking, and the woman came and with her

own hands gave him more of the cordial against the shocks that ran through his nerves, gave him enough that his raw throat was soothed and his head spun while the man worked in soft, steady blows.

Surely they took good care for the body they claimed. There was something terrible in such careless use of their rich things, in the gentle touch of the woman's hand as it rested on his shoulder, and in her soft reassurances: "He will not hurt you."

It was one with the other madness, and Chei's senses spun, so that he was not sure whether the ground was level or not. The soft ringing of the metal resounded in his skull, the pain ran up from the bones of his leg and into his hip, till the iron fell away, and the man very delicately, with his knife, slit the stitching of his boot and said something to the qhal in words which made no sense—but Chei was far gone in the pain that began about his ankle from the moment it was free of its confinement, an ache that made him wish the chain back again, the boot intact, anything but that misery which made him vulnerable. He tried not to show it, he tried not to react when the man probed the joint; but his back stiffened, and he could not help the intake of breath.

The world was dim for a time after that shock. They went away from him. He was glad to lie still and not heave up the moisture they had given him; and he thought that he would, for a time, if he lifted his head at all. But the man brought a wet cloth warm from the fire, and washed his face and his neck and his hands with it.

"Do you want more water?" the man asked.

He did. He did not ask. It was a trick, he thought, to make him believe them, and he did not want to talk to them. Somewhere in the distance, wolves howled, and he shivered at the chill of water rolling down under his collar; that small twitch he could not suppress. For the rest he did nothing, lay still and cared as little as possible what they did.

Until he felt the man's hands at his armor buckles, unfastening them.

"No," he said then, and flinched from under that touch.

"Man, I will not hurt you. Let me rid you of this and wash the dirt off—only the worst of it. Then you can sleep till morning."

"No," he said again, and blinked the man clear in his vision—a human face, faintly lit by fire. The place was real, like the woods overhead, branches the fire lit in ghostly ways. He flinched as the touch came at his shoulder again, and struck feebly at it, being desperate.

"Man—"

"No. Let me be."

"As you will. It is your choice." Another touch, this time on his wrist, from which again he moved his hand. "Peace, peace, rest, then. Rest. Whoever did this to you is no friend of ours. You can sleep."

The words made no sense at all to him. He thought of the wolves, the ones he had named—he had known their faces, he had known their ways. They were terrible, but he knew them, what they would do, when they would do it: he had learned his enemy and he had known the limits of his misery.

But the qhal he could not understand. They would guard his sleep, fend away the wolves, do him whatever kindnesses pleased them: they would do no terrible thing until they had brought him to the gate, or to their own lands. There was no limit, then, no mercy such as the wolves would have shown.

"He might be a murderer," Vanye said, at the fire with Morgaine, sitting on his heels in that way that years out of hall made comfortable enough for him. "But so am I," he added with a shrug. "Whoever put him there—God requite."

"He will run," Morgaine said.

"Not with that foot. At least tonight. God in Heaven, *liyo*—"

Vanye hugged his arms about him, in the scant warmth of the fire they risked, and shook his head, and cast a glance toward the dark lump that was their guest, lying just beyond the firelight. It was a fair, green land they had left the other side of the gate. Their friends were aged and gone, a kinsman of his— was dust, he thought, for he once had thought the gates led only between lands; but now he knew that their span was years and centuries; and knew that if he looked up away from the fire he would see the too-abundant stars in no familiar pattern, the which sight he could not, this moment, bear. The breath seemed choked in him.

"We do not let him free," Morgaine said harshly. The fire shone on the planes of her face, winked redly from the eyes of the dragon sword. It had not left her side. It would not, this night.

"No," he said. "That I do know."

He felt cold, and bereft, and victim of a cruel choice which was Morgaine's doing—that she asked everything of him, every possession, every kinship, every scruple, the sum of which choices brought him here, where men fed each other to wolves. *I had everything I thought that I had dreamed of. Everything was in my hands—honor, kinship, a home that was mine—within the arrhend. There was peace—*

But Morgaine would have gone on without him. And with her, the warmth in the sun would have gone. And no one could ever have warmed him again, man or woman, kinsman or friend. The essential thing would have left his life, and beyond that, beyond that—

He had ridden into that dark gulf of the gates—it had been this morning, a bright meadow, a parting with his cousin, last save Morgaine herself who could speak the language of his homeland, last save Morgaine who knew his customs, knew the things he believed, remembered the sights of home. And it was already too late. Was dust, between two strides of the horses that bore them.

He shivered, a convulsive twitch as if a cold wind had blown over his back; and he bowed his head and rubbed the back of his neck, which the warrior's braid made bare. Honor demanded. Honor, he had back again. But he did not put off the white scarf, which made him *ilin*, a Claimed warrior, soul-bound to the liege he served; and when he asked himself why this was, his thoughts slid away from that question as it did from the things Morgaine tried to explain to him, how worlds circled suns and what made the constellations change their shapes.

So he thought, listening to the wolves, thinking that they were not alone, that this world had touched them already. They had in their care a man who depended on them for life, and who in someone's estimation had deserved to die by a terrible means.

He wished that he knew less than he did, or had seen less in their journeying.

"We cannot leave him; Heaven knows we cannot make speed carrying double. And Heaven knows—fever may take him by morning."

Morgaine stared at him, a flash of her eyes across the fire, out of a brooding silence. So he knew he had gotten to the heart of her thoughts, that she dismissed his worry for their guest as short-sighted, the matter of one life. She weighed it against other things.

"We will do what we have to," she said, and beneath that was: *I will do, and you will, or our ways part.*

There was always that choice. It was knowing that, perhaps, that made him choose to stay within *ilin*-oath and keep himself from other, more damning choices. He could not take another direction, in a strange land and outside the law he knew. And where was honor— when a man chose a woman, and refused to leave her even for his honor's sake; and a liege, and must not desert her, else he had no honor at all; and that woman and that liege lord, being one and the same, would never turn left or right for his sake, being bound by an oath still more dreadful than his.

He had no wish to serve what she served. Serving her, he served that terrible thing, as much as a man could and hold out any vestige of hope for his soul. Being Kurshin, and Nhi, and honorable, he sought after absolutes of law, and right; and that truth of hers, which killed the innocent and shattered law and right, shimmered beyond all his horizons, stark as the sword she bore—*here is absolute truth, man, here is truth beyond truths, which makes all justice void.*

Morgaine understood it. Morgaine did all that she did for that thing she served, did all that flesh and blood could do, woman or man; and took so little care for herself that she would not eat or drink, at times, would forget these things if he were not there to put food into her hand and to protest that he, he, being a natural man, needed rest even if she did not. He distracted her from her pursuit from time to time. And so few things could.

He gave her such comfort as he could, and they were not even lovers, Heaven knew and few guessed. They had shared a blanket in the beginning with her sword between, lately without so much as that caution to stay them; which was intolerable and gave him the more reason to chafe at this unwanted guest, and the demands of his own stubborn honor.

"I think," Vanye said quietly, "that he has no love of qhal."

"He is human," Morgaine said with a shrug. "And we do not know who left him to die."

I am not qhal, she was wont to insist, as long as he had known her—for in his own lost land the qhal were dreaded and damned; *halfling* had been Morgaine's ultimate admission to him, when at last he won a little of truth from her, none so many days ago as their time ran.

Now she let the implication of qhalur blood pass without a protestation. Perhaps she was preoccupied; perhaps she finally believed him enough to give up the lie—that pretense which had begun perhaps in kindness on her part and lasted in doubt of him.

Was that the last test, that I should ride this gate with you? But did you doubt me, liyo, *that I would keep my word?*

"Go, rest," she told him, brushing the last crumbs of their dinner into the fire. "I will watch a while."

He shifted his eyes to their guest, in the shadows. "If he has need of anything, wake me; do not go near him."

"I have no such notion," she said, and slid the pan into her saddlebag, there by her side, as if they could leave in the morning with their guest as weak as he was. But it was only prudence. They had not survived this long by leaving gear behind, if attack came on them. "If he has need of anything in your watch," she said, "you will wake me, the same."

"He is one man," Vanye said with a little indignation, and she frowned at him.

"Wake me," she said, being unreasonable on the matter.

So this land had frightened her too. And she grew irrational in little things.

"Aye," he said, and shrugged. It was little enough concession.

He loosened his armor, and wrapped himself in his cloak, wrinkling his nose from the stink the cloth had taken on from its little contact with the man, and thinking that he might never have it clean again.

In the morning, in the daylight, after sleep, he thought, the man might be reasonable—Heaven help them, they had no means to deal with a madman.

He must see what could be done to salvage the man's gear—as long as they were not traveling.

But for his part he was very weary, and his bones ached. So with his liege, he thought; but she had thinking to do, and he had none—it was Morgaine chose their way, Morgaine who decided matters, it was Morgaine who told him what he should do, and therefore he did not worry about that—only about the little matters—the horses, the gear, and how they should do what Morgaine had set them to do. And he was content enough with that arrangement.

Morgaine threw her own blanket over him as he lay there, a little settling of added warmth, in the which, his head pillowed on Arrhan's saddle, he relaxed. She patted his ankle as she let down the blanket, a gentle good night, a comfort at which he sighed, and thought after that, staring into the dark—for she had a way of doing that to him—that perhaps that gesture of hers had been intended for more than that, that if not for the damnable matter of their uninvited guest, if not for this world that threatened them and set them to sleeping turn and turn about, in their armor, that cursed, familiar burden which seemed to settle on heart and soul, with all its habits of fear—

So close they had been to being lovers. So very close.

He sighed again, but not for the same reason, and tried with all his mind to go quickly to sleep, with that good sense he had learned on this trail—that unbroken sleep was precious as food and water, and very often harder come by.

A hard lump pressed beneath his armor, against his heart. He felt after the chain which held it and pulled it loose for his comfort . . . careful of the case, for it was a perilous thing within, more perilous still as near the Gate as they were camped. The stone in it might tell him the way to another Gate. It might find another stone of its kind which was near enough. That was the virtue in it, which held so much else of danger.

It had been a parting-gift, from a man he had begun to love, one he had wished had been his father. But in Morgaine's service there were only partings—and deaths. Only the small stone and the white horse, these he owned, besides his gear, both of which he knew for foolishness and dangerous vanity—a mare, and white at that; and a stone which marked him equal to a qhal-lord—and reminded him of the arrhend.

That land they had traded irrevocably for this one, where the gates themselves threw out power enough to misshape the trees and make all their vicinity unwholesome.

It was that lost, beautiful forest and another, less wholesome, which haunted his sleep. He dreamed that Morgaine had left him and he could not overtake her.

He dreamed of a ride wherein he had seen a dragon frozen in the snow, beyond which time nothing had been ordinary in his life. For the most part, he thought, folk chose to be where they were born, with familiar dangers. It might be a terrible place or a good one, might be love or hate that came to them, they might

have their freedom merely by turning their faces from
what they knew and walking straight ahead—yet they
would not go, not though the place where they were
would kill them. He might have been such a man as
that. He had hovered for two years close about the
region of his exile, when he was eighteen and an
outlaw, despite his danger: he had imagined nothing
beyond that.

Till Morgaine had found him.

She had shown him things which made no sense in
the world he knew. And like the dragon which perished, bewildered, in the snow—he had known he was
out of his element from the moment he had begun to
follow her.

Therefore he dreamed of endless following. Therefore he waked with his fist clenched on the stone; and
lay bewildered, wondering where he was; and where
Morgaine was; and was terrified until he had found
her, a familiar shadow, beneath the ancient and twisted
tree, in more starlight than any world he had yet seen.

He drifted off again. The horses remained quiet.
The wind blew and rattled the branches, and there was
no sound that did not belong.

But—a brief darkness then; and a snap like a burning log, that brought him out of his sleep reaching for
his sword, aware first that Morgaine was at his left and
that their guest was to his right and moving, staggering
to his feet and reeling away among the trees at no
slight speed. Fire burned in the leaf mold. That was
the result of Morgaine's weapon: he knew it well
enough—knew that was the sound that had waked
him; and he scrambled up sleep-dazed as he was and
overtook the man before he had gotten as far as the
horses he strove to reach—overtook him and seized
him at the shoulders, bearing him down in a crash to
the leaves at the very hooves of the gray warhorse.

The gray reared up with a challenge and Morgaine's
whistle cut the dark. "Siptah!" she shouted, as Vanye
shielded his head with his arms, the prisoner with his
body, and the iron-shod hooves came down, flinging
dirt and leaves into his face and clipping his shoulder,

thunder of hooves all about them as the warhorse scrambled over them, missing them with every stride but one. The prisoner beneath him did not move.

"Is thee hurt?" Morgaine was asking. "Vanye, is thee hurt?"

Vanye gathered himself up off the man and caught his own breath in great frightened gasps, looking up at his liege, who had caught firm hold of Siptah's halter rope. He flexed the shoulder as he rose and thanked Heaven the hoof had clipped only leather and a mail shirt.

"He could have had a knife," Morgaine raged at him. "He might have had any sort of weapon! Thee did not know!"

He thought the same, now it was done; more, he thought of the hoof-strike that had missed his head, and his knees went to water. The big gray had shifted balance in mid-attack and all but fallen trying to miss him; that was what had saved them.

At his feet the prisoner moaned and moved, a half-conscious stir of his limbs. Vanye set his foot in the man's back when he tried to get an arm under him and pressed him flat, not gently.

"He is not altogether lame," Morgaine observed dryly, then, having recovered her humor.

"No," Vanye said, still hard-breathing. The deserved reproof of his mercy stung more than the bruise did. "Nor in any wise grateful."

Chapter Two

Dawn light grew in the clearing, and Vanye probed the ashes of their fire with a bit of kindling, as he had fed it from time to time in the hours of his watch. Yellow threads of fire climbed and sparked in the threads of inner bark of something very like willow. He added a few other twigs, then arranged more substantial pieces, deliberate in his leisure. It was a rare moment in which nothing pressed them, in which he knew that they were not riding on, and all he needed think on was the fire, the mystery that was always homelike, no matter what the sky over him, or the number of moons in it. The horses grazed in the clearing on the riverside, where the twisted trees let in enough light for grass—faithful sentries both, dapple gray Siptah wise to war and ambushes, Arrhan forest-wise and sensible. Something might escape human ears, but the horses would give alarm—and they found nothing amiss in this morning. Catastrophe had attempted them in the night—and failed.

On the other side of the fire, the glow falling on slender hand and silver hair, Morgaine slept on, which small vision he cherished in that same quiet way as he did the fire and the dimly rising sun.

"Sleep," he whispered when she stirred. Sometimes, in such rare leisure, she would yield him the body-warmed blankets, so he might sleep a little while she made breakfast—or he yielded them to her, whichever of them had sat the watch into dawn.

She half-opened her eyes and lifted her head, nose

above the blankets. "Thee can sleep," she said, in the Kurshin tongue, as he had spoken—but it was an older accent, forgotten by the time he was born. It was a habit she had when she spoke to him alone, or when she was muddled with sleep.

"I am full awake," he said, which was a lie: he felt the long hours of his watch in a slight prickling in his eyes, his bruised shoulder ached, and the blankets were tempting shelter from the morning chill. But he saved her from hardship when he could—so often that it became a contest between them, of frowns and maneuverings, each favoring the other in a perpetual rivalry which tilted one way or the other according to the day and the need.

"Sleep," he said now. Morgaine sank back and covered her head; and he smiled with a certain satisfaction as he delved into their saddlebags and brought out a pan for mixing and cooking.

The prisoner too, lying prone in his cloak, showed signs of life, rolling onto his side. Vanye reckoned what his most pressing need likely was, and reckoned that it could wait a time: shepherding an escape-prone madman out to the woods meant waking Morgaine to put her on guard; or letting their breakfast go cold—neither of which he felt inclined to do, considering the prisoner was healthy enough to have sprinted for the horses last night, and considering he had won a stiff arm for his last attempted kindness.

Morgaine bestirred herself as the smell of cakes and bacon wafted into the air—enough to draw the hungry for leagues about, Vanye reckoned—the most of them bent on banditry, if what they had seen was any guide.

And another glance toward the prisoner showed him lying on his side, staring in their direction with such misery and desolation that Vanye felt his eyes on him even when he looked back at their breakfast.

"I should see to him," Vanye muttered unhappily when Morgaine came back from the riverside. He poured tea into their smallest mixing bowl, wrapped a cloth about it to keep it warm, and set out a cake and a bit of bacon on the cloth that wrapped his cooking-gear, while Morgaine sat down to eat. "Have your own," he said, "before it cools."

It did not look like a madman who stared up at him as he came over to his place among the tree-roots. It looked like a very miserable, very hungry man who hoped that food truly was coming to him. "I will free your hands," Vanye said, dropping down on his heels beside him. He set the food down carefully on the dead leaves of the forest floor. "But not your feet. Meddle with that and I will stop you, do you understand? For other necessities I trust you can wait like any civilized man." It was the qhalur language he spoke, and it did not go so lightly over his tongue as it ought. He was not sure, at times, what hearers did understand of him. "Do you agree? Or do I take the food back?"

"The food," the man said, a faint, hoarse voice. "Yes."

"You agree."

A nod of the head, a worried gnawing of the lip.

He turned the prisoner over and gently worked the knots free on his hands. The man only gave a great sigh and lay still on his face a moment, his arms at rest beside him, as a man would who had spent the night with his hands and shoulders going numb.

"He is quieter," he reported then to Morgaine, in his own tongue, when he settled down to breakfast beside her. He took a cup of tea and considered his hands, where he had touched the man. It was death-stink, lingering: the man was that filthy; and he could not eat until he had walked down to the river and washed his hands.

It was overdone bacon then; Morgaine kept the breakfast warm for him on the coals, along with the tea which by now was bitter-edged. He drank and made a face.

"I should have gotten up," Morgaine said.

"No," he said. "No, you ought not. I will take care of him. I will have him down to the river before the sun is much higher, and I swear to you he will be cleaner before you have to deal with him."

"I want you to talk to him."

"*Me?*"

"You can manage that."

"Aye—but—"

"Not?"

"I will do it." Rarely nowadays she put any hard task on him: and he took it, distasteful as it was, likely as he was to make a muddle of things. "But—"

"But?"

"He can lie to me. How should I know? How should I know anything he told me? I have no subtlety with lies."

"Is thee saying I do?"

"I did not say—"

She smiled, a quirk of her mouth, gray eyes flickering. "Man and man; Man and Man. That is the fact. Between one thing and the other I am not the one of us two he will trust. No. Learn what brought him here. Promise him what thee sees fit to promise. Only—" She reached out and laid a hand on his arm. "He will not go free. We cannot allow that. Thee knows what I will give—and what I will not."

"I know," he said, and thought as he said it that he had chosen the road that brought him to this pass— thought suddenly how more than one land cursed Morgaine kri Chya for the deaths she brought. He had tried in his life to be an honorable man, and not to lie.

But he had chosen to go with her.

It was far more warily the man regarded him on his return, tucked up with his back against a tree, eyes following every move he made—a filthy, desperate figure their guest was by daylight, his nose having bled into his white-blond mustache and down his unkept and patchy beard, dirt-sores and crusted lines on his face, a trickle of dried blood having run from under the matted hair at his temple—a reminder of the night previous, Vanye thought. Likely more than the man's arms ached this morning.

But he had not touched the binding on his ankles. He had eaten every bit of the cake and the bacon off the cloth, down to the crumbs. And there was still a look on his face, as if having eaten off their charity, he felt there was a chance something else of hope might happen, but much doubted it.

"I will tell you," Vanye said, sinking down on his heels, arms on knees, in front of him, "how I am. I hold no grudge. A man in the dark and fevered—he may do strange things. I reckon that this was the case last night. On the other hand, if I you take some other mad notion that endangers my liege, I shall not hesitate to break your neck, do you understand?"

The man said nothing at all. There was only a stare of wary blue eyes, beneath the tangled hair, and the stink of filth was overwhelming.

"Now I think you have been a warrior," Vanye said. "And you do not choose to be filthy or to be a madman. So I should like to take you down to the water and give you oil and salve and help you present a better face to my lady, do you understand me at all, man?"

"I understand," the man said then, the faintest of voices.

"So you should know," Vanye said, taking out his Honor-blade from his belt and beginning to undo the knots which bound the man's feet, "my lady is herself a very excellent shot, with weapons you may not like to see—in case you should think of dealing with me." He freed the knot and unwrapped the leather, tucking it in his belt to save. "There." With a touch on the man's bare and swollen right foot. "Ah. That did the swelling no good at all. Can you walk?—Have you a name, man?"

"Chei."

"Chei." Vanye rose and took his arm, and pulled the man up to take his weight on his left foot, steadying him as he tried the right. "Mine is Vanye. Nhi Vanye i Chya, but Vanye is enough outside hold and hall. There. Walk down to the water. I warn you it is cold. I would have heaved you in last night, with that gear of yours, except for that. Go on. I will find you down by the water. I *will* find you down by the water—or I will *find* you. Do you hear me?"

Thoughts of escape passed through the man's head, it was clear by the wariness in his eyes; then different thoughts entirely, and fear, the man being evidently no fool. But Vanye walked away from him, going back after his kit by the fire.

"Be careful with him!" Morgaine said sharply, as he bent down near her. *Her* eyes were on the prisoner. But he had been sure of that when he had turned his back.

Vanye shrugged and sank down a moment to meet her eyes. "Do as I see fit, you said."

"Do not make gestures."

He drew a long breath. So she set him free and then wanted to pull the jesses. It was not her wont, and it vexed him. But clearly she was worried by something. *"Liyo,* I am not in danger of a man lame in one foot, smaller than I am and starved into the bargain. Not in plain daylight. And I trust your eye is still on him—"

"And we do not know this land," she hissed. "We do not know what resources he may have."

"None of them came to him on that hilltop."

"Thee is leaving things to chance! There are possibilities neither of us can foresee in a foreign place. We do not know what he is."

Her vehemence put doubt into him. He bit his lip and got up again. He had never quite let his own eye leave the man in his walk downhill, save the moment it took to reach her; but it seemed quibbling to protest that point, the more so that she had already questioned his judgment, and justly so, last night. Beyond this it came to opinion; and there were times to argue with Morgaine. The time that they had a prisoner loose was not that moment.

"Aye," he said quietly. "But I will attend him. I will stay in your sight. As long as you see me, everything is well enough."

He gathered up one of their blankets for drying in, along with his personal kit. He walked down the hill, pausing on the way to lay a hand on Siptah's shoulder, where the big gray and white Arrhan grazed at picket on the grassy slope. He reckoned that Morgaine would have that small black weapon in hand and one eye on him constantly.

It was not honorable, perhaps, to deal with hidden weapons in the pretense of being magnanimous; but Morgaine—she had said it—did not take pointless chances. It was not honorable either, to tempt a frightened man to escape, to test his intentions, where keeping him under close guard would save his life. And other lives, it might well be.

But the man had not strayed—had attended his call of nature and limped his way down to water's edge by the time Vanye had walked the distance downslope, and he had never dared bolt from sight of them or wander behind branches. That much was encouraging. Chei had bent down to drink, with movements small and painful, there on the margin.

"Wash," Vanye said, and dropped the folded blanket beside him on the grass. "I will sit here, patient as you like."

Chei said nothing. He only sat down, bowed his head and began with clumsy efforts to unbuckle straps and work his way out of the filth- and weather-stiffened leather and mail, piece after piece of the oddly fashioned gear laid aside on the bank.

"Lord in Heaven," Vanye murmured then, sickened at what he saw—not least was he affected by the quiet of the man sitting there on the grass and taking full account, with trembling hands and tight-clamped jaw and a kind of panic about his eyes, what toll his ordeal had taken of his body—great, deep sores long festered and worn deep in his flesh. Wherever the armor had been ill-fitted, there infection and poison had set in and corruption had followed, deepening the sores, to be galled again by the armor. Wherever small wounds had been, even what might have been insect bites, they had festered; and as Chei pulled the padding beneath the mail free, small bits of skin and corruption came with it.

It was not the condition of a man confined a day or even a few days. It bespoke something much more terrible than he had understood had happened on that hill, and the man sat there, trembling in deep shock, trying stolidly to deal with what a chirurgeon or a priest should attend.

"Man—" Vanye said, rising and coming over to him. "I will help."

But the man turned his shoulder and wanted, by that gesture, no enemy's hands on him, Vanye reckoned—perhaps for fear of roughness; perhaps his customs forbade some stranger touching him; Heaven knew. Vanye sank down on his heels, arms on his knees, and bit his lip for self-restraint, the while Chei continued, with the movements of some aged man, to peel the leather breeches off, now and again pausing, seeming overwhelmed by pain as if he could not bear the next. Then he would begin again.

And there was nothing more than that, that a man could do, while Vanye watched, flinching in sympathy— Lord, in Ra-morij of his birth, a gentleman would not countenance this sort of thing—chirurgeon's business, one would murmur, and cover his nose and go absolve himself with a cup of wine and the noisy talk of other men in hall. He had never had a strong stomach with wounds gone bad.

But the man doggedly, patiently, worked out of the last of it, put his right leg down into the water, and the left, and slipped off the bank, to lose his balance and fall so suddenly that Vanye moved for the edge thinking he had gone into some hole.

Chei righted himself and clawed for the bank—held on in water only chest deep as Vanye gripped his forearm against the grass. Chei was spitting water and gasping after air, his blond hair and beard streaming water, his teeth chattering in what seemed more shock than cold.

"I will pull you out," Vanye said.

"No," Chei said, pulling away. "No." He slipped again, and all but went under, fighting his way to balance again, shivering and trying to pull free.

Vanye let him go, and watched anxiously as the prisoner ducked his head deliberately and rubbed at ingrained dirt, scrubbing at galled shoulders and arms and body.

Vanye delved into his kit and found the cloth-wrapped soap. "Here," he said, offering it out over the water "Soap."

The man made a few careful steps back to take it and the cloth; and wet it and scrubbed. The lines about the eyes had vanished, washed away with the dirt. It was a younger face now; tanned face and neck and hands, white flesh elsewhere, in which ribs and shoulder-blades stood out plainly.

More of scrubbing, while small chains of bubbles made serpentines down the rapid current. There was danger of that being seen downstream. But there was danger of everything—in this place, in all this unknown world.

"Come on," Vanye said at last, seeing how Chei's lips had gone blue. "Come on, man—Chei. Let me help you out. Come *on,* man."

For a moment he did not think the man could make it. Chei moved slowly, arms against his body, movements slowed as if each one had to be planned. The hand that grasped Vanye's was cold as death. The other carefully, deliberately, laid the soap and the cloth in the grass.

Vanye pulled on him, wet skin slipping in his fingers, got the second hand and drew him up onto the grass, where Chei might have been content to lie. But he hauled Chei up again and drew him stumbling as far as the blanket, where he let him down on his side and quickly wrapped him against the chill of the wind, head to foot.

"There," Vanye said. "There—stay still." He hastened up again, seeing Morgaine standing halfway down the slope, there by the horses: and recalled a broken promise. He *had* left her sight. He was shamefaced a second time as he walked up to speak to her.

"What is wrong?" she asked, fending off Arrhan's

search for tidbits. There was a frown on her face, not for the horse.

He had turned his back on their prisoner again. But: "He is too ill to run," Vanye said. "Heaven knows—" It was not news that would please her. "He is in no condition to ride—No, do not go down there, this is something a man should see to. But I will need the other blanket. And my saddlebags."

She gave him a distressed look, but she stopped with only a glance toward the man on the bank, a little tightening of her jaw. "I will bring them down half-way," she said. "*When* will he ride?"

"Two days," he said, trying to hasten the estimate; and thought again of the sores. "Maybe."

It was a dark thought went through Morgaine's eyes—was a thought the surface of which he knew how to read and the depth of which he did not want to know.

"It is not his planning," he said, finding himself the prisoner's defender.

"Aye," Morgaine said quietly, angrily and turned and walked uphill after the things he had asked.

She brought the things he asked back down to him, no happier. "Mind, we have no abundance of anything."

"We are far from the road," Vanye said. It was the only extenuation of their situation he could think of.

"Aye," she said again. There was still anger. It was not at him. She had nothing to say—was in one of her silences, and it galled him in the one sense and frightened him in the other, that they were in danger, that he knew her moods, and her angers, which he had hoped she had laid aside forever. But it was a fool who hoped that of Morgaine.

He took what she gave him and walked back to the bank, and there sat down, a little distance from their prisoner—sat down, trying to smother his own frustration which, Heaven knew, he dared not let fly, dared not provoke his liege to some rashness—some outright and damnably perverse foolishness, he told himself, of which she was capable. She scowled; she was angry; she *did* nothing foolish and needed no advice from him who ought well to know she was holding her temper very well indeed, Heaven save them from her moods and her unreasonable furies.

The focus of her anger knew nothing of it—was enclosed in his own misery, shivering and trying, between great tremors of cold and shock, to dry his hair.

"Give over," he said, and tried to help. Chei would none of it, shivering and recoiling from him.

"I am sorry," Vanye muttered. "If I had known this, Lord in Heaven, man—"

Chei shook his head, clenching his jaw against the spasms a moment, then lay still, huddled in the blanket.

"How long," Vanye asked, "how long had you been there?"

Chei's breath hissed between his teeth, a slow shuddering.

"Why," Vanye pursued quietly, "did they leave you there?"

"What are you? From where? Mante?"

"Not from hereabouts," he said. The sun shone warm in a moment when the wind fell. A bird sang, off across the little patch of meadow. It meant safety, like the horses grazing above them on the slope.

"Is it Mante?" Chei demanded of him, rolling onto his back and lifting his head, straining with the effort.

"No," Vanye said. "It is not." And reckoned that Mante was some enemy, for Chei seemed to take some comfort in that, for all that his jaw was still clamped tight. "Nor anywhere where they treat men as they treated you. I swear you that."

"She—" The man lay back and shifted desperate eyes toward their camp.

"—is not your enemy," Vanye said. "As I am not."

"Are you qhal?"

That question took the warmth from the daylight.

"No," Vanye said. "That I am not." In Andur-Kursh the fairness of his own brown hair was enough to raise questions of halfling blood. But the one who asked was palest blond; and that puzzled him. "Do I look to be?"

"One does not need to *look* to be."

It was, then, what he had feared. He thought before he spoke. "I have seen the like. My cousin—was such a man."

"How does he fare?"

"Dead," Vanye said. "A long time ago." And frowned to warn the man away from that matter. He looked up at a motion in the edge of his vision and saw Morgaine coming down the hill toward them, carefully—a warlike figure, in her black and silver armor, the sword swinging at her side, either hand holding a cloth-wrapped cup she was trying not to spill.

Chei followed his stare, tilting his head back, watching her as she came, as she reached the place where they sat and offered the steaming cups.

"Thank you," Vanye said, as he took his cup from her hand, and took Chei's as well.

"Against the chill," Morgaine said. She was still frowning, but she did not show it to Chei, who lay beneath his blanket. "Do you need anything?" she asked, deliberately, doggedly gracious. "Hot water?"

"On the inside of him will serve," Vanye said. "For the rest—the sun is warm enough when the wind falls."

She walked off then, in leisurely fashion, up the hill, plucked a twig and stripped it like some village girl walking a country lane, the dragon sword swinging at her side.

She was, he reckoned, on the edge of a black rage.

He gave Chei his cup and sipped his own, wrinkling his nose as he discovered the taste. " 'Tis safe," he said, for Chei hesitated at the smell of his. "Tea and herbs." He tasted his again. "Febrifuge. Against the fever. She gives us both the same, lest you think it poison. A little cordial to sweeten it. The herb is sour and bitter."

"Qhalur witch," the man said, "into the bargain."

"Oh, aye," Vanye said, glancing at him with some mild surprise, for that belief might have come out of Andur-Kursh. He regarded such a human, homelike belief almost with wistfulness, wondering where he had lost it. "Some say. But you will not lose your soul for a cup of tea."

He had, he thought when he had said it, lost his for a similar matter, a bit of venison. But that was long ago, and he was damned most for the bargain, not what sustenance he had taken of a stranger in a winter storm.

Chei managed to lean over on his elbow and drink, between coughing, and spilled a good amount of it in the shaking of his hands. But sip after sip he drank, and Vanye drank his own cup, to prove it harmless.

Meanwhile too, having considered charity, and the costs of it on both sides, he delved one-handed into the saddlebags and set out a horn container, intricately carved.

And perhaps, he thought, a scrupulous Kurshin man would regard the contents of that little container as witchcraft too.

"What is that?" Chei asked warily, as he finished his cup.

"For the sores. It is the best thing I have. It will not let the wounds scab, and it takes the fire out."

Chei took the box and opened it, taking a little on his fingers and smelling of it. He tried it on the sore on the inside of his knee, his lip caught between his teeth in the patient habit of pain; but soon enough he drew several deep breaths and his face relaxed.

"It does not hurt," Vanye said.

Chei daubed away at himself, one wound and the other, the blanket mostly fallen about him, his drying hair uncombed and trailing water from its ends. Vanye took a bit on his own fingers and covered the patches that Chei could in no wise reach, those on his shoulders, then let Chei do the rest.

"Why?" Chei asked finally, in a phlegmy voice, after a cough. "Why did you save me?"

"Charity," Vanye said dourly.

"Am I free? I do not seem to be."

Vanye lifted a shoulder. "No. But what we have we will share with you. We are in a position—" He drew a breath, thinking what he should say, what loyalties he might cross, what ambush he might find, all on a word or two. "—we do not want to make any disturbance hereabouts. But then, perhaps you have no wish to be found hereabouts—"

The man said nothing for a moment. Then he reached inside the blankets to apply more of the salve. "I do not."

"Then we do have something to talk about, do we not?"

A pale blue stare flicked toward him, mad as a hawk's eye. "Have you some feud with Gault?"

"Who is Gault?"

Perhaps it was the right bent to take. Perhaps the man in his turn thought him mad—or a liar. Carefully Chei took a fresh film of salve on his fingers and applied it, and winced, a weary flinching, premature lines of sunburn and pain around the eyes. "Who is Gault?" he echoed flatly. "Who is Gault. Ask, *what* is Gault?—How should you not know that?"

Vanye gave another shrug. "How should we? I know great lords aplenty. Not that one."

"This is his land."

"Is it? And are you his man?"

"No," Chei said shortly. "Nor would I be." He lowered his voice, spoke with a quickening of breath. "Nor, unlike you, would I serve the qhal."

It was challenge, if subdued and muttered. Vanye let it fly, it being so far off the mark. "She is my liege," he said in all mildness, "and she is halfling, by her own word. And in my own land folk called her a witch, which she is not. I should take offense, but I would have said the same, once."

Chei occupied himself in his injuries.

"It was this Gault left you to die," Vanye said. "You said that much. Why? What had you done to him?"

It was that hawk's stare an instant. There was outrage in it. "To Gault ep Mesyrun? He lives very well in Morund. He drains the country dry. He respects neither God nor devil, and he keeps a large guard of your kind as well as qhal."

"Tell me. Do you think he would thank us for freeing you?"

That told. There was a long silence, a slow and evident consideration of that idea.

"So you may reason we are not his friends," Vanye said, "and my lady has done you a kindness, which has so far gained us nothing but an alarm in the night and myself a few bruises. Had you rather fight us to no gain at all? Or will you ride with us a space—till we are off this lord Gault's land?"

Chei rested his head in his hands and remained so, sinking lower with his elbow against his knee.

"Or do you mislike that idea?" Vanye asked him.

"He will kill us," Chei said, and lifted his face to look at him sidelong, head still propped against his hand. "How did you find me?"

"By chance. We heard the wolves. We saw the birds."

"And by chance," Chei said harshly, "you were riding Gault's land."

The man wanted a key—best, it seemed, give him a very small one. "Not chance," Vanye said. "The road. And if our way runs through his land, so be it."

There was no answer.

"What did you do," Vanye asked again, "that deserved what this Gault did? Was it murder?"

"The murder was on their side. They murdered—"

"So?" Vanye asked when the man went suddenly silent.

Chei shook his head angrily. Then his look went to one of entreaty, brow furrowed beneath the drying and tangled hair as he looked up. "You have come here from the gate," Chei said, "if that is the way you have come. I am not a fool. Do not tell me that your lady is ignorant what land this is."

"Beyond the gate—" Vanye considered a second time. It was a man's life in the balance. And it was too easy to kill a man with a word. Or raise war and kill a thousand men or ten thousand. There was a second silence, this one his. Then: "I think you have come to questions my lady could answer for you."

"What do you want from me?" Chei asked.

"Simple things. Easy things. Some of which might suit you well."

Chei's look grew wary indeed.

"Ask my lady," Vanye said.

It was a quieter, saner-seeming man Vanye led, wrapped in one of their two blankets, to the fireside where Morgaine waited, Chei with his hair and beard clean and having some order about it once he had wet and combed it again. He was barefoot, limping, wincing a little on the twigs that littered the dusty ground. He had left all his gear down on the riverside—Heaven knew how they would salvage it or what scouring could clean the leather: none could save the cloth.

Chei set himself down and Vanye sat down at the fireside nearer him than Morgaine—in mistrust.

But Morgaine poured them ordinary tea from a pan, using one of their smaller few bowls for a third cup, and passed it round the bed of coals that the fire had become, to Vanye and so to Chei. The wind made a soft whisper in the leaves that moved and dappled the ground with a shifting light, the fire had become a comfortable warmth which did not smoke, but relieved what chill there was in the shade, and the horses, the dapple gray and the white, grazed a little distance away, in their little patch of grass and sunlight. There was no haste, no urgency in Morgaine.

Not to the eye, Vanye thought. She had been quiet and easy even when he had come alone up the hill bringing the cups, and told her everything he could recall, and everything he had admitted to Chei—"He knows the gates," Vanye had said, quickly, atop it all. "He believes that is how we got here, but he insists we lie if we do not know this lord Gault and that we must know where we are."

Morgaine sipped her tea now, and did not hasten matters. "Vanye tells me you do not know where we come from," she said after a moment. "But you think we should know this place, and that we have somewhat to do with this lord of Morund. We do not. The road out there brought us. That is all. It branches beyond every gate. Do you not know that?"

Chei stared at her, not in defiance now, but in something like dismay.

"Like any road," said Morgaine in that same hush of moving leaves and wind, "it leads everywhere. That is the general way of roads. Name the farthest place in the world. That road beyond this woods leads to it, one way or the other. And this Gate leads through other gates. Which lead—to many places. Vanye says you know this. Then you should know that too. And knowing that—" Morgaine took up a peeled twig to stir her tea, and carefully lifted something out of it, to flick it away. "You should know that what a lord decrees is valid only so far as his hand reaches. No further. And I have never heard of your lord Gault, nor care that I have not heard. He seems to me to be no one worth my trouble."

"Then why am I?" Chei asked harshly, with no little desperation.

"You are not," Morgaine said. "You are a considerable inconvenience."

It was not what Chei had, perhaps, expected. And Morgaine took a slow sip of tea, set the cup down and poured more for herself, the while Chei said nothing at all.

"We cannot let you free," Morgaine said. "We do not care for this Gault; and having you fall straightway into his hands would be no kindness to you and no good thing for us either. Quiet is our preference. So you will go with us, and somewhere we shall have to find you a horse—by one thing and the other I suppose you are familiar with horses. Am I wrong?"

Chei stared at her, somewhere between incredulity and panic. "No," Chei said faintly. "No, lady. I know horses."

"And our business is not truly needful for you to know, is it? Only that it has become yours, as your safety has become conditional on ours—as I assure you it is. We will find you a horse—somewhere hereabouts, I trust. Meanwhile you will ride with Vanye—as

soon as you are fit to ride. In the meanwhile you eat
our food, sleep in our blankets, use our medicines,
and repay us with insults." All of this so, so softly
spoken. "This last will change. You have naught to do
today but lie in the sun, in what modesty or lack of it
will not affect me, I do assure you. You do not move
me.—How wide are Gault's lands? How far shall we
ride before we cease to worry about his attacking us?"

Chei sat there a moment with a worried look. Then
he bit his lip, shifted forward and pulled a half-burned
stick out of the coals to draw in the dirt with it. "Here
you found me. Here the road. Back here—" He swept
a wide, vague area with the stick. "The gate from
which you came." The stick moved on to inscribe the
line of the road running past the hill of the wolves,
and up and up northward. "On either side here is
woods. Beyond that—" He gestured out beyond the
trees, where the river was, and where meadow shone
gold. "The forest is scattered—a woods here, another
there, at some distance from the road."

"You are well familiar with this lord's land,"
Morgaine said.

The stick wavered, a shiver that had no wind to
cause it. "The north and the west I know. But this last
I do not forget. I watched where they took us." The
stick moved again, tracing the way, and slashed a line
across the road. "This is the Sethoy, this river. It
comes from the mountains. A bridge crosses it, an old
bridge. The other side of it, northward across the
plain, lord Gault's own woods begin; and his pastures;
and his fields; and there is his hold, well back from the
old Road. In the hills, a village. A road between. He
has that too. There are roads besides the Old Road,
there is a track goes across it from Morund and up
again by the hills; there is another runs by Gyllin-
brook—that runs along these hills and through them,
up toward the village. None of these are safe for you."

"Further over on either side," Morgaine said, and
moved around the fire to indicate with her finger the
left and the right of the road. "Are there other roads?"

"Beyond the western hills." Chei retreated somewhat from her presence, and used his stick to trace small lines.

"Habitations?"

"High in the hills. No friends of any strangers. They keep their borders against every outsider: now and again the lords from the north come down and kill a number of them—to prove whatever that proves. Who knows?"

There was perhaps a barb in that. Morgaine did not deign to notice it. She pointed to the other side. "And here to the east?"

"Qhalur holdings. Lord Herot and lord Sethys, with their armies."

"What would you counsel?"

Chei did not move for a moment. Then he pointed with the stick to the roads on the west. "There. Through the woods, beyond Gault's fields. Between Gault and the hillmen."

"But one reaches the trail by the old Road."

"There, lady, just short of Gault's woods. I can guide you—from there. I *will* guide you, if you want to avoid Gault's hold. I want the same."

"Where are *you* from?" Vanye asked, the thing he had not said, and moved close on the other side. "Where is your home?"

Chei drew in a breath and pointed close above Morund land. "There."

"Of what hold?" Morgaine asked.

"I was a free man," Chei said. "There are some of us—who come down from the hills."

"Well-armed free men," said Vanye.

Chei's eyes came at once back to him, alarmed.

"Are there many of your sort?" Morgaine asked.

Fear, then. True fear. "Fewer than there were," Chei said at last. "My lord is dead. *That* is my crime. That I was both armed, and a free Man. So once was Gault. But they took him. Now he is qhal—inside."

"Is that," Vanye asked, "the general fate of prisoners?"

"It happens," Chei said, looking anxiously from one to the other side of him.

"Tell us," Morgaine said, shifting position to point at the road where it continued. "What lies ahead?"

"Other qhal. Tejhos. Mante."

"What sort of place?" Vanye asked.

"I have no knowledge. A qhalur place. *You* would know, better than I."

"But Gault knows them."

"I am sure," Chei said in a hoarse small voice. "Perhaps you do."

"Perhaps we do not," Morgaine said softly, very softly. "Describe the way north. On the old Road."

Chei hesitated, then moved the stick and drew the line northward with a large westward jog halfway before an eastward trend. "Woods and hills," he said. "A thousand small trails. Above this—is qhalur land. The High Lord. Skarrin."

"Skarrin. Of Mante." Morgaine rested her chin on her hand, her brow knit, her fist clenched, and for a long moment were no more questions. Then: "And what place had Men in this land?"

Unhesitatingly, the stick indicated the west. "There." And the east, about Morund. "And there. Those in the west and those who live in qhalur lands. But in the west are the only free Men."

"Of which you were one."

"Of which I was one, lady." There was no flinching in that voice, which had become as quiet as Morgaine's own. "You are kinder than Gault, that is all I know. If a man has to swear to some qhal to live—better you than the lord that Skarrin sent us. I will get you through Gault's lands. And if I serve you well—believe me and trust my leading when you come near humans, and I will guide you through."

"Against your own," Vanye said.

"I was Gault's prisoner. Do you think human folk would trust me again? There have been too many spies. No one is alive who went through Gyllin-brook, except me. My lord Ichandren is dead. My brother is

dead—Thank God's mercy for both." For a moment
his voice did break, but he sat still, his hands on his
knees. "No one is alive to vouch for me. I will not
raise a hand against human folk. But I do not want to
die for nothing. One of my comrades on that hill—he
let the wolves have him. The second night. And I
knew then I did not want to die."

Tears spilled, wet trails down his face. Chei looked
at neither of them. His face was still impassive. There
were only the tears.

"So," Morgaine said after a moment, "is it an oath
you will give us?"

"I swear to you—" The eyes stayed fixed beyond
her. "I swear to you—every word is true. I will guide
you. I will guide you away from all harm. On my soul
I will not lie to you, lady. Whatever you want of me."

Vanye drew in a breath and wrapped his arms about
him, staring down at the man. Such terms he had
sworn, himself, *ilin*-oath, by the scar on his palm and
the white scarf about the helm—outcast warrior, taken
up by a lord, an oath without recourse or exception.
And hearing that oath, he felt something swell up in
his throat—memory of that degree of desperation; and
a certain remote jealousy, that of a sudden this man
was speaking to Morgaine as his liege, when he knew
nothing of her; or of him; or what he was undertaking.

God in Heaven, liyo, *do you trust this man, and do
you take him on* my *terms—have I trespassed too far,
come too close to you, that now you take in another
stray dog?*

"I will take your oath," Morgaine said. "I will put
you in Vanye's charge."

"Do you believe him?" Morgaine asked him later,
in the Kurshin tongue, while Chei lay naked in the sun
on a blanket, sleeping, perhaps—far enough for decency on the grassy downslope of the riverside, but
still visible from the campfire—sun is the best thing for
such wounds, Morgaine had said. Sun and clean wind.

Not mentioning the salve and the oil and the matter

of the man's fouled armor, which there was some salvaging, perhaps, with oil and work.

"A man swears," Vanye said. "The oath is as good as the man. But," he said after a moment, kneeling there beside the dying fire, "a man might sell his soul, for something of value to him. Such as his life."

She looked at him for a long time. "The question then, is for what coin, would it not be?"

"He believes," Vanye said, "in witchcraft."

"Does thee not, now?"

Vanye lifted his shoulders, a small, uncomfortable movement, and shifted his eyes momentarily toward the dragon sword, which had never left her side, not in all this perilous day. Its ruby eyes gleamed wickedly in the gold hilt; it reminded him of that stone which he carried against his own heart, a foreign, a dangerous thing. "I have never seen any witch-working. Only things qhal have made, most of which I can manage—" A sense of dislocation came on him, a sense of panic, fear of what he had become, remorse for the things that he had lost. "Or I have become a witch myself," he murmured. "Perhaps that is what witchcraft is. Chei ep Kantory would think so."

There was a great deal, he thought, on Morgaine's mind. But for a moment he had distracted her, and she looked at him in that way that once had made him vastly uncomfortable. Her eyes were gray and clear to the depths of that gray like the devouring sea; her lashes were, like no human and no qhal he had ever seen at such range, dark gray next the lid and shading to pale at the tips, and that shading was on her brows but nowhere about her hair, which was altogether silver. Halfling, she had said. Sometimes he thought it true. Sometimes he did not know at all.

"Thee regrets?"

He shook his head finally. It was the most that he could say. He drew a great breath. "I have learned your lesson, *liyo*. I look around me. That is all. Never back."

Morgaine hissed between her teeth and flung a bit

of burned stick, that with which Chei had drawn the map. It was more than her accustomed restlessness. She rested with her arms about her knees, and shifted to hunch forward, her arms tucked against her chest, gazing into nothing at all.

He was silent. It seemed wisest.

It was their lives she was thinking on. He was sure of that. She was wiser than he—he was accustomed to think so. He missed things, not knowing what he should see, things which Morgaine did not miss. She had taught him—skills which might well horrify their prisoner: the working of gates, the writing of qhal, the ideas which qhal held for truth—who swore by no god and looked (some of them) back toward a time that they had ruled and (some of them) forward to a time that they should recover their power, at whatever cost to the immortal souls they disavowed.

Qhal in most ancient times had taken Men, so Morgaine had told him, and changed them, and scattered them through the gates, along with plants and creatures of every sort, until Time itself abhorred their works and their confusing what Was, and mixed all elements in one cataclysmic Now—the which thought chilled his much-threatened soul, and unhinged the things Holy Church had taught him and which he thought he knew beyond any doubt.

Qhal had taken Men to serve them because they were most qhal-like . . . and thereby the ancient qhal-lords had made a dire mistake: for Men in their shorter lives, multiplied far more rapidly, which simple fact meant that Men threatened them.

In his own land, in Kursh and Andur, divided by the mountain ridge, the snowy Mother of Eagles—there qhal had been reduced virtually to rumor, hunted for the most part, tolerated in a few rare cases—so frost-haired Morgaine had been tolerated by the High Kings a hundred years before his birth, while in his own ruined age even his own hair had been too light a brown for Nhi clan's liking. And in this place—

In this place, qhal had adjusted that balance. *The*

*lords from the north come down and kill a number of
them*—Chei had said of qhalur raids on the hillfolk. To
prove whatever that proves. Who knows?

Vanye knew. He knew it along with the other things
that a man like Chei would not, he hoped, comprehend. That understanding of callous murder, that per-
spective which allowed him to fathom qhalur motives—
seemed to Vanye a gulf like the gulf of life and death,
the knowledge that everything behind them was dust.

What became of your cousin? Chei had asked. But
he could not answer that either: he could explain to no
one, except the likes of lord Gault, behind whose
human eyes, Chei had said, resided a qhal—

—an old one, Vanye thought. Or one wounded or
sick to death. A qhal who had learned a single way to
overcome humankind, by the gates and the power
they had to conserve a dying mind in a body not its
own.

Qhal who use the gates, he thought suddenly, and
felt a touch of ice about his heart.

"*Liyo*," he said. "If qhal are using the gates here—
what will prevent them going where they will?"

"Nothing prevents them," Morgaine said, and looked
toward him, a sharp, quick look. "Thee understands—
nothing—prevents them. It is possible they know we
are here, it is possible they are tracking us already,
since we disturbed the gate. These are not gentle folk.
We have seen the proof of that. I will tell you what I
notice: that our friend yonder is not much amazed at
our horses or our gear or our companying together.
Nor astonished that we should come from the gates,
the precise location of which he does not know. Now,
that he is not astonished may be that he knows nothing of the gates, but if the qhal in this world do come
and go by that one gate, then they have considerable
mastery of the other one." She gestured about them.
"There are the trees, do you see? That twisting does
not happen in one use of the gates. It is frequent that
this one gate throws out power. It is not working well.
But that they cannot mend it does not mean that they
do not use it."

It was not a comforting thought. "Then they might come behind us."

"If what our friend believes is true, yes. They can. And if by chance someone in Mante or Tejhos was warding that gate when we came through, then they do know that it was used."

He cast a sharp look toward the man sleeping in the sun, and experienced a feeling of panic.

It was a guide *he* did not trust, a burden to slow the horses. Easiest to abandon the man, trust to speed, remembering that the man was lame in one foot and incapable of running.

—There were, to be sure, the wolves.

There was no pain finally—nothing but the wind and the sun on his bare skin, and Chei lay with his eyes shut, the light glowing red through his lids, the delirious play of sun-warmth alternate with the cool wind—in abandonment and safety unimaginable in all his life. He ought to feel shame at his nakedness, but there was little left in a man who had suffered Gault's dungeons. He ought not to be so well content, but he had learned to put all his mind into a moment, even into the trough between two waves of pain, and to find his comfort there, trusting that another such respite would come—if he ignored the pain between.

So with this day. Hell was on either side. But the day was the best he had known since the other side of Gyllin-brook, and if there was hell to come, perhaps— only perhaps—it would be like the waves of pain, the first signal of a rhythm he only now discovered in his life.

That was how he reasoned with himself. Perhaps he had grown mad on his hilltop, conversing with the wolves and calling them by name. But he was very sure that his life was better now; and that tomorrow might well be the same. He had grown comfortable indeed if he could plan for two whole days at once.

Beyond that he refused to think at all. There was danger in such thoughts—danger the moment he began to believe the earnestness in the man's eyes or the easy way this man and this qhalur woman spoke together, argued, shrugged and gestured—everything about them being the way of two comrades in the field, except the little frowns, or the small gestures that said male and female—

As if that could be. As if a human man could willingly go to a qhal—

That a qhal could laugh and trade barbs with her servant, and that a qhalur woman sat here in the woods, secret from Gault and all his doings—a qhalur witch with one human servant and a power which could burn iron—this was a matter that ranged far beyond the things that Chei wanted to think about.

It was only certain that they meant him to go with them; and for the moment that meant he had hope of evading Gault's patrols and a return to that hilltop. That was worth the *lady* and the bowing of his head, and even—more dangerously—the least small wondering if there was not another kind of qhal, and if the bargain this qhalur lady offered might be real—or if her human servant might wish to be his friend.

The most perilous thing, the most dangerous thing, was to give way to that manner of thinking and even once, even a moment—think that the qhal might take him on the same terms as her servant, or that in her—in the slender person of this qhalur woman—might be safety without compromise, safety such as he experienced now—even power such as a Man could have. If a man could find a qhal-lord so free with her servants—was a man not a fool to refuse to shelter in that shadow, when he had come to the point he would not have lived, otherwise? Was there shame in that?

He did not want to think of that overmuch either. The comfort he was in was sufficient for the day, sufficient for many days. He should turn onto his face and avoid burning his skin. That was the most onerous decision he needed make.

In a little while he moved to the shade and was content to lie still, wrapped in his blanket, his head pillowed on his arm. He slept, and waked to find the smell of cooking on the breeze, at which he wept, a foolish leaking of tears from his eyes and a desire to gather his courage and walk up the hill to them and sit down at their fire and be welcomed there—but he lay there weeping instead, and shaking with fear of trying that, fear that there would be no welcome for him, and that they would only tie him again and his aching shoulders could not bear the pain of another night like the last.

And he did not know why he should weep and shiver like a fool over the smell of cakes on the fire, except he was still alive; and others were not, his brother was not, which thoughts ranged back to the hill and the noise of wolves feeding in the dark—a safe sound, a sound with nothing at all of grief in it, because life shrank to the night, the moment, the instant . . . in which the wolves were fed and he was still alive.

That was the safe thing to remember. That was a cold time, a numb, down-to-the-rock time, when a man learned that only life was valuable, and only his own life was truly valuable. His comrades kept the wolves from him. That was all. They were there to talk to and fill the silence while they were alive, but a man only wanted to be alive a little longer at the last; and if a friend was the price of that, then a man learned he would pay that, would pay the wolf-price with his dearest friend or with his own brother. That was the safe thing to remember . . . when the smell of bread and the sound of voices waked something so painful, so terribly painful it might shatter him and make him a man again.

So quickly then, the aching knot untied itself, and the tears dried in the wind, and he lay smelling that cooking and thinking that he would sell his soul for a morsel of fresh bread and a little of human laughter. There was so little of it left to sell, so very little of what he had been. He was damned as the qhal and as this man who served her, and if they would take another soul for a little ease and a little food and a betrayal of his own kind, then he was apt enough for that trade.

He might have tamed the wolves, finally, and if they would let him be a wolf, then he need not fear Gault, or anything in the world—for a while. They might well be Gault's enemies: rumor was that the thing which was Gault had no love lost with his Overlord. They might be from Mante, or from somewhere—the woman had said it—that he did not understand; but if they let him be a wolf, if they took him among themselves and there was a kind of man who could walk among the qhal free as that one walked, and still in his own right mind—then there was hope . . . .

He shivered again, seeing Ichandren's head outside Gault's gates, seeing that dungeon again, and hearing the screams wrung from a man who was the bravest and strongest he had ever known, before they reduced him to a red and terrible lump of meat and struck off his head . . . .

. . . There was revenge. Gault would never know him by sight. It was a random choice had selected the few for the wolves. He was no one, that Gault should single him out for any personal revenge.

But if he was a wolf, there was a time Gault would learn to fear him and to curse the day he met him.

That was an aim even worth a man's soul.

For the first time the chance of a future opened up before him, like a mist clearing.

But he had met the woman's eyes by accident across the fire, and after that avoided—after that, avoided remembering, too closely, that he had felt himself in bodily danger from her. It was *that* kind of feeling, that a man did not expect to feel with a woman, that was unmanly to feel with a woman, and that one would never admit to; but if ever he remembered it, afterward, when he was with a woman, then he would have no power with her . . . no more with any woman, ever . . . .

She was indeed a witch, he thought. He knew folk who called themselves witches, and made a great deal of muttering over their herbs and potions, and midwived babes and horses into the world. A man did not cross them, or did so only if he had bought the token of a greater one for stronger luck—and too great a one might, the priests said, taint a man's soul.

Such great power he had felt in this one. He knew that it was. And it was better mercy by far had he gotten from her than Gault had gotten from Mante— the Gault they had honored before the qhal had taken him up with talk of peace; the Gault who had been Ichandren's friend, and worked the same ploy on Ichandren—God help them all.

Truce. Truce—Gault had said.

That was the faith qhal kept.

The man Vanye came down the hill finally: Chei watched him come—and trembled, as if in a dream; and walked with him at his invitation to share their fire.

Thereafter Chei sat wrapped in his blanket and took a meal he could not eat his share of, so weak his stomach was. But they were easy with him, the man and the woman both, and asked him few questions, and afterward let him lie over near the fire, while the witch took the pans down to the water to wash them like any woman of the bands; and Vanye after she had returned, led the horses down to water them, from their picket higher on the hill.

After that, while daylight faded, they worked on what Chei recognized for his own gear, picking bits of rust from the links of his chain-mail, scouring the metal with water and river sand, finishing it with oil.

His boots were already done, the one split as it was, but with a length of harness-leather lying looped about it, sufficient to wrap several times about the ankle and hold it.

He saw all these things, lying on his side, with only the blanket to clothe him . . . watched them work, even the witch, on these menial tasks which seemed to be for his benefit—for him, since they had no conceivable need of a pair of ruined boots or armor much poorer than the wonderful close-linked mail and supple leather that they wore.

In the deep night, when they said to each other that it was time to sleep, the man dragged his saddle and his bedding over by the horses and lay down there, while the witch wrapped herself in a dark cloak and settled against an old, thick-boled tree, to keep night-watch. They left him the warmth of the coals. They said no word to threaten him. They did not tie him.

Chei lay in the dark thinking and thinking, watching and drowsing by turns, observing every smallest move they made. Hope trembled through him, that they had already accepted him, for whatever reasons. He wept, in the dark, long and unreasonably.

He did not know why, except their kindness had broken something in him which all Gault's threats had never touched, and he was terrified it was all a lie.

Chapter Three

It was fish, the next supper they shared. There was not a rabbit to be had—the wolves, Vanye reckoned, who sang to them nightly, had seen to what hunting there was about the gate; although why the wolves themselves stayed in such an unwholesome place, he wondered.

It was the mountains to the south, Chei said; and humans; humans to the west and north; qhal to the north and east; and in all, Vanye reckoned, the wolves were as shy of habitations as they were in other worlds.

Excepting only, Chei said, the half-wolves. Gault's pets.

Or once, when war had made chaos of the middle lands—then Chei remembered the wild wolves coming down to human camps and villages to take the sheep. He remembered his folk moving a great deal—where, he did not know, except it had been in the hills.

"Then," Chei said, looking mostly at the fire, as if his thoughts ranged distant, "then we settled in Perot's freehold, in Aglund. We felt safe there. But that only lasted—at most, a year. Then Gault was fighting along with the other lords. I was a boy then. I remember—I remember wars, I remember having to move and move again. I remember the winters, with the snow chest-deep on the horses—and people died, many died. We came to Gault's freehold, in Morund. We were borderers, for him. Those were the good years. I rode with Ichandren. My brother, my father and I. They are dead. All."

He was silent for a time, then.

"Mother?" Morgaine asked.

Chei did not look at her. His throat worked. But the eyes never shifted from their wide gaze on the fire. "I do not know. I saw her last—" A lift of one shoulder. "I was thirteen winters. That was before Morund fell and Gault went north. He came back . . . Changed. After that—after that, he and the qhal from the north killed most of the human men at Morund-keep. Killed most everyone, and brought in men from the east. They would fight for Gault. Some of those from Morund might have wanted to, but if they took them at all, they marched them west, to serve the other qhal-lords. Gault would never trust men who had served him before he was qhal. Aye, nor women either. They put them all on wagons. We lost—twenty men trying to take the women from the guards. My father died then. There were just too many."

There was more of silence. The fire snapped and spat.

"But I doubt very much my mother was alive," Chei said. "Even then. My father believed it. But no one else did. She was not a strong woman. And it was a bad year."

Twenty men lost, Vanye thought, amid a man's grief, and thought by the way he had said it that twenty had been a devastating loss. *There were just too many. . . .*

He met Morgaine's eyes across the fire and knew that she had added that as quickly and set things somewhat in proportions—she, who had taught a young outlaw something beyond woodcraft and ambush; his lady-liege, who had ridden to war and sat in the affairs of kings a hundred years before he was born.

But she had led him into both war and kings' councils since then.

He rested his arms on his knees and probed the coals with a stick, watching it take fire.

"The trees," Morgaine said. "Do you mark them, Chei, how they twist here? Yet there is no present feeling of unease in this woods. Birds come here. They tolerate the gate-force very little. Why do you suppose this is?"

"I do not know," Chei said faintly.

Morgaine did not answer.

"Why would it be?" Chei asked her then.

Morgaine shifted the dragon sword to her lap, tucking one knee up, and hugged that knee against her. "If I cast leaves in the fire, it would flare. Would it not?"

"Yes, lady."

"And you would move back. Would you not?"

"Yes," Chei said, more faintly still, as if he regretted ever asking into qhalish lore.

"Quickly?"

"Yes, lady."

"So the birds would fly for their comfort if that gate yonder opened this moment. And you would feel it in your bones."

Chei flinched, visibly.

"So this is a very good place for a camp," Morgaine said, "for us who have no desire for unannounced visitors. How frequently do you suppose this gate is used?"

"I would not know."

"Perhaps not. So of that use we would have warning. If we ride from here we have Gault to concern us. How long—might we ride, slowly, on the road itself, before we came to his notice?"

"If we left after sundown—" Chei's breath came rapidly. "We could make the western road and be deep in the woods before daybreak. Lady, I do not know where his riders may be, no one could say that, but I know where they are likeliest not. We could make a safe camp in that woods near his lands, stay there the day, and pick up the west road. No one would be traveling that at night; and by one more morning we can reach the hills. We rest during the day, we travel at night. That is the best thing to do."

"So," Morgaine said, and glanced Vanye's way, a quick shift of her eyes. "We can reach the woods before the dawn," she said, looking back at Chei. "You are sure of that."

"A-horse, I know that we could."

"Then we will go," she said quietly. "If our guest swears he can bear the saddle, we had best leave this place. We do not know how long our welcome will last."

Vanye nodded, agreeing, with misgivings he knew she shared, and with a quiet as carefully maintained.

The place, true, had a ward as great as any fabled witchery could provide—that they would feel any disturbance in the gate.

But it held danger too: it was remotely possible—that that flaring of power could simply take them, at this range, if there were some unshielded gate-stone to which the force might reach—and if their enemies had found them.

Vanye had one change of clothes, cloth breeches and a fine shirt—the one for those times they could lay aside the armor, which did not look likely here: light and fine, delicately sewn—a waste to wear such a gift on the trail; but the giver had insisted.

Now he laid all this at Chei's side, along with the mended boots, as Morgaine was meticulously packing and weight-measuring with their bags.

"You could not bear the armor on your shoulders," Vanye said. "My liege will carry it; I will carry you on my horse. We are taking your word we can make cover before sunrise."

Chei took up the fine cloth and frowned in surprise. Well he might, Vanye thought; and went to prepare his own gear, and to saddle the horses in the dark. *They* knew that there was a journey to come, and stamped and shifted in impatience at this meddling about.

He saddled them both, and hung his sword at Arrhan's right side, where he would not carry it on a ride like this, except he had Chei at his back. He tied a folded blanket flat under thongs bound to the rings that ordinarily held it rolled, scratched Arrhan in the soft underside of her throat, and Siptah under his chin, snatching his fingers from the stud's half-hearted nip—trouble, he thought. Siptah had been trouble of one kind before, well-trained as he was; now that he had acquired the mare, Siptah had other thoughts in his head, and Arrhan had like ones.

"Fool," he muttered to himself, that ever he had taken her, that ever he had brought her to a land like this. He was Kurshin, was a horseman from his birth. And he had been, a handful of days ago, under a fair sun, too willing to hope—Heaven save them—for something other than this.

Fool, he thought again. For disaster went about the gates. Where power was, there the worst men gathered— too rarely, the best. He had ridden out among the twisted trees, among ruins, into murder and wars—

And all his subtle plans—for Morgaine was mad, at times, and drove them too hard and wore herself to bone and will—all his plans, ill-thought that they were, involved a means to travel at a saner pace. For that, he had accepted the mare, knowing there was a risk— but hoping for a more peaceful passage, for leisure and time, even to drop a foal of the Baien stud: such thoughts the arrhend had made reasonable, and now they seemed mad.

Now it was his own instincts urged they run.

He hugged the mare about the neck, pressed his head against her cheek, patted her hard, all with a pang of bitter guilt. "So we go," he whispered to her. She ducked her head free and nosed him in the side with a horse's thoughtless strength.

No stopping the stallion or the mare. No stopping any horse from what it truly willed to do, even if it was a fatal thing. It was always their own vitality that killed them, a horseman knew that.

He heard a step behind him, and turned his head. It was Morgaine, bringing the saddlebags. She let them down at his feet, then, standing close, rested her hand on his shoulder, and walked away, so startling him by that gesture he simply stood and stared at her retreating back.

What was that? he wondered.

Apology, of a kind? Sympathy?

She did these things to him, and walked away in her silences, and left him to saddle the horses and wonder, in a kind of biding panic, what had moved her to that.

He did not even know, Heaven witness, why he should be disturbed, or why his heart was beating in panic, except it was the old familiar business of snatched sleep and arming by dark and riding through hostile lands, sleeping by turns in the daylight, tucked close in some concealment.

Except it was Morgaine who, like Heaven, decided where they should go and when; and there had been all too much of comradely understanding in that small gesture—as if she had confessed that she was weary, too, and there were no miracles.

From his liege, he did not want such admissions.

He finished his work. He overtook her at the buried fire, leading the horses; and having the horses between him and Chei, he took his Honor-blade sheathed from his belt and gave it to her without a word—for safety's sake. She knew. She slipped it into her belt next her own ivory-hilted Korish blade, and pulled and hooked the belt ring which slid the dragon sword up to ride between her shoulders, before she took Siptah's reins from his hand and climbed into the saddle. The gray stud snorted his impatience and worked at the bit.

Vanye set his foot in Arrhan's stirrup and settled himself in the saddle, reining her about, where Chei waited, dressed in his borrowed clothing and his own mended boots, and holding his sleeping blanket rolled in his arms.

"You will want that on the ride," Vanye said, taking the blanket roll into his lap, and cleared his left stirrup for the man. Chei set his foot, took his offered hand as Arrhan shifted weight, and came astride and well-balanced so quickly that Vanye gave the mare the loose rein she expected. It made the mare happier about the double load; she pricked her ears up and switched her tail and took a brisk stride behind Siptah.

Through the trees and down along the river which had guided them—by the light of an incredible starry heaven and a slivered moon, so brilliant a night as the sunlight left the sky utterly, that the pale grass shone and the water had sheen on its darkness.

Behind him, Chei wrapped the blanket about himself, for the breeze was chill here in the open; and Vanye drew an easier breath, bringing Arrhan up on Siptah's left—the left, with Morgaine, shield-side and never the perilous right. She had her hair braided for this ride: not the clan-lord's knot to which she was entitled, but the simple warrior's knot of clan Chya of Koris, like his own. *Changeling's* hilt winked moonlit gold beside the silver of her braid; bright silver sparked and flashed along the edge of her sleeves, where mail-work shone the like of which later ages had forgotten. Moonlight touched Siptah's illusory dapples, the pale ends of his mane and tail.

They were enspelled—not with magics, but with the sense of change, of passage, the night sky's softening influence that made them part of a land to which they did not belong.

And Chei had sworn, on his life, that they might expect peace for a time on this ride.

They took the same slow pace when they had come to the Road, with its ancient stone bridge across the stream. Woods gave way briefly to meadow and to woods again, a tangled, unkept forest. A nightbird called. There was the sound of their horses' hooves—on earth and occasionally on stone, and eventually on the stone and damp sand of a ford which crossed a stream, perhaps tributary to the river they had left.

"I do not know its name," Chei said when Vanye asked. "I do not know. I only know we crossed it."

They let the horses drink, and rode further, in wilderness cut well back from the road, but unthinned beyond that. No woodsmen, Vanye thought, no caretaker. It was still wild woods, overgrown and rank with vines and thorns. But the trees grew straight and clean. Gate-force did not reach to this place. They were beyond the region in which they would know if the gate were used; and they were beyond the region in which some weapon of that nature could reach to them.

He felt Chei lean against him, briefly, and recover himself; felt it again; and again the same recovery; a third time: "No matter," he said. "Rest," and: "No," Chei murmured.

But in time Chei slumped a while against him, till they faced a stream-cut to go down and up again. "Chei," Vanye said, slapping him on the knee.

Chei came awake with a start and took his balance. Arrhan took the descent and the climb with dispatch then, and quickened her pace till she had overtaken Siptah.

They were still on the Road. It began to stretch away across a vast plain, country open under fewer and fewer stars, exposed to view as far as the eye could see, and Morgaine drew rein, pointing to the red seam along the horizon.

"Chei. That is the sun over there."

Chei said nothing.

"Where are we?" she asked.

"It is still the Road," Chei protested; and: "Lady, this is not the land I know. Northward—yes. But here—I have never been but the once. We are still on the Road—we will make it—"

"How far does this go?" Her voice had an edge to it, a dangerous one. "Wake up, man. You know what I would know. You swore that you did. Do you want your enemies' attention? Or do you tell me full and free that you do not know where you are?"

"I know where I am! There is a kind of ruin, I do not know how far—I swear to you, we will reach it by morning." Chei's teeth chattered, and his breath hissed, not altogether, Vanye thought, of exhaustion and the night chill. "It was our starting-place misled me. The river must have bent. I know it is there. I swear it is. We can still come to it. But we can go wide, now." He pointed over westward, where the plain rolled away to the horizon. "We can pick up the trail yonder in the hills. Off Gault's lands."

"But equally off our way," Morgaine said, and held

Siptah back, the dapple gray backing and circling. "How is Arrhan faring?"

"She will manage," Vanye said, and looked uneasily toward the lightening of the sky in the east, over low and rolling hills. "*Liyo*, I do not say yea or nay, but I had as lief be off this road. West is likely the best advice at this point."

"North," she said, and held Siptah still a moment, when he would have moved. "By morning, he swears. It is very little time."

She swung about and went on, not quickly, saving the horses.

"*Are* you mistaken?" Vanye asked of Chei.

"No," Chei said; and shivered, whether with cold he could not tell.

Morgaine had said it; there was only one way, ultimately, that they could go; and less and less he liked delay along this road, less and less he liked the prospect of a long journey aside, and more and more he disliked their situation.

"Best you be right, man."

Morgaine dropped back to ride beside. They went perforce at Arrhan's double-burdened pace, under an open sky and fading stars.

Chei hugged his blanket about him. It was terror kept him awake now. It was nightmare as dread as the wolves, this slow riding, this pain of half-healed sores and the slow, steady rhythm of horses which could go no faster, not though Gault and all his minions come riding off the horizon.

The sky brightened, the few wispy clouds in the east took faint and then pinker color, until at last all the world seemed one naked bowl of grass and one road going through it, unnaturally straight track through a land all dew-grayed green. At times Vanye and the lady spoke in a language he did not understand, a harsh speech which fell on the ear with strange rhythms, but softly spoken, little exchanges of a word and a few words. There was a grim tone to it. There was discontent. He imagined it involved him, though he dared not ask.

"Where are these ruins of yours?" Vanye asked then, and slapped him on the knee when he failed to realize that it was to him he had spoken.

"I know that they are there," he said, "I swear to you."

"Neither does the sun lie," Vanye said.

There was the beginning of daylight. There was the hint of color in things. And the white mare was weary now. Did their enemies find them, Chei thought, there was no way that the mare might run.

Did their enemies find them. . . .

But on that terrible hilltop, like a dream, he recalled light coming from Morgaine's fingers, and recalled chain melting and bending, and how Vanye had shielded him from that sight.

Weapons you may not like to see, Vanye had warned him.

He looked at the open land around him, and the treacherous roll of hills which might mask an army.

They would kill him first, he thought, if they suspected ambush. There was no doubt but what they would; he had failed them. They had cause to be angry.

The sun came up full. The land went gold and green.

And as they crested a rise of the plain and looked on a darkness that topped the rise ahead he felt a moment's dread that it was some band of riders—till his eye adjusted for the scope of the land and he knew it was woods that he saw.

They camped among ancient stones, beside a stream which crossed the low point among them, under the branches of trees which arched over and trailed their branches waterward. Among the ruins, a sparse and stubborn grass grew, on a ridge well-shielded by the trees; and there the horses grazed.

They ventured a fire only large enough to heat a little water, and ate bread Morgaine had made at the

last camp, and fish they had smoked; and drank tea—
Chei's prepared with herbs against the fever.

Chei had borne the ride, Vanye reckoned, very
well—was weary, and only too glad to lie down to
sleep, there in the sun-warmth, on the leafy bank. So,
then, was he, leaving the watch to Morgaine, and
listening to the water and the wind and the horses.

"It has been quiet," she whispered when she waked
him, while Chei still slept. "Nothing has stirred. A
bird or two. A creature I do not know came down to
drink: it looked like a mink with a banded tail. There
is a black snake sunning himself down on that log."

These were good signs, of a healthier vicinity. He
drew a deep breath and yielded her up the blankets,
and tucked himself down again in a nook out of the
wind. He had a bite to eat, a quarter of the bread he
had saved back from their breakfast; and a drink of
clear water from the stream which ran here, more
wholesome than the river had been.

And when toward dusk, Chei stirred from his sleep,
he rose and stretched himself, and put together the
makings of a little fire—again, hardly enough to warm
water, quick to light and quick to bury, and a risk
even as it was.

Morgaine roused them for tea and day-old cakes
and smoked fish, and sat against the rock, sipping her
portion of the tea and letting her eyes shut from time
to time. Then her eyes opened with nothing of somno-
lence about them at all. "We might stay here a day,"
she said. "We have put distance between ourselves
and the gate—which is very well. But this is the last
place we may have leisure. Another night's riding—
and we will be beyond Gault's holdings. Is that not the
case?"

"That is the case," Chei said. "I swear to you."

"Bearing in mind that hereafter I will not permit
Vanye's horse to carry double, and tire itself."

"I will walk. I can fend for myself, lady."

"Are you fit to walk? I tell you the truth: if you are
not fit—we will give you that day's grace. But there

may be other answers. Perhaps you know something
of Morund's inner defenses."

Chei's eyes widened in dread. "Guarded," he said.
"Well guarded."

"I," Vanye said, and rested his chin on his forearm,
his knee tucked beneath his elbow. "I have stolen a
horse or two in my life. I suppose Morund has pastures hereabouts. And for that matter, *liyo,* I can
quite well walk."

Morgaine glanced his way. So he knew that he had
guessed her intention all along, by that calm exchange.
And he had had a queasy feeling in all this ride, good
as the reasons were for quitting the last camp: Arrhan
might carry double at a very slow pace, but not in
haste—his liege not being a fool, to press one of their
horses to the limit.

But that she risked them this far on this man's word
had bewildered him, all the same—until she asked of
Morund.

"Or," he said in the Kurshin tongue, "we might let
our guide walk these trails he claims to know—alone.
And we go the quicker way, the two of us, by night
and by stealth, *liyo*, and get clear of this place. That is
my opinion in the matter."

She gave him a sudden sidelong glance.

He gave a little lift of his shoulder. No frown was on
her face, but that, he thought, was because there was
a witness.

"I will have a word with thee," she said, and motioned off toward the streamside.

But: "I do not think there is overmuch to say," he
said, and did not rise. "I am *ilin.* Ask. I will do it.
Steal a horse? That is nothing. Perhaps I should take
Morund. You hardly need trouble yourself."

"Thee is unreasonable!"

"I do not think I am unreasonable. Everything you
wish, I will do. Can a man be more reasonable? Take
Morund. Better that than walk in there. *Far* better
than drag this poor man in there, since you are set on
stirring up a trouble we could ride around. We have
come this far on this man's advice. Take the rest of it,

I say, and go where he bids us go, and let us go around this place."

For a moment she did not speak. There was sullen anger in the look she gave him. Then: "Oh, aye, and trust to luck and half a score human bands, shall we?"

"Better luck than this Gault, *liyo*. And what will we, do general murder? Is *that* what you want? It is what you lead us to. Someone will die, likest myself, since I have to shield you. I have a bruise the size of my fist on my right shoulder—"

"Whose fault, that?"

"—and a man by me I do not trust; or we do trust him, enough to let him free where he could cry alarm; or we do murder outright on this man—Which is it, do we kill him, do we tie him to a tree for the wolves and his enemies to find, or do we trust him to go free? Or if we trust him for that, why in Heaven's sweet reason do we not trust him down the back trail ourselves, and take ourselves clear of this damnable place before we raise hue and cry from here to the north?"

She rose abruptly to her feet and walked off. It left him Chei's frightened stare.

"We are having a dispute," Vanye said, "regarding the ease of finding horses."

Chei said nothing at all. He looked from one to the other of them, and for a long while Morgaine stood by the streamside, arms folded, staring off into the gathering dark.

Vanye buried their fire, and went down to wash the single pan they had used.

"Thee confuses me," Morgaine said, standing behind him as he rinsed the pan. "Thee considerably confuses me."

It was not, precisely, what he had expected her to say.

"Then," he said, "we confuse each other."

"What will you?"

That was not the question he was prepared for either—or it was the earnestness of it which confounded him.

"What will *you*?" He turned from the stream, for he

sensed her precisely where she was, her back turned to
their prisoner and the horses; and all manner of mis-
chief possible. "I have no idea—"

"Thee does not kneel."

"I am washing the cursed dish," he retorted, "and
you have your back to the man. Do you trust him that
much?"

"Now thee is watching. I *trust* that thee is watching.
What will thee? To let him free? Ride in among his
folk, on his guidance? *Or* do we kill him or leave him
for the wolves?"

"Ah. I thought it was his oath we trusted."

She drew in a sharp breath, and said nothing at all
as he got to his feet. They were of a height. He stood
lower on the bank. And for a long moment he did not
move.

"Or," he said, "do you think we should *not* trust his
guidance? Lord in Heaven, you took his oath. Did you
count me so lightly? I do not recall my pledge was
much different."

"Thee is *Kurshin*," she said, and recalled to him
what he had forgotten: that it was more than the
language she spoke, that she was, perhaps to a greater
extent than he had thought—Andurin, out of the wood-
land cantons of his own land.

"You will not let me remember it," he said, and
jutted a clenched jaw toward the man who waited by
the dead fire. "He is human. But it is not considering
my scruples you took his oath. You deceived him and
you refused to confide in me. Why?"

"I do not deceive you."

"You do not tell the truth."

"*Thee* pleaded for his life."

"*I* had as soon have left him at the last camp, where
he had some choice where to go. *I* had as soon gone
further west from the beginning and come up through
the hills."

She pressed her lips together in that way she had
when she had said all she would. So their arguments
tended to end—himself with the last word, and Morgaine lapsed into one of her silences that could last for

hours and evaporate at the last as if there had never been a word of anger.

But always Morgaine did as she would—would simply ride her own way, if he would not go with her; there was no reasoning with her.

"I will get your cursed horse," he said.

She drew a sharp breath. "We will go *his* way, by the trails."

He felt his face go hot. "So we walk turn and turn."

"I did not ask that."

"That is a wounded man. How much do you think he can do?"

"I am willing to wait here. Did I not say as much?"

"Wait here! With the enemy over the next hill!"

"What would you?"

Now it was he who found no words. He only stood there a moment, half-choked with anger; then bowed his head and walked on past her, back to put the pan with their gear.

Chei looked at him with the same bewilderment, his eyes jerking from one to the other—lastly toward Morgaine, who came and sat down on her heels beside them.

Vanye sat as he was a moment, jabbing at the ground with a stick between his knees. "I reckon," he said mildly, "that we could make the back trails. If Chei and I rode and walked by turns."

Morgaine rested her arms on her knees, her brow on the heels of her hands. Then she dropped her arms and sat down cross-legged. "Myself," she said, "I am not of a mind to be inconvenienced by this Gault of Morund."

A touch of renewed panic hit him. *"Liyo—"*

"On the other hand," she said, "your suggestion is reasonable. Unless our guide knows where we might find horses, otherwise."

"Not except we raise the countryside," Chei said in a faint voice.

"How far a journey—clear of his lands?"

"By morning we are clear."

Vanye rested the stick in both his hands. "In the

name of Heaven," he said in the Kurshin tongue, "he will tell you whatever he thinks will save his life: he was wrong this morning, and we rode under sun and in the open."

"Trusting him is thy advice, and first it is aye and then nay—which do I believe?"

"I am a Man. I can trust him without believing him. Or trust him in some things and not in others. He is desperate, do you understand. Wait here. I will go and steal you a horse."

"Enough on the horse!"

"I swear to you—"

"Vanye—"

"Or lord Gault's own cursed horse, if you like! But I should not like to leave you with this man. *That* would be my worry, *liyo*. Leaving you here, I *would* tie him to a tree, and I would not take his word how far it is across this cursed lord's land. I will tell you what I had rather do: I had rather do without the horse, strike out due west, far from here, and come north well within the hills."

"Except it needs much too long."

"Too long, too long—God in Heaven, *liyo*, it *needs* nothing but that we ride quietly, carefully, that we arrive in our own good time and disturb no one. I thought we had agreed."

"He named a name," Morgaine said.

"What, he? Chei? What name?"

"Skarrin, in Mante. This lord in the north."

His heart clenched up. "Someone you know?"

"Only an old name. We may be in great danger, Vanye. We may be in very great danger."

For a moment there was only the sound of the wind in the leaves.

"Of what sort?" he asked. *"Who?"*

"In the north," she said. "I am not certain, mind. It is only a very old name—and this north-lord may be an old man, *very* old, does thee mark me. And once he knows his danger, there are measures he might take which could trap us here. Does thee understand me?"

"Who is he?"

"I do not know who he is. I know *what* he is. Or I guess. And if I bind this man by oaths and any promise I can take from him—I do not loose him near that gate behind us, does thee understand? From Morund I might gain something. From Morund I might draw this north-lord south, out of reach of his own gate. But thee may be right—there is the chance too that this Gault is mad, and that there is no dealing with him."

"With a man who feeds his enemies to wolves?"

"With a *devil*, there is dealing—sometimes far easier than with an honest man. And by everything Chei has told us, there are Men enough among the qhal and not the other way about, so we need not worry for thy sake. But thee says trust this Man, and trust ourselves to his folk—"

"I did not say that!"

"What does thee say? Leave him? Kill him? Is that what thee is asking? Or ride on with him? We are too far into this to camp, and if this lord Gault finds us skulking about without his leave, that brings us to a fight or to Morund-gate, under worse terms."

Vanye raked his hair out of his eyes, where it fell forward of the braid, and raked it back again, resting his elbows on his knees.

In Andur-Kursh, Men would shoot a qhal on sight.

"Has Chei ever heard my other name? Did you by any chance tell it to him?"

"I do not know," he said, dismayed. "The one the Shiua used?" And when she nodded: "I do not know. I think not. I am not sure. I did not know—"

"Do not speak it. Ever. And do not ask me now."

He glanced at Chei, who stared at him and at her as his only hope of safety—his life, Chei surely sensed hung in the balance in this dispute he could not follow. It was a sensible man, Vanye thought, whose eyes followed all their moves, but who had the sense to hold his peace. "He is surely wondering what we say— Heaven knows what he understands of us—but in God's good mercy, *liyo*—"

She rose and walked back to Chei; and he rose and followed.

"Can you walk?" Morgaine asked in the qhalur tongue, looking to Chei. "Do you think you can walk through the night?"

"Yes," Chei said.

"He is telling you anything he thinks he must," Vanye said in the other. "He fears you. He fears to refuse any qhal, that is the trouble with him. Let him ride and I will walk, and let us go the trails he says he knows, quietly as we may. That is my advice. That is all the advice I have. Quickly and quietly, and without bruising a leaf. It is *Men* here I had rather trust. And you know that it is not my human blood makes me say it: I had no such feeling in the arrhend, and you well know it."

"My conscience," she named him. "And has thee forgotten—it is a world's honest men who will always fight us. I dread them, Vanye, I do dread them, more than the Gaults and all the rest."

"Not here," he said with conviction. "Not here, *liyo*. Nor, let me remind you, in my land, where you found me."

"Ah, no. Thee saw only the end of it. In Andur-Kursh I did my very worst. And most I killed were my friends." It was rare she would speak of that. There was a sudden bleakness in her face, as if it were carved of bone, and as if there were only the qhal-blood in her and nothing else. "But thee says it: this is not Andur-Kursh. Thee trusts this man, and I had rather be where I know what a man stands to gain—have I not said I have no virtue? But so be it. I do not say I have always been right, either. We will go his way."

He was frightened then, with a fear not unlike the moments before battle.

The north, she had said—an *old* enemy. And he argued against her instincts which had saved them a hundred times over, however unlikely her choices.

Heaven save them, *who* in this land could know her name, when they had never passed this way in their lives, nor had aught to do with the people of it?

"We are going on," he said to Chei, who looked at them with bewilderment. "I will walk. You ride. My liege thinks it too much risk to venture Morund for a horse."

There was still the bewilderment in Chei's eyes. And gratitude. "She is right," he said, in innocence.

He did not want to take it for omen.

He went up to the ridge and fetched the horses down. He saddled them, and arranged their gear.

"Get up," he said then to Chei, who waited, no more enlightened than before. "I am leading the horse. From time to time we will trade places."

"And hereafter," Morgaine said, touching Chei on the shoulder before he could get to the saddle, "should we meet anyone, if you have heard any other name than Morgaine and Vanye—consider your own safety and forget that ever you heard it: there are those who would do worse to you than ever Gault did, to have their hands on anyone who knew different—and you could not tell them what they would want. Do not ask me questions. For your own sake."

"Lady," Chei said to her, half-whispering. He looked straight into her eyes close at hand, and his face was pale. "Aye, lady."

Vanye walked, the qhal-witch rode, when they had come down the streamside and found that trail Chei knew—that narrow track the fey-minded deer and determined borderers took which ended, often with like result, on Gault's land.

Chei watched them from his vantage—the qhalur witch, the man who deferred to her at most times and argued with her with a reckless violence that made his gut tighten instinctively; a man knew, a Man knew lifelong, that the qhal-lords were not patient of such familiarity—or Vanye himself had deceived him, and was not human. But he could not believe that when he looked in Vanye's brown and often-worried eyes, or when Vanye would do him some small and unnecessary kindness or take his side—he knew that Vanye had done that—in argument.

What these two were to each other he still could
not decide. He had watched all their movements,
the gestures, the little instants that an expression
would soften, or she would touch his arm at times
when she gave an order—but never did he touch her
in that same way or truly bid her anything, for all he
might raise his voice and dispute her.

They are lovers, he thought sometimes. Then he
was equally sure that they were not—not, in the way
the man deferred to her: *my lady*, Vanye would say;
or *my liege*, or a third word he did not understand, but
which likely signified the same.

Now they raged at each other, argued in voices
half-whisper, half-shout, in which debate he—Vanye
had said it—was undoubtedly the center of matters.

It was not the threat to his life that bewildered him.
It was that there was argument possible at all. And
between arguments he saw a thing he had never, in all
his life, beheld. He watched them in a fascination
which, increasing, absorbed his fear.

Unholy, he thought. But there seemed profound
affection between them. There was more than that—
but not in the way of any man and any woman he had
known. It was that loyalty which bound the bands
together.

It was that devotion for which men had followed
Ichandren till he died.

It was that motion of the heart which he thought
had died in him; and it ached of a sudden, it ached so
that he rode along with the branches and the leaves
raking him, and the tears running down his face—not
fear such as he had felt in the night, but a quiet ache,
for no reason at all that he could think of except he
was alone.

He reckoned even that it was a spell the witch had
cast over him, that from the time she surprised him
with that look into his eyes, from that moment his soul
had been snared. Now he found himself weeping
again—for Falwyn and the rest, and for Bron and
Ichandren his lord, and even for his father, which was
foolish, because his father was many years dead.

He was weak, that was all. When the lady reined back and the man stopped the horse under them, saying they would rest, he was ashamed, and pretended exhaustion, keeping his face toward the horse as he climbed down.

So he sat with them, at the side of what had become a dirt track, and tucked his knees up and bowed his head against his arms so he should not have to show his eyes damp.

He should find some means to get a weapon and break from them—in this night, in this tangle he knew and they did not. The man he had once been would have done something to resist them, be it only slide off the horse and hope that he could put brush between them and him, and lie hidden.

But he let go his hopes in all other directions. He began truly to mean the oath that he had sworn. He wiped his face, disguising tears as sweat, despite the night air, and took the cup of water they passed him, and took their concern—for all that he had thought Vanye's earlier anger was half for him, Vanye's hand was gentle on his shoulder, his voice was gentle as he inquired was he faint.

"No," he said. "No. I will walk a while."

"Horses will fly," Vanye muttered to that. "We have half the night gone. What do we look to find ahead?"

"I will know the border," he said. "We have come halfway."

"As you knew the plains yonder?"

"This, I know," he insisted, anxious, and found the stirrup as the lady mounted up. He heaved himself into the saddle and took his seat as the horse started to move, Vanye walking ahead on the road, defined in a ray of moonlight and gone again, ghostly warrior in forest-color and mail and leather, the white scarf about his helm, the sheen of the sword hilt at his shoulders the most visible aspect of him. And the lady was no more than gray horse and shadow: she had put on her cloak and the dark hood made her part of the night.

Only he himself was visible, truly visible, to any

ambush—helmless, in a pale linen shirt and astride the white mare that shone like a star in the dark. He thought of arrows, thought of the gates of Morund which lay beyond the woods, across the ancient Road.

He thought of Ichandren's skull bleaching there, and the bodies of the others cast on Morund's midden heap, and shivered in the wind, taking up his gray blanket again and wrapping it about himself partly for the cold and partly that he felt all too visible and vulnerable. He trembled; his teeth chattered if he did not clench them, and every measured tread of the horse beneath him, the whisper of the wind, the small sounds of the night—seemed all part of a terrible dream begun at Gyllin-brook.

He had ridden this way, part of Ichandren's band. In those days they had been Gault's allies; in those days they had won victories. For a few years there had seemed to be a turning in their fortunes against the northlord.

It was the same road. But the boy who had traveled it, keen on revenge for both mother and father, on winning a sure victory against the thing Gault had become . . . had become a thin and beaten man, much the wiser, in the company of strangers and on a journey which at one moment seemed swift and full of turns, and in this forever-lasting night—such a peak of terror that it could not last; as the things they did to his comrades could not last; as the nights atop the hill could not last: there was always a morning, and done was done, and a man survived somehow, that was all—but O God, the hours between, that a man had to live . . . .

They rested yet again. Quietly the woman spoke—some suggestion which Vanye refused: perhaps, Chei thought, it was to put him off the horse and make him walk a time. And Vanye would not, whatever it was, which imagined kindness reassured him and made him warmer in the long night.

But he was afraid with a growing fear—that he had not accurately reckoned their pace: the rides he recalled had been swift and none of them had been afoot. Once he had misjudged the plains: that was the mistake of a shock-dazed memory. But now he misjudged again—he knew that he had, and that safety was further than daylight at the pace they were setting; and more difficult than he had thought, for the shock was done and the mind began reckoning clearly again, that since Ichandren was lost—any situation might prevail and the borders might have moved as they did after battles: things might not be what they had been and it was not to a known land that he was returning.

Nor was it any longer a known land in which he was both guide and hostage.

And to confess to them the fact that he had twice mistaken the distance—or given them false assurance –

He moistened his lips. He shifted his weight in the saddle. "Man," he whispered. "Vanye."

Then something else came to his ears beyond wind and leaf-whisper and the sound of their own horses. Vanye stopped the horse. The lady reined back and circled back toward them, then stopped again in mid-turn.

The woods felt wrong. Hairs lifted at his nape, and he shivered again, looking about him as Vanye did, at thicket and nightbound silence. The mare stood steady, hard-muscled under Vanye's touch. The gray stud yonder had his ears up, and they angled back and twitched as he shifted round, restless and with nostrils flared.

Of a sudden, in that silence—was another definite sound, faint and far ahead.

"Get down," Vanye whispered faintly. "Get down, man. Take cover. Quietly."

Chei looked at him in panic. "Gault's men," he whispered, with one wild thought of driving in his heels and seizing control of the horse—weaponless as he was, with Gault's hunters abroad.

"My lady has a weapon aimed at you," Vanye said, "and you will get down."

Chei looked in startlement. He saw no weapon at all, only the cloaked form and the lady's face. And in that instant, quick as a snake striking, Vanye had one hand entangled in his breeches-leg, and the mare was shying the other direction—the night suddenly, irrevocably upended and his shoulders and the back of his head meeting the ground before his hips and his legs did.

Colors exploded in his skull. He was helpless for the instant, the breath driven out of him; he saw Vanye leap to the saddle, saw the white mare shy over in quiet, mincing paces and move back again as Vanye carefully, quietly, drew his sword and lifted the fallen blanket from the dust.

Vanye flung it at him off the sword-tip, and he caught it, dazed as he was; flung himself over and scrambled for the brush and safety, hugging the blanket to him as he sprawled belly down.

The white and the gray horse had moved too, like ghosts over amongst the trees, a wisp of illusion, a pallor which did not belong and which a searching eye must see.

Chei wrapped the blanket about his own white shirt and made himself part of the ground, next a deadfall, next the smell of decaying leaves and rotting wood and the pungent, herbal stink of centurel that he had bruised in lying there.

Such a small accident could kill a man. A waft of wind. A breeze. A silence when no silence should be—as there was now; or the smell of crushed leaves reaching an enemy. He held himself from shivering, pressed as tight to the cold earth as if he could by willing himself, sink into it.

Chapter Four

The sound grew in the night—riders on the road, a goodly number of them, Vanye reckoned, knee to knee with Morgaine there in the dark; and a tremor went through his muscles, the chill that was no chill but a desire to move. He felt the heavy press of Siptah's shoulder against his right leg, heard the small sounds as the warhorse pulled at the reins and worked at the bit.

Arrhan stood—arrhend-foaled and trained to stand silent at a pass of a hand over her neck and a careful hand on the reins. So the Baien gray was trained to stand and hold silent; but that was not all his training, and Morgaine's little distractions with the bit only availed so far with him. It was oil and metal, was the presence of a mare and the smell of strangers and strange horses the warhorse would have in his sensitive nostrils, and it was only a skilled and familiar hand could hold him as still as he was, frothing the bit and sweating.

It would happen, Vanye thought; horseman that he was, he felt it in the air—sensed it in the number of the horses coming, the agitation at his right, which infected the mare under him and made her shiver and work the bit—it was in the way the road lay and the startlement likely when the riders turned that bend and the shifting and fickle breeze carried sound and scent to the horses, was in the growing sound of hooves and metal, not the sound of peaceful folk, but of riders in armor, in the night and moving together.

A horse whinnied, on the road before the turning. Siptah snorted and gave half an answer before he answered to the rein, rising on his hind legs and breaking brush on his descent; Arrhan shied over and fidgeted, complaining.

There was quiet again, both their horses and the ones down the road, deathly quiet in the woods.

"That has it," Morgaine hissed, hardly above a breath. "They have stopped. They will sit there till daylight if we are lucky—and send a messenger back to their lord if we are not."

Vanye slid his sword into sheath. "My bow," he said, and made a sign in that direction.

She leaned and loosed it from her gear, along with the capped quiver, and quietly passed it over to him. The horses bided quiet, the damage done. Siptah ducked his head and worked to free more rein, but Arrhan stood steady as Vanye stepped carefully down from the saddle and felt for footing among the undergrowth. He cleared Arrhan's reins and lapped them round a sapling that might hold when Siptah moved, Heaven knew.

He took off his helm with its betraying sheen and passed it to Morgaine before he slipped past Siptah's head with a reassuring touch on a sweaty neck and insinuated his way into the brush.

It was not alone Myya deer he had hunted when he had been an outlaw. The instincts came back, with the memory of Myya arrows and hunger: a desperate Nhi-Chya boy had learned of the only tutors he had, his enemies, and was still alive, when some of his Myya kinsmen were not.

He heard them, as quiet as half a score of riders could be, all drawn aside into brushy cover—no one of them so quiet as a single Kurshin hunter could stalk them. He saw them, himself motionless and themselves as still as they could hold their horses, vague shadows in the starlight. He moved carefully beyond them. The horses knew he was there. They jerked at the reins and fretted. The men cast about them anxiously, beginning to look back they way they had come, at the woods about them.

In moves soft and still he set his bow against his instep and strung it; he uncapped his quiver and took out three arrows, brushing the protected fletchings to be sure of them in the dark. There was not an arrow he had he did not know as sound. There was not a crooked shaft or a marred feather in the lot.

He nocked the first and chose the clearest and the nearest target, rising from the thicket: there was no mail forged might stand against an arrhendur longbow full-bent at that range. His bruised shoulder held sound. The arrow flew, thumped in a solid hit and the man fell.

The others turned to look. He had another arrow nocked while they were amazed, and a second man went down with an outcry as a horse broke free and went shying off into the road.

Third arrow: the men scrambled to mount and ride, and one of them cried out and fell even as he made the saddle.

Vanye snatched another arrow from the quiver braced against his leg. He took a fourth man in the back as the troop bolted away from his fire, toward Morgaine.

Then he snatched up his quiver and ran past the fallen, caring nothing for concealment as he raced down the road after them, his heart hammering against his ribs.

He heard the outcries and the crash of brush before he reached the turning; and beyond it as he rounded the bend was Siptah and his rider in the moonlight and horses still shying off from the calamity that had spilled their masters lifeless in the dust. He saw Chei scramble from cover, bent on seizing one of the loose horses, saw Morgaine with deadly aim wheel instead toward himself and knew a moment of stark terror.

"*Liyo,*" he called out, holding the bow wide.

Then she knew him, and spun the stallion about to ride after Chei as he swung up onto the captured horse with more strength than a sick man ought to show.

He thought then that she would kill Chei outright or

shoot the horse under him, and he ran with a dread
like ice in his gut—he could not cry out, not stay her
from what had to be: he was afoot, and Chei escaping
on horseback, and she had no strength to grapple with
him hand to hand—there was no way that Morgaine
could stop him, else. He ran, breathless and armor-
weighted, down the middle of the roadway.

But Chei was reining hard about, the panicked horse
going wide on the turn and fighting the bit; and
Morgaine reined back, bringing Siptah to a stop facing
him.

Chei rode back to join them, of his own will. Vanye
reached Morgaine's side with a stitch in his side and a
roaring in his ears, sweat running beneath his armor.
He saw the terror on Chei's face, the terror of a man
who had just seen the deaths he had seen—and knew
what might have overtaken him an instant ago and
what might befall him now. But Chei had made his
decision. By riding back—he had declared something,
at least.

And there were eight dead back there, four dark
lumps in the roadway, others where he had left them
beyond the turning. There were seven horses headed
wherever those horses thought to go—home and stable, eventually, with empty saddles and trodden reins.

"Did any escape?" Morgaine asked, not taking her
eyes from Chei.

"No," Vanye said, "if none passed you."

"None," she said in that hard, clipped tone, "but
we have horses loose and dead men lying here with
marks on them that will raise questions in Morund—
Chei! Whose are they? Are they Gault's?"

"Gault's," Chei said in a low voice.

Vanye drew a ragged breath. "The marks I can care
for." The blood was still up in him. In an hour he
would be shaking. Now the grisliest tasks seemed possible. "If it is the sword Chei's people favor."

"It will not hide the burning well enough," Morgaine
said; and coldly: *"Fire* will. *Fire* in these woods will
occupy them no little time. Move the bodies deep into
the brush."

"God," Chei murmured in a tone of horror. "Burn the woods? Burn the land?"

"Vanye," Morgaine said flatly.

Vanye set the bow against his foot and unstrung it; and handed that and the quiver to Morgaine's left hand, the while she hardly took her eyes from Chei.

"Help him," she bade Chei in a voice still colder. "You seem fit enough."

"If any are alive—" Vanye said. The numbness was still about him. It frayed suddenly; and he tried to hold onto it, tried not to think at all except in terms of what he must do.

"Find that out," she said.

Beyond that she did not give him orders. Beyond that, surely, was her own numbness, as essential as his own. It was cowardice to ask what he should do in that case, cowardice to cast the necessity onto his liege by asking for instruction, when he knew as well as she that they could afford no delays and no second and hostile encumbrance. He walked back toward the men on the ground, slipping his sword to his side, unhooking and drawing it. He heard the two horses walking at his back, heard one rider dismount and delay a moment; he had no attention for anything but the supposed dead—men armored much as Chei had been, in leather and chain.

There was no doubt of the four Morgaine had taken. He went into the woods where Arrhan stood fretting— the white mare, the cause of so many deaths. He recovered his helm from where he had left it, freed the mare and rode back beyond the curve of the road where he had left the rest of the company, those his arrows had accounted for.

One of them was qhal. All of them were dead.

Thank Heaven, he thought; and was horrified at his own blasphemy.

He tied Arrhan by the road and dragged the dead men as far into the brush as he could manage; and rode back to Morgaine and Chei, where Chei tried to do the same, staggering and panting with the effort of hauling yet another armored corpse off into the brush of the roadside.

Vanye lent his help, himself staggering by the time that they had laid out the last of the bodies well within the woods.

Chei said not a word in all of it—worked with his face averted and grim, his gasps after breath the only sound except the breaking of brush as they trod back to the open road.

"Wind to the east," Morgaine said as they mounted up. Under her, Siptah sidled toward Chei or his horse and she curbed that. "I trust this road tends north, Chei—rapidly."

"Yes," Chei answered.

"On your life," Morgaine said then, and lifting her arm toward the roadside fired the black weapon she carried, taking no trouble now to conceal it, from a man who had seen it and seen the wounds it made, burning through flesh and bone.

Now it was the dry leaves it burned, and a thin line of fire traced itself along the ground where it aimed. The fire increased with a dry crackling. The horses fretted and complained at the smell of smoke, and they let them move.

All along that curve of the road as they went, Morgaine raised fire. That behind them blazed bright when Vanye looked over his shoulder.

The dawn itself was not so bright. It was well beyond the fire that they could see the sun coming, a lightening of the east that had nothing to do with that ominous glare in the woods behind them.

"It is Gault's woods," Chei muttered when they let the horses breathe, looking back from a height and a turning of the wooded road. "It is his woods we are burning, and the wind will bring the fire to his fields."

Vanye stared at the line of fire below them that now rolled smoke into a dim but increasingly sunlit sky. For himself he wanted clean water, in which he could wash his hands and wash his face and take the stink of death and burning out of his nostrils.

Lord in Heaven, there were horses loose down there,

in that, no knowing whether the road would take them to safety. And the land itself—

Burn the woods? Burn the land?

He was not sure where it weighed, against ambush and murder of unsuspecting men who might, Heaven knew, have run from the sight of them; or a lord who fed his enemies to wolves; or the obscure terrors which Morgaine feared, which involved the gates and things which she tried in vain to make him comprehend.

The gates opened too far, into too much, and it was possible, Morgaine had said, that they could unravel all that was and take it into themselves. Perhaps that was so. He did not conceive of things in the way Morgaine did—he did not want to conceive of them, in the same way he did not want to know why the stars shifted, or where they were when they were between the gates and there were neither stars nor substance.

But he had felt the gate-force in his bones. He had stared into the void often enough to know it was hell itself that beckoned there.

He knew what made a man like Gault. He knew that there was, for himself and his liege, no honor such as the world counted it, and that the most irresponsible thing in the world was to have let a man of that company back there escape alive, to bring pursuit on them, for if they should fall—Morgaine had told him—the deaths would be . . . everything: all that had ever been and might be. In this she was telling the truth as she believed it, though she had lied to him in lesser things. On this one item of faith he committed himself body and soul. He even hoped—in the secrecy of his heart—that God might forgive him. For all the murder, God might forgive him and forgive her, if it was somehow right, what they did, and they were not deceived.

But he wished with all his soul, that he could feel as keen a remorse as once he might have felt for the men he had killed back there. He could not find it again. There was only horror. There was keenest anguish— but that mostly for the horses; and very little for the men, even of his own kind. He was afraid when he knew that, as if something were slipping irrevocably away from him, or he from it, and he did not know his way back from this point.

"Where have we gotten to?" Morgaine asked their guide when they had come still a little higher up the road, up where the road bent again away from the dawn and toward the still-shadowed sky; and the fire below them was a rolling of white smoke across the tops of trees. "Can we get off this road and onto the old one?"

"It is not safe," Chei said. His face by the dawning light was haggard and his hair wild, with bits of dead leaves stuck in it. His eyes held a feverish look, as well a man's might, which had seen what they had. "If you want ambush, lady, that is where to find it."

"Where were they going before dawn?" Vanye asked harshly, for that was the thing that made no sense to him; it outraged him, that men had been so foolish, and he had had to pay them for it. He felt *that*, when he wished to Heaven he could feel something like conscience.

One of them, Mother of God, had been hardly more than sixteen; and tears stung his eyes, at the same time he could have struck anything in his path.

"I do not know," Chei said. "I do not know."

"We assume they had reason," Morgaine said shortly. "We assume it was on this road and we may yet meet it, to someone's sorrow—do you understand me, Chei?"

"I do not know," Chei protested, shaking his head.

"You took a great chance," Morgaine said, "running for that horse back there in the woods. If not for that white shirt, you would be dead. Eight men are— lest they betray us. Do you still understand me, Chei?"

"Yes, lady," Chei said in a faint voice.

"Are we yet off Gault's land? Where is his border?"

"I do not know.—It is truth! We fought north of here. My lord Ichandren—is dead. Gault's forces are on the road at night—God knows, God only knows, lady, what they were doing, or where more of them are—That fire will draw them, but it will draw other attention too—God knows who, or whether they will think it an accident or set. It is Gault's land down there. His men would not burn his own land. Neither—" He hesitated a breath. "Neither have we ever fired the land we move in. That road will be Gault's when it has burned out. It will be black sticks and open to the eye, and it will be so much more land he can march through."

It was indignation, that last. Vanye leaned on the saddlebow and frowned—it was a change in Chei's voice and bearing, was even daring of a Man toward a qhal who threatened him, and with corpses a-smolder in the forest to prove it. "What," Vanye said, "'we'? Friends of yours? And how will *we* fare with them?"

Chei's mouth stayed open an instant. There was a wild flicker in his eyes, only the briefest of moments. Then his glance settled from him onto Morgaine and back again. "The same as I," he said. "They will kill us all, you on sight, me when they recognize me for one of Ichandren's men. Prisoners do not come back. But if we go back to the Old Road, they will take us for Gault's and kill us just the same."

It was wretched enough to be the truth.

"And where are they?" Morgaine asked. "Close enough to cause that band of Gault's to ride at night? What are we going into?"

"War," Chei said, "war, lady, beginning with that fire down there and eight men dead. If things had settled to any truce before—Gault will lay that fire to the account of human folk, and human folk will know that when they see the fire. Up there in the hills they will know it, and they will move down to strike while they can, while Gault's men are occupied putting it out—Gault knows *that* too; and he will throw every man he can spare out toward the hills to prevent it. That is the way things are. We must go up, by the remote trails, we must keep moving by night, and hope we do not have to give account of ourselves— there will be ambushes laid on every road Gault's men will take."

It seemed like the truth. It seemed very much like the truth, after so much of deception and mistake.

"Should we believe you?" Morgaine asked. "You are twice *wrong*, Chei."

"I do not want to die." Chei's voice trembled. He leaned forward in the saddle, shirt-clad shoulders taut in the chill wind. "Before God, lady—if we go the way you want we will run head-on into ambush. I know that I have been wrong. I have no excuse, except I hoped we could go faster, except—I lied—how well I knew the land down there. Here, truly, here is the place I know. I have lived to get here. And I will not, on my life, be wrong again. I swear it to you."

"We dare not tire the horses," Vanye muttered. *"Liyo,*—whatever we meet, we cannot push them now."

Morgaine looked at him. For a moment there was that look in her eyes he knew and dreaded—that impatience that would kill them. Then reason returned.

"I know a place," Chei said very quietly, "not far from here, to camp."

It was a place well-hidden among the trees, where a spring broke from the rocks of the hill—not a great deal of water, Vanye saw as they rode in, but sufficient. He climbed down from the saddle, finding suddenly that his very bones ached, and that the mail weighed far more on his shoulders than it had when he had put it on two days ago. "Let me," he said, catching up Siptah's reins while Morgaine dismounted: the gray stud had decided on war with the stolen bay gelding, and his ears were back and his movements full of equine cunning—not outright challenge, but going toward it, in little increments of aggression that meant all three of their horses unsettled.

"He hates that horse," Morgaine said, and reached and jerked at the gray's chin-strap, turned his attention and rubbed the nose the stallion offered her like a maid's fat pony. "I will take him in hand, no mind. It is Arrhan has him disturbed."

A heat came to his face. It was as close to reproach

on that score as she had come, and it flew straight to a sore spot.

While Chei, wisely, drew his horse well off out of reach in the little clearing among the pines—for pines they were, at last a tree like trees of Andur-Kursh; and a little scraggle of grass among the rocks.

But the while he unsaddled the mare, Vanye shot glances Chei's way, past Arrhan's shoulder—"Heaven knows," he said to Morgaine, "what is in that gear he has gotten along with the horse."

"We will find out," Morgaine said quietly, the while she took down Chei's armor, which Siptah had carried this far. "He will have his own gear to carry when we ride on, that much I know.—Hush, hush." She reached and smothered a nicker from the gray stud, and gave several sharp tugs at the halter-strap. "Do not thee make us trouble, thou."

The Baien gray muttered and shook his head and Arrhan fretted beside him. "It is the fighting," Vanye said. "Among other things."

"It is the other things," Morgaine said, and looked at him in a way that, vexed as she was, said that nature was what it was—the which stung twice over.

"I will be rid of her."

"I did not ask."

More than Chei's horse was inconvenient. He clenched his jaw and took off the mare's saddle and rubbed her down from head to foot, the while Morgaine did the same for the gray and put him in better humor.

Then Chei came walking over, bringing the saddle-bags which belonged to the bay.

And with a harness-knife in his hand.

Chei lifted that hand and held it out hilt-foremost, letting the saddlebags to the ground. "I do not think you want me to have this," he said; and as Vanye reached out and took it: "Search the bags if you like. Or myself."

Vanye stood staring at him. It was a point of honor Chei put in question.

"Do that," Morgaine said, having no compunction in such things.

Or because her liegeman hesitated.

"Come with me," Vanye said to Chei. That much courtesy he returned, not to shame the man. He took him aside, against the rocks, and ascertained, to their mutual discomfort, that there was no second knife.

"I would like," Chei said, staring past him while he searched, "to borrow a razor. I would like to shave. I would like to have a knife to defend myself. I would like to have the blanket that came with this gear. I lost yours in the woods. I am freezing."

"Take the blanket," he said; and, finding nothing: "As for the razor—" He thought more of the man's suicide with it, and discarded the idea. It was not the choice of a man so determined to live. Nor was the choice which had brought him back to them—mere cowardice, in a man who had survived what this one had. "I will lend you mine.—I will search the rest of the gear, understand."

"I did not doubt it," Chei said.

Smoke drifted up in a general haze about the hills; Vanye perched low on the rocks to see what he could of the direction of the fire, and climbed down again to Morgaine's side, where she worked. "Our cookfire will draw no notice," he said.

"Is it burning east?"

"East and quickly east. There is a great deal of undergrowth. I do not think they will be able to stop it till it comes to open fields." It still troubled him, about the burning; and most, the thought of the horses haunted him. "They may not get *through* those roads if the wind shifts. Nothing may."

Morgaine said nothing for the moment, as she stirred a little salt into the meal. Then: "Would we could assure that."

Vanye dropped down to his heels and rested his arms on his knees, thinking of that map Chei had drawn for them, how far they had come and how far there was yet to go, northward to a place called Tejhos, where a gate stood, and into a land utterly qhal.

And never quite did Chei leave his attention, as he

was under Morgaine's observation from where she sat working.

It was a stranger that emerged from under that blond thatch of hair and straggling beard. With one of their cooking-pans full of water from the trickle of a stream that served them, with the borrowed razor, the lump of soap, and Morgaine's tortoise-shell comb, Chei had washed his hair and braided the sides of it and the crown of it, which the sun was drying to its straw color; and sat thereafter leaning forward and doggedly scraping the lathered beard off.

It was a lean face, sun-darkened above and a little paler where the beard had covered it. It was a well-favored face, and unexpectedly young—hardly more than two score years, if that: nothing of madness about it, nothing but a young man of whom no one would expect an older man's experience, and who showed a meticulous if oddly timed determination to present a better appearance to them. Chei was shivering the while, wrapped in his blanket as far as his waist, in the thin shirt above, and scraping his skin raw with a keen razor and cold water, his wet braids dripping water onto his shoulders and adding to his chill.

Perhaps it was his new freedom, given a horse, given the wind of his own hills blowing on his face.

A man of Andur-Kursh could understand such a feeling . . . who knew he would never come to his own highlands again; who found something familiar in the chill of the wind and the smell of pines and the manner of a young man who for some reason had recovered his pride again—and perhaps his truthfulness.

Chei came back to them, to return the razor and the pan and the comb, bringing his blanket with him and settling with a shiver at the tiny fire.

"Here," Vanye said, and offered him his own cup of tea—receiving a look of earnest gratitude in return, so natural an expression, of a face so changed and eyes so strangely shy of them now Chei had restored what must be his proper self—

—A golden meadow . . . a parting. His cousin riding away, last friend, save his liege.

And there was something so like himself in this young man who attached himself to them, whose glances toward him were earnest and worried and wanting—perhaps nothing more than friendliness. A man could grow that desperate.

He remembered—remembered his house, and his brothers, and being the bastard son, gotten on a Chya prisoner in a Nhi house and lodged under the same roof as his father's heirs. Generally both his brothers had tormented him. More rarely his middle brother had mitigated that. And to him, in those days, that had seemed some sign that brother secretly loved him.

Strangely—in their last meeting, there had been something of that left, small as it had always been.

Now it was that desperate gesture Chei had made, that glance directed at him, which touched that recollection: see, this is myself, this is Chei, am I not better than what you thought of me?

It ached, deep as an old wound. On so small a thing, his heart turned around and found the man no threat at all—which was foolish, perhaps; he told himself so. He was always too forgiving; he knew that of himself, that his brothers had set that habit in him—a foolish conviction that there was always the hope of a hope of something changing, a misguided faith which had kept him in misery all those years.

And helped him survive all they had done to him.

He ventured a dark and one-sided smile Chei's direction, a gesture, a reassurance on the side Morgaine might not see; and saw that little shift of hope in Chei's eyes—ah, it was the same pool and the same poor desperate fish come to the bait: poor boy, he thought, Heaven help you, Heaven help us both, it was Morgaine who pulled me out. Who will save *you?* God, is it *me* you look to?

He passed Chei the cake Morgaine passed him, cut a bit of cheese and passed that too, then a bit for Morgaine and for himself.

It was a small thing, the precedence of a guest, but it was not lost on Chei. His eyes lightened. He settled easier and adjusted the blanket about himself so he could lay his meal in his lap; it was a healthy appetite he had gained, too.

There had been food in the saddlebags Chei had appropriated: that went into common stores. It was rough-ground grain and a flask of oil and a bit of salt, all welcome. A sort of jerky along with it. A change of linen. And a pan and a cup, a whetstone, a rasp and blunt scraping blade, oddments of rope and leather, with a harness ring—valuable, all; a packet of doubtful herbs, the which Morgaine spread out beside her now, and asked Chei the name and properties of each.

"That is yellowroot," he said of one twisted, dry sliver. "A purgative." And of others: "Lady's-cap, for the fever. Bleeding-root, for wounds."

It had value, then. So had the blanket, since Chei had lost one of their two in the fire.

"The riders did not come from very far, or intend to stay long," Vanye said, "reckoning what they carried with them."

"No," said Chei, "they were a patrol, that was all. A few days and back to Morund land." He swallowed a mouthful of cake, and waved the back of his hand toward the hills. "There is always trouble."

"But now more of it," Morgaine said. "Very much more."

The hand fell. Chei's ebullience vanished as he looked at Morgaine. For a moment the fear was back, and what thoughts went through his head there was no knowing.

"I mean no harm to your folk," Morgaine said. "I will tell you something, Chei: *what* I am I will not argue with you; but by what you have told me, there is no harm I will do you . . . unless you have some reason to love the lord in Mante."

"No," Chei said softly.

"Nothing I intend will harm your folk in these hills," Morgaine said. "Perhaps it will do you a great deal of good. Qhal have reason to fear me. You do not."

"Why—" Chei's face had gone still and pale. "Why should they?"

"Because I will be sure there are no more Gaults—no

more comings and goings through the gates. No more of what gives them their power over you. Humankind has only to draw back and wait. In time, you will outnumber them. And of that—they know the end. *That* is why they war against you."

Chei surely knew that he had heard a perilous thing. For a long moment he hardly seemed to breathe; then his glance flicked desperately Vanye's way.

"It is true," Vanye said. But it was not, O Heaven, so simple as that, it could never be. And surely a man grown to his manhood in war—knew that much. Morgaine was lying—by halves and portions.

"What will you do?" Chei asked of Morgaine, bewildered. "What will you do, alone?"

"I shall shut the gate. I shall tell you the absolute truth: when I do that, Vanye and I shall pass it, and we will destroy it behind us, with all its power and all its harm. Serve me as you swore you would and I will give you that same choice: pass the gate or remain behind, in this land, forever. To no one else will I give it. I shall counsel you against accepting it. But at some time you may desire it, desperate as your situation is; and if you do choose it, I will not deny you that right, if you have kept your word to us."

For a moment Chei rested still, lips parted, eyes fixed on her. Then he broke the spell with a desperate, humorless laugh. "Against Mante?"

"Against Mante and against Skarrin who rules there, if that is what opposes us. Against anything that opposes us, qhal or human. Our motives are very simple. Our solutions are very direct. We do not argue them. We pass where we will and best if we meet no one and share no hospitality of your folk, however well-meant."

Chei caught up the blanket that had fallen from his shoulders, as if the wind were suddenly colder. His face was starkly sober.

"Now, Chei, I have given you my truth. I will listen to yours, if there is anything that presses you to tell it me, and not hold it against you, but beyond this I will hold any omission worth your life. Does anything occur to you, Chei, that you ought to tell me?"

"No." He shook his head vehemently. "No. Everything is the truth. I told you—I told you I had lied; but I did not mean to lie—"

"A second time I ask you."

"I have not lied!"

"Nor omitted any truth."

"I guide you the best that I know. I tell you that we cannot go back to that road, we have no choice but go through the hills."

"Nor claimed to know more than you do."

"I know these hills. I know the trails—*here*, here I do know where I am. This is where I fought. You asked me guide you through the other and I had only been that way the once, but here I know my way—I am trying, lady, I am trying to bring us through to the road beyond the passes; but if we go that road, through those passes, they will catch one glimpse of your hair, my lady, and we are all three dead."

"Human folk, you mean."

"Human folk. They watch the road. They pick off such as they can. They ambush qhal who come into the woods—"

"In this place where you lead us."

"But they expect qhal to come in numbers. They expect humans serving the qhal, in bands of ten and twenty. They do not expect three."

"It must happen," Vanye said, "that your folk fall to the qhal; and that such as Gault—know these self-same trails; and that Gault's folk have guides who bring them very well through these woods."

"So my people will assume I am," Chei said. "That is exactly what they will think. That is why we do not go on that road. That is why moving quietly and quickly is the best that we can do. I am no safety to you. And you are a death sentence for me."

"I believe him," Morgaine said quietly, which was perhaps not the quarter from which Chei expected affirmation. He had that look, of a man taken thoroughly off his balance.

"So you will show us how to come on these folk," Morgaine said, "by surprise."

"I will show you how to avoid them."

"No. You will bring us at their backs."

Vanye opened his mouth in shock, to protest; and then disbelief warned him.

"To prove your good faith," Morgaine said.

Surely Chei was thinking quickly. But every hesitation passed through his eyes, every fear for himself, every hope sorted and discarded. "Aye," he said in two more heartbeats. "Ah. Now you have lied to me," Morgaine said.

"No." Chei shook his head vehemently. "No. I will bring you there."

"You are quick, I give you that; but a mortally unskilled liar, and you have scruples. Good. I wondered. Now I know the limit of what I can ask you. Rest assured I intend no such attack. Do you understand me?"

"Aye," Chei said, his face gone from white to flushed, and his breath unsteady.

"I shall not overburden your conscience," Morgaine said. "I have one man with me who reminds me I have one." She began to smother the fire with earth as if she had never noticed his discomfiture. "Have no fear I shall harm your people. You will carry your own armor when we ride out tonight—on your horse or on your person, as you choose. I have some care of your life, and, plainly put, I want the weight off my horse."

The flush was decided. Chei made a little formal bow where he sat—a quick-witted man, Vanye thought, and shamed by that deception of him, shamed again by a woman's kindly, arrogant manner with him. That she was qhal made it expected, perhaps—to a man attempting a new and unpalatable allegiance.

It was not a thing he could reason with, knowing Morgaine's short patience, and knowing well enough that she had that habit especially with strangers who put demands on her patience—blunt speech and a clear warning what her desires were and what she would have and not have.

She gave him the pots to scour; she re-packed the

saddlebags. "Go to sleep," she bade Chei, who still sat opposite her. He was slow to move, but move he did, and went over where his saddle lay, and tucked down in his blanket.

"You are too harsh with him," Vanye said to her, returning the pans wet from the spring.

"He is not a fool," Morgaine said.

"Nor likes to be played for one."

She gave him a moment's flat stare, nothing of the sort she gave Chei. It was a different kind of honesty. "Nor do I. Lest he think of trying it."

"You are qhal in his eyes. Be kinder."

"And test his unbelief twice over?"

"You are a woman," he said, because he had run out of lesser reasons. "It is not the same. He is young. You shamed him just then."

She gave him a second, flatter stare. "He is a grown man. Let him manage."

"You do not need to provoke him."

"Nor he to provoke me. He is the one who needs worry where the limits are. Should I give him false confidence? I do not want to have to kill him, Vanye. *That* is where mistakes lead. Thee knows. Thee knows very well. Who of the two of us has ever laid hands on him?"

"I am a—"

"—man. Aye. Well, then explain to him that I did not shoot him when he ran and that was a great favor I did him. Explain that *I* will not lay hands on him if he makes a mistake. I will kill him without warning and from behind, and I will not lose sleep over it." She tied the strings of the saddlebags and shifted *Changeling's* hilt toward her, where it lay, never far from her. "In the meanwhile I shall be most mildly courteous, whatever you please. Go, rest. If we *trusted* this man, you and I both might get more sleep."

"Plague take it, if you heard any—"

Across their little shoulder of rock and soil, the horses lifted their heads. Vanye caught it from the tail of his eye and his pulse quickened, all dispute stopped in mid breath. Morgaine stopped. Her gray eyes shifted

from horses to the woods which shielded them from
the road, as Chei lay rolled in his blanket, perhaps
unaware.

Vanye got up carefully and Morgaine gathered herself at the same moment. He signed toward Chei's
horse, tethered apart: that was the one that he worried
might call out, and to that one he went while Morgaine
went to their own pair, to keep them quiet.

The bay gelding had its ears up, its nostrils wide. He
held it, jostled the tether as he would do with their
own horses, held his hand ready should it take a
notion to sound an alarm. It might be some predator
had attracted their notice, even some straying deer,
granted no worse things prowled these pine woods.

But in moments he heard the high clear ring of
harness, of riders moving at a deliberate speed—down
the road, he thought, and not ascending, though the
hills played tricks. He ventured a glance back at
Morgaine as he held his hand on the bay's nose and
whispered to it in the Kurshin tongue. Between them
Chei had lifted his head: Chei lay still and tense with
his blanket up to his shoulder—facing him, his back to
Morgaine, who was the one of them close enough to
stop some outcry, but not in a position to see him
about to make it.

Chei made no move, no sound. It was the horse that
jerked its head and stamped, and Vanye clamped his
hand down a moment, fighting it, sliding a worried
glance Chei's way.

It was a long, long while that the sounds lasted in
the wind and the distance, the dim, light jingle of
harness, the sound of horses moving, in full daylight
and with, perhaps, Heaven grant, more attention on
the part of the riders to what was happening in the
valley and what they might meet on the road, than to
the chance someone might have occupied this withdrawn, rocky fold of the hills.

Thank Heaven, he thought, the fire was out, and
the pots were washed, and the wind was coming off
the road to them and not the other way.

There was quiet finally. A bird began to sing again.

He gingerly let go the horse he held, looking at Chei all the while.

He nodded at Chei after a moment.

And Morgaine left the horses to walk back to the streamside.

Chapter Five

The roan horse shied back from the fire and the rider applied the quirt, driving it through the smoke, where human servants labored with axe and wet sacking and mattocks to keep it from passing the Road. Others rode behind him, both qhal and the levies from the villages.

Gault ep Mesyrun was not his name: it was Qhiverin; but at times he forgot that fact, as he did now, that the rebels assailed the land itself. In this unprecedented attack on the forest, Gault's will and the self that had been Qhiverin's were of one accord.

The land burned. They had seen the plume from Morund, long before the first of the riderless horses came wandering into the pastures. There was no reasonable cause of fire on a clear night, but one; and Gault had roused the levies, rung the bell to turn out the villagers, and sent out his couriers breakneck for the east, where his fellow lords held an older and firmer control over the land. Southward to the gate, to take a shorter route to the north, he sent his lieutenant Kereys—for the change in tactics that set human folk to war against the land itself was a considerable one, and the high lord in Mante preferred too fervent a zeal for reports rather than too much complacency.

It was a humiliation of a kind Gault did not intend to let pass, more, it was an embarrassment before Skarrin, with whom he had little favor; and nothing but justice on the rebels would redeem him. He had broken the back of the rebellion at Gyllin-brook, elim-

inated his former ally Ichandren as a trouble-maker
and made examples; and since that time the man who
rode beside him, on the piebald gelding, was not the
human he looked to be.

His name had been Jestryn ep Desiny, but that was
not the mind which lived behind that handsome, sword-
marred face. It was Gault-Qhiverin's old friend Pyverrn,
who had taken too grievous a wound at Gyllin-brook;
and who had chosen a human shape, gate-given—one
of Ichandren's own, his cousin.

There was a certain irony in it, Gault-Qhiverin
thought—that two old friends rode side by side bent
on vengeance, Jestryn being Gault's ally and guide in
this foray to the highlands as they had once, when
they were human, ridden against qhalur enemies at
Ichandren's side.

Their friendship thus had, as Gault counted it, a
certain double poesy.

It was onto the road at dusk, and the road which
began in the lowlands as a track carts used, became a
narrow trail cut through the pines, a pale line eroded
and slotted by horse or foot, grown up in wispy grass
along the margin so that it was easy to mistake some
thinning of the trees for a spur off it.

There was no room, where it crossed difficult places,
to have two riders abreast; and it was all too easy a
place for ambush.

Ambush crossed Vanye's mind—constantly. He little liked these close spaces, little as he had liked the
prospect of the open road, knowing what Chei had
warned them. It was Chei in the lead now, Morgaine
bringing up the rear, in this dark, pine-spiked shadow,
and Chei did not have the look of a man contemplating a run for freedom: Chei had declined to wear the
armor Morgaine had returned to him—the scabbed
sores were still too painful, Chei had said: it was hard
enough to bear the riding.

But Chei was armed again, after a fashion: he had
the harness-knife, small as it was, a gesture Morgaine

had made to him at their setting-out; for peace, Vanye reckoned. Or it was another test of him.

Certainly Chei had looked confused, and then: "My lady," he had said, in a respectful, astonished tone, the while Vanye's gut had knotted up and his hand clenched tight on his own blade-hilt, considering how close Morgaine stood to Chei, with the knife in his hand.

But Chei had put it away in its sheath on his saddle-skirt, and tied his armor up behind his horse with his blanket and his saddle-bags; and rode now to the fore of them, conscious, surely of his sword and of Morgaine's weapon at his back, if treachery ever crossed his mind.

It was a wooded track, Chei had assured them. It was a way they would stand less chance of being seen.

It was also a track in which they could not see the turns ahead in the nightbound forest, in which they did not know the way and were utterly dependent on their guide, the same one who had twice mistaken his way—he swore.

Vanye himself had argued for this. Morgaine would have walked brazenly into Morund and demanded hospitality, and thrust Chei into Gault's very hold and hall and forced Gault to take him for a guest . . . backed by power enough to deal with any qhalur hedge-lord.

He had persuaded her otherwise, into this, with the land afire and men dead, half a score of them, and a twice-mistaken guide holding their lives in his hand—

Lady, Chei called her now, not witch. If Chei thought of sorcery it was surely tempered, living near qhal as he did, by the knowledge that what qhal did came not entirely from empty air and ill intent; it was not a thoroughly superstitious belief, and Chei surely knew by now that there was a qhalur weapon involved. When it came to fine distinctions beyond that—

—When it came to that, Vanye himself was not well sure whether it was witchcraft, or what it was he carried against his heart, or what that blade was that Morgaine carried, and both guarded and hated with all that was in her.

If they had met some innocent folk family on the valley road, if some children—

God help them, he thought; God help us.

And tried to forget the face which lingered behind his eyes, the sixteen year old boy, open-eyed and startled and dead in the starlight of the road.

It stood for everything that had gone amiss.

He rubbed his eyes that stung with weariness—short sleep, trading watches, with the smell of smoke still hanging about the hills and the surety that by now there was commotion behind them, deadly as a river in spate—Heaven send it was not in front of them as well.

At a point where the road reached the turning and the climbing was steep to the shoulder of the hill, Chei drew rein and hesitated, drawing his horse back about in the starlight, coming even with them.

Then he gave his horse his heels and took the ascent with the impetus it needed.

I am not eluding you, that gesture was to say. *Follow me.*

Morgaine sent Siptah after; Vanye allowed the big gray the room he needed on the narrow track, then gave Arrhan the touch of his heel.

For a moment they were in starlight, climbing that slot among the rocks; then they came among the pines again, and into thicker brush, where boughs whispered in a ghostly voice above the creak of harness and the sound of the horses, a climb for a long, long distance until the way began to wind down again, through deep shadow, such as it was in this land where the stars shone in such numbers and so bright, and white Arrhan and even the Baien gray and his gray-cloaked rider seemed to glow by night.

Then they broke out upon a broader track, and Chei's gelding struck a faster pace, along a streamside and across shallow water that kicked up white in the night-glow.

Morgaine suddenly put Siptah to a run, so that Vanye's heart skipped a beat and he kicked Arrhan in the same moment that Arrhan leapt forward on her own: the mare cleared the water in a few reckless strides to bring him up on Morgaine's flank as she overtook Chei and cut him off with Siptah's shoulder. The gelding shied off, scrambling up against a steep bank and recovering its balance at disadvantage. Chei drew in, his eyes and hair shining pale in the starlight.

"Slower," Morgaine said. "Where do you think to go, so surely and so fast? A trail you know? To what?"

"It is a way I know," Chei said, and restrained his horse as it backed against the bank and shied and threw its head. "Where should I lead you? I swear I know this place."

"That also I wonder. We are making far too much noise for my liking."

"Vanye," Chei appealed to him, "for God's sake—"

"Liyo," Vanye said, and eased Arrhan forward, his heart beating so the pulse seemed to make his hands shake. No man called his name. Few in his own land had cared to know it; excepting Nhi and Chya and Myya, and his Chya cousin, who was not wont to use a Kurshin name when he could help it, and called him only *cousin* when he was kindest. But in Chei's mouth it was not a curse, it was like a spell cast on him, was the way Morgaine used it.

Fool, he told himself. And his heart moved in him all the same.

"Where are we going?" he asked Chei.

"Where I told you from the beginning—across the hills to the road. Before God I have not lied. Vanye, tell her so. Tell—"

What sound it had been Vanye could not identify, even in hearing it. But it had been there; and none of them moved or breathed for the instant.

The black weapon was in Morgaine's hand, beneath the cloak. Vanye knew it, as well as he knew where sky and earth was. *Changeling* rode at her side tonight, since she went hooded; and there was power enough in her hand to deal with any single enemy.

Chei shook his head, faint movement. His eyes rolled toward the woods, a gleam of white in a shadowed face. "I do not know," he whispered, ever so faintly. "I swear to God I do not know who that is, I did not plan this—Please. Let me go, let me ride to them. It may be they are human—I expect that they are. If they are not, you can deal with them. If they are, then likely I can ride in on them."

"And tell them what?" Morgaine asked in a flat voice.

"After that—God knows. They may kill me. But likeliest they will want to know what they can find out." His voice trembled. His teeth were chattering, and he drew in a rough breath. "Lady, if we go on we will ride into ambush and they will raise all the hills against us. We have no choice! Let me go to them!"

"You are supposing we would ride in after you," Morgaine said.

"I am supposing," Chei whispered back, "nothing. Except we are too few to threaten them. That is all the safety we have. I can talk to them, I can tell them you are no friend of Gault's—Let me *try*, lady. It is the only way. They are bowmen. We will not have a chance if they begin to hunt us."

"He is brave enough," Vanye said in his own language.

"Brave indeed," Morgaine said. "He has courted this, curse him."

It might well be true. Honest men, Morgaine had warned him.

"What can we do now," Vanye asked with a sinking heart, "that costs less?"

"Try," Morgaine said to Chei.

"Hold." Vanye edged Arrhan up next the gelding to pull the ties free which held the heavy bundle of mail and leather atop Chei's other gear. He pulled it free and handed it to him. "Put it on."

In the case, he thought, that Chei was on their side.

Chei did not argue. He took the offered help, and took the mail on his arms, ducked his head and slid it on, leaving it unbelted.

Then he took up the reins and urged the gelding quietly ahead, up the bank and into the woods.

In a moment more there was a whistle from that

direction, low and strange. Siptah threw his head and Morgaine held him steady.

It was not a safe vantage they had. Vanye interposed himself and his horse between her and the woods, on the side the bank did not shelter; but their backs he could not defend.

There was nothing then but the dark and the bubbling of the stream behind them, the sighing of the leaves.

Another sound, from their side: Morgaine unfastened the hook which held *Changeling* at her side, and brought it sheath and all, to rest crosswise on her saddle.

Doomsday. His hand went on reflex to that pyx he had beneath his armor, and he felt it like a coal against his heart.

Destruction.

Once that sword was drawn there was no peace in the world. Once that was drawn there would be deaths heaped up and uncountable.

He sat his horse still, thinking of archers beyond the trees; and that by now Chei had either fallen to some silent killer, or found the allies he had led them to, for whatever purpose.

The movements were virtually silent, the rustle of a branch, the brush of a body against leaves. The gelding shifted and snorted and stamped, breaking twigs and working at the bit; and Chei held him in place.

"Who are you?" came a voice hardly above the wind.

"A human man," Chei answered in a normal voice, and did not turn in his saddle. "Ep Kantory. Chei ep Kantory, asking passage. There are three of us, no more, two at the streamside. One of us is qhal."

There was long silence, very long. He heard a whisper, and another, but he could not hear the words. He did not turn his head.

"Get off your horse," the whisper came.

He did that, and drew a whole breath, though his legs wanted to shake under him. One qhal, he had told them. It was enigma enough to confuse them and make them ask further. He had made himself defenseless. He had ridden without true stealth. Therefore he was still alive. He stepped down in the little clear space and held his horse close to the bit, forestalling its nervous shifting as branches stirred and a shadow afoot came out of the brush into filtered starlight only slightly better than the forest dark.

That shadow came to him and took his horse's reins and led it away from him. He did not resist.

He did not resist when others came up behind him and took his arms in a painful grip.

"It is passage I ask," he said to them in a hushed voice. "The qhal with me is a woman, alone with one human man. They are enemies of Gault's. Gault is hunting us."

A slight weight rested on his shoulder, and moved till the cold, flat metal of a sword-blade rested against his neck. "Where do you come from?"

It was death to move. It was death to give the wrong answer, and for the moment he could think of nothing at all, the forest air seeming too thin, his senses wanting to leave him as if the world had shifted again, and he should be back on that hilltop, all that he had to tell them become a dream, a delirium. He could not even believe, for one dizzy moment, in the companions he had left on that streamside, or in the things that had happened to him, at the same time that he knew he was back among human men.

The sword turned edge-on against his neck.

"I am still human," he said. "So is the man with her. She is here on business of her own. It would be well—to find out what that is. They have told me something of it—enough I knew I ought to bring them here. I swear you have never seen anything like her. Or like the man with her—he *is* a Man, and from somewhere I do not know. Let me go back to them and I will lead them to the falls. There is no way out of that place but back. You know that there is not. We will camp there and wait, and you can ask what questions you want."

There was another long pause. Then: "Ep Kantory," the whisper in front of him said, "your brother is with us."

His heart lurched. As a trick, it was cruel. "My brother died at Gyllin-brook. Ichandren at Morund. I am the last alive."

"Bron ep Kantory is alive," the whisper said. "He is with Arunden. In our camp."

He did not know whether, then, he could stand on his feet. He was numb. He felt his breath short and anger blinded him and hope came by turns, between the conviction they were lying and hope—remotest and terrible hope, that it might be true.

"Who is this," the same voice continued to ask, "that you travel with?"

He could not speak. He could not find his voice. He had been better than this when Gault's men led him to the hilltop. He had been better than this in the depths of Morund-hall when Ichandren died. His senses came and went, as if he would faint, and here and there wavered.

"Did you think that you could do this?" the whisper asked him. "Did you think that you could deceive us?"

"I am Chei ep Kantory. My brother's name is Bron. He fell at Gyllin-brook—"

The blade pressed against his neck. A strong grip drove the blood from his hands.

"And who else are you? What other name?"

"Tell Bron I am here. Bring him. Tell him he will know if I am still his brother. Tell him that!"

A long time passed. He told himself that it had been a test. He had failed it. At any moment the one in front of him would give the order and the blade would slit the vein—or worse, they would take him with them, and ask him questions alone—

There was a chance, O God, a chance: if Bron had lain alive on Gyllin's bank, if Arunden's men had heard the rumor and had been able to reach that place before the night and the scavengers—

If only once, if he died for it, he could see his brother again—

"Let him go," the voice said.

Vanye had both hands on his own sword, across the saddlebow, as he heard the stir of a rider in the forest. Arrhan shifted nervously, and Siptah stamped once and worked at the bit.

Then one rider in unbelted mail came out into the starlight and down the slope at an easy pace. Two others followed, shadowlike, at either side and behind him.

Chei reached the flat and stopped face to face with them, then carefully got down from his horse and left it to stand while the others waited at his back.

It was to Vanye's side he walked, leftward, away from Morgaine, and it occurred to Vanye it might be attack, some means to take him down and leave Morgaine's back undefended: there was the harness-knife, for one; and Heaven knew with what Chei was armed now.

But he saw nothing in Chei's hands—Chei held them both outward from him in the starlight, and when Chei came up at Arrhan's shoulder and laid a hand on his stirrup:

"They have agreed to talk," Chei said in a low voice. "They want you to come. There are others in the woods. There are arrows aimed at us. Likely they will aim for the horses if we try to run." Strong emotion trembled in his voice. "They say my brother is alive. I do not know. It might be true. If it is—if it is, then he might convince them—whether to listen to me."

That they were surrounded was credible. The rest of it . . . Heaven knew. He was sure that Morgaine heard what Chei was saying: her ears were sharper than anyone's he knew, and likeliest she heard whatever was in the brush as well. She said nothing, and a sense of panic came over him—man and man, she had said, Man and Man, trusting his instincts to deal with this many-turning youth.

"I beg you," Chei said, and caught at his hand where it rested on his leg, gripping it hard. "I beg you. I am not sure of these trails, enough to run the horses here. It is a tangle ahead, rock and root. The stream leads to a falls and there is no way out. But if we go with them, there is the chance they will listen, and it will likely be closer to the road anyway. These men belong to Arunden ep Corys, and if they are not lying, my brother will know whether or not to believe me. Come with them. If things go wrong I will fight *with* you, I swear it under Heaven."

"And your brother? What of him?"

"I want his life. His. That is all I ask. And you have me. Heart and mind—I swear it, only so you save him and take no life you can spare. Listen to me: this is the last place free Men hold. It is the land I am fighting for, it is the land, and your lady says she has hope for us—but if becomes a war of fire, Gault and the lady—for God's own sake, Vanye—listen to me and come with me and take them for allies. They will not ask you give up your weapons. They are not unreasonable men. And when we reach their camp my brother will stand with us. I know that he will."

"As you knew the way across the plains? And the woods? As you led us here?"

Chei's hand was cold on his, cold and strong. "In the name of God, Vanye. I am your friend. You have been mine. I never betrayed you. I only wanted to live to get here; and we are here—and I am begging you—take what I give you. I have lied, I admit it. But not of malice—only of too much hope. And now I swear to you I am not lying. I have brought you where there was hope of getting through, and now that has failed us—there is this, and it is the best one, the best I could have hoped for—"

"All your hopes diminish, friend. And this one if it goes amiss, has your people's blood on it."

"There is nothing else," Morgaine said beside him, and in the Kurshin tongue, "that we can do, but see where this leads."

His advice, he thought, had brought them to this—as

much as Chei's. "Aye," he said heavily. And to Chei: "My lady agrees; we will go."

Chei's hand clenched on his, desperately hard. Gratitude shone in his eyes, starlight aglimmer on tears unshed. "I swear," Chei said. "I swear to you—I am with you in this. I will not betray you. Not for my life. I know what you can do. Take me first if I betray you."

Vanye felt an unaccustomed, half embarrassed impulse, let his fingers twitch, then clench in human comfort as he looked into Chei's shadowed face.

"My brother will help us," Chei said. "I swear that too. And you will not harm him."

"We will harm no one who does not threaten us."

"And your lady—"

"Take Vanye's word," Morgaine said. "He does not know how to lie. And in this I take his advice."

The way lay up the bank, into the forest by trails only Chei and the shadowy horsemen knew; and it was well enough certain that there were other watchers about, on foot and ahorse on trails following and crossing theirs.

It was like the arrhend, Vanye thought; or the men of Koris, of his own land. One did not hope to take such a land cheaply, in lives or in time—except an enemy did the unthinkable; except it was not the land or the wealth of the woods a conqueror valued, and he was willing to use fire.

We ought not, he kept thinking with every stride of the horses, every whisper of the leaves, we ought not, we ought not to have brought the fire.

There was that in him which ached, thinking of it, as greenwood and the forest damp took the stench of smoke away—as more and more the land was like coming to his own home again, even to the smell of the trees.

O my liege, I might have stopped you from setting the fire. Why did not I speak? I am a Man. And this is a human place. Did it not occur to me?

Or am I become something else?

The trails made a maze, a narrow track down one

hill and up another through one and another little dell completely unremarkable in the dark.

Chei went foremost behind their first guide. Morgaine rode at Chei's back and Vanye at hers, with the second of their mounted guides going hindmost; and at times in the shadow of the thicket there was only the sound of the horses and the creak of harness and jingle of chain; and at most the pale flash of Siptah's pale rump and white-tipped tail to keep him aware which way they were turning, each horse following the other.

To such a land Arrhan had been foaled, and there was a lightness in her step and an alertness to her busy ears as if she were reading signals no human ear heard. She was not alarmed, not yet; but by the prick of her ears and the set of her head she advised where her apprehensions were and where some sound went which he did not hear.

There is no way out of this, he kept thinking, the further and the deeper they went. Whether Chei is witting of it or no, it is a trap, this narrow passage.

Heaven help us. The last hold of free Men. Chei has lied to us; and fair enough for that: Morgaine has lied to him in turn—and we are all in the web, they and we alike.

No more deaths. No more children, Mother of God, no more mistakes, and no more blood. I dream of them.

At last Morgaine stopped; for ahead of her Chei and their guide had paused. Arrhan came up with her head against Siptah's flank and crowded closer still as the big gray threw his head and snorted warning.

"It is soon," their forester guide said. "Be patient."

It was, Vanye reckoned, a boundary of a sort, and they were about to cross it: someone ran ahead to tell others what came visiting.

There was silence after. There were only forest sounds and the slow, fretful shifting of the horses. Morgaine did not question. Chei did not say anything, nor had he spoken since they began this ride. Their guides volunteered no word beyond that simple directive.

Somewhere a nightbird cried.

"Come," their guide said then, and turned his horse sedately and went ahead at the same deliberate walk he had used for some little time. So Chei went and so Morgaine; and himself and the last man, as the trail followed the shoulder of a wooded hill and climbed again, up among tall trees and down once again, onto the other side of the hill.

For the first time, on that breath of wind, Vanye picked up the scents of smoke and habitation. No lights showed as they came down, first into thinner trees and then among brushy lumps—huts which seemed more like thickets than dwellings—but nature never grew them, Vanye thought, as they rode sedately down the steep slope and past one such that was high as horse and rider together, a rounded shape against the straight trunks of the trees.

Not a stirring hereabouts. Not a breath of a voice, no gleam of fire. From a pen, withdrawn among the trees, came stable-smell and a restless shifting of horses, as they rode out into the clear midst of this low place.

Then their guide dismounted. "Get down," he said.

"Best we do that," Chei said, and slid down.

Well indeed, if there were archers in question. Morgaine got down from the saddle, with *Changeling* hung at her side, and Vanye did, at the same time as Chei did; and dropped the reins to let the horses stand.

Then came a little movement, and more than one shadow gliding out from among the trees and the huts.

One came and crouched on the ground in the starlight in the midst of the large clearing at the center of the huts, and poked round in a familiar way with a stick, after which coals came to a sullen glow, and a slight gleam showed: the man then piled on tinder and wood. So the village folk had taken precautions and now felt encouraged enough that the one man squatted there with the firelight leaping up brighter and brighter on his heavy-jowled face.

"My lord Arunden—" Chei said in a plaintive way, and walked forward a pace or two; and stop as the man at the fire looked up at them with an underlit scowl.

The man called Arunden stood up, and drew the short sword that hung at his belt. The fire limned them both, Chei all dark, fire glancing on the edges of his mail; the older man all light, shadow about his features and his leather and furs and braids.

"Strange guests," Arunden said, and the voice matched the face, heavy and rough. "Stranger still that you bring them here. What does Gault want?"

"Is my brother truly alive, my lord?"

"Answer."

"Gault wants our lives, theirs and mine, my lord. I am human. So is the man. The lady is qhal, but she is no friend of Gault's."

"The land is burning, below. What do we do for this? How did this happen?"

Chei had no quick reply for that.

"It happened," Morgaine said, drawing a startled look from the man, and walked forward to stand, gray-cloaked and hooded figure with arms folded, the dragon-sword out of sight, riding at her hip, and Heaven knew where her other weapon was, but Vanye well guessed as he moved to take his place at her left shoulder. "The qhal of your land have no courtesy," Morgaine said to the lord, "and I have found more with this young human. So I have come to you. As for the burning—a matter of war, my lord, else worse would be at your borders."

There was stark silence from lord Arunden . . . stark silence too from the shadowy figures which appeared among the trees behind him. Vanye's heart began to pound in dread, his mind to sort rapidly what he could see of those about them, mapping which way they should go—what their path of escape should be, where cover was.

There would be, Chei had assured them, archers.

"Who are you," Arunden asked sharply, "riding here with your minions? What are you, Gault's jilted doxy?"

That was the limit. Vanye slipped the ring. The

weight of the sword hit his hip as Morgaine lifted one empty, white hand, forestalling him without even looking to see what his move had been, and let back her hood, spilling her pale hair free to the light.

"No," she said softly, "I am not. Would you guess again, my lord Arunden?"

"My lady," Chei said, stepping between. "My lord—"

"Is she here to make threats?" Arunden asked. "Or to spy out the hills, with you for her guide?"

Morgaine glanced Chei's way with chill disdain. "You vowed this was a reasonable man."

"I am no fool!" Arunden shouted, and stamped his stick into the coals, so that coals scattered and sparks flew up.

"I am out of patience," Morgaine said to Chei, and turned aside.

"Stay," Chei said. "Wait—my lord Arunden. Do not make a mistake."

"I make no mistake. It is *your* mistake—"

"Chei!" a voice called out of the dark, and a man was coming down the slope of a sudden, limping and making his way with difficulty on the uneven ground among the trees and huts.

Vanye let his sword surreptitiously back to its sheath, as Morgaine had stopped near him, her hands shrouded in her cloak and her jaw set.

"Bron, it is not your brother," Arunden shouted uphill as that man came on, and waved him to stand off.

But: "Bron," Chei said, quietly. "O Bron—"

The man came resolutely forward, limping somewhat—unarmored, wearing only breeches and shirt and boots, weaponless; he came and he stopped in doubt a little the other side of the fire; as Chei for his part stood still—wisely, Vanye thought, with that prickling between his own shoulder-blades that weapons at his back set there.

"I am not Changed," Chei said in a voice that scarcely carried, a voice which trembled. "Bron, Ichandren is dead. Everyone is dead. Gault gave the last of us to the wolves. Myself, Falwyn, ep Cnary—"

His voice did break, quiet as it was. "They died. That was what happened to them. I thought you had died on the field."

"What do you want here?" Bron asked, in a voice colder than Arunden's. "What is it you want?"

Chei turned his face away as if it he had been dealt a blow, and shook his head vehemently.

"What do you want, Chei?"

"Passage," Chei said after a moment, looking back toward his brother. "Safety. I am sworn, Bron, my lord was dead, you were dead, the lady and this man found me, they took me away from the wolves, healed my hurts—He is not qhal, Bron, he is a man like I am and *she* set me free and gave me a horse and tells me things that Arunden ought to know, that all of us ought to know, Bron—I swear to you, I know there is no way to prove anything I say. But you know me, you know everything I could know—try me, whether I have forgotten anything. Bron—for the love of Heaven—"

Bron's face worked, somewhere between desperation and grief.

And suddenly he held out his open arms.

"No," Arunden cried. "Fool!"

But Chei came to him, slowly, carefully. They embraced each other, and wept, for very long, till Bron set Chei back by the shoulders and looked at him as if he could discover the truth by firelight.

Vanye watched with a pang of his own—the which he could not comprehend, only something in him hurt, perhaps that a man could come home again; or that brothers could prove true.

Or that Chei had just deserted them for a deeper loyalty, whatever the issue of this place.

Fool, he thought. Well that there *be* some help for us here.

There was Morgaine beside him, who was all his own concern; and Chei at the moment was hers, he reckoned, their guide and the source of everything they knew in this world. She would wreak havoc to keep him safe, Chei was very right; had Arunden attempted to stop him or to strike him or his brother, Morgaine would have acted, fatally for Arunden and half the village before she was done.

But she and Arunden and all of them stood baffled by this, that Bron ep Kantory took his brother into his arms without being sure what he was embracing: he made himself a hostage to stop those who cared for either of them, and by one move held them all powerless.

Chapter Six

"Come," Bron said, his hands on Chei's shoulders, while Chei's thoughts reeled between one side and the other of the forces gathered there at odds. There was the lady and Vanye and there was Arunden ep Corys, a sudden and hard-handed lord. Calamity was possible at any instant.

But Bron held to him as if there were no chance in all the world that he was a piece of Gault's handiwork. "Come," Bron said gently, as if there were no lunacy at all in his arriving in camp in company with a qhalur witch and a man in strange armor. "Tell me; tell me what I can do; O my God, Chei—" Of a sudden Bron hugged him tight again and pressed his head against his shoulder; and Chei embraced him a second time, appalled at how thin his strong brother had become, how there was so little between his hands and Bron's ribs, and how there was a fragile, insubstantial feel about him.

"I am not theirs," Chei insisted, over and over again. "Not theirs. I am not lying, Bron, I swear to you I am not Changed."

"I believe you," Bron said. "I know, I know, what shall I do, what do you want me to do?"

"Just swear for me. *Talk* to Arunden."

"Tell him what? Who are they? What are they?"

"Friends. Friends to us."

Bron set him back and stared at him, bewildered, desperate—at his little brother who was a fool and could not think of anything but seeing him, until now,

131

now that he knew what he had known from birth, that
Bron would do the same as he—would believe him
because he wanted to believe, and become another
fool for his sake, risking his life and his soul for the
remotest hope Chei was alive and still his brother.
That was what was in Bron's eyes, that was the struggle to believe, while his hands trembled on Chei's
arms and strayed once and twice to his face and his
shoulders as if he could not believe he was flesh and
blood.

"You *look* tolerably well," Bron said.

"They have been good to me, Bron, truly—they
have. You—?"

"Well enough, I am well enough."

"You limp."

"Ah, well, that will mend, it will mend. So do
you.—My God, my God—"

"There was a brooch Mama had—it was a marsh
rose. There was a place in the wall we used to hide our
special things—"

"O *God,* Chei—"

"—I gave you that scar on your chin; I hit you with
a harness buckle—you teased me about a girl; her
name was Meltien. She died in the winter march—"

"Brother—" Bron hugged him to silence. They wept
together; and when he could speak again:

"Bron, I have sworn to take them north on the
Road; and I have to do that—"

"There are arrows aimed at us." Bron took his face
between his hands and looked again at him, intensely.
"Who are they? You will have to tell me. I do not
understand. God knows Arunden does not. What shall
we do?"

"I will talk to them. *They* will talk with Arunden if
he will listen—"

"He will listen," Bron said; and hugged him close
against his side, so that they shielded each other as
they went to Arunden, Bron armorless as he was,
himself in a mail shirt that was in no wise proof against
the lady's weapons.

But a man barred their way, a man with a drawn

sword and the emblem on him of Holy Church; and Bron stopped still, his hand clenched on Chei's shirt.

"If you will not kill it," the priest said, "*I* will. Your soul is in danger, Bron ep Kantory."

"Your *life* is," Chei answered, and would have pushed Bron behind him, but Bron stood fast. "My lady!"

"Hold!" Arunden said.

"My lord," the priest protested.

But Arunden walked into the matter, and waved the priest off. And Chei stood with a weakness still in his knees, uncertain which of them was supporting the other. Words froze in his throat. They always did, at the worst of times.

"There is a curse in him," the priest said. "It is a curse has come to us in a friend's shape. It is Gault's gift. Kill them. Have no words with them."

"Then we would know nothing Gault wants," Arunden said. "Would we, priest?—Talk, boy. What have we here? What do you bring us, eh? More of Gault's handiwork?"

"The lord is talking, at least," Vanye said in a low voice, seeing what transpired, with the brothers and Arunden and two armed men. His hand was still on his sword, from the first Chei had called out.

And he thanked Heaven that Arunden had moved to stop the man.

"Hope that this brother's word has some weight," Morgaine said in the Kurshin tongue. "I should not have let us leave the road. That was the first mistake. Stay to my left."

"Aye," he murmured, feeling the sting of that, and his heart was pounding, the old, familiar fear, the nightmare of too many such choices. But Chei came toward them and fear shifted to a frail, desperate hope, seeing that Bron continued to talk to Arunden.

"He will speak to you," Chei said, casting an anxious glance between him and Morgaine. "I swear to you—Arunden is not a treacherous man: God witness, he is not a careful one, either—he is afraid of you, lady, and he cannot admit it. Be patient with him.

That is a priest of God—that one, with the sword. Be careful of him."

Vanye looked a second time. It did not look like a priest. He drew in a quick, anxious breath. It had been long since he had found anything of the Church; and there had been so much doubtful he had had to choose on his own: so far he had come, and changed so much—and a priest—

He was starkly afraid to face anything of the Church nowadays: that was the proof that he was damned, and he did not need a priest to threaten him with Hell.

Or to threaten Morgaine, or curse her with curses she would not regard, but which would all the same bring no luck to them.

"We do not need the priest," he muttered. "Send him away."

"I do not know," Chei said in evident consternation. "I do not think—I do not see how . . . my lady—"

"No matter," Morgaine said. Gold flashed in the seam of her cloak. She rested *Changeling's* cap on the ground, her hands on the quillons of the dragon grip. "If it saves us time, let us be done with this."

Vanye opened his mouth to protest. But it was not that Morgaine did not know the Church. There was nothing he could tell her. There was nothing he knew how to tell her.

He longed—God in Heaven, he longed for someone to tell him he had done right, and that his soul was not so stained as he thought it was, or a gentle priest like those in Baien-an or even old San Romen, who would lay hands on him and pray over him and tell him if he did thus and thus he was not damned.

But this priest did not have any gentle look. This one was damnation and hellfire, and met them with the uplifted cross of a sword.

"No further," the priest said, and drew a line in the dirt, between them and his lord. "Talk behind that."

Morgaine grounded *Changeling* just behind that line, the dragon hilt in her hands, and a hell between them that the priest could not in his wildest dreams, imagine.

"Do we talk to this?" she asked scornfully, looking past the priest to Arunden. "Is he lord in this camp? Or are you?"

"My lady," Chei cautioned her, and Bron, who had come halfway between Arunden and his brother, stopped still and looked appalled.

"I will talk with whoever is lord here," Morgaine said. "If it is this man, so be it. His word will bind you. And I will take it for yours."

"If I say talk with the camp scullions, you talk with them!" Arunden snarled.

Vanye went stiff, but Morgaine's hand was up, preventing him, before the lord Arunden had even finished speaking.

"Well and good," she said. "To *them* I will offer my help, and turn this camp upside down, lord Arunden, when they profit from what I have to say. *Or* you can listen, and profit yourself and yours, and not come to Ichandren's fate or have to ask advice of your servants."

"You are in a poor place to threaten us, woman! Have you looked around you?"

"Have *you*, my lord, and have you not noticed that qhal are taking your land and killing your people? I might make some difference in that. Let us talk, my lord Arunden! Let us sit down like sensible folk and I will tell you why I want to pass through your land."

"No passage!" the priest cried, and people murmured in the shadows. But:

"Sit down," Arunden said. "*Sit,* and *lie* to us before we deal with you."

More and more people appeared out of the dark and the woods, coming down into the light: a man or two at first, who stood with Arunden within the priest's line; and young women in breeches and braids, who scurried about seeing to the fire and bringing out blankets to spread by it—an appearance of decent courtesy, Vanye thought, standing by with his hand on his sword-hilt and a dart of his eye toward every move around the shadows on their own side of the line.

On his, the dour, broad-bellied hedge-lord stood by

with a clutch of his own men and with Bron and Chei both across that line and talking urgently to him—he had his arms folded, and scowled continually; but made no overt gesture of hostility, only repeated ones of impatience.

The priest, for his part, drew another line when the rapidly-forming circle took shape about the fire, a mark in the dust with his sword and a holy sign over it, the which sent a cold feeling to Vanye's gut.

"Poor manners, these folk," he said to Morgaine, looking constantly to their flanks and refusing to be distracted by the priest's doings.

"No saying where the archers may be posted," Morgaine said. "I will warrant there is one or two with clear vantage—that ridge yonder, perhaps. Mark you, we do not give up the weapons—hai, there—"

One man was moving to take the horses. Vanye moved to prevent it, one hand out, one hand on his sword; and that man stopped.

Chei's horse had strayed loose, uncertain and confused, and apt, Heaven knew, to bolt; but their own had stood where the reins had dropped, where Siptah now stood and jerked his head and snorted challenge, a wary eye on the man approaching.

"I would not," he advised the man, who measured the warhorse's disposition and the owners' resolution with one nervous glance and kept his distance. "I would not touch him at all, man."

That stopped the matter. The man looked left and right as if searching for help or new orders, and edged away, leaving the warhorse and the mare and all their belongings to stand unmolested. Vanye whistled a low and calming signal, and the Baien gray grunted and shook himself, lifting his head again with a wary and defiant whuff.

"My lady," Chei came saying then. "Come. Please. Keep within the line."

Morgaine walked toward the fire. Vanye walked after her, and stood behind her—*ilin's* place, hand on sword, within the wedge-shaped scratch in the dirt that made a corridor to the fire.

So Arunden stood, with his priest, and his men—all men: the only women were the servants, who came and went in the shadows.

"Sit," Arunden muttered with no good grace, and sank down to sit cross-legged.

So Morgaine sat down in like fashion, and laid *Changeling* by her, largely shrouded in the folds of her cloak—which movement Arunden's eyes followed: Vanye saw it as he stood there.

But: "Vanye," Morgaine said, and he took her meaning without dispute, and sank down beside her, as others were settling and gathering close, Chei and Bron among them, on Arunden's side of the line, but beside them on Vanye's side.

"So you found this boy with the wolves," Arunden said. "How and why?"

"We were passing there," Morgaine said. "And Vanye did not like the odds."

"Not like the odds." Arunden chuckled darkly, and with his sheathed sword poked at the fire so that sparks flew up. "Not like the odds. Where are you from? Mante?"

"Outside."

There was long and sober silence. The fire crackled, the burning of new branches, the flare of pine needles.

"What—outside?"

"Beyond Mante. Things are very different there. I do not give my enemies to beasts. I deal with them myself."

There was another long silence.

Then: "Cup!" Arunden said.

"My lord," the priest objected vehemently, scrambling up.

"Sit *down,* priest!" And as the so-named priest sank down with ill grace: "Close up, close up, close up! Does a qhalur *woman* frighten you? Close up!"

No one stirred for a moment. Then Chei edged closer on Vanye's side. After that there was a general movement, men moving from the back of the circle forward on Arunden's side, edging closer on either side of them, blurring and obliterating the line the priest had drawn, two rough-looking men crowding close on Morgaine's side, so that Vanye felt anxiously after his sword-hilt.

"You!" Arunden jabbed his sheathed sword toward him across the fire. "Sit *down!*"

"Sit as they do," Morgaine said quietly, and Vanye drew a second nervous breath and came down off his heels to fold his legs under him, sitting cross-legged and a cursed deal further from a quick move. Morgaine reached and touched his hand, reminding him it was on the sword-hilt, forbidding him, and he let it go, glaring at Arunden with his vision wide on everything around him.

But a young woman brought a massive wooden bowl and gave it to Arunden: he held it out to the priest. "Here," he said. *"Here!"*

The priest drank. Arunden did, and passed the massive bowl to his right.

So from hand to hand it passed, all about the gathering on that side before it came to Bron and to Chei.

There was utter silence then, a profound hush in every movement in the circle.

And from Chei, as he gave it to Vanye's hands, a frightened look, a pleading look—What, Vanye wondered. That they not refuse? That there was some harm in it?

"Take it," Chei said. "You must take it."

It was honey drink, strong-smelling. Vanye looked doubtfully toward Morgaine, but he saw no likelihood of poison, seeing others had drunk, seeing that the moisture of it shone on Chei's mouth. *"Liyo?"*

She gave a slight nod, and he drank one fiery and tiny sip, hardly touching the tip of his tongue to it.

"Drink," Chei whispered from his left. "For God's sake, truly drink. They will know."

He hesitated, feeling the sting of it, tasting herbs. Panic touched him. But they would insist for Morgaine too, he thought; if there was harm in it, she had to know. He took a mouthful and swallowed it down, tracing fire all down his throat.

He passed it slowly, amid the soft murmur of those about the fire. He held onto the bowl a moment, feeling that fire hit his stomach, tasting it all the way down with the sense that he knew to use on bitter berries, unfamiliar fare at strange table. Slowly he let her take it, while the murmur grew; and there was a troubled frown on her face—full knowledge what he had done, and why.

So she looked at him and drank a very little, he thought that she truly did, her own judgment: but she was a woman, she might be delicate in her habits; it was his place to convince them, and he thought that he had, sufficient good faith for the two of them.

She passed the bowl on to the man at her right, and so it went on.

The murmur grew.

"Is there something remarkable in it?" Morgaine asked then, civilly.

"There is fen-wort in it," Arunden said. "And neverfade."

"To loosen tongues," Chei said in a small voice, at Vanye's left, "and to bring out truth."

"*Liyo*—" Vanye said, for there was of a sudden too much warmth on his tongue for one sip of honey-mead. She glanced his direction.

"It is harmless—" Chei said. The cup was finishing its course. A young woman brought a skin and filled it, and it began a second passing.

The crowd-murmur grew. "Another bowl!" the priest objected. "It is unclean, unclean—"

But the bowl went to him. "Drink," Arunden bade him, and clenched his hand in the priest's hair and compelled him, at which there was rough laughter, at which Vanye took in his breath and stared in horror, not knowing what to do, not knowing what the priest might do, or some man who respected him.

But no one did anything.

"*Liyo*," he said, wishing them out of this.

"Is thee all right?" she whispered back, past the laughter and the noise.

"I am all right," he said, and it was true, as the moments passed and the cup went round and the priest wiped his mouth and frowned. He felt Chei take his arm and press it—"—no harm," Chei was assuring him. "No harm in it—"

He reached that conclusion in his own reckoning, that it was very strong, that his stomach had been empty, but it was well enough: he thought that he would not fall if he rose, nor sleep if he sat, but that if he sat still a little while his head might not spin and his judgment might come back.

Chei's hand rested on his shoulder then, heavily, a friendly gesture, offering him the cup in the next round. Every detail seemed to stand out with unnatural clarity—like the effects of *akil,* very like that, but milder. There were more and more cups offered about, bowls passed hand to hand, drink poured from skins, blurred voices murmuring words indistinct to him. More than one bowl came his way. He drank only a little and passed them on.

It was mad. There seemed no hostility in it, but it was all balanced on the knife's edge, a peculiar sort of intimacy in this passing of drink round and round. Yet another bowl came his way, and he only pretended to drink now, and gave it on to Morgaine, who likewise feigned drinking, and passed it on again.

"Say on now," Arunden said, whose mustache glistened with beads of liquid in the firelight. *"Now* we talk. My lady qhal, fine lady, who shares my drink and shares my fire—what is it you want in my land?"

"Passage through."

"Through, through, *where* through? To what—to *Mante?"*

"It is the gates," Chei said unbidden. "My lady—*tell* him."

"Chei means to say," Morgaine said quietly, in a silence that had grown so sudden and so hushed there was only the wind in the leaves about them, among a hundred, perhaps a hundred fifty men, and words rang in the air like a hammer on iron: "that Vanye and I came through the southern gate and we are going out the northern one, against the interests of the qhal in this world. We will pass it, we will seal it, and there will be no more taking of men and changing them, there will be no more coming and going out the southern gate, with Gault bringing whatever he likes at your backs while the north brings war against you. There will be no more gate-force. Once I am done with them, they cannot bring them back to life."

A great murmuring grew in the silence she left. "Ha," Arunden cried, and gestured to one of the women, who filled a bowl. He drank deeply, and wiped his mouth. "Who will do this?"

"No great band of men will do it," Morgaine said. "No force of arms. A Gate is far too dangerous to assault head-on."

"Aye, there you say!" He took another deep draft. "So who will do it?"

"I am enough."

"Ha!" He waved his hand. *"Drink* for our guests! *You* are enough! Woman, m'lady qhal, how do you propose to do that? Seduce Skarrin?"

"Liyo," Vanye said, but her hand rested on his arm, and she slid her hand to his and pressed it hard.

"Gate-force," she said. "I am qhal—am I not? The most they have to fear—is one of their own with hostile intent."

"Who says there has never been? Qhal feud and fight. And what has it ever done? You are lying or you are mad, woman."

"Feud and fight they may. But they will not go that far. I will. They have no chance against you then. Do you see? I will give you the only chance you will ever have."

"And the fires—the fires—in the valley!"

"The only chance," Morgaine repeated, "you will ever have. Else Gault will widen his territory and yours will grow less and less. I set that fire—else Gault would be warned and warn his lord, and after *that,* my lord, you would see a hunt through these hills you would not wish to see. I will advise you: shelter me and mine tonight, and pass us through these woods in the morning as quietly and quickly as you can. Beyond that I can assure you the qhal will have other concerns; and beyond that you can do what you have

never, I would surmise, been able to do: to come at
Gault from the wooded south. That gate south of
Morund will cease to be active. There will be no
power there. Begin to think in those terms. Places you
have not dared to go. Enemies you will not have when
these present shapes age and fade—it is *that* which can
make a qhalur enemy a most deadly threat, do you
understand? It is the experience of a half a score
lifespans fighting in the same land, against human folk
who know only what they can learn in twenty years.
That will cease. You will see them die. You will find
their successors fewer and fewer. They do not bear
half so frequently. That is what I offer you."

Arunden wiped a hand across his mouth. The bowl
tilted perilously in his hand. From time to time as
Morgaine spoke the gathering murmured almost enough
to drown her voice, but it was quiet now.

Arunden was entirely drunk, Vanye thought. He
was drunk and half numb and the visitor he had tried
to ply with drink and drug had spun a spell enough to
muddle a man's mind—that was the witchery Morgaine
practiced. He had seen her work it on more than one
man with his wits about him; and he watched now a
desperate and inebriate man trying to break the strands
of that web, with sweating face and glittering eyes and
quickened breath.

"Lies," Arunden said.

"Wherein?"

"Because you will never do it! Because no one can
get through."

"That is my worry. I have said: shelter for the night.
Safe passage through to the Road. That is all."

"That is easy done," Arunden said, wiping his mouth
again. He held out the bowl which had come to him.
"It is empty!"

A woman hastened to fill it. There were a great
number of bowls filled, and a general and rising commotion among the onlookers. Chei's hand a second
time rested on Vanye's shoulder.

"Quiet!" Arunden shouted, and took another deep
draft of the bowl. "Quiet!"

There was a slow ebb of noise. Wind sighed in the leaves, and bodies shifted anxiously.

"Gault will move against us," Arunden said, and motioned violently toward her with the bowl, spilling the liquor. *"That* is what you have done!"

"He may," Morgaine said.

"What does a woman know about strategy?" Arunden cried then, and seized by the shoulder one of the women who rested near with the skin of drink, and shook at her. "Eleis here—a fair shot and a fair cook, till she comes to bearing, eh, pretty?—a good many of our girls come down to the marches for a few years, but lead? Carry a sword? This arm here and mine—d' you want to go a pass with me, Eleis?"

There was rude laughter.

"What do *you* say?" Arunden asked then, and jutted his chin and waved the bowl toward Vanye.

Morgaine laid her hand on his arm again. "Patience," she said, and the laughter sank away a little.

"Go a pass with you?" Vanye asked in measured tones. "Aye, my lord. Gladly. When you are sober."

There was a moment quieter still. Then Arunden broke out in laughter, and others laughed. He pushed the young woman roughly aside, and the woman caught her balance and got up and left the circle.

"Are you human?" Arunden asked him.

"Aye, my lord."

"Your speech is strange as hers."

"That may be, my lord. I learned it of her. My own I much doubt you would understand."

"What clan are you from?"

"Nhi. I am Kurshin. You would not know that land either, my lord. It had gates—which my liege sealed. There have been others. There have been those who attacked my liege. Many of them. *She* is here with you."

That, perhaps, took some thinking for some of them. It evidently did, for Arunden, who sat frowning in a sudden quiet and perhaps wondering whether there was an affront somewhere mixed in it.

"Ha," Arunden said then. "Ha." He lifted the bowl and drained it. "So. Hospitality."

"That is what we ask," Morgaine repeated patiently. "Weapons."

"That we have, my lord."

"Men. You need—three thousand men to storm Mante. Four thousand!"

"I need one. I have him. That is *all*, my lord. *You* will reap the benefit of it—here. You will need those three thousand men, *here*, in the hills, to wait till the qhal grow desperate. That is what you have to do."

"You tell *me* strategy?"

"I could not possibly, my lord. No one could."

"Ha!" Arunden said. And: "Ha! Wise woman. Witch! Is that a witch?" He elbowed the priest with his bowl. "That is a witch, is she not?"

"That is a qhal," the priest muttered, "my lord."

"That is the way out of these hills. That is the way of *winning* against the whole cursed breed! Qhal against qhal! Qhalur witch—that, they send, slip into Skarrin's own bed, hey—is that how you will do it?"

"My liege is very tired," Vanye said. "We have been days on the road. She thanks you for your hospitality; and I thank you. I would like to find her a place to rest, by your leave, my lord."

"Too much to drink, eh?"

"Travel and drink, my lord." Vanye gathered himself to his feet in one smooth motion: such as the drug had done, rage had dispelled. He reached down his hand and assisted Morgaine to stand, taking matters beyond Arunden's muddled ability to manage. "Good night to you—gracious lord."

"See to it," Arunden said, waving his bowl, and women leapt up and hurried as seated men edged aside, opening a path in their circle for the course they were about to take. Shouts went up. More drink splashed into bowls.

But Chei was on his feet too, and Bron. Vanye escorted Morgaine through the press, toward the horses, with Chei at his heels; and young women intercepted them, managing to come not at either of them, but at Chei: "This way," one said, "come, tell them come—"

"Our horses," Vanye said, and ignored the summons, he and Morgaine, walking back to where Siptah and Arrhan stood, while the crowd behind them muttered with drunken dismay. *"Liyo,* let me tend them," Vanye said. "They should not see you do such a thing."

"One of them can tend them," Morgaine said shortly. "But not with our belongings."

"Aye," he said, understanding the order to stay close by her; and caught his breath and went hurrying ahead of her, between the horses, snatched thongs loose and retrieved their saddlebags and their blankets, finding female hands all too ready to take anything he would not hold back from them, and Siptah bothered enough to be dangerous. "Take them," he said, and threw the reins at Chei's brother, who limped within range. "Get someone to rub them down—*both,* else you call me." This last because Siptah was on the edge of his temper, and he was not sure whether any man in camp was sober enough to trust with a twenty year old packhorse, let alone the Baien gray.

"They have vacated a shelter for the lady," Chei said, at his elbow.

O Heaven, he thought, get us clear of this. And aloud: "See the horses picketed near us, Chei, Bron, I trust you for that. And have our gear near us."

"Aye," Chei agreed.

He turned away, after Morgaine and the women, as they tended out of the firelight and toward the shadow of the woods, as the uproar around the fire grew wilder and more frivolous.

There was more to-do as they came to the ill-smelling little shelter of woven mats and bent saplings. Women offered blankets, offered water, offered bread and a skin of liquor. "Go," he said shortly, and pushed the ragged wool flap aside to enter the shelter where Morgaine waited. Firelight entered through the gaps in the reed walls. After a breath or two his eyes found it enough light to make out more than shadow, the glow of her pale hair, the glimmer of silver at her shoulders as she dropped the cloak, the shape of her face and her eyes as she looked at him.

"I would kill him," he said. He had done very well up till now. He found himself shaking.

She came then and embraced him, her cheek against his for a moment, her arms about his ribs; then she took his face solemnly between her hands. "You were marvelous," she said, laughing somewhat; and touched her lips to his, the whole of which confounded him in that way she could do. Perhaps it was the drug which still muddled him. It seemed only courteous not merely to stand there, but to hold to her and to return that gesture, and perhaps it was she who pressed further, he was not sure—only that he did not want to let her go now she had gotten this close and she did not let him go, but held to him and returned him measure for measure till the world spun.

"Vanye," Chei's voice came from outside the shelter, and he caught his breath and his balance and broke apart from her with a whispered curse; at which a second touch of Morgaine's hands, lightly this time, on his arm, sliding to trail over his fingers—

"What?" he asked, far too harshly, flinging back the door-flap.

Perhaps there was murder in his look; perhaps his rapid breaths said something; or perhaps the firelight struck his face amiss, for Chei's expression went from startlement to thorough dismay.

"I was about to say," Chei said, above the uproar from about the fire, "I have told them where to picket the horses, yonder. I am going to go back to the fire, if you—I think I should—Bron and I. . . . Your pardon," Chei said suddenly, and backed and made a hasty retreat, not without a backward look; and a second, and a third, before he suddenly had to dodge a tree and vanished around it.

Vanye caught his breath and, muddled somewhere between outrage and embarrassment, let the door-flap fall again.

Morgaine's hands rested on his shoulders, and her

head against the back of his neck. "We had best take the sleep," she whispered, her breath disturbing the fine hairs there.

"Aye," he said with difficulty, thinking that sleep was not going to come easily despite the liquor and the drug and the exhaustion. "They are fools out there. At least ninety and nine of them. I cannot credit that Chei is a fool with the lot of them—"

"I do not think he is," she said. "I think he has found his brother, that is all. Let him be."

Fire and clangor of arms, one brother lying dead at his hand, the other lying under the knife in hall—and after that, after that was exile, *ilin*-ban, and every kinsman's hand against him. The old nightmare came tumbling back again, of bastardy and years of torment before he reacted, once, frightened—no, *angry*—cornered in a practice match.

Kandrys had not intended his death. He had reasoned his way to that understanding: it would have been only another baiting—except it was the wrong day, the wrong moment, Kandrys' bastard brother grown better and more desperate than Kandrys knew.

And he had always wanted most that Kandrys would forgive him his existence and his parentage.

He drew a sudden, gasping breath, as if a cold wind had blown out of that dream, and brought the grave-chill with it.

"Vanye?"

"It is that cursed drink," he murmured. "Likely Chei has his ear to matters out there—my mind is wandering. I am hungry, but I think I am too tired to get into the packs. Did you drink anything of it?"

"No more than I must."

"They have left us more of the stuff. What kind of fools raise such a noise, living as they do? That is a *priest* out there—"

She leaned her head against him. "This is not Andur-Kursh. And they are fools who have fought their war too long," she said. "Fools who are losing it, year by year, and see a hope. If they are not thinking how to

betray us *and* do Gault harm. How far can we trust
Chei, do you think? For a few leagues still?"

"I do not know," he said. He slipped her grasp,
turning to look at her, as laughter and shrieks rose
from the gathering at the fire. "He may. There is no
honor for a man here. He is too good for this. This is a
sink, *liyo,* a man who could not hold his folk, except
he binds them with that—out there. That is the game
this hedge-lord plays. Only he is gone in it himself.
Heaven knows about Chei's brother."

"Heaven knows when Chei knew about his brother,"
Morgaine said. "Curse him, he forced this, *he* has
gotten us into this tangle; I do not say he was not
taken by surprise, I do not know whether he wanted
this from the beginning, but there is disaster everywhere about this place. They have left us bread yonder; and meat; likely it is safe enough; and we will
take what food we can and prevail on Chei and his
brother at least to see us to the Road. That is all we
need of him, and there is an end of it."

"Aye," he said forlornly, and with a sense of anger:
"It is a waste, *liyo,* this whole place is a waste. Heaven
knows we could do better for him."

"Or far worse," she said.

"Aye."

She caught him by the arm and held him so. Perhaps her eyes could see him in the dark. She was
faceless to him. "If he ties himself too closely to us—
will they ever forget? If he stays then, is he or his
brother safe, when once the gates die, and powers
start to topple? Or if we take them with us—*where* are
they then? Can you promise them better? Best, I say,
we let him go. The eight down in the valley are only
an earnest of what we shall do here. When power falls
here, it will fall hard."

"Lord in Heaven, *liyo*—"

"Truth, Nhi Vanye, bitter truth. That is the ciphering I do: thee knows, thee knows I have no happier
choices—except we leave him, here, near a great fool,
who will vaunt his way to calamity with the power he
imagines he has; and Chei, being Chei, will know

when to quit this hedge-lord—or supplant him. *That* is the best gift we can give him. To leave him among his own kind and kin."

He drew several large and quietening breaths. "Aye," he said again, reasoning his way through that. "In my heart I know that."

"Then be his friend. And let him go."

"Is it that clear?"

"Vanye, Vanye—" But what else she would have said, she did not say, not for some little moment. Then: "Did I not tell thee, thee could leave me? I warned thee. Why did thee not listen?"

He said nothing for a moment, in confusion, a sudden hurt, and deep. He traced it several times, trying to understand how she had gotten to that, or what he had said or done to bring her to that offer again.

Then he realized it for her wound, not his—a doubt she could not lose.

"There will never be a time," he said. "There will never be. *Liyo*, when will you believe it? I cannot leave you. I could never leave you. When will you trust me?"

There was long silence. He wished that he could see her. The very air ached.

"I do not know," she said finally, in a voice hushed and faint. "I do not know why thee should love me."

"God in Heaven—"

But it was not a simple thing that she meant. It was all that she was. It was the whole that she was.

Chei, then, was not the one she had meant—*be his friend. Let him go.*

He took her face between his hands. He kissed her on the brow, and on either cheek, as a man might his kin. He kissed her a third time on the lips, not after the same fashion. It was desperate; it became passionate, and her arms came around him, while the tumult went on outside.

Then he remembered she had not wanted this, and he heard the arrival of the horses out beside the shelter; and reckoned that there was too much of ill in this place and too much chance of disturbance and too much that they risked. Perhaps she had the same sense of things. He separated himself from her in consternation, and she touched his face.

"I think they have brought the horses," she said, foolish for the moment as he was, one heartbeat, one way of thinking, one intention between them, and all of it sliding in that way a dream might—coming apart and passing into the ordinary.

"Aye," he said, feeling himself still breathing in time with her, and all the world having shifted in its balances, and still reeling. He drew another breath. "Best I see where the rest of our gear is."

And outside, with the horses, dealing with the several men who tried with little success to deal with the gray—"Let him be," he said, and took the reins himself. "Put the tack over there—" He gave orders while the figures at the fire moved darkly against the glare, and shouts rang out, and his mind was dangerously busier with his liege than it was with Arunden's men and with Chei and Bron, who had deserted them.

"Whoa, whoa," he whispered to the gray stud, and to the mare, the both of which were unsettled by the place, the fire, the strangers about them. He spoke to them in his own tongue, he stroked them with his hands.

It was strange that he could suddenly be so content to stay a night in this wretched place, or that he could suddenly put the matter of Chei and Chei's betrayals out of his mind. He went back in, he shared a supper of yesterday's bread and a little honey and a sip of their own arrhendur liquor, and somehow they sat closer together than they were wont, and leaned together, armored that they were—and not, after all, fools enough to shed it, whatever the temptation.

"There is time," she said against his cheek, when they were also fools enough to lie down together, because it was easier than to move elsewhere.

And what she had said somehow frightened him, like an ill omen.

There was a third presence by them, an unliving thing. She had laid *Changeling* on her other side, that fell thing without which she never slept, and with and without which she could not rest.

Against that, against the things which had begun to move in the world, he knew he had no power.

Chapter Seven

There had been quiet in the camp for some time, in Vanye's restless sleep. The tumult around the fire had sunk away. Now a milky daylight was streaming through the reed walls, and he lay with his eyes open a moment content only to breathe and to feel Morgaine's warmth against his side, and to know that it was no dream that had happened. Sleep, she had bade him finally: if there was harm here they would have done it—only sleep lightly. It had thundered in the last of the night, a little flashing of lightning, a little sifting of rain against the reed roof, no more than that.

He drifted again, in that half-sleep in which he had spent the little of the night they had had left, alternate with Morgaine, when she would shake at him and tell him it was her turn for an hour of deep rest.

It was more rest, at least, than sitting awake and battling exhaustion during a first watch: as the course of things had gone, it was rare luxury, considering the weather and the night chill.

But he came wide awake again at the simultaneous realization that there was a quiet stirring in the camp, and that Morgaine had shifted onto her elbow.

"They are awake out there," he said reluctantly; and she:

"We had best take our leave of this place, gather Chei, and go."

"I will find him."

She rested her hand on his chest. "Do not stray from here." Fingers tightened on his harness. "The horses first. Then we both find Chei, if he does not come to us. We can break our fast on the way."

She was always cautious. This had other cause. He sensed that suddenly, wider awake than a moment ago, though he did not know which cause of many he could think of.

"Aye," he said. He understood it for something of instinct; he did not take his own such impulses lightly, when they came; and Morgaine's, which were reliable, set a chill into him and cleared his head faster than cold water.

He gathered himself up and moved.

All the world outside was gray and wet, in a hanging fog—except he had kept the blankets dry, and seeing the likelihood of dew, even if he had not foreseen the rain, had thrown a reed mat over the good leather of their tack—being of mountainous Morija, where heavy dew and sudden rains were ordinary. The horses blew and stamped and threw their heads when he came to saddle them, and shifted skittishly as he worked, liking the drying-off, all the same.

Around the dead fire below, the women labored, wrapped in blankets, strange moving shapes like their own huts gone animate in the mist, among the less energetic forms of men who had begun to rise and wander about the peripheries of the camp similarly shrouded.

Morgaine came out with their packs and slung them over Siptah's saddle, pausing to cast a glance downhill toward the fire-site and the moving figures.

"There will be aching heads this morning," Vanye muttered, pulling Arrhan's girth tight; and heard some-one walking near them, through the brush, the which sound set his heart beating a little faster in apprehension. "Who will that be?"

Morgaine made no answer. She had her cloak slung on one-sided against the cold; and because of the weapons she had. She carried *Changeling* at her back; and she stood by Siptah's side looking in the direction of that quiet tread—more than one man was there, that much was certain.

It was Chei that came out of the mist and the trees, with Bron limping behind him.

"We are leaving," Morgaine said quietly. "Chei, one last journey and I release you from your word— guide us as far as the Road. Beyond that—you are quit of us and you can go where you like, with our thanks."

"Lady," Chei said, "you mistake me. Where I want to be, is with you and with Vanye. Myself and Bron, together. We have both decided. He understands everything. He agrees."

"There is no need," Morgaine said with a shake of her head. "Believe me: that one service is all you need do us, and then go back, find some other place, do as you choose."

"I am not helpless," Bron declared fervently—a man much like his brother in all points, but taller. It was the identical anxious look. "Lady, I limp, but I am a whole man on horseback—I shall not slow you; it is my leg that is wounded, that is all, and it is healing. I will not be lame, I have my gear, and I will not slow you."

The silence went on then, painfully. "No," she said then.

The man drew in his breath, slowly. "Then at least—do not cast Chei off for my sake."

"You do not understand," she said.

"*You* do not understand," Chei said, and held out his hand toward Vanye with that same expression. "Vanye—we were worth something to our lord, Bron and I; Bron—Bron was the one he used to say—had no fear of the devil himself. You see he is wounded; but he will heal—*I* will heal; you have never seen what I can do, and the two of us—you will never regret taking us, we will fight for you, Bron and I, against *any* of your enemies, human or qhal; we will never find a better lord, I believe that, and Bron believes it—He knows what you might have done here, and did not, and how you dealt with Arunden—and how you

dealt with me—Tell her, Vanye. Tell my lady we will
repay everything she spends on us. We will earn our
keep. We are worth having, Nhi Vanye!"

"It is not your worth she disputes, Chei."

"Then what? Do you doubt us? I brought you through
this. I have gotten you safe passage. I swore to you.
What do you think—that I have not kept my word?
Bron and I—will go with you on our own. We will
prove to you what we are worth. Take us on those
terms. You owe us nothing. Only for God's sake do
not leave us in Arunden's debt."

Entanglement showed itself, unguessed and dark,
an obscurity of honor and obligation. "You mean that
Arunden has some claim on you."

"For Bron's life," Chei said. "For mine, if you leave
me here; I will have to trade him everything I own;
and most of everything that comes to me or Bron; and
then we will never be free of him. One or the other of
us he will always find a way to keep in his debt—that
is the way he is. Lady, I swear we will manage, we will
take nothing of your supplies—have I not brought you
my own horse and gear already? Bron has his gear, he
has a good horse—he traded his small-sword for it last
night. He has his other. We will not slow you. We will
earn our way, every step of it."

"Foolishness," Morgaine said harshly. "Two wounded
Men and qhalur territory ahead of us. And you *would*
use our supplies. We have no time for hunting."

"We have them! We have provisions—we—"

"Chei. Chei, no. This much I will do, if you have
some debt here. Ride with us, both as far as the Road.
I will at least get you free of here. You will see us as
far as the Road and then we are quit of each other.
You will have no debt to me or to Arunden, and that
is as much as I can give you. I claim nothing of you."

"Did you not promise—*promise* to me—that you
would take me through the gate if I chose?"

Morgaine stopped for once with her mouth open,
caught. Then she shut it abruptly and frowned. "That
had condition, condition you cannot meet. You know
nothing about the land further on."

"I thought it was for my life's sake—for my protection. Not a few nights gone. *I will not deny you that right,* you said."

"I said I would advise you against it."

"But I will go, lady, and my brother will."

"*You,* I said. No other!"

Chei's face went paler still. "Both of us. You will not hold me to that. You will not deny me for Bron's sake, you would not do that, lady."

"You do not know *what* I would do, fool!"

"I know I will follow you. And Bron will. Both of us. And you will not turn us back. Please."

A long moment she stood still. And Chei was next to weeping, Bron's face pale and set. "You are not afraid for *that?*" She swept her hand toward the camp, the dead fire, Arunden's place and others'. "You have no fear of your priest and his curses?"

"We will follow you."

"We will talk about it again before Tejhos. By then, you may have another opinion."

"Lady," Chei said fervently, and knelt down and seized her hand, his brother after him kneeling and taking her hand and pressing it to his brow, the which she endured with a look of dread on her face.

"We are leaving," Morgaine told the brothers. "Arm and saddle and take everything you can. I would dispense with any long leave-takings with Arunden, if we can avoid that, Chei. Or if you have to deal with him, say we will remember him kindly—say whatever will keep him content and keep him off our trail."

"Aye, lady," Chei said, and Bron murmured the same, rising with a great effort not to falter in the act. Chei delayed for him and then the both of them went off directly across the camp in all the haste Bron could use.

Morgaine swore beneath her breath and shook her head.

"It is freedom you offer them," Vanye said. "Evidently they are beholden for whatever they take at Arunden's hand."

"If that is all they want," she muttered, and turned to Siptah to tie the thongs that held her blanket roll.

"What would they want?"

She cast him a frown over her shoulder. "Glory. Whatever else you name it. Power. I have seen it before." She finished the tie with a vengeance. "No matter. I could be wrong."

"You do not understand them. I think that is a good man, Chei's brother. I think that Chei is trying to be. He is young, *liyo*, that is all, and too proud, and he knows too little, and acts on it too soon, that is the trouble with him. I have done that, now and again."

"Then thee generally did it younger. No, likely I do not understand: men and Men, did I not say it from the beginning? When did I say I kept my promises? I lie; thee knows I lie; *tell* this boy."

"Why am *I* always the messenger?"

"Because thee is the honest man in this company. Did I not tell thee how trouble looks for an honest face?"

"I cannot tell him—"

"Peace, peace, forbear. We will settle it later. I only want us away from here. We are already delayed. Now we have these two making noise in the camp—"

"And it is trouble if we slip out without it. You will shame this Arunden if you leave with no courtesy to him."

"A wonder, something that would shame Arunden. No, I will pay him courtesy; and well enough it were short courtesy, and ourselves well away from here." She took Siptah's reins and flung herself to the saddle, reining back as the horse started forward. "Before noon, I hope."

Vanye mounted up more carefully, and leaned to pat the white mare's shoulder as she stood quietly at Siptah's side. In the camp in general there were more folk up shambling about their private business. A little tongue of fire gleamed through the mist, where blanket-shrouded figures crouched.

And in a very little time there was the sound and the ghostly shapes of two riders coming back again through the mist, but they were not alone. A handful of bearish figures went after them afoot.

"*There* is trouble," Morgaine said between her teeth, about the time the riders broke free and came cantering their way.

They did not shake the followers. A loud shout rang through the misty air and dark shapes jogged at the riders' heels, others rousing from fireside and shelters and every occupation in the camp.

The brothers did not bring the trouble that far. They turned their horses about and stopped there, in the face of the oncoming crowd.

Morgaine sent Siptah forward and Vanye touched his heels to Arrhan, overtaking her as she reined in alongside Chei and Bron, in the face of Arunden himself and his priest, and by the size of the crowd that was rallying there, of every man in camp.

"You do not take them only," Arunden shouted at her, waving an arm at the brothers. "Here is a man in debt to me—I release him! I make no claim against him or his brother for his keep! But if it is my safe-conduct you want, by Heaven, lady, you do not have it through my land with these guides, and you do not have it without my riders. That is no lie, lady, God knows what they have told you to send you riding out like this, with no farewell cup and no advisement to me, but you are ill-advised to listen to them."

"My lord Arunden, I counsel *you*, I am traveling with all speed, and the more speed and the fewer and the more silence the safer."

"Arrows are quicker than any horse," Arunden said, and set his fists on his hips, walking forward. Siptah snaked his head for more rein and Vanye sent Arrhan sidestepping closer on his side, forming a solid wall, whereupon Arunden stopped in his tracks. "My lady Morgaine—Yonder is no trail for any qhal, much less a woman and a handful of men, two of them such as I would never send out on a ride like this, and who do not have leave to come and go in my land. My warders will stop you, and at best hail you back here, and at worst shoot without asking questions! Whatever these two scoundrels have told you, *I* will tell you, you do not pass through these woods or any other without a good number of reliable men around you, and you before God do not ride that road without there be good human men around you, and men my warders know, or before Heaven, someone will take that hair of yours for a target! First cover that head of yours before someone takes you for some of Gault's own, and stand down and wait while we break camp. We will rouse you more than one clan, my lady, and I will personally see you to the Road!"

"We need no help," Morgaine said. "The four of us are enough. Do not press me, my lord Arunden. Pay your attentions to Gault, southward."

"Do not be a fool," Arunden said, and stalked off a few paces to give a wave of his hand at his gathered men. "Break camp."

The men started to obey; and froze and scrambled back as red fire cut through the mist and smoke and then flame curled up at Arunden's feet. Arunden stood confused a moment, looked down and retreated in alarm as the tiny fire grew to larger points. Then he looked back at Morgaine, wide-eyed, and Vanye settled back in the saddle with his hand still on his sword-hilt.

"Witch!" Arunden cried; and his priest held up the sword.

"You have been my host," Morgaine said coldly. "Therefore I owe you some courtesy, my lord. Therefore your land is untouched. But do not mistake me. Here I am lady, and these are men of mine, and whoever rides with me takes my orders or Vanye's orders. There are no other terms with me, and I am sure they are not to your liking. If you would have my gratitude—my lord—then be sure of that southern border, where Gault is very likely to be no little disturbed by what we have done in his lands."

A series of expressions fleeted through Arunden's eyes, from fear to other things less easy to read.

And the priest thrust himself forward with his sword for a cross, chanting prayers and imprecations at them, at the crowd, at Heaven above. *Witch*, was the general murmur in the crowd that was melting backward; and there was fear in Bron's eyes too, as he controlled his horse and glanced her way. At the priest's feet the fire had spread to a small circle, faltering in the wet grass, and he kicked at it suddenly with a vengeance, stamping it underfoot as Arunden and his men murmured behind him. "Fire," the priest cried, "such as took the woods down in the valley. Fire of your making. Who burns the woods is cursed of God! Cursed be all of you, cursed who ride with you—"

Vanye crossed himself. So Bron and Chei made some sign, and backed their horses, when the priest pressed forward with his sword uplifted hilt to Heaven; but: "Hai!" Vanye cried, seeing he was going at Morgaine, and rode forward and shouldered the priest back and back.

"Cursed and damned!" The mailed priest's sword wheeled and came down at Arrhan's neck. Vanye swung his sheathed sword up and struck the blade up, then kicked the priest sprawling in the smoking grass, the priest howling and writhing instantly with the heat of it. "Damned!" he shouted, "Damned!"—scrambling up and after his sword.

Arunden brought his foot down on the blade as his hand reached the hilt, pinning it to the blackened ground.

"Is this your help?" Morgaine asked dryly. "I shall do without, my lord Arunden."

"You will take what I give!"

"I said that I was Gault's enemy. I have told you what I will do, and where I am going, and I will have done it before Gault spreads the alarm to his masters if you do me the grace to do what I have said. I should take that advice, my lord, if it were my lands bordering Gault. But far be it from me to say what a free Man should do. That is your choice—to help or hinder."

"Do not listen to her," the priest cried, and snatched up the sword Arunden's stride released.

Arunden turned and interposed his arm at the same time Vanye bared steel; and grasped the priest's sword-hilt in his hand and wrenched it away, disarming the man and flinging the sword far across the grass. "My lady," Arunden said, "Take my advice. I will not argue strategy with you. I will go with you myself, with ten of my men. My lieutenant will go south and close the road, others east and west and advise the other clansmen. Ichandren's skull is bleaching on a pole at Morund, and it is only my word and yours that tells my warders these lads are still human or that *he* is. I can vouch for you, and get you to Tejhos-gate never touching the Road. My word carries weight in these hills with bands beyond this one—there is no one says *I* am one of Gault's minions—ha? Ha, priest who eats my food and warms at my fire? Take the curse off. *Off*, hear?"

"God remembers," the priest muttered, and made a sign, half with an eye to Arunden.

"Well enough," Arunden said. "See? We are friends."

"Liyo," Vanye said in his own language. "There is no mending this man. You will regret any good you do him. And much more any help he gives. Do not have any part of his offer."

Morgaine was silent a moment, in which Arunden stood looking up as solemn and sober as he had yet been.

"You will not regret it," Arunden said. "Time will come, you will need us, my lady—you will need someone the other clans know, a man they will listen to."

"Then prove it, now" Morgaine said. "Send messengers to the clans and prevent Gault from your land and from the southern gate. Three of your men can manage our safe-conduct. But all this land will regret it if Gault learns what I am about, he or his neighbors; and if one of Gault's men reaches that gate in the south and brings help from Mante—do me that grace, lord Arunden, and I will freely own myself in your debt."

Arunden's face darkened, suffused with a flush. He gnawed on his lip and raked a hand back through his disordered hair, where it had come loose from its braids.

"Whoever commands that position," Morgaine said, "will command the south. When that gate dies—you will feel it in the air. When it dies you will know that I have kept my promise; and you will sit as lord at Morund. That I offer you—that and anything you can take and hold. The south will need a strong lord. I will have those three men you offer. I will send them back to you when I have cleared your lands. My own, I keep!"

She wheeled Siptah then and rode, as Arunden stood open-mouthed and with a thousand hostile and avaricious thoughts flickering through his eyes. Vanye did not turn away from him. "Go with her," he said to Chei and Bron, who had moved up beside him; and the brothers turned and rode after Morgaine, leaving only himself facing Arunden and his folk.

"My lord," Vanye said then sternly. "Your three men."

Arunden came free of his astonishment and called out three names, at which Vanye inclined his head in respect to Arunden. "I trust," Vanye said, without a trace of insolence in his tone, "that your men can track us."

Then he whirled about and rode after Morgaine and the ep Kantorei.

"Damned, who defies the priest of God!" the priest shouted after him. "Cursed are ye—!"

He cast a look back. No weapons flew. Only words. Ahead of him Morgaine waited on the slope, Bron and Chei on either side of her, dim figures among the ghosts of tall trees.

"Was there trouble?" Morgaine asked him as he reined in.

"My back is unfeathered," he said, and refrained from crossing himself. He felt more anger than distress.

"He is not much of a priest," Bron said. "No one regards him. It is only words."

"Well we were out of here," Morgaine said, "all the same." And motioned Bron and Chei to lead. "Vanye?"

Vanye drew Arrhan to a walk beside Siptah as Chei

and Bron led them out of the misty clearing and in among the trees.

"Do we have the escort?" Morgaine asked.

"He did not refuse it," he said. "I said they should find us on the trail."

"Good," Morgaine said. Then, in the Kurshin tongue: "Did I not tell thee? Power. Arunden does not know what I am. He thinks he knows, and fills in the gaps himself. At least it is honest greed. And it is rarely the first rebel in any realm who ends by being king. There will far worse follow."

He looked at her, troubled by her cynicism. "Never better?"

"Rarely. I do not put treachery past him—or the priest."

"The three he is sending?"

"Maybe. Or messengers he may send ahead of us and behind."

He had reckoned that much for himself. He did not like the reckoning. He thought that he should have forced a challenge and taken off Arunden's shoulders all capacity for treachery.

He was not, he knew all too well, as wise as Morgaine, who had improvised a use for this man: but Arunden, last night, had touched on an old nightmare of hers: he had felt it in the way she had clenched his hand at the fireside.

They would not listen, she had said of that moment human lords had broken from her control; *because I am a woman they would not listen.*

And ten thousand strong, an army and a kingdom had perished before her eyes.

That was the beginning of that solitude of hers, which he alone had breached since that day. And what they had almost done in the night was very much for her—Heaven knew any distraction was a risk with that burden she carried, dragon-hilted and glittering wickedly against her shoulder as she rode, and trust was foreign to everything she did—trust, by her reckoning, was great wickedness.

So he was resolved, for his part, not to bring the

previous night into the day, or to be anything but her liegeman under others' witness, meticulous in his proprieties.

Wet leaves shook dew down onto them as they maintained their leisurely pace and refused to give any grace to Arunden's laggard men. A fat, strange creature waddled away from the trail and into the brush in some haste, evading the horses' hooves: that was all the life they saw in the mist. Trails crossed and recrossed in the hollows, along ravines and up their sides, in this place where Men seemed to have made frequent comings and goings.

Eventually the sound came to them of riders behind them on the trail. Morgaine drew rein. The rest of them did, waiting in a wide place on the shoulder of a low hill.

"They took long enough," Morgaine said with displeasure. She slipped *Changeling* to her side and adjusted and put up the hood of the two-sided cloak the arrhendim had given her; wrapping herself in gray— gray figure on gray horse in the misty morning; and in the next moment one and the next and the third rider appeared through the thicket across the ravine. They seemed unaware until the next heartbeat that they were observed; then the leader hesitated to the confusion of his men and their horses.

"Well we are no enemy," Vanye said under his breath as the men came on ahead, down the slope and up again toward them.

"Lady," the older of the three said as he reined in, and ducked his head in respect, a stout man with grizzled braids and scarred armor.

"My thanks," Morgaine said grimly, leaning on the saddlehorn. "I will have one thing: to go quickly and quietly. I want to find the road where it enters qhalur lands, and that with no harm to anyone, including yourselves. I do not need to say the other choice. Ride well ahead of us. When we come to the road, your duty is done and you will return to your lord. Do you question?"

"No, lady."

She nodded toward the trail, and the three rode on
into the lead at a brisk pace. Her glance slid Bron's
way, and to Chei, as she reined the gray about; and
last she looked to Vanye.

"If they do not cut our throats," he muttered in the
Kurshin tongue, and stayed close by her as they rode.
The riders ahead had already hazed in the mist, and
Bron and Chei were hindmost on the narrow trail.
"Bron," he said, reining back half a length. "Do you
know those three?"

"The one is Eoghar," Bron said, "and the others
are his cousins—Tars, they call the dark one; and
Patryn is the one with the scarred face. That is all I
know, m'lord—no better and no worse than the rest of
them."

"Well when we are quit of them," Chei said for his
part, "but just as well we have them now. In that
much Arunden told the truth."

The rain began to fall again, a light, chill mist that
alternately blew and clung. The noon sun had no
success with the clouds, nor was the afternoon better.
Streams trickled in the low places they crossed; the
rounding of a hill gusted moisture into faces and down
necks, and showed the wooded flanks of further hills
all hazed and vague.

It was steady progress they made, but not swift, and
Morgaine chafed in silence—Vanye knew that look,
read the set of her mouth and the sometime impatient
glances at the sky, with frowns as if she faced some
living enemy.

Time, he thought. It was time and more time lost.

"How far is it?" she had asked Chei early on; and:
"Two days," Chei had said, "down to the road again."
Then: "Maybe more."

Now their guides halted, waiting for them on the
trail, all wrapped in their cloaks and with their horses
back-eared and unhappy in the blowing mist.

"We should make camp," their leader said—Eoghar,
Bron had named him. He had a wretched look, a
pained look, squinting against the rain that dripped off

his hair, and Vanye recalled the last night, and the campfire, and the amount of drink that had passed even before they quit the gathering.

"No," Morgaine said, and, "No," again when Eoghar argued the weather and the horses and the slickness of the rocks and the slopes. "How much worse does it get?" she asked then, looking at Chei and Bron, who had ridden up close behind them.

"More of the same," Chei said, himself in worse case, having only his blanket for a cloak, and its gray fibers beginning now to soak through. "No worse, my lady. Certainly no better."

Only looking at him and at Bron did Morgaine's frown go from annoyance to a more complex thing—worry, Vanye thought. But: "Move on," she said to Eoghar and his cousins.

"Lady," Eoghar protested, and his mustached lips shut themselves and the voice faded into something very like fear at whatever look Morgaine then sent him. "Aye, lady." And Vanye took his hand from the sword-hilt as three wet and unhappy men turned their horses about and kept going down the exposed and down-sloping trail.

To Morgaine he ventured no word, knowing her moods well enough, that a black anger was roiling in her, and he knew well enough what kind of look had likely set the men moving.

Yet she delayed a moment, looking back at Chei, and there was worry again. "Are you bearing up?" she asked.

"Well enough," Chei said, and drew a little breath, straightening in the saddle. "My lady."

It was not gratitude shone in Chei's fair eyes, with rain-chill whitening his face and the water running from his hair. It was something like adoration.

Vanye lowered his head and kept his eyes on the trail as they rode after their guides, gazing down on the tops of trees and the depths of a ravine that fell away beside Arrhan's sure, careful steps.

He did not know why that expression of Chei's should trouble him so. It was not the look of a man with a woman he wanted. He had seen it—he recollected—in chapel, candlelight off painted wood, face after identical face—

He did not know why that image out of childhood and Church came back to him again and again, stronger than the world around him, of gray mist and mist-grayed pines and slick granite, or why he thought then of Chei when he had first come to them, that fevered, mad glare that had nothing to do with the clean-faced, earnest youth who spoke so fair to Morgaine and looked at her since this morning as if she were some saint.

But he understood with a little chill of fear—knowing that behind Morgaine's careful question, that kindly, out of the ordinary question to Chei when she was otherwise distracted—Morgaine was indeed disturbed.

I am not virtuous, she was wont to say, again and again to him, warning him. I cannot afford to be.

And again, in the night: How can you love me?

And this morning: I lie; thee knows I lie; *tell* him—

It was fear he felt in her, that was what moiled in his stomach at the moment; it was a rising sense of panic, between her acceptance of Chei for his sake and Bron for Chei's sake; and the changes between himself and her; and this priest and this cursed gift from a hedge-lord. It was no time to think of such things, riding on a high trail in the company of men they could not trust, in a land which might offer ambush: he was derelict to think of anything but where they rode and what things the forest might tell him and the attitudes of the men in front of them. But it was not in the forest that he felt the danger. It was beside him, in Morgaine's silence, in the way she looked at Chei and at him.

Perhaps she mused on things the two of them had done and promised and said to each other, in the thunderous dark.

Nothing seemed now so simple or so clean now as then. He did not know what he should have done differently this morning or how he could have protected her or what he ought now to do.

Persuade Chei and his brother to leave them, that was the first thing, before worse happened.

But to cast them out in these hills, when Chei was known to have been in qhalur hands, and when both of them were known to have ridden with Morgaine kri Chya—that would be a death sentence for these two, for these honest, too-young men who had neither lord nor family to protect them, and not, he sensed, the ability to wrest power unto themselves.

Honest men, Morgaine had said.

Chapter Eight

The rain came down in wind-borne mist by sundown, under skies flickering and glowing with lightnings, as they rode within the shelter of a rocky retreat which had not, perhaps, been a streambed until the rain fell, but which now had a waterfall spilling off the heights above the cut and boiling white along the rocks to yet another falls.

There was a sheltered camp here, Chei and Bron supported the guides in that assertion, and Vanye was only glad to hope for the overhanging cliff face Bron described or anywhere out of the wind. "There is no way out of the place but one," Bron had admitted, "but with your weapons no one could force it from the front or from above."

Vanye had had second thoughts at that description, and looked at Morgaine: warfare in world and world and world had taught him half a score of ways to attack such a place; Morgaine surely knew as many more. But Morgaine had made no objection except a misgiving glance, wet and miserable as the rest of them in this storm that mixed cold mist with the breaths they took.

Now they rode in the last of the light, into this narrow place where a waterfall thundered above the rain, and where some previous user had left standing a woven brush-work against the rock. He did not like the look of it; but the horses were spent after rough going on the slick trails, they were chilled to the bone, and the whipping of the wind up the heights and the

171

scattering of water off pine boughs in soaking drops,
threw water at them so many directions there was no
fending it off: it ran down necks and got under cloaks
clenched in numb hands; and that brush shelter beckoned with the promise of dry ground and rest and
respite.

But: "No," Morgaine said then, ready to refuse it
after all, "no more of guesting—"—at which Vanye's
heart both sank in weariness and resolved itself she
was altogether right. But: "It is a hunter-shelter,"
Chei said. "I do not expect anyone is there."

"Find out," Morgaine said to Eoghar, and with
more zeal than he had done anything in the last hour,
Eoghar spurred his horse up the bank to hail the place
and then to dismount, draw his sword, and look into
it.

Eoghar turned then and waved to them to come
ahead, murky flash of his sword-blade in the dark.
Vanye gave a sigh of relief and guided Arrhan carefully after Eoghar's cousins, to have an eye on them
and keep his sword between them and Morgaine, should
they have any notions of treachery in this dark hole.

But when they had come up and dismounted beside
the shelter:

"One cannot hear in this place," Morgaine objected,
the last of them still ahorse, her voice thinned by the
roar of the water pouring down and running over
rock. "I do not like this."

Vanye looked up at her from across Arrhan's rain-
wet saddle. "Aye," he said hoarsely, knowing a second time she was right, but he felt the weight of the
mail on his back and the cold of water down his neck
and soaking his boots and breeches. It was her second
quibble with this place. He respected her instincts; but
there was in him a heart-deep vexation—Heaven save
us, *liyo,* you have three men you can trust, he thought
to shout at her.

But there were Arunden's three, and those men
large and strong, and if they would not mutiny in the
night, they were bound to if she bade them go on now.

And he, God help them, had to enforce her orders,

or she had to do murder on them; and he was not sure he had a fight left in him—

"Do we ride on, *liyo?*" he asked with a deep and weary breath.

She glanced back, a shifting of her eyes toward Chei and Bron, who were already taking gear off their horses in the lightning-flashes and the mist, Chei trying in vain to keep the sodden blanket from flying in the wind, his cloth breeches wet through in places where it had blown as he rode. They were spent, man and youth both thin and worn, both recent from wounds, both vulnerable to chill and staggering with exhaustion.

"No," she said, then, in a voice weary as his own. She slid down from Siptah's back, and led him toward the shelter. "We will have a fire if we can find wood enough. At least the rain will drown the smoke. If anyone disturbs us tonight it will be his own misfortune."

It was dead branches broken off the trees back along the rocks, that they had for their fire; and the black weapon's power to set it burning, for which Vanye was earnestly grateful, for nothing but sweat and all a woodsman's skill could have gotten such a fire alight tonight, even considering the heart of the wood was dry. A quick touch of that red light into a little fibrous tinder pulled from the underbark of the nether side of the branches, a little encouragement with dead leaves pulled from the inside of the woven shelter, and there was instantly a cheerful if smoky little flame that grew with twigs and grew with kindling and branches and quickly underlit her face and the fearful countenances of their companions.

A man grew to rely on such comforts.

"It has other uses," Morgaine said to the men who watched in horror. One—Patryn, it was, signed himself. None of the three looked reassured.

To the good, Vanye thought. Chei was not troubled; he tucked his wet blanket about him and huddled close to the qhal-made fire, whereat Bron relaxed and even gave a shy grin between his own shivers as he pulled his boots off to dry them.

With Eoghar and his kin it was another matter—but so was their situation, men passed off by their lord into a witch's keeping, despite their priest's objections. They huddled together a little separate, and hugged themselves against the cold. The cousin named Tars sneezed mightily, and buried his head a moment in his arm, and sneezed again.

If they had begun the day with aching heads, Vanye reflected, their misery was surely complete by now. He was even moved to pity for them—not enough that he turned his back on them, but he brought them some of the wood, and brought them burning tinder in a wedge between two sticks, and left them to nurse it along and to go out in the rain if they wanted more firewood in the night: "My charity," he said dourly, "stops at the shelter's edge."

Thereafter Eoghar and Patryn took their turn out in the driving mist, wood-gathering, and he went back to Morgaine and the brothers, loosed his armor buckles and his belts, tucked himself up in his wet cloak next the fire, and rested with Chei and Bron, close by Morgaine as she boiled up tea, his back against the rock and his left shoulder next the dry leaves of the woven branches which made one wall of their shelter.

Outside, the horses complained of the rain, and Siptah snorted his displeasure either at two wet strangers wandering about outside or at the geldings picketed apart from him and the mare.

The wood-gatherers returned with their arms full, before their fire died. Inside, under the shelter of the stone overhang and the woven walls, the warmth increased. By the time there were a few coals and the first pannikin of tea had boiled, there was a closer, less peevish feeling in the air and Chei had unfolded himself somewhat and ceased to shiver.

There was smoked meat, fowl, venison, and the bread they had taken from the camp: they did not use their carefully prepared trail rations while there was that choice, and with food that would not last there was no stinting. There was tea to warm them; and by their own fire at the opposite and shallower end of the shelter, Eoghar and his cousins saw to their own supper with the supplies they had brought.

"Ah," Chei said with a little wince when he had drunk his cup, and he sighed as he leaned back against the rock wall by his brother. Bron pushed at him with an elbow, grinned, and Chei pushed back, then clapped Bron on the shoulder in a brief embrace, a glance, a quick and tender look passed between them such as brothers might exchange, who found each other alive against all expectation.

Then Chei burst into tears, and turned his face into Bron's shoulder, and the two of them held each other fast, at which Vanye found himself the fire to look at, and then Morgaine's face—as she looked distressedly toward him, and then found occupation for her hands with repacking.

There was no cursed place for privacy, except the rain. And Chei fought hard for his dignity, who was, Heaven knew and events had witnessed, not prone to tears.

After, Chei bent and rested his forehead on his knee, his braids covering his face, for a long time in which he met no one's eyes. Only Bron's hand rested on his back, until he wiped fiercely at his eyes.

It was safety did that to a man. That was all. The lifting of some terrible burden. The knowledge of trial passed. As if this place, with the rain beating down and the wind whipping outside, offered what the secure camp had not.

Freedom, perhaps. Or a brother's life.

"I am all right," Chei declared, and wiped his eyes and drew a breath and clasped his hands on the back of his neck, taking his wind.

Bron held him by the shoulder and rocked at him. There was a sheen on Bron's eyes too, as he rubbed Chei's back and wound his fingers in Chei's hair and tugged at it with a familiarity from which Vanye averted his eyes in embarrassment.

But perhaps they felt they had found kin.

"You did not know," Morgaine said, "that your brother was there. Truly."

"No," Chei said, a small, quick breath. And looked up, as if he then understood that question. "I swear I did not."

"But took us to land you knew—to friends' territory."

A frightened shift of Chei's eyes mistrusted the listeners. But there was the waterfall to cover their voices. "Ichandren's. My own lord's."

"Ah," Morgaine said, and did not glance at Eoghar herself; and Vanye dared not, putting it together, how Arunden who held a sick man in debt, had moved right gladly into a dead ally's lands.

"This Arunden seems quick to gain," he muttered.

"From everything," Chei said fiercely. "He is known for it."

"I had wondered," Morgaine said in a low voice, "how we happened to find Bron. Coincidence is the most remote chance in all the world—good coincidence even rarer. I do not trust men who seem to have it all about them. And strokes of luck are worst of all."

It was honesty. When Morgaine became obscure it was an offered confidence. Honesty with her was one thing and the other. It was Chei she meant, and Chei she looked at, and Chei looked confused as a man might. "I—do not think I have had luck, lady, except you brought it."

"Any man might have been there, at the gate. Luckier for your friends if we had been a fortnight earlier. It is finding Bron I mean."

"I had no hope of it," Chei said earnestly. "I only went home. I wanted no more mistakes. I thought—I thought—there was no way to get through without meeting ambush. When you told me—what you told me—I knew there was hope in talking. So I did not try to slip around the long way. I brought you up the short way, and took no pains to be quiet, you were right, lady. But we were dead, the other way. It was all I could do."

"And did not tell me."

There was long silence. Chei looked at her, only at her, and his face was pale in the firelight.

"But you did not know," Morgaine said, "that Bron was there."

"No, lady. On my soul, I did not know."

"He could not have known," Bron said. The fire snapped, wet wood; and scattered sparks.

"Arunden took you up," Morgaine said.

"I fell in the fighting," Bron said. "Arunden's folk came down to collect the gear. To *steal* anything they could. That is what they are."

"Gault's men leave their enemies' gear?" Vanye asked. "For others to take up?"

"This time they did," Bron said, and drew a long and shaken breath. "I do not know why. Probably they had wind of Arunden's folk close by. They took up prisoners—I saw them. I fainted then. I thought they would gather up weapons and they would find me alive and finish me. When I woke up it was one of Arunden's men had found me, that is all I know. And Gault's men had taken none of my gear."

"You were fortunate," Morgaine said. "Did I not just say how I abhor good fortune?"

Bron looked anxiously at Chei, last at Vanye, a worried look, a pleading look.

"It is truth," Bron said. "That is all I know."

Vanye shifted position, having found his arm cold from the wind gusting through the woven-work. He found his heart beating uncomfortably hard. "Arunden was an ally of your lord's?"

"We were ambushed on our way to join with him. The qhal may have known he was there—" The thought seemed to come to Bron then. His mouth stayed open a moment. His eyes darted and locked.

"And withdrew," Morgaine said.

Bron had nothing to say. He darted a look of his own Eoghar's way and back again. Chei's breath was rapid.

"No one would—" Bron said.

"You say yourself, changelings are not uncommon. A man too close to qhalur lands, a scout, a hunter—"

"We are not that careless!"

Heaven save us, Vanye thought. And aloud: "Is your enemy without guile? Or luck?"

Both the brothers were silent. At their own fire, Eoghar and his cousins talked among themselves, voices that did not carry over the water sound.

"It would be easy, then," Morgaine said, "for messengers of all sorts to come and go. From the camp, for instance."

"We do not know it is so!" Chei said.

"No," Morgaine said. "It might be coincidence. Everything might be coincidence."

Bron exhaled a long slow breath. "A treaty with Gault?"

"Possibly," Morgaine said, "you were only fortunate. There *is* chance in the world. It is only very rare—where profit is concerned."

Bron ran his fingers back through his hair and rested, his hands clenching his braids. Then he looked at Vanye and at Morgaine. "Are you, after all, from Mante? Is this something you *know?* Are you having games with us?"

"We are strangers," Morgaine said. "We are not from Gault and not from Skarrin. We do not know this land. But of treachery and of greed we have seen altogether too much. Perhaps it has occurred to you— that there is profit to be had. We do not withhold it. Anything you can gain from us, take. We will have no need of power in this world. Do you want Gault's place? Or any other—take it."

Bron caught a breath. "Everything," he said in a faint voice, "that Chei has told me about you I believe. I never—in all my life—In all my life, I never— never knew I would—come to—to owe—"

"A qhal?" Morgaine asked.

Bron swallowed the rest of that speech. His face was bone-white, his pain-bruised eyes set on her as if he could not find a way to move. "But," he said after, "it is you I will follow. I do not think we will live long. I do not think we will live to see Mante. But for what you did for my brother I will go with you; for what you did for both of us, I will do everything I can for you. I do not deny I am afraid of you. There is a cost—to serving qhal—and I do not know what you would choose, between us and others. But what you say you will do—if you seal the Gates—is a chance for every man alive; and we never had one till this. It is *worth* a life. And mine is spun out longer than I expected, since Gyllin-brook. Chei's, too. Where else shall we find a place for us?"

Morgaine looked at him long; and turned then and began to pack away their belongings. "I do not know. But I would you could find one." She looked up at them. "When we reach the road, turn back. Go somewhere far, and safe. Two more humans will be a hazard to me—only that much more likelihood that someone will know me for a stranger."

Chei had opened his mouth to protest. He shut it as she spoke and he caught a breath. "But," he said then, "they would take us for the Changed, that is all. There is no reason not."

"It is that common."

"Half the qhal in Morund—have human shape."

"So," she said softly, and her frown deepened and darkened. She put a last packet into the saddlebags and wrapped the ties tight. "They are using the gates that often."

"I do not know," Bron said, looking as bewildered as his brother. "I do not know how often they come and go."

"No one knows," Chei said. "None of us go south. When they want to come and go—they use Morund-gate. They do not need to ride through our land."

"Frequently?"

"Maybe—several times a year. I do not know. No one—"

"So a message has already gone to Mante."

"I think that it would have," Chei said. "When the woods burned. I think they would send for that. Gault is not friendly with Mante. With his lord. So they say."

"Rumor says," Bron amended. "Men who come and go off Gault's land. Some do, still."

"Too much here is tangled," Morgaine said; and Vanye shifted his mailed and weary shoulders back against the rock and picked up the thongs that depended from his belt, beginning to braid three of them.

"As to changelings," Vanye said, "we do not do that, with friend or enemy. You are safe with us, as safe, at least, as we are. And we intend to reach Mante, and go beyond it. But that—that, has no return. You should understand that. My lady advises you turn back. There is reason. You should listen to her."

There was silence after, except a discordant muttering from Eoghar and his cousins, about their separate fire. A little laughter drifted from them, about their own business. Doubtless Chei and Bron were distressed. He did not look up.

"Lady," Chei said.

"For your sake and ours," Morgaine said firmly.

Again there was silence, long silence, with only the noise from the other fire where, Vanye saw with a shift of his eye, the three clansmen had unstopped what he reckoned was not a waterskin, and began to pass it about. He did not like it. He did not want the quarrel now, either, with unhappiness enough in their camp. "*Liyo,*" he said in a low voice and when he had her attention, shifted his eyes to indicate the matter.

She frowned, but she said nothing. They were not boisterous at the other fire, only men taking their ease of the dark and the rain in a way as old as men on any earth.

And finally: "I do not understand you," Chei said.

Vanye jerked the braiding loose and looked up at him, frowning. "There is Hell between the gates, Chei, and we will ride through it. There is a new earth the other side, but fairer or fouler than this one, neither of us knows. Heaven knows how the worlds are ordered, but the gates bind them together in ways dangerous for all life. When we are gone it will not be the same sun that rises over us. That is all I understand of it. But that is where we will be—as if we were dead,

Chei, and the other side of Hell, and you cannot go back or change your minds then, and nothing you knew will be true. That is what will become of you. This land is your home. And fair or foul, it is what you understand. Think on that. And you still will not know the extent of what will happen to you. Nothing you know will be true."

"But you go. And you are a Man. Are you not?"

Vanye shrugged. The question went deep, troubling him. "It will not matter," he said. "I cannot even reckon how old I am. The stars are not the same. I do not know where I am. I do not know how long ago my cousin died. And it was only a handful of days ago I left him. Now only my liege speaks my language. All the rest are gone." He looked up at two bewildered, sobered faces. "That is the plainest I know to tell you. There is nowhere we come from. There is nowhere we are going. We only go. Come with us if you will. Leave us, the other side of the gate. It may be you will find peace there. It may be we will fall straight into Hell, and die there. We have no way to know. If it is to glory you hope to follow us—or wealth—there is none to offer you. And whether we are right or wrong in anything we do, I do not know. I cannot offer you that either. My liege cannot. So you would be wisest to stay here. Truly you would."

"I do *not* understand you," Chei said.

"I know. But I am telling you the truth. Go with us as far as Tejhos, that is all. Then ride west. Lose yourselves in the hills, hide and wait. There will be wars. In that time—you will find a lord worth following. That is my advice to you."

"Are you a witch?" Chei asked.

"I suppose that I am."

"But not qhal."

"No. Not qhal."

"You are my friend," Chei said, and reached and pressed his arm.

He could not look at Chei. It hurt too much. He gave a sigh, and ripped out his braiding.

From the men beyond there was a burst of laughter,

muted; Bron turned himself about to see what they did and looked back again, frowning, as if he were thoroughly remiss not to forbid that.

But he was not, at present, in any mind to fight with men who, whatever their lord was, brigands or no, were cheerful again, after sullenness all day.

"They will sleep the better for it," Vanye said. "And if their heads ache in the morning, that is their misfortune."

They neither one said more than that. How their thoughts ran now he could not say. They sat together, leaned together. Bron touched his brother's hair as no man would touch another, casually, even were they kinsmen, but he reckoned this was only affection, and foreign ways. They understood hospitality; their fire seemed sacred enough, and the passing of food and drink; and there were priests to confess them; and yet a lord could claim a wounded man who came to him for protection, and not let him go again. He had met men far more strange to him, whose customs troubled him less, because they were utterly strange.

Yet he reckoned they might trust two watches tonight to these brothers, and know their throats would stay uncut, and their backs defended, if it came to that. If these two were not arrhendim and did not have Kurshin ways, still they were decent men, and he felt his supper uneasy at his stomach, somewhere between regret for having them along and the fear that they would go, and the sorrow that he had finally found a friend staunch enough to stay by them—

—and it was not a man he could trust.

That Chei could lie and never know he was lying— that was a flaw he did not know how to mend. Chei simply did not know what truth was.

And he himself was Nhi as well as Kurshin, wherefore a man who deceived and twisted and turned with the agility that seemed native to this land, set his teeth on edge, in an anger at once familiar and terrifying— and he remembered suddenly why.

It was only his brothers had evoked that peculiar ambivalence in him.

And he had killed one and all but killed the other: clan Myya was his legitimate half-brothers' clan—hill bandits turned noblemen, who did not know a straight way through any door, that was Nhi's proverb for them; and again: thicker than feuds in Myya.

He opened his eyes again. It was only pale-haired Chei, and Bron, whose faces showed hurt and whose eyes sought some answer of Morgaine, since he had shut them out.

"I will take first watch," Morgaine said, rescuing him from the chance that they would go on with him. "Go to sleep. We will be on our way before light; best you all take what you can."

"Aye." He reached at his side and loosed his armor buckles, and found a place the rock fit his shoulders. He unhooked his sword from his side and laid it across his lap, considering Eoghar's company yonder. "Quiet," he shouted at those three, making a small shocked silence, astonishing himself profoundly that they looked so daunted. "Men are going to sleep here."

The trouble was in himself, he thought in the quiet that continued, who invented worries and conjured up calamities—you think too much, his brother Erij had told him once upon a time, chiding him for cowardice.

It was truth. He fell into old habits. It was fear which did that to him, fear not of enemies, but of friends. His brothers had taught him that lesson—beaten it into him, flesh and bone and nerve.

He clasped his sword to him, nevertheless, in both arms, so that Eoghar and his cousins would go on understanding their situation, if there remained any doubt.

The rain subsided to a light patter on the ground outside, an occasional gust carrying it into the shelter, but there was enough heat from the two fires and the presence of seven bodies to keep the chill away. It would have been a good night under other circumstances, Chei thought glumly, lying curled toward the fire warmth, back to back with Bron, but a different kind of cold had crept in among them, and Chei could

not reason why, except somehow the lady, always cold
and obscure, turned kind to them; while Vanye suddenly refused to look him in the eyes, for reasons
which Chei did not, after thinking and thinking on the
matter, understand . . . .

What do you want of me? A prisoner, a slave,
someone to be grateful for whatever crusts you will
give me?

Why could he not say once that he was glad for me,
that Bron is alive?

Could not he manage anything but that scowl for it?

The thoughts turned over and over in him like peb-
bles in a current, one abrading the next; and one atop
and then the other. He ached inside. It angered him
that the man he admired turned away from him, and it
mattered in a personal way—when he ought to worry
only for the consequences of being cast out masterless,
as a sane man ought.

He might, he thought, appeal to the lady who sat
there in the glow of the coals, beautiful and terrible in
her fire-stained pallor, herself embodying every fear
he had had from childhood; and every mercy he had
found in extremity. She leaned on the sword that she
bore, which had a fantastical beast for hilt and quillons. Her eyes gazed toward the glow of the coals, and
her face was pensive, even gentle—it tempted a man
to think she might listen to him.

He was mad, perhaps: a man who began to hope
against the general ebb of human fortunes in the world,
and who began to believe in miracles—was he not
mad?

But he would not have believed at all, till he looked
up from the wolf-pack snarling about him and saw first
the swordsman bearing down on him and then the
silver-haired woman—demons out of Hell he had
thought them first, that the ordinary world had rent in
twain and death had come for him. He thought of that
in bleak moments of terror which intervened in his
other thoughts: but he was not dead, his delirium had
left him, and it was a familiar woods he rode, with
Bron back from the dead and in company with these

two who moved out of pattern with the world and promised him humankind need not, after all, perish.

He had ridden a knife's-edge of hope and terror thus far; and that it all should unravel on the spite of a man he had begun to rely on in ways he had only relied on Bron—he could not accept that. He could not believe that Morgaine would in truth send them off to die. He could not believe, now he thought about it, that Vanye, who had dealt kindly with him when it had not been necessary—could turn so vindictive. He must, he thought, have done something or said something—or it was Arunden's offense against the lady; or things had not gone well between Vanye and the lady when he had walked in upon them—

He built a score of desperate structures in the blink of an eye, each more and more fantastical, until he found his hands clenched and his heart thumping against his ribs, and at last rose up on his elbow.

"My lady," he whispered, very softly, not to disturb the others. His hands were sweating as she gazed at him, a figure of shadows in the light of the coals; his arm shook under him, which might have been the chill and the hour. He had everything prepared to say.

Then there came a sound from outside, the low mutter of a stallion that might be bickering with the other horses, but it was the gray: he knew the timbre of it, and where that horse was, just outside the woven wall.

So Morgaine's eyes shifted, and she became still as stone. So he was, till the horse complained a second time and one of the others, further toward the falls, made a complaint of its own that was echoed farther away.

Of a sudden, with her the only one waking, cipher that she was, he was afraid. "Something is out there," he said; and by now Vanye was rising and putting the blanket aside, and Bron had waked, all the while Morgaine sat very still, with the ornate sword against her, her long fingers curving about the hilt as her eyes shifted from him to Vanye.

Vanye gathered himself to his knees and tightened

the buckles of his armor. There was no sound now but the roar of the falls and the rain-swollen waters, no light but the afterglow of the coals. Chei trembled and cursed his own cowardice in the uncertainty of the hour; but he was lost, he did not know what was on them, whether it was Arunden's treachery or some hapless hunter of the clan they would have to deal with as the lady had said, more murder they had to commit, this time on innocent men; and his tongue seemed paralyzed.

"I will go out there," Bron said, and moved. "If it is human they are late on the trail—or if they are Arunden's—"

But Eoghar and the others still slept, none of them stirring.

"I will go with you," Chei said. No one prevented him. Eoghar and his cousins snored on, lost to every sense. He walked out into the drizzling rain and stood there blind to the dark and with himself and then Bron silhouetted against the fire-glow, however faint.

A rock turned, click of stone on stone, and the horses close at hand snorted in alarm.

"Arunden!" a voice called out, hoarse above the roar of water. "Eoghar!"

It was sure then that Eoghar had led them along the route where Eoghar had been told, and Chei dived back inside. "My lady—" He found himself facing the black weapon and froze in mid-motion. "It is Arunden's men," he said then, against the risk of her fire and Vanye's half-drawn sword.

But outside someone was coming, and Bron was left to meet that advance. He risked a move to escape and joined Bron out in the drifting mist, out in the dark in which some rider came down the streamside and toward them in haste.

"Who are you?" Bron called out sharply.

"Sagyn," the voice called back. "Ep Ardris."

"I know him," Bron said to Chei as the rider stopped just short of the ledge that was their shelter and slid down off his horse to lead it. "Stop there," Bron said, but the man did not.

"Riders," the man gasped out, staggering to them over the gravel. "Gault's."

"Where?" Bron asked, and drew his sword about the time Chei reached after his own knife, misliking this approach. "No closer, man, take my warning!"

"Truth," ep Ardris said, a thin and shaken voice, and stood there holding the reins of a rain-drenched and head-drooping horse. "It was Gault came on us—Gault, in the woods—"

Chei felt a sense of things slipping away. He heard the movement behind him, he heard the curses of Eoghar and his men, awakened to news like this and by now standing outside; he knew the lady's anger, and the uncertainties in everything, all their estimations thrown in disorder.

Except the lady had fired the lowland woods and begun a war as surely as Gault had come to answer it.

In Chei's hearing ep Ardris was babbling other things, how their sentries had alerted them too late, and Arunden had attempted to attack from the cover of the woods, but Gault's men had been too many and too well armed. The clan had scattered. Arunden himself was taken. Ep Ardris did not know where the others were or how many had survived.

"What of my father?" Eoghar came from the shelter with his two cousins, and laid hands on the man—and if there was a man of the lot not dissembling, it was Eoghar, whose grip bid fair to break the man's shoulders. "Did you see him? Do you know?"—to which ep Ardris swore in a trembling voice that he did not know, no more than for his own kin.

And at Chei's side, all sound of her coming drowned in the roar of the falls, the lady walked up and doubtless Vanye was behind her. "So Eoghar told his lord the places we might camp."

"He would know," Chei protested, "lady, any man of his would know—"

"So, now, might our enemies," Morgaine said darkly. "We have no way of knowing *what* they know. Saddle up. Now."

Chei stood frozen a moment, lost in the water-sound and the nightmare. Others moved. A hand closed hard on his arm.

"Come on," Vanye said harshly, as he had spoken when they had been enemies; and in his muddled sense he heard ep Ardris protesting that Gault's riders might be anywhere—Arunden was innocent, he thought, of the worst things; but if any of Arunden's folk was in Gault's hands, there was very much that they knew.

"They do not know the forest," Chei protested, the least frail hope he could think of, but no one listened, in the haste to break camp. Gault and his men had gotten *into* the forest, plainly enough.

He could not account for all of Ichandren's men. He had not thought of that for very long, since he had sat waiting for the wolves—that there were worse fates than Gault had meted out to him, and that it was Gault's spite of his own Overlord that chained healthy and fair-haired prisoners to die within reach of Morund-gate—when there might be someone in Mante with use for them. It was defiance Gault made of his master.

But he had no idea who had died on the field, who in the prison, and who might not have been taken to Morund's cellars at all.

Or who—as the lady had said—of their hunters and scouts of whatever clan might not have strayed into Gault's hands. For that reason a man never went alone to the border; for that reason they left no wounded, and carried poison among their simples and their medicines.

Someone had betrayed them, either living or dead. Someone who knew the ways in.

The roan horse picked a narrow path among the rocks, a course that others followed in the dark. They made no night camp, only took such rests as they had to have, and few of those.

There was fear in Gault ep Mesyrun, and therefore he drove them. At times thoughts surfaced in him which Gault himself would have had, and not Qhiver-in—to that extent he was disturbed; and he knew that Jestryn-Pyverrn who rode near him was much more than that, to the extent that he feared for Pyverrn's self. A profound shock could affect a mind newly settled in a body, and old memories might surface, like bubbles out of dark water, from no knowing which self of the many bodies a man might have occupied, no knowing whether it might not be the latest and strongest self reorganizing itself, disastrous in a mind distracted by doubts.

Therefore Jestryn-Pyverrn himself had laughed, when first the priest had told them what they had to deal with—had looked into Gault's face with a laugh and a desperation in his eyes that quickly died, more quickly than Arunden's priest, who been all too willing to talk, for hate, it seemed, a genuine hatred of a qhalur woman and a man for whose sake he had suffered some slight; and thought that he had something to trade to them for his life. "That might be," Jestryn had said, "except we have no need of a priest—"

At which the priest had called out Arunden's name, pleading with him as a Man—wherefore Gault asked Arunden, the quisling they had set over the borderlands: "Dealings with Mante, now, is it?"

"They are from outside," Arunden protested, as the Man had protested everything, disavowed the firesetting, wept and sobbed and swore he had never betrayed them, only the woman was a witch and might read everything he did.

Therefore Arunden had been compelled to entertain them, therefore he had dealt with them and had sent men with them—this woman who proposed to attack Mante.

"From outside," Gault had said then, beginning to believe this lunacy, though they had long thought there was no outside, and the very thought that there might be, implied a tottering of the world—challenging the power in Mante, of Skarrin himself, over whose death neither he nor the men of his company would shed tears.

But an incursion from outside—

But a threat, babbled in a human witness's confused

terms, against the very gates—and a qhal counseling humans about things which humans did not well guess—

The priest went on babbling, pleading his usefulness and his sacrosanctity. "Silence that," Gault said, and had meant that one of the others should do it.

Quick as the drawing of a sword, Jestryn cut the priest's throat and stepped back, his face all flecked with blood: Gault had seen that moment's horror, and well knew the reason the Pyverrn-self had desired that particular execution.

Exorcism, the humans would say.

They had come in the space of an hour from anger at human attack to suspect a far greater danger. "We cannot get a message south," Jestryn had said, meaning one that should pass the southern gate and speed north with the speed of thought. "There is Tejhos-gate."

"They will know that," Gault had said, and had dispatched one small part of his forces back toward the road to sweep north, under a man he trusted—which would have been Jestryn, had he thought Jestryn reliable at the moment.

Perhaps, he thought now, Jestryn had mustered anger enough to overcome his confusion. Perhaps luck would be with them and Jestryn could guide them on these trails, now they knew where their enemy had gone.

But he did not trust to Jestryn's sanity.

"Take him with us," he had said of Arunden. "Kill the rest." And headed for his horse at a run.

There was a Weapon loose. What the priest and Arunden had described could only be that. It was that which had lent absolute credence to a tale otherwise incredible.

Skarrin himself was challenged. The trouble had passed Morund with only a trifling attack. It was possible that the high lord had stirred up some trouble which bade fair to destroy him and to take the world down to chaos—it answered to things which in qhalur lore were only dimmest legend, that there had been such visitations once, and time itself might shift, and all reality alter.

He did not count himself a virtuous man. He did not know one—Skarrin being Skarrin and only the favored few of his lords profiting from Skarrin's rule; but Gault found himself with no choice and no one but himself to look to.

He rode without heed of the night or the rain that should keep them prudently camped. He trusted himself and his men to the guidance of a traitor and a bloodstained man struggling for sanity, because there was no time for anything else.

The war he had started out to fight was for a woods, a handful of deer and rabbits and revenge on a quisling human he thought had betrayed him.

But in a few words from a human's lips he found himself in a war for survival.

Chapter Nine

"It might be a trick," Vanye said to Morgaine, beside her as they saddled in desperate haste, there by the woven wall of the shelter. He worked by feel on gear rapidly becoming rain-soaked, with their horses unsettled by the visitor out of the dark and ill-tempered at taking the trail again. It had the feel of old nightmares.

And there were Arunden's men with them; Eoghar and his lot, and ep Ardris, Bron and Chei over with them, flinging saddles onto wet, angry horses, ep Ardris' beast standing with hanging head, unfit for the trail.

"They might be waiting for us out there."

Morgaine said nothing, only flung her saddlebags over Siptah's saddle and jerked the ties tight.

"Let me go up on that ridge and have a look," Vanye said. "*I* can climb it—"

"Aye, and it would take considerable time and mesh us in a battle and separate us if the least thing went amiss."

"Nothing would go amiss. There is the water to cover the sound—"

"No," she said sharply. She finished the last tie on the other side and took up Siptah's reins, stopping face to face with him as he took up Arrhan's. "If they would be on us out in the open, they could save themselves the trouble and fire down from the ridge. Thee is too careful, thee is always too cursed careful. Let us be out of here!"

His face went hot. But there was no leisure for

193

argument and less profit in it at the moment. "Aye," he said sharply, and threw Arrhan's reins over, on his way to the saddle.

She caught his arm with a hard grip. "Vanye." And as he stopped and looked full into her face there in the misting dark: "Take care for *thyself*, not for me, does thee hear me? I need no more fools tonight!"

"I am none," he retorted; "you mistake me,"—their voices being muffled in the sound of the falls; and she turned quickly to mount.

It was Chei she meant, Chei and Bron and every other encumbrance which had seized on her and weighed on her: that panic in her came of delays and entanglements and mortal frailties—he knew well enough that pitch of rage that he had begun to sense growing in himself, the understanding of dangers winding them about like threads, more and more of entanglements.

He flung himself to horse and reined in beside her. "If so happen," Morgaine said more sanely, "if so happen the qhal *have* Arunden for whatever cause— then it is speed will save us now, and we cannot reckon otherwise. There is the gate at Tejhos; and if Gault does come behind us, then we can reckon that from the hour he reaches either gate, north or south, the lord at Mante will know everything Gault knows."

Then, he thought, there was little now that conscience would stay her from. An old and familiar chill lapped him about, more penetrating than the rain and the wind. Morgaine turned Siptah's head and rode forward, the paler tip of Siptah's dark tail moving like a will o' the wisp above the ground and the horse himself like illusion: it was white Arrhan would draw the most attention of all their company—fool, he thought again, that he had ever taken such a gift; and he drew his sword as they rode, quietly passing the rest, sweeping up Chei and his brother with him, devil take the rest who were rising to their saddles. "Stay close," he said as they passed, half lost in nightmare. "Whatever happens, keep close."

Chei said something which he did not hear in the

rush of the stream near them and in the sighing of the trees on the ridge. He blinked the water from his eyes and took his own pace from Morgaine, staying to her left, always to the left, shieldside, as the way out turned onto a narrow trail and the water-laden wind laden came blasting up the mountainside, under his cloak and into his eyes.

There the stream took a precipitate course and plunged down the mountain in a second falls as the land opened out. Morgaine took the right-hand bend around the rocks, close against them as possible, toward the wooded track that led higher up, and Vanye glanced behind them as they turned, to see the tail of their column leave the narrows and bolt the other way.

"Liyo," he exclaimed, and reined Arrhan about as Chei and Bron also turned, drawing the weapons they had.

"My lady," Bron called out. "Arunden's men—"

"Let them go," Morgaine hissed, as she drew back even with them.

"We did not know—"

"Do you know the way from here to the road, that is what I care for!"

"We know it," Chei said with no doubt at all in his voice. "Let us to the fore, my lady. At least in this rain we will have less chance of meeting any watchers."

"Go to it," she said, and with no delay at all Chei and his brother urged their horses past and on. "Do not thee stray far back," she said then to Vanye. "Stay with me."

That suited him well enough, thinking of qhalur riders at their backs—of whom Eoghar and ep Ardris and the rest could have joy, he thought in dark rage: they had made no decent request to go back to their kin, if that was where they were bound, and it was as likely they were deserting outright to hide in the hills.

For his part he recollected that great westward jog in the road Chei had drawn. He tried to think where the sun and been and where they might come to it and where Gault might; and he did not like the reckoning.

He dropped back as the trail narrowed, and wended

up again among the rain-dripping trees, cold, large drops falling more unpleasantly than did the fine mist, branches raking them with wet bristles where limbs pressed close on the trail.

It was climbing for a while and descent for a while, and eventually rest for the horses, who suffered with the rain and the uncertain footing, the lee of a hill being the only respite they could find on this side of the ridge.

"How much further?" Morgaine asked of Chei and Bron. Their horses, even Siptah and Chei's gelding, huddled together as they took their breath, breaking the force of the wind off each other as it skirled about them. "Do we get there tonight? Tomorrow?"

"Far yet," Chei said, at which Vanye's heart sank in greater and greater despair.

"How far for Gault's folk?" Morgaine asked. "If he sent a messenger up to Tejhos or back to Morund-gate—can we reach Tejhos first?"

"I *think* we can," Chei said. "Lady, God knows! We do not know how long ep Ardris hunted for us—we do not know how long Gault will delay—"

"The Road bends our way up ahead," Bron said. "He cannot send one of his own back to Morund except with a guide, and he has hit his own ally, if Arunden has betrayed us. He may not have men he can spare who know their way up here: they say it is not every Changed can remember—that is what has saved us before this: they get few of us and most of those remember nothing who they were—"

"Do not count on that," Morgaine said darkly. "It is *not* the case. Believe that he will have every help he needs, *curse* your optimism!"

"We are on the high trails," Chei said. "A large force cannot make good time where we are going: if there are any of Arunden's warders left, they may have to fight their way through—"

"And Arunden himself may be their safe-conduct *and* their guide and the warders may find us instead! Man, quit making excuses for our troubles and quit making allowances for our enemies! *Do* what I tell you and get us to the Road!"

"It is at least another day to get there!" Chei shouted. "For them and us—and there is no shorter way than this—I swear there is not! We can turn and fight them—"

"*If* we could trust that they have not gone straight east to the Road, *if* we could trust ep Ardris told half the truth—It is *time* we do not have: do not question me, Chei! Do not make me delays or excuses! Lead! We will find a secure camp, rest and move on when we can make more time. That is all we *can* do now."

It was in a weary haze Chei rode at last—fending branches in the dark, feeling an uncertainty in his horse's legs as they negotiated a descent. Of a sudden the animal skidded and went down on its haunches and clawed its way sideways on the muddy hill so that he had to let the reins down and let it fight its own battle.

The horse recovered itself facing uphill and with its hindquarters braced, unmoving as the other riders came down the straightforward way, but not so steeply. Chei found himself trembling the same as the horse, weak in the legs as he dismounted there on the slope and slipped and slid to lead it around and safely down. The mail had rubbed his shoulders raw; he knew that it had, working wet cloth against wet skin; and that pain brought back the hill, and the wolves, so vividly at times he did not know this woods from the other, or remember the intervening time.

But Bron was with him. Bron urged him on, promising him rest, saying that there was shelter, and he bit his lip and concentrated on the pain there and not in his arms.

"Soon," he agreed, teeth chattering, "soon."

"We need not lose a horse," Vanye said, to which Morgaine said something Chei could not understand; but they got down where they were, on the leaf-slick floor of the ravine, and led their horses an increasingly difficult track in this dark and rain, off the main trails, all of them walking now, descending the next muddy slope and ducking low under the branches.

"Straight on," Chei said, his heart suddenly lifting as lightning-flicker showed him an ancient pine he knew. He recognized his way again. He pulled at the weary horse, taking it sideways on the slope and down again, around the boggy place between the slopes and up another rise, up and up a pine-grown slope to the crest of the hill.

It was a hunter's shelter below them, looming up like nothing more than a massive brush-heap in the constant flicker from the clouds; but Chei knew it, and when Bron said that he would go down to it: "I will go," Chei murmured, and led his horse along with Bron, down the incline as Bron hailed the place.

There was no answer. There was only the dark mass of the shelter; and neither horse seemed shy of it, which was the best indication nothing had sheltered there. Only some small creature skittered away in the brush, at which his weary horse hardly reacted, a little jerk at the reins.

"Hai-ay," Bron called out again, and with no answer and no answering hail, led his horse into the lee of the hut.

It was enough. Chei reached the place, leaned against his horse and managed the girth; and had him half unsaddled before Vanye and Morgaine had ridden in.

He dried off his horse vigorously with the blanket and rubbed down its legs, such care as he could give to ease it and protect it from soreness; and looked and saw Bron's horse unattended, which carelessness his brother would not countenance on a night like this and after such a ride.

Then he spied Bron sitting on the ground, and went to him quietly. "Bron?" he whispered, dropping down to face him, and laid a hand on Bron's shoulder.

"It is hurting," Bron said. Chei could not see his face in the dark, could hardly make out the pallor of skin and hair in the dark, but he gripped Bron's shoulder in a brotherly way and felt a cold about his heart.

"How bad is it?"

A whisper of leather and metal, a shrug beneath his hand. "Hurting," Bron said, and drew a breath. "I will make it tomorrow. They will not leave me. They will not. I will not slow you down."

He embraced Bron, hugged him tight a moment as he reckoned Vanye and the lady were paying no attention to them. "Give me your cloak," he said; and unfastened it from Bron's neck, slung it on and rose to tend Bron's horse, trying not to think of the fear, only of necessity—not turning his head, only doing his work and praying neither Vanye nor the lady would notice in the deep shadow beside the hut and the confusion of two bay geldings and two blond men and a borrowed cloak, that it was the same man on his feet.

But Vanye walked near him, leading the two pale horses into that shadow, and behind him; and stopped.

Chei dropped down and rubbed at the gelding's legs, head tucked. But he heard the step in the wet mold, heard the light ring of metal as Vanye went past him and knelt down by Bron.

He got up then and went over to him. "I am all right," Bron was saying, where he sat against the wall in the wet and the decaying leaves. And Chei, desperately: "He is all right. I will tend the horses, the gray too if he will stand—"

"We cannot go much more of this," Vanye said, and touched Bron's shoulder and rose and laid a hand on his, gently shaking at him. "My lady has her reasons. How much farther?"

"Tomorrow," Chei said. His heart was beating hard. He found himself short of breath, not knowing what was in Vanye's mind. "We will get there tomorrow."

"My lady is grateful. Truly."

"What does she want of us?" he asked desperately; and did not believe that the lady had said it at all: the lady was angry with them, had been angry since they had broken camp, and everything seemed the wrong thing with her. Now Vanye came to them, on his own, for Vanye's reasons, catching them in another deception, and fear swept over him—irrational, for they could go no faster and no further, and the lady on that iron-winded gray could not so much as find the road without them.

But honor meant very much, when there was neither clan nor kin; and the lady cursed them and shamed them, even Bron: he had brought his brother to this, and the lady cursed them for mistakes he himself had made, and shamed Bron for things not Bron's doing—

"We will make it," Vanye said. "Chei—"

"Aye," he said, and jerked his shoulder free, turning his face to his work again.

"Chei. Listen to me." Vanye put his hand on the other side of the horse's neck, stood close against its shoulder, close beside him. "She has one manner with everyone. With me as well. She is thinking, that is what she is doing, she is thinking, and what talks to us is not herself when this mood is on her. That is all I can tell you."

Chei listened in anger, down to the last, that a tendril of cold slipped into his heart. Then he recalled that they were pacted not only with a qhal, but with a witch. He gave a twitch of his shoulders, less angry, and more afraid, and no more certain where honor was in anything.

"She never remembers her tempers," Vanye said. "Do the best you can do. When she knows what you have done she will be grateful. *I* thank you. She would want me to. She would want me to tell you—get us as far as the Road, and if you have changed your minds, go aside: we will see to Gault."

"Mante," Chei said. "We are going to Mante."

"Do you know what is there? Do you know what we face?"

He shook his head. He had no wish to know. "The gate," he said. "Somewhere else."

"Maybe a worse place."

"It could not be. For us it could not be." He seized Vanye by the arm and drew him well aside, over by the trees, into the dark and the wind. "Vanye, my brother—he is a great man, he *is*, Vanye: he *will* be; Ichandren himself used to say that in his life he had never seen any man promise so much—"

"For whose sake are you doing this? For his? Then leave us at the road."

"That is not what I am saying!"

"There is nothing to be had from us. There is nothing we can give you. You mistake us. We have no place to go to. You are chasing after what does not exist."

"We will not go back to live like bandits! We will not find another clan! We will make a name for ourselves—we—Bron and I. Do not shame us like this."

Vanye was silent a moment. "I only try to warn you. You cannot ask too much of her. I will not let you."

"You are her lover."

An intake of breath. "What I am is my concern."

"I only mean that I know. We know you are her right hand. We do not dispute you. Only do not let her speak like that to my brother."

"My lady will speak how she chooses, to me, to Bron, or to you!—But I will talk to him."

"Do that," Chei said. The wind touched him. He shivered, having gotten less than he wanted. But he had pushed too far; he saw that.

Vanye walked away from him. Chei stood with his arms and Bron's cloak about him, waiting, while Vanye found Bron looking after the horses himself, cloakless and stubborn.

They had words together. It did not last long, but they parted with a mutual touch at shoulders, and Vanye took their own two horses in charge, while the lady stayed in shelter.

"Here," Chei said to Bron, when he had walked back to the arbor. He slung the cloak about Bron's shoulders. "Get out of the wind." And: "Did he say anything?"

Bron shrugged. "Only courtesy," Bron said. "He offered qhalur medicines. I said I was well enough. Do not trouble him, Chei."

*   *   *

The morning brought fog again, a general murk that made it uncertain exactly when it ceased to be night and began being daylight; but Vanye levered his aching bones up when there was light enough to see by, in a watch he judged by his own time-sense. "Stay and rest," he said to Morgaine: it was his watch last—they were the better by Chei and Bron having their turn at waking, in the small part of the night they had had left—and he left her and the brothers to drowse away the last few moments while he sought after their gear and carried it up to saddle up.

But Chei was up as quickly, moving about in the gray and the damp, seeing to his horse and his brother's.

"I meant to let you sleep," Vanye said, attempting to mend matters.

"We will manage," Chei said shortly.

So a company grew irritable, weary as they were, friends more quickly at odds than utter strangers. His face still burned when he recollected Chei's remark of last evening, and how Chei thought he knew more of their affairs than he knew.

Ilin and liege—and he was not sure whose doing it was, after all this time. He tried to protect their honor; but Chei—

Chei, being Chei, trod straight in on a matter that would have gotten challenge outright and unexplained, if Chei were of his own people.

But Chei, being Chei, had not understood, no more than he himself understood more than the surface of Chei's thinking. Bron had seemed dismayed when he went to ask his pardon, had seemed embarrassed, if nothing else. "Chei ought not to have done that," Bron had said. "Forgive him."

Now Bron came out into the daylight, limping pronouncedly in the first few steps; and concealed that with a grasp after one of the support poles of the shelter.

Vanye paid it no attention and offered no help. He wanted no more misunderstandings. He flung Siptah's saddle up and tightened the girth.

"We will break our fast on the trail," he said as

Chei passed him; Chei nodded and said no word to him. Perhaps it was only the reaction of a man with his jaw clamped against the chill.

Or it was the reaction of a man who felt betrayed.

Morgaine came out, wrapped in her cloak, gray side out, her pale coloring one tone with the fog.

"Tonight for the open road," she said in a quiet voice, taking Siptah's reins. "So we dare not push the horses today."

"Aye," Vanye agreed, thanking Heaven one of them at least had come back to reason.

They rode out, with breakfast in hand, a little waybread and water from their flasks, ducking water-laden branches, but with the sun bringing a little warmth through the mist, and the wind having stopped. There was that for comfort.

"Here," Jestryn said, and urged his horse down a trail hardly worthy of the name, a narrow slot of stone and dirt among pines that clung desperately to a crumbling slope. Some of the men murmured dismay, but Gault followed, nothing loath, for the Road passed near a village hereabouts, a straight bare track below the truncate hill: the ancients had carved mountains, disdaining to divert their Road for any cause; and yet bent it sharply west in open ground, for reasons that no qhal living knew.

Now the descendants of the builders rode quietly as they could, making better time than they had been able to make in the fog, reliant on Jestryn-Pyverrn's human memory and on Arunden's thoroughly human one, under the threat of Jestryn's knife.

"I swear to you," Arunden had cried, "I swear to you—I will guide you! I am your friend—"

"Impudent Man," Jestryn had said, and laughed, as Pyverrn would, with his human, guttural laughter. "You are not *my* friend before or *after* I was human; and God knows you were never Gault's—"

Jestryn kept such human affectations, and swore and used human oaths qhal did not. But the sparkle in his eye was Pyverrn—past the sword-cut that raked one handsome cheek. It did not distract from his looks. Next to him, Arunden was a clumsy, shambling brute; and Arunden's wit matched his outward look.

"You will lose a finger," Jestryn had said, "for every annoyance on this trail; I counsel you, *tell* me where the warders are, and what the signals are, or you will find out what pain is,—my lord Arunden."

They had taken three of the watchposts. Arunden snuffled and wept about it and protested they were disgracing him and ruining his usefulness.

But a flash of Jestryn's knife stopped the snuffling.

"You either serve us," Gault had said then, "or not. Decide now. We *can* do without you."

"My lord," Arunden had said.

Now they rode quietly as they could, with bows strung and arrows ready.

Jestryn gave a quiet call, a kind of lilting whistle, and a like signal answered it from down the slope.

The horses picked their way down with steady, small paces, to a place where the trail widened. A Man waited there, whose eyes betrayed shock the moment before Gault's arrow took him. Perhaps it had been the sight of Jestryn, back from the dead. Perhaps it had been the sight of Arunden himself, who was their own lord, beside Gault, who had been lord over the human south, not six years gone: Men to the outward sight, and armored like Men, he and Jestryn, Qhiverin and Pyverrn—both archers of Mante's warrior Societies and both deadly.

Jestryn grinned at him, an expression light and pleasant as ever Jestryn-the-Man could have used, past Arunden, who sat his horse in apparent shock.

"Let us go," Gault said, and motioned to the men who followed.

They rode forward, closer to the human camp, with the stench of its midden all too evident. It was that garrison which guarded the road; and there was dangerous work at hand—We must take them, Jestryn had said, and reach the Road there: that is the quickest way.

If only, Gault thought, they did not bog down in

some day-long siege; but Jestryn promised not: Arunden would hail them out once their archers were positioned.

Gault chose three arrows as he rode quietly at Jestryn's back: he did not ride the roan, which was too well known—but on a borrowed sorrel. The rest of the column overtook them on this flat ground as the shapes of huts appeared among the pines. Gray smoke drifted up as haze in that clearing, from fires about which humans pursued domestic business, the weaving of cloth, the grinding of grain doubtless bartered or plundered from Gault's own storehouses.

There was hardly reason at first that these humans should take alarm at human riders arriving in their camp, since those riders had had to pass their sentries, even if the riders carried bows at their sides.

They could only be mildly alarmed when their own lord Arunden rode forward of the three, and in a ringing voice ordered everyone to the center of the village.

Only when those bows lifted and bent and the shafts went winging to drop those who obeyed, then the cries went up and humans rushed to the attack of two solitary archers.

Then the rest of Gault's troop appeared from the brush around the camp, and arrows came from every direction.

It was unfortunate that Arunden was not quick enough, and that a stray shaft tumbled him from his horse.

Beyond this there was little resistance. Certain humans escaped into the brush and saved their lives: do not pursue, Gault had told his men. We have no time.

When there was quiet in the clearing Gault changed horses again and rode where Jestryn beckoned him, where the height on which the village sat, dropped away sheer, and the Road showed as patches of white stone in an otherwise grassy expanse of rolling hills.

Jestryn led them down the slope of the hill to a track which human feet had worn, going and coming,

laying bare the roots of pines and stripping those roots
of bark, a natural series of steps in the muddy slope
which gave the horses somewhat surer footing on their
way down to the plains.

There was no dread of arrows now. Only of what
they followed.

He could not understand why they had burned his
woods and sheltered with humans; why, if they were
hostile they had not attacked Morund; why, if they
were not, they had not approached it. The woman
whom Arunden had abundantly described was surely
no halfling and the tall Man with her doubtless hosted
some qhalur mind: they would have been welcome in
Morund, if they were Mante's enemies, some shadow
out of Skarrin's traffic in the gates.

But they had one and now two of Ichandren's lot to
advise them: that too, Arunden had told them, among
other things. That one of them was Chei ep Kantory
surprised him: the pale-haired wolf-whelp had cozened
Morund-gate's wolves then, longer than he would have
thought: Kantory's get was hardy as its sire, whatever
might presently house in that human frame—for it was
well possible the strangers had taken his offering at
Morund-gate.

But that the other Man was Bron ep Kantory distressed him: Bron who had carried off Gault's serfs
and raided his storehouses three times in the last two
years. He had thought he had taken care of that matter at Gyllin-brook, along with the rest of Ichandren's
rebels.

Bron could not be qhal, having been near neither
gate; and therefore Chei was not likely to be. Bron
would have suspected a changeling—they never would
have deceived him. No, it was a question of humans.

And qhal who dealt with them in preference to
legitimate authority, for whatever purpose.

It was a ride on which Gault-Qhiverin had had
ample time to think; and the thoughts which chased
one another through his mind held only greater and
greater uncertainty, whether he could hope to find
common ground with these strangers, Mante's likely

enemies, or whether he should only strike and kill and hope for reward as Skarrin's savior.

Which would last, he thought, about as long as it took for Skarrin to arrange his assassination. Gault-Qhiverin the exile was something Skarrin could ignore. Gault the hero of the south—was not.

He reached the road just behind Jestryn and with room to run, the red roan overtook Jestryn's bay with a vengeance, weary as they all were.

"We will catch them," Jestryn said. "There is still time."

It was Tejhos Jestryn was thinking of; so were they all. That was the place the enemy was going, and that was the place they would find them.

The trail led down by the last of the twilight, and deeper still the twilight under the great trees which overshadowed the trail in the descent. "Not far, not far," Bron assured them, when once Morgaine asked. Bron's face was pale in the half-light and sweat glistened on it. Constantly Chei had a worried look, but Bron did not ask to stop; neither did Chei, though Bron's riding now was generally with his shoulders hunched in pain, his hands braced against the saddlehorn against the jolts of the descent: his leg by now must be agony and Vanye hurt with a sympathetic pain, who had endured similar miserable rides.

But suddenly their trail reached a level place, and in a little more of riding the trees began to thin: the forest edge gave way to open land and hills the like of the hills in the south, open grassland.

Between the last trees, under a clearing and fading sky, a rain-puddled bit of white stone, the trace of the Road; and looking up from it, toward the hills in the dusk, it was easy to see it, a line where ancient builders had sundered hill from hill, letting nothing divert it from here to the horizon.

Exhausted as they were, the horses picked up their pace somewhat on this level ground, and they grouped two and two, Bron and Chei to the fore and himself and Morgaine behind, with all the open hills before them and the sunset at their left.

"We will make it," Bron said, dropping back a moment to ride with them. "My lady, we will make it there very soon."

"Tejhos is on the road itself," Morgaine asked him, "is it not?"

"Yes," Bron said.

"We can find our way, then, from here. Go back. Take my advice."

"No," Bron said, "my lady."

"I have warned you." She shifted in the saddle. "That is all I will do."

"I know the reports of the road," Bron said. "I have never ridden it, but I know something of where it goes. I know something of the lord in Mante. I have these things to trade. Lady—"

"As far as you will," Morgaine said after a moment, and heavily. "As far as you can. I will keep my word to you."

Chei had dropped back with them. There was heavy silence as they rode.

Chei's eyes sought toward Vanye as if even then he questioned; and Vanye shrugged and looked away, denying him any help or any encouragement.

Morgaine laid her heels to Siptah and rode from between them.

"It is kindness she meant," Vanye said, and lingered a moment more to reason with them, holding Arrhan as she made to follow Siptah, reining her about again. "That is all."

Chei answered something. Vanye held steady, sweeping his eye back to a thing in the dusk beyond Chei's shoulder, a darkness that had not been on the horizon the instant before. It might have been a rock or a tree in the first blink of the eye.

But it moved. It vanished from the horizon.

Chei and Bron turned their horses about, fallen silent. "God in Heaven," Vanye murmured, and turned and rode after Morgaine. "*Liyo,*" he said as she turned half about. "They are behind us. Someone at least—is on the Road."

She looked, and reined back somewhat. "Ground of our choosing," she said in a low voice, and brought Siptah to a halt as Chei and Bron overtook them.

She slipped the hook on *Changeling's* sheath and laid it across the saddlebow.

Chapter Ten

"I cannot see them now," Vanye said, straining his eyes against the gathering dark, holding Arrhan steady as she would stand with Morgaine's big gray chafing at the bit and stamping the ground beside her. "We have lost them out there."

"They will come to us," Morgaine said, while Bron drew his sword and Chei waited weaponless except for his knife.

"Their horses may be no more rested than ours," Bron said.

"Then again," Morgaine said, "they may be."

"This is mad," Chei cried. "There is the woods over there. We might make it."

"Again," Morgaine said, "we might not. Put away the sword."

"My lady—"

"Do as I say, Bron. Put it away."

"My lady, for our lives—listen to me. Vanye—"

"Never ride on my lady's right," Vanye said quietly. He was excruciatingly conscious of the stone at his heart, inert and harmless as it was at the moment. He had his own sword unhooked and resting across the saddlebow, as Men would parley who met under uncertain circumstances; but he did not reckon it likely that this world knew that sign of conditional peace.

"Vanye," Chei protested, riding close, "for God's sake—"

"Have done!" He whipped the sheathed sword across Chei's chest and stopped it a finger's width from his shoulder. He glared at Chei with temper flaring in him; but this time the sword was sheathed; this time he had the control to hold it, trembling, short of touching. "There will none of them live if we come to blows. Do you understand me? Not the innocent and not the purest. We cannot let them to the gate. We cannot let one escape. It is clear targets we want, range where their archers are useless and none of them can escape. Will that satisfy you?"

Chei's face was stark and wide-eyed in the twilight. Bron had frozen in place. Vanye withdrew the sword and laid it back across his saddlebow, with a second and challenging glance toward one and the other brother.

"The dark will help us," Morgaine said quietly. Vanye did not see her face. He did not want to see it. There was in his vision a boy, staring up at him from a dusty road as if death had greatly astonished him. He saw candles and a nightmare room in Ra-Morij, his brother's face all white and still.

He concentrated instead on the rolling land in front of them and on the hills about them, a constant pass of the eyes, lest the riders arrive at their flank or bring archery to bear from the hill nearest.

"I hear them," Morgaine said, and a moment later he heard them too, horses coming at considerable speed for horses long on the trail. Their own blew and shifted, and Arrhan's ribs worked less strenuously between his legs. That was the simple strategy of their position: the enemy chose to exhaust their horses overtaking on the uphill; they rested theirs by waiting.

It was a small band, ten to twenty, that crested the hill. *Where are the rest of them?* Vanye thought in a moment's cold panic. Then the rest poured over the hilltop, forty, eighty, a hundred and more riders sweeping out on either side of the road.

Steel rang as Bron began to draw.

"No," Morgaine said calmly. "Wait. Both of you keep constantly to Vanye's left. Do *nothing* until I tell you. I have scant patience and less charity today.

Vanye—" She changed suddenly to Kurshin accents. "Do not attempt the stone. Here!"

He had reached after his bow. She flung him *Changeling*. He caught it one-handed across its sheath, in a rush of cold fear, first because she had thrown it; then that it was in his keeping—the one of her weapons that he knew how to use. He had only to look at the odds and know why.

"Chei!" he said, and flung his own arrhendur sword to Chei in the same fashion, as accurately caught, while a familiar panic loosened his joints.

He drew several breaths more, hoping neither man saw; hoping more that Morgaine did not. It was his besetting weakness, that set his palms sweating on *Changeling's* hilt and gray sheath, and his heart pounding to the hoofbeats of the oncoming riders.

Heaven save us, he thought as the line began to spread wide.

Beside him, Morgaine signaled. He reined over, and Bron and Chei took a place at equal separation in their meager line.

The centermost riders drew to a halt. The rest kept moving, a half-ring about them, still closing. *Move us,* he thought, *for the love of Heaven, backward, forward,* liyo, *one or the other!*

Morgaine leveled her hand toward their center, where the most of the qhalur riders were. "Halt!" a man called out, and that envelopment ceased on the instant, everything stopped, except the breathing and stamping of the horses and the leathery creak and jingle of armored riders.

Morgaine's hand did not lower. It stayed aimed at the center of the qhalur ranks.

"My lady," the man said to her, human face, human voice.

"Gault," Chei's voice rasped. "That is Gault, on the roan. The man by him is Jestryn ep Desiny—he was one of our company—"

"My lord Gault," Morgaine shouted back. "What have we to say to each other that you follow me so far from home?"

"We might have discovered that had you come to me." Gault rode forward a few paces and drew the roan to a halt again. "You take strange allies, my lady. Brigands. Rebels. You set them free from my justice. You burn my lands and kill my game. Am I to take this for a friendly gesture?"

"I rarely practice justice. Outright slaughter, yes. I do not call it pretty names, my lord Gault."

"What is that you hold?" Gault's big roan surged forward and he curbed it, reining aside.

"That which seems to make you prudent, my lord. Justifiably so. I see you have talked to my enemies."

"And is your report of me so foul?" Again Gault paced the horse the other direction, weaving a slow, distracting course in the deepening dusk, which Morgaine's hand followed constantly.

"It is your death, my lord. My patience is lessening with every step you take. Do you want to discover which is the fatal one?"

Another three paces. "He is delaying," Vanye muttered, scanning the hills with constant attention. "There is something else out there, and he is waiting for the dark."

"My lady," Gault called out. "You and I might have more to speak of than you think likely. And perhaps more in common than you think." Gault's voice grew gentler, and he curbed his horse's straying. "I take it that it is you I deal with and not this gentleman by you."

"It is myself," she said. "Have no doubt of that."

"What is he?"

"This is delay," Vanye said. *"Liyo,* seek no more of him. Let us be out of here."

"My companion," Morgaine answered Gault. "So— you do not know everything about me."

"Should I?" Again the horse surged forward and Gault reined it back. "You are no visitor out of Mante. Your name is Morgaine. So the humans say. Mine is Qhiverin—among others."

"Liyo. Break away—now! Do not listen to this serpent."

"You are a stranger here," Gault said. "A wayfarer of the gates. You see I am not deceived. You have threatened Mante. Now you will kill me and all my men, lest I reach Tejhos. You think that you have no choice. But here am I, come to parley with you when I might have stayed safe in Morund—or turned prudently south to Morund-gate, once I learned what you are. I did not. I have risked my life and my lord's favor to find you. Is this the action of an implacable enemy?"

"Do not believe him," Bron said. "My lady, do not listen!"

Gault held up one hand, took his sword from its hangings and dropped it ringing to the ground. "There. Does that relieve your suspicions?"

"Withdraw your men," Morgaine said.

Gault hesitated, seeming uncertain, then lifted his hand to the darkened sky.

A black and moving hedge crested the hill eastward.

"Riders on our left!" Vanye cried, and ripped *Changeling* from its sheath.

The air went numb and Arrhan shied under him as that the blade came free, an opal blaze till its tip cleared the sheath and whirled free.

Then a darkness greater than the night formed at *Changeling's* point, and drew in the air all about them. Wind shrieked and keened; men cried out in panic, and the dark lines went to chaos, some breaking forward to meet him, some turning to flee.

"Gate," he heard cry throughout the enemy ranks, *"Gate!"*—for gate it was, leading to Hell itself. He swung it and a horse and rider together went whirling away into dark, screaming with one terror. Others collided with each other in their attempt to escape his attack, and them he took in one stroke and the next, merciless, for there was no stopping it, there was no delicacy in it—it ate substance and spun it out again, streaming forms of living men away into Hell and cold—

—one and the next and the next as Arrhan cut a

curving swath through attackers who trampled each other trying to flee it.

"Archers!" he heard cry. It was for his liege and his comrades he had concern. He reined aside to bring the hell-thing to the defense of his own—taking missiles askew with the wind, trying to shield his liege if he could find her in the unnatural light and the blinding wind.

"*Liyo!*" he shouted, desperate, fighting when he must, when some rider rushed him. The gate-force quivered through his arm and his shoulder and deafened him with its screaming; his eyes grew full of the hell-light and the sights and the faces till he was numb and blinded.

"*Liyo!*"

"*Vanye!*" he heard, and went to that thin sound, turning Arrhan, forcing her with his heels as the mare faltered in blind confusion.

Riders swept toward him. He swung the sword up at the nearest and saw the horrified face in the light of the blade, saw the mouth open in a cry of disbelief.

"*Bron!*" he cried, wrenching the blade aside, veering so that Arrhan skidded and fought wildly for balance.

Bron was gone. The bartered horse thundered past riderless.

He guided Arrhan about in a stumbling turn, and saw Morgaine beyond, silver and black, and Siptah's eyes wild in the opal fire.

"Follow!" she ordered him, and reined about and rode for the dark and the road.

He did not even think then; he followed. He drove his heels into Arrhan's flanks and swept to her right and behind, to keep Morgaine safe from what he did not know and could not see for the shock to his soul and the blinding of his eyes. If there were enemies still behind he did not know. He held *Changeling* naked to his right, protecting them both, for in that howling wind no arrow could reach them.

Up, up and up the steep slope, until horses faltered

on the wet grass, and Siptah came about and Arrhan slowed, blowing froth back from her bit.

"Sheathe it," Morgaine cried. "Sheathe it!"

He discovered the sheath safe in its place at his side: he had done that much before he lost himself, reflexive and unremembered act. He took the sheath in a trembling hand and turned the other numbed and aching wrist to wobble the point toward safety, the only thing that would contain *Changeling's* fire.

That small aperture was a goal he suddenly feared he could not make without calamity. His hand began to shake.

"Give over!" Morgaine said in alarm.

He made it. He slid the point home and the fire dimmed and died, so that he was truly blind. His right arm ached from fingers to spine. He had no strength in it nor feeling in his fingers. "I killed Bron," he said with what voice he could manage, quite calmly. "Where is Chei?"

"I do not know," Morgaine said, reining Siptah close to him. There was hardness in her voice, was very steel. He could not have borne any softer thing. "We did not take them all. Some escaped. I do not know which ones."

"Forgive—" His breath seemed dammed up in him. "I—"

"We are near Tejhos. There is a chance that Mante will mistake one gate-fire for the other. At least for the hour." She turned Siptah on the slope and rode, Arrhan followed by her own will, dazed and blind as he.

"Too near the gate," he heard her say. "Too cursed near. We must be nearly *on* Tejhos-gate. I should *never* have given it to you."

"Bron is dead," he said again, in the vague thought that she might not have understood him. He had to say it again to believe it. The fabric of the world seemed thinned and perilously strained about him and what he had done seemed done half within some other place, unlinked and without effect here. Things that Were could not be mended piece to piece if he did not

say it till it took hold of him. "Chei may have gone
with him—O God. *O God!*"

He began to weep, a leakage from his eyes that
became a spasm bowing him over his saddle.

"Is thee hurt?" Morgaine asked him sharply, grasp-
ing Arrhan's rein. They had stopped somehow. He did
not recall. "Is thee hurt?"

"No," he managed to say. "No." He felt Siptah
brush hard against his leg and felt Morgaine touch him,
a grip on his shoulder which he could hardly feel through
the armor. He was alone inside, half deaf with the
winds, blinded by the light which still swung as a red
bar passing continually in his vision. He was drowning
in it, could not breathe, and he was obliged to say:
"No. Not hurt," when next he could draw a breath,
because she had no time for a fool and a weakling who
killed a comrade and then could not find his wits again.
He pushed himself up by the saddlebow and groped
after the reins.

"Give me the sword," she said. "Give it!"

He managed to wind the reins about his numbed
right hand and to pass *Changeling* back to her with his
left.

"Brighter," he remembered, competent in this at
least, that his mind recollected something so difficult
amid the chaos. He indicated with a lifting of his left
hand toward the northeast, as the road ran. "There.
There will be Tejhos gate."

She stared in that direction; she hooked *Changeling*
to her belt and they rode again at all the pace the
horses could bear. His right arm ached in pulses that
confused themselves with the rhythm of the horses or
with his heartbeats, he could not tell which. He worked
the fingers desperately, knowing the likelihood of enemies. He scanned darkened hills the crests of which
swam with the blurring of his eyes.

"Gate-force," Morgaine said in time. "We are very
near. Vanye, is thee feeling it?"

"Aye," he murmured. "Aye, *liyo*." It was inside
the armor with him, was coiled about his nerves and
his sinew, it crept within his skull and corrupted sight

and reason. They must go near that thing. Perhaps ambush waited for them.

We will lose everything we have done, he thought, everything she has suffered this far—lost, for a fool who mishandled the sword. I should have sheathed it when it went amiss. I should have ridden back. I should have—

—should have—known what I struck—

O God, it could as well have been her.

"Vanye!"

He caught himself before he pitched. He braced himself against the saddlehorn and felt Siptah's body hit his right leg, Morgaine holding him by the straps of his armor, though he was upright now without that.

"Can thee stay the saddle? Shall I take the reins?"

"I am well enough," he murmured, and took the reins in his left hand and let his numbed right rest braced between him and the saddlebow. If he could do one thing right this cursed night it was to dispose himself where he could not fall off and compound his liege's troubles.

Siptah took to the lead then; and the mare lengthened her stride to match him, struggling now, on heart alone.

Where are we going? he wondered. Is it enemies she fears? Or do we go toward the gate, to hold it?

His very teeth ached now with the emanations, and he felt a pain like knives driven into every joint of his right arm, an ache that crept across his chest and into his vitals. He wished he had respite to faint away or to rest; and dutifully fought not to, for what use he was. The pain reached his spine and his skull, one with the pounding of the mare's gait, the jolts which threatened to take him from the saddle.

Hold on, he told himself, slumped over the saddle when other thought had ceased, hold on, hold on.

The roan horse came to a slow halt where the battle had been, and Gault clutched after its ties and its stirrup, letting himself down by painful degrees to stand amid the field. He did not know the weapon that had struck him, which had pierced through his left arm and burned across his back. But here he had fallen in the battle, here his ranks had broken in terror of the gate-weapon, and there were appallingly few corpses remaining.

Here he had flung himself at the roan horse as the slaughter started and managed to get back astride— when the gate-force broke loose and sane men quit the field as quickly as they could.

Such of them as survived had rallied again—qhal, and a scattering of terrified humans—most of all, that the squad he had sent wide before they came to Arunden's camp, had overtaken them now, having swept up the deserters; and had found him on the road.

Now they walked as he did, probing among the dead that were thickest here, where the only the red fire had come, where the woman had wielded what they had mistakenly thought the chiefest of weapons they faced.

That was the fire that had touched him. He understood that much. He stumbled among cooling bodies and found one living, who hoarsely called his name— "Rythys!" Gault called out, "your cousin!"—and Rythys left his desperate searching and came in haste, one of the few fortunate.

But Gault sought Jestryn on the field, and found him finally—Pyverrn the wit, Pyverrn the prankster, Pyverrn who had done an unhumorous thing at the last, and flung himself and his horse between Gault and the killing fire.

"Pyverrn," Gault-Qhiverin said, feeling after a heartbeat, and finding none, finding Jestryn's face already cold in the night wind. "Pyverrn!" he cried, for that was the oldest name, the name by which they had been friends in Mante, and fought the Overlord's battles and intrigued in the Overlord's court through their last life. *"Pyverrn!"*

He hugged the body to him, but it was only cooling human clay against his own borrowed flesh, a body Pyverrn had worn, but never truly mastered.

This was the last death, the irrecoverable one: not Tejhos-gate nor any other could save a life, once the life was gone; and Gault would have murdered one of his own men to have hosted Pyverrn's self again—he would have taken one of his own kind; his other and dearest friends.

He would have—such was the bond between them—accepted what only a few had dared to save a fading life: he would have gone into the gate with his friend and taken him into his own self, risking madness, or obliteration.

That was his love for Pyverrn.

But there was nothing left to love. There was only the cold flesh that Pyverrn had wrested from its previous owner, and no way to restore it.

His men came round him where he knelt and wept. None ventured a word to him, until he himself let the body go and stood up.

"Tejhos-gate," he said. *"We are going after them!"*

Doubtless there were some few who would have fled, had they had a choice. He knew the cowardice of some of them, that had had to be herded back. But in the southern lands there was nothing to hide them should they fail him—and now they knew he was alive.

"Two of you will go to Mante," he said when they were mounted again. "The rest of us will ride after these invaders. We will have them. *I* will have them, him and her, and they will wish they had been stillborn."

"Better?" Morgaine asked; and Vanye, sitting with his back against a standing stone, leaned his head against that unforgiving surface and nodded with his eyes shut. He did not remember much of the ride that had brought them this far. He knew that he had been upright in the saddle, but so much of it had been that kind of pain which the mind would not believe could last so keenly, so long. All that time seemed compressed; yet he knew it was leagues beyond that place where he had almost fallen. Tejhos-gate was far behind them.

And the cessation of that force left him drained, void, as if he had been gutted.

Beside them the horses caught their breath and began to show a little interest in the grass under their feet, now they had drunk of the little creek and had their legs rubbed down. He had done that much for his horse, while Morgaine saw to the Baien gray. He was a horseman from his birth: he would have done that for the brave mare with his heart's blood, after the course she had run; and Morgaine—whatever she was—had no less care for the gray.

Now she leaned against another such stone facing him—not stones of power, mere markers along the roadside. One knee propped the sword on which she leaned, the sight of which he could hardly bear and the weight of which he remembered in his bones: not balanced like an ordinary blade, the crystal length within that sheath rune-written with the secrets of the gates—for the sake of a successor, she had told him once. She had taught him writing and ciphering more than a lord's bastard needed—for what purpose he knew, and loathed, and thought about no more than he had to.

But he could read those runes. They were burned into his soul like the light into his eyes.

"Water?" she asked him.

He drank from the flask she gave him, struggled with his left hand and his right to hold it without shaking. The pain was still there, but only a dull ache, against the memory of the living blade in his hand. He gave the flask back, drew a breath and looked about him at the rolling hills, the stones, the road pale in the starlight.

"We should have gone over to Tejhos," he murmured.

"Thee could not," she said.

It was bitter truth. He would have left her to hold the place alone, would have fallen—Heaven knew where he would have fallen, or how long the fire would run in his bones if he lay within that influence.

The drawing of the sword was a dice-throw, a power either felt in Mante, if they were wary; or was mistaken for ordinary—O Heaven—*ordinary* use of the gate, in which case Mante would do nothing, until their enemies reached it and passed it and told Mante otherwise—which they would, assuredly.

Therefore they ran. Therefore they paced themselves to last now, with all the speed they could make, while they might make it.

He had a cold lump of fear at his gut. Coward, he had heard from his brothers, and from his father, and most of Morija—You think too much, his brother had told him. He had never been like them. In all too many respects.

If a man thought—if a man let himself think—backward or forward—

"It is not the first friend the sword has taken," she said finally. "Vanye, it was not your fault."

"I know," he said, and saw in his mind the harper-lad of Ra-morij, who had thrown himself between that blade in her hand and his threatened kin—had flung himself there to be a hero, and discovered Hell in the unstoppable swing of Morgaine's hand.

"They rode to your right," she said, "against all our warnings."

The excuses she made for him were doubtless those which armored her, the only and best wisdom she had to give him. He sensed the pain it cost her to expose that. And there was nothing to say against those excuses that she did not, beneath those reasonings, know—

—except the harper had known the report of the sword: who in Morija had not?

But Bron had not known, had not guessed how far its danger extended. They had never told him.

He shut his eyes, clenched them shut, as if it could banish the terrified face that was burned across his vision; or bring back the sun, and end this terrible night where visions were all too easy. The priest, he thought, had cursed him, cursed Bron, cursed Chei. He did not say that to Morgaine. But he feared it. Heaven had answered that creature, and he did not know why, except Heaven judged them worse—

Harness jingled, the sudden lifting of Siptah's head, the clink of slipped bit and snaffle ring that his ears knew before his eyes lifted. The stallion stood with ears pricked, gazing toward the road.

Morgaine rose instantly and moved to take the horses in hand and lead them inward of the stones for cover from the road.

He rose shakily to his feet and held the reins, soothing them, stroking one nose and the other—"Quiet, quiet," he said to them in the Kurshin tongue, and Siptah strained at his grip and shivered, one long twitch up his foreleg.

"One rider," Morgaine said, venturing a quick look from the edge of the stone.

"One man makes no sense."

"A good many have cause to follow us."

"Past the gate at Tejhos? Alone?"

She drew the black weapon. It was a dead man rode that track, and did not know it. He leaned his shoulders against the stone and looked out past it, as the stone was canted at an angle to the road.

The rider came on a dark horse. Mail glinted about him in the starlight.

Vanye's heart leapt and jolted against his ribs. For a moment he could not breathe. "Chei," he said, and reached for Morgaine's arm. "It is Chei."

"Stay here!"

He turned his head in dismay to look at her, at the weapon still in her hand. *"Liyo,* for the love of Heaven—"

"We do not know that it *is* Chei. Stay here. Wait."

He waited, leaning against the rock and breathing in shorter and shorter breaths as the faltering hoofbeats came closer.

"Liyo," he whispered in horror, seeing her arm lift.

She fired as the rider came past them, a red fire breaking out in the meadow-grass; and the exhausted horse shied and fought for balance as the rider reined up and about, facing them.

Chei slid down, holding to the saddlehorn and clinging to the reins.

"Chei," Vanye said, and left the horses, walking out from between the stones.

"Stop," Morgaine said; and he stopped.

Chei only stood there, as if he were numb.

"Bring your horse in," Morgaine said. "Sit down."

Chei staggered toward them and led the horse as far as the first stone. "Where is my brother?" he asked. "Where did Bron go?"

It was not the question Vanye had expected. It took the breath out of him.

"Bron is dead," Morgaine said.

"Where did he *go?*"

"*Changeling's* gate has no other side."

Chei slid down the face of the stone and leaned against it, his head resting against the rock. Vanye sank down facing him.

"Chei—I could not stop it. I did not know him— Chei?"

Chei neither moved nor lifted his head. There was only silence, long and deep, in which Morgaine at last moved and retrieved her flask from Siptah's saddle.

"Here," she said, offering it.

Chei looked up and took it as if his hands and his mind were far separate. He fumbled after the stopper and drank, and slowly, as if it were a thoroughly unfamiliar task, stopped it again and gave it back.

"I feared," Vanye said desperately, "that it was the both of you. I could not see, Chei."

"Rest," Morgaine said, and came close and stood with *Changeling* folded in her arms. "So long as we rest. After that, go back to your own land."

"No," Chei said with a shake of his head.

"Then take my order. You will go no further with us."

Vanye looked around at her in dismay, at a face implacable in the starlight, a figure that had as well be some warlike statue.

"*Liyo—*"

"He is a danger," she said in the Kurshin tongue. "There is a gate yonder. Has thee forgotten?"

"There is not enough time!"

"Tell me how long it takes. There were wounded aplenty back there."

"It is Chei! Would a qhal come asking where his brother was? Is that the kind of question a qhal would ask first, who *knows* what the gates are?"

"Barring other chances, there is the matter of bloodfeud. Of revenge."

"Revenge? God in Heaven, has the man come seeking revenge on me? I wish he would—I wish he *would* say something—"

"In time to come, at some point of crisis—yes. Being what he is, he may well think of revenge, when he wakes from the shock of it. I will not have him with us, at your back—or mine."

"For the love of God, *liyo!* No! I refuse this. I will not have it."

"We gave him what chance we could. Here is an end of it. He goes, Vanye."

"And where is my voice in this?"

"Thee is always free to choose."

He stared at her in shock, numb. It was the old answer. It was forever true. It was real now, an ultimatum, from which there was, on this plain, near the gates—no return within her trust.

"You will go," she said to Chei.

"Lady—"

"Life I have given you. Use it."

"You have taken my brother's!"

"Aye, and spared yours just now. Do not stay to rest. Take your horse and go. *Now.*"

"Vanye—" Chei said.

"I cannot," he said, forcing the words. "I cannot, Chei."

Chei said nothing for a moment. Then he struggled toward his feet. Vanye put out a hand to help him and he struck it away, fumbling after his horse's reins.

"At least," Vanye said to Morgaine, "let him rest here!"

"No."

Chei did not look at him until he was in the saddle, and then he was all shadow, there between the menhirs.

He rode away without a word, whipping the exhausted horse with blows Vanye felt in his own flesh.

"*Liyo,*" he said then to Morgaine, without looking at her, "I know your reasons. I know everything you would say. But, Mother of God, could we not have let him rest, could we not have tried him—?"

"Pity," she said, "will be your undoing. *I* did this. I have spared you the necessity. For your sake—and mine. And I have given him cause to hate me. That is my best gift. Best he lose his zeal for us altogether—before it kills him. *That* is the pity I have for him. And best it come from me rather than you. That is all the mercy I have."

He stared at her in the darkness, somewhere between numbness and outrage. Now it was temper from her. Now she was righteous. "Aye," he said, and sat down abruptly, deciding that numbness was better, for the night, perhaps for a good many days to come.

There was a pain behind his eyes. He rested his head on his arm and tried to make it go away, or the pain in his heart to stop, or the fear in his gut; and none of them had remedy, except that Morgaine knew that pain, Morgaine was still with him, Morgaine was sunk in her own silence and Morgaine was bearing unto herself—she had told the truth—all the cruelty of which he was not capable.

The road stretched on and on in the starlight, unremitting nightmare, and Gault-Qhiverin clung to the course with what followers he had left to him. There was a wetness all down his side, the wound broken open again, though he had bound it, and the roan horse's gait did nothing to lessen the pain of his wounds.

"Go back," his captain said to him. "My lord, let us continue. You go back. We dare not lose you—" Which was true: there were many in Gault's household who were there for reasons which had much to do with court and intrigue and the saving of their lives—lose him they dared not, for fear of who might replace him in Morund.

But they were not mortal wounds, that bled down

his side and across his back. He would live to deal
with consequences, and he had said things and com-
promised himself in front of witnesses, in ways that
required personal action to redeem him: no, my lord,
treason was never my purpose. I only queried them to
learn their business: my offers to them were a lie.

Form meant a great deal in Mante, whatever the
Overlord knew of true purposes.

There was most of all, most of all—revenge. And
the saving of his reputation: Gault was never without
double purposes, even in something so precious to him
as his best friend's life. There were ways and ways to
accomplish anything; and revenge was always best if it
accomplished more than its immediate aims.

This was the common sense that had settled into
Gault now the blood was cool and the purpose formed:
alliance was not possible and therefore he would be
virtuous, serve his own interests in the other way—and
survive to deal with his and Pyverrn's enemies.

The pair of them first for himself; and, failing that,
for Mante and Skarrin's gentle inquiries. That was the
object of his ride.

But there was something before him on the road, a
single moving darkness that advanced and gained detail at the combined speed of their horses.

"What is that?" one of his company asked. *"Who* is
that?"—for Tejhos was behind them on the road, where
the two members of their own company had gone
message-bearing and asking after troops. This could
be no answer Mante had sent—from upland, from that
direction.

Closer and closer the rider came, on a horse weary
and faltering in the night.

"Lord Gault!" the rider cried. "Lord Gault!"

Gault spurred the roan forward of the rest. "Who
are you?" he yelled back at the oncoming rider.

And had his answer as the pale-haired rider came
straight for him with a howl neither human nor qhal.

"Gault—!"

A sword glittered in the starlight. He whipped his

own out and up, and metal rang on metal as the fool tried to leave his saddle and bear him off the horse.

But a knife was in the other hand. It scored his armor and found a chink in his belly, and he yelled in shock as he brought his own sword-hilt round, the only weapon he could bring to bear at too close a range, battering at his enemy who was ripping the knife upward in his belly before his men could close in and pull the man off.

"My lord," his men cried, holding him in their arms, lifting him from the saddle, as he clamped a hand to his gut and stared down at the wild man the rest of them had caught and pinned.

"Do not kill him!" he managed to say, while his gut leaked blood through his fingers and the chill came on him. "Do not kill this one."

The Man screamed and lunged at him, trying before the others could stop him to tear him down by the feet, by the knees; but they held him.

"Do not hurt him," Gault said again, and the man struggled and screamed at him, calling him butcher and coward and what other things Gault's dimming hearing lost track of.

"I am Chei ep Kantory," the man yelled at him. "Try again, Gault. Do you want a shape to wear? Do you need one? I will give you one—I will give you mine."

"He is mad," someone said.

"What do you want?" Gault asked, fascinated despite the pain that racked him and the cold that came on him. "What price—for this partnership?"

"For my brother," ep Kantory said. His sobs stilled. He became quite calm. "We have a common enemy. What is it worth to you—to have me willing?"

Chapter Eleven

It was a procession as fraught with fear as the last trek Chei had made with Gault and his company—the same, in that many of these were the same men that had taken him to Morund-gate; but here was no one stumbling along afoot: they let him ride, and though he was bound, none of them struck him, none of them offered him any threat or harm, and their handling had put not so much as a bruise on him.

They went now with what speed they could, such that it must cost Gault agony: Chei knew and cherished that thought for the little comfort he could get from it.

Mostly, in this dreadful place of barren hills and night sky and stars, he thought of his own fate, and from time to time of Bron, but not Bron in their youth, not Bron in better times, but Bron's face when the sword had taken him. That horror was burned into his sight, every nuance of it, every interpretation of what word Bron had tried to call out and for whom he had meant it, and whether he had known what was happening to him as he fell away into nowhere at all.

And it was all to no purpose, serving allies who despised them both, who killed Bron and then cast off the faith he had tried to keep for his brother as if it was some soiled rag, himself qhal-tainted, henceforth not to be trusted—so much the clans might have done, for their own safety—but *something,* something, they could have said, something—anything, to make Bron's death noble, or something less horrible than it was.

They might have offered regret—Forgive, they could have said: we dare not trust you. Forgive me, Vanye could have said: could have prevailed with the lady—the man who had taken him from the wolves, been his ally—

—killed Bron.

—then cast him out with a shrug of his shoulders, seeing the lady threaten him with death by fire—with the sword itself.

But that was not the fate that he had chosen.

He felt power in the air as they passed the shoulder of a hill—felt it stronger and stronger, so that the hair stood up on his head and his body, and the horses shied and fought the bit.

Men dismounted; some led Gault's horse and some led his after this, though the gelding fought and re-sisted and Gault's roan horse threw its head and tried to turn away.

"Not far now," one said; and Chei felt cold inside. "Not far—" As they passed that hill and the black menhirs rose up like teeth against the stars.

Beyond, atop the hill, the gate of Tejhos itself hove up against the sky, monstrous and dark, a simple square arch that framed a single bright star.

Then Chei's courage faltered. Then, his exhausted horse led perforce toward the base of that hill, he doubted everything that he had purposed, whether any revenge was worth this. He pulled furtively at the cords that held him and found them secure. He looked about and measured how far he could ride if he should kick the horse and startle it free—but the horse was doing all it could to free itself already, as men held it close by the bit and crowded it close.

Suddenly other figures came into their path, from among the rocks, accosting Gault; words passed; swords were drawn. What is this? Chei wondered numbly. It occurred to him that something threatened Gault him-self, and that some other presence had arrived that had the guards all about him reaching for weapons. It was too complex. He had come into a qhal matter, and their deviousness and their scheming threatened to swallow him up all by accident.

But the difficulty seemed resolved. The qhal who had met them broke their line and allowed Gault to pass. Then they began to move again, toward the hill. They passed between the masked warders themselves, strange helmed figures with visors in the shape of demons and beasts, with naked swords that gleamed silver in the starlight.

This was Hell, and he had come to it of his own accord. They left the warders behind, he and the men who led his horse and surrounded him with force. The gate loomed above them. There was no way back and no way of escape, and he had done everything knowing that such would be the case, knowing himself now, that he was not a man who could die simply or easily, or lay down his life of his own accord.

At every step of this he had planned that they would take care of the matter for him: they would shoot him down on the road—Gault would be dead or refuse to fight him, and the whole band would ride against him—he would find them scattered on the road and kill a few of them before the odds ran out—or he would ride all the way to Morund-keep itself, and hail out qhal one after the other till they killed him.

Or his first purpose would succeed, Gault would answer his challenge and Gault would skewer him outright or he would kill Gault before Gault's men killed him—

And last of all they might take him prisoner and use him as they planned to now, if there was desperate need—

That was the bargain he ventured. He had heard while he was in Gault's prisons, that when they took a body, sometimes the qhal who tried it lost, and utter madness was the end; or now and again (so they whispered, devising vague hopes and schemes in that stinking dark) the war inside that body went on for years, mind and mind in the same flesh.

There was not a clan in the hills would have him now. There was nothing going home could offer him.

But this . . . this offered something.

He had planned this when he drove himself straight at Gault and gotten his way past Gault's guard by sheer berserk desperation, and driven a harness-knife for Gault's vitals, even while half a hundred men moved to stop him.

He kept believing it possible, as the horse fought and jolted under him, and men whipped it and forced it.

War on different grounds, he thought, you and I, inside, with no escape for either of us—I shall embrace you, Gault-my-enemy. That leaves us your hate and mine, and my anger and yours; and what I want and what you want, and which is stronger, qhalur lord?

Was Gault-the-Man afraid when you took him? But I am not. I welcome you. I shall welcome this fight with all my damned soul, Gault-my-enemy. I came back from Hell once, where you sent me. Do you think I will not come back again?

"A little farther," someone said.

Or seemed to say. But it was harder and harder to think at all, in the jolting steps the horse made under him in its struggles, in the sensation crawling like insects over his skin. The gate loomed nearer and nearer, and the horse shied and faltered under him, so that the men finally stopped it, as it stumbled nearly to its knees. "Get down," that voice said, and they pulled him from the saddle, their hands no longer gentle, everything passing further and further from the familiar and the known.

He looked up at the span of the gate and saw that the roan horse had gone further; but now the men lifted Gault from his saddle and carried him, while others seized his own arms and started him toward that height, toward the night sky shimmering like air over fire, within the towering frame of the gate.

Closer and closer, until he could see nothing but the sky past those pillars, and a single star within that arch, a point of light that quivered and danced in the air. There was a singing in the wind, the thrum of bowstrings, of voices, spectral and quivering in his bones.

Closer yet. The sky seemed to shift *downward* within the gate, and the thrumming was in his brain. His bowels turned to water in him, and his knees quaked, and the men holding him were all that enabled him to walk. O God, he thought, God, what can a Man hope to do here, with them?

And again: Fear is Gault's weapon. I must not be open to it. I dare not let fear in. Hate is all I have. Hate greater than his—

They reached the crest almost together, Gault holding his hand pressed to his belly, but walking at the last, leaning on the men who attended him. The black pillars seemed to throw off a kind of light, none for themselves, but a white hell-glow that played about the ground and that ran up the legs and the bodies and the faces of men who passed within its compass. Small sounds were swallowed up. The sky twisted and writhed like a gaping pit.

As far as the pillars that dwarfed them, Gault went, and leaned against the left-hand stone holding to it for his support, laying his hand on one place and another as if it were a living thing, and himself in communion with it—qhalur wizardry, Chei thought, breathing with difficulty, watching with small jerks of his eyes and knowing that his face betrayed terror; but so was there terror in the grip of hands which numbed his arms and held him upright despite his failing knees. They were all afraid, he, the qhal themselves—it was a strange reliance he began to have on them, who would defend his safety now with their own lives, who were there to hold him and keep him from failing his resolution or from tumbling untimely into that place—A little longer, a little longer, he told himself; and concentrated on the little pain they caused his arms as the only saving of his sanity:

Help me, do not let me go; we are all flesh, and flesh does not belong next this thing—

They gathered him up; they brought him closer, and

Gault staggered forth to meet him in front of that dark archway, on the edge of the sky.

"Free him," Gault bade them, and a rough sawing cut the cords on his hands. They let go their grip on him, and Chei lurched out of balance, staring at the sky which now had lost all stars, which did not show the hills beyond, or anything but night—stared helplessly at Gault's face, suddenly, as Gault caught his arms. Hell-light shimmered over them, turning flesh dead white; Gault caught him closer, as suddenly the air began to move about them, stirring Gault's hair, howling with the force of summer storm.

The gate was opening, greater than the gate the sword had made, louder than the howling of the winds which had taken Bron.

"Have you changed your mind?" Gault asked, and embraced him closer still. "Is it still willingly?"

Chei fought down his gorge and nodded, and his heart pounded in shock when he felt Gault seek his hand and press the hilt of a knife into his cold fingers. "Then you may do what you so much wish so much to do," Gault said, and slid his hand to the back of his neck, winding fingers into his hair, holding him tight. "Friend."

Chei rammed upward with the knife in a spasm of outrage, under Gault's jaw, toward the brain.

Someone pushed him. He felt the hands strike him, and the hill fell away under him and the man who was locked with him in a sickening fall of cold and wind and void.

Something began to go wrong then, his senses going out one by one: he saw things he could not name, and was blinded by light that was pain. He screamed and screamed as he fell, alone now, falling slower—a drifting dark, in which something else walked, and that thing was a thought that waked in him and called itself Chei, but it was not himself. It remembered dying, remembered the shock of a blade in its bowels, and one beneath its jaw, stopping breath and speech; the pain was all for a moment.

Then it ebbed, retreating to the past, safe and bearable.

He knew then what had happened to him, and that realization itself was fleeting, shredding away from him in the dark as something he dared not reconcile, except that he had died—he knew that recent memory had his death in it, and he did not want to delve into that, here, in the dark, naked to the winds and the cold.

He had use for his life. He discovered it and clung to it. He called it Bron and he called it Jestryn and Pyverrn, and he could not remember whether it had been brother or friend, or whether the man or the woman had killed him, but it was one and the same. He had a revenge to take, and that it was the one thing that had brought him north or south on that nightbound road, whichever direction he had been traveling, whichever horse he had been riding.

Then, having discovered his heart was whole, he was less afraid. He felt other things slipping away, pieces that might matter, but he was no longer in doubt where his course was and that the men waiting for him would follow him.

He knew all of Morund. He knew the hills. He knew Mante. He saw a hold set in the mountains, and the great Gate which ruled all gates, and knew the intricacies of politics which had sent the warders who waited below the hill: the Overlord Skarrin had received his first message and sent this handful of his underlings to guard the approach and to discover what they could, while Skarrin questioned at length the messengers he had sent. Skarrin's men had tried to bar him from use of the gate, until he could have permission of the high lord.

They had hoped, perhaps, that he would die.

But now, in his recollections, he had something indeed to tell them, which would stir Skarrin out of his lethargy and bring forces south.

Tell them the urgency of it he would, but he would not tell all he knew—nor stay for them or wait on Skarrin's pleasure. He had been Qhiverin Asfelles. He and Pyverrn had fought in these lands between Tejhos and Mante, against various of the high lord's enemies; he knew the secret ways into the hills, off the Road and back to it. He had utter freedom of the land, the high lord himself had cause to fear him and his connections within the warrior Societies, and he was as likely as any to profit by the present chaos—by whatever means turned up under his hand.

He drew a breath.

He felt the winds again, when a moment before had been only cold that numbed all feeling.

He heard the sounds, when a moment before had been only stillness. It was as if a ripple were sweeping through the dark, bearing him closer and closer to the shores of the world.

He moved his limbs, finding himself weaker than he remembered, lighter of limb. It was a young body. It was skilled and agile and had a long-muscled, runner's strength different than the slower, mature power of the body he recalled as Gault's—was far more like Qhiverin's; was nearly as fair as a qhal; and that pleased him.

He had a mature mind, too, that took the skittish thoughts of a younger and impulsive man and calmed them and spread wider and further into connections from which he shied back, of a sudden: there was too much memory, and it needed long meditation to reconcile it.

Witch-mind, a part of him said.

Nature, said the other, nature and knowledge.

God! part of him cried.

The other part said: Nature.

Vision cleared in a shimmer like the surface of a pond. The hill grew firm under his feet and the men who gathered anxiously to meet him were all friendly and familiar to him.

"Hesiyyn," he said, and laid his hand on a tall qhal's shoulder with easy humor, knowing how Hesiyyn loathed humankind.

"Lord Chei," Hesiyyn hailed him with deep irony.

It was custom. It was the penalty of the twice-and-three-times-born.

The Men among them would be confused. They would murmur things about souls, which Chei dismissed and refused to think about. But tall, elegant qhal had no hesitation in bowing the head and offering homage to him, to Chei ep Kantory, lord of Morund— the intimates of his household, his servants, the remnant of the human levies, even the troublesome and arrogant warders from Mante, who waited below, with their captain.

He felt wounds on him. He felt bruises. His knees ached with exhaustion. That was the penalty this body brought with it. None were unbearable.

He sought weapons—the sword which the Man had given him: that was one weapon he did not intend to lose. It was qhalur-work, and foreign—from further, he was sure, than merely overseas, and he delighted in it when he tried its balance.

He took his own bow; and the red roan; the lame gelding he turned out to fend for itself: perhaps it would recover.

But he declined more weapons than that, and declined to go in more than the breeches and mended boots and light mail that came with the man.

"This is the shape they will expect," he said to Hesiyyn.

"Wake," Morgaine's voice whispered out of nowhere, and muscles jumped and body tensed all in one spasm as on the edge of a fall—But it was stone at Vanye's back, and he pressed himself against it, controlling his breaths and blinking at the shadow that stood between him and the horses. "I might have hit you," he said. "Oh, Heaven—" He caught his breath and brushed loose hair out of his eyes with a trembling hand. "I dreamed—" But he did not tell those dreams, that took him back to old places, old terrors. "I did not mean to sleep."

"Best we move."

"Is there—"

"No. Only shortness of time. A little of the night left. We travel while we can."

He glanced around to see were Chei and Bron awake then, one instant's impulse, and remembered everything like a blow to the stomach; he drew a breath then and rubbed an unshaven face, and quickly gathered himself to his feet, trying not to think on anything but the road.

Fool, he thought. Do not look back. Look around you. *Look around you.* That is what caused this sorry business, nothing more and nothing less than losing track of things.

He wanted to weep. He adjusted Arrhan's gear and reached out to hold Siptah's bridle for Morgaine as she prepared to mount. "Do not be seeing to *me*," she said sharply, taking back the reins, by which she meant do not be twice a fool.

It stung. He was not in a mood to bear her temper, and she was not in a mood for debating what she wanted. He turned and flung himself to horse, and waited on her, since she was in such haste.

She mounted up and rode without a backward look. She was fey and doom-ridden, and the loss of a comrade and the driving away of another—the excessive cruelty of it, like her ultimatum to him with Chei, was all one thing.

It was because of that blade she bore. It was because of the lives it took. It was because of the things she knew that he did not, and the madness—the madness which distracted her, and which, this morning, beckoned both of them.

Her moods had been tolerable while he had been no more than *ilin* and now were enough to drive him to black, blind rage, anger to match her own.

She spoke finally. It was to remark on the land, as if there had never been a quarrel.

"Aye," he said, and: "Aye, my liege," choking down his temper—for hers was gone, vanished. That was the way of her. He was Nhi on one side of the blanket and Chya on the other and temper once it rose was next to madness, it blinded and it drove him—

even to fratricide; after which he had learned to smother it under *ilin*-law. O Heaven, he thought, *ilin* to a temper-prone woman was one thing. Both lover and shieldman to a woman half-mad and geas-driven was another.

He had the warrior's braid back. The cool air on his neck, the high-clan honor that forever reminded him he could take another path, the *ilin's* oath that bound him to a liege he could in no wise leave—unwise, unwise, ever to tangle matters further, unwise to have drifted closer and closer until she could wound him, and drive him mad, and then absently forget she had struck at him at all.

But it had happened. He was snared. He had been enspelled from the beginning.

And she left him with his ghosts—thinking at one time he heard more horses than their two, thinking at another moment that Chei and Bron were behind him. They haunted the tail of his eye so that a bit of brush, a stone, a trick of the rising sun, persuaded his sight that they were there.

Both.

Chei is dead, he thought with a chill, and crossed himself. *Chei is dead.*

And he could not say why he suddenly believed this, or why it was two riders that haunted him, except it was guilt, or foreknowledge what they had sent Chei to, in a land where he had qhal-taint on him.

He wept, the tears running down his face, without expression. Beside him, Morgaine said some word.

"Vanye," she said then.

There was no place for a man to go, except to turn his face away.

She was silent after. The wind dried his face. There seemed nothing to say, that would not lead to things he did not want to discuss. He only gave a sigh and shifted in his saddle and looked at her, so that she would know that he was all right.

The sun came up by degrees in the sky and showed them other ghosts, the heights of hills which had not been there, showed them a land of crags and rough land ahead of them, all painted in shadows of gold and cloud.

"Rest," she said again, when they had come to water, a little pond between two hills, and this time again he took Siptah's bridle as she dismounted.

She laid her hand on his back as she walked past him, as he slipped the horses' bits to let them graze and rest a little. He felt it faintly through the armor, and it set the thoughts moiling in him, a little of relief, a great deal of reluctance to do or say anything with her. It was not a quarrel of woman and man. It was, he decided finally, that their blood was up, both, that they had killed, that she had fighting in her mind and so did he, and to expect any gentleness or to offer any was unwise.

He went and washed his hands and his face and his neck in the pond, wetting his boots in the boggy grass.

"Do not drink," she said from behind him, reminding him of cautions that he knew as well as she, and he turned half about with a sudden, trapped fury in him.

He said nothing, and rose and walked back to sit down on his heels and press his wet hands to the back of his neck and to his brow.

"Sleep," he said without looking at her. "You are due that."

"I should not have chided thee."

"No, you should have let a fool drink from standing water. It is not Kursh, or Andur, *liyo*. I know that. I was not that much fool."

"Thee can take the rest. Thee has more need."

"Why, because I am short-tempered? I have killed a man. I have killed one man I held for a friend. And we have lost the other. No matter." He wiped the hair back from his stubbled face, the wisps that had come loose from his braid and trailed about brow and ears, and he had not the will left to do more than wipe them out of his way. "I am learning."

Then the reach of what he had said shot through him. He glanced up at her face. *My God, why did I say that?*

The mask had come back over her countenance,

pale as it was. She shrugged and looked aside at the ground. "Well that we save our shafts for our enemies."

"Forgive me." He went to his knees and she moved so suddenly he thought she would strike him in the face, but it was his shoulder she caught, hard, with the heel of her hand, before he could even think to bow to the ground as reflex made natural. He met her angry stare and there was nothing woman-gentle in the blow that had stopped him from the obeisance. He had meant to make peace. Now he only stared at her.

She looked dismayed too, finally, the anger fading. Her hand went gentle on his shoulder and trailed down his arm. "There is no way back," she said. "If you learn anything of me, learn that."

He felt his throat tighten. He drew breaths to find an adequate one and finally shook his head, and turned aside and got up clumsily, since she gave him no room.

"I am sorry," he said with his back to her. The arm that had wielded the sword ached again, and he rubbed at the shoulder she had struck. "I have my wits about me, better than you see. God knows, we are going to need our rest. And I do you no service to rob you of yours. I am not the first man mistook a friend in a fight, God knows I am not—" He remembered the harper, with a wince. He could not but wound her, no matter what he did or said; no more than she with him. He could not think where they would find rest, or where he would shake the phantoms in the tail of his eye, and of a sudden panic came over him, thinking what odds mounted against their passing those mountains ahead.

It was speed they needed. And human bodies and exhausted horses could only do so much before hearts broke and flesh failed.

"They are my mistakes," she said. He heard her move, and her shadow fell past him and merged with his on the thin grass, "to have taken them with us, to have given thee the sword. It was thy own strength betrayed thee, that thee kept using it. Never—*never* bear it till it wields thee. That is what happened. That,

I did not make thee understand. It has happened to
me. Thee learns. And sometimes even then—"

She did not finish. He looked half around at her and
nodded, and refused to regard the phantom that beckoned him from the tail of his eye, a shadow on the
horizon of the road. Her hand rested on his arm and
his pressed hers.

Until that phantom insisted, and this time he must
look, seeing a horseman atop the ridge.

"Liyo!" he hissed. "On the road—"

He leapt up and she did; and hurried for the horses,
to tighten cinches and refit bridles: he caught Siptah
first, his duty to his liege, and she left him to that for
economy of motion and did the same for Arrhan, still
working as he led Siptah to her.

A last buckle and she was done. He cast a glance
over his shoulder and saw the oncoming riders, twenty,
thirty or more.

"They are Gault's or they are out of the gate,"
Morgaine said, and set her foot in Siptah's stirrup. "If
the latter, we have no knowledge *what* weapons they
have, and I do not like this ground—Ride!"

He sprang to the saddle and reined to her left as
they made the road. There was no question but that
they were seen by now, but the narrowing of the road
left them little choice—and that in itself put a fear into
him. Many things about the gates bewildered him, but
crossing from *here* to *there* did not, and if Gault's men
had gone from Tejhos to Mante and back, Mante itself
was warned and might have riders coming south to
head them off.

It was more and more of narrow passage ahead of
them: the rising sun had limned rougher land stretch-
ing eastward and north, and that meant fewer and
fewer choices of any sort.

They had won so many battles. The odds grew and
the land shaped itself against them. "Get off the road,"
he shouted at Morgaine as he rode alongside. "For
Heaven's own sake, *liyo*, we cannot win straight
through—we cannot outride them behind and before!
Let us get into the hills, let them hunt us there, let

them hunt us the winter long, if that is what it takes to let them grow careless—"

It was an outlaw's counsel. He had that to give. He looked at Morgaine and saw her face set and pale in that unreason that drove her. He despaired then.

"We make as much ground as we can," she called across to him, "as long as we can."

He looked back over his shoulder, where their pursuers made a darkness on either margin of the road, running beside the sporadic white stone.

"Then stop and fight them," he said. *"Liyo,* in Heaven's name, one or the other!"

"There might be others," she shouted back, meaning overland, through the hills; and he caught the gist of her fears and reckoned as she reckoned, on Mante, and stones, and gates.

The riders so easily seen might be a lure to delay or herd them.

Still, still, she was the elder and warier of them.

They crested a hill and for a time they were running alone, at an easier gait, for a long enough time that he looked back once and twice looking for their pursuers; and Morgaine looked, her silver hair whipping in the wind.

They were gone.

"I do not like this," she said as they rode.

The road which had held straight so far, through so much of the land, took a bend toward the east which Chei had never mapped.

And his own instincts cried trap.

"Liyo, I beg you, let us get off this!"

Morgaine said nothing, but of a sudden turned Siptah aside into a fold of the hills, keeping a quick pace on grassy and uneven ground, down the course the hills gave them.

Deeper and deeper into land in which they no longer had a guide.

They rode more quietly at last, finding their way by the sun in a wandering course through grassy hills, brush and scrub forest.

They watched the hilltops and the edges of the thickets, and from time to time looked behind them or stopped and listened and watched the flight of birds for omens of pursuers.

Morgaine did not speak now. He rode silent as she, senses wide and listening, for any hint of other presence.

Only as the sun sank: "The dark is their friend tonight," Morgaine said, "more than ours, in a land we do not know. We had best find ourselves a place and lie quiet a while."

"Thank Heaven," he muttered; and when they had found that place, a deep fold of the hills well-grown with brush, and when they had gotten the horses sheltered up against an overhang of the hills and rubbed them down and fed them, then he felt that he could breathe again and he had a little appetite for the fireless supper they made.

"Tomorrow," he said anxiously, "we will camp here, and I will go a little down the way and bring back forage for the horses—I do not think we ought to stir out of here for a few days. Listen to me!" he said, as she began to answer him. "Whatever you ask, I will do, you know that. But hear me out. Time will serve us. If it takes us months—we will live to get to Mante."

"No," she said. "No. We have no months. We have no days. Does thee understand me? This Skarrin—this lord in Mante—" She fell silent again, leaning her chin on her arm, resting on her knee, and there was a line between her brows, in the fading of the light. "There are qhal and there are qhal, and Skarrin's is an old name, Vanye, a very old name."

"Do you know him?"

"If he is what I think he is—I know *what* he is; and I tell thee there is no risk we have ever run—" Her fist clenched. "Only believe what I tell thee: we have no time with this man."

"*What* is he?"

"Something I hoped did not exist. Perhaps I am wrong." She sighed and worked the fingers of that hand. "Talk of something else."

"Of what?"

"Of anything."

He drew a breath. He cast back. It was Morija came to mind. It always did. But darker things overshadowed it—a keep surrounded with flood. A forest, haunted with things which did not love human or qhal. Of his cousin. But that was a memory too fraught with dark things too.

"At least we are warmer," he said, desperate recourse to the weather.

"And dry," she said.

"Good grazing here. A few days," he said. *"Liyo,*—we can rest a few days. The horses will not take more of this."

"Vanye—"

"Forgive me."

"No, thee is right, but we have no choice. Vanye—I *had* no choice."

It was not their moving on that she meant. Her voice trembled.

"I know that," he said, no steadier.

She looked at him and reached out to his arm, a light touch which jolted him like hot iron, drew him out of despair and absorbed his attention so thoroughly a score of enemies could have ridden down on them and come second in his mind.

No, he had wit to think, but not much beyond that. Her arms clenched about him. Her mouth met his. There was precious little more to do, surrounded by enemies, under arms, with no rest to be had and no leisure to spend unwary.

There will never be a time, he thought, in a chill of panic, and held her the tighter, as she held him, in an armored grip become harsh and desperate, with nothing of gentleness about it. *Everyone else has failed her. Too much she has lost, too many dead—For that reason she armed me more than herself, gave me her chiefest weapon; and what did it win us but calamity to our friends, and rage at each other?*

They slept finally, turn and turn about, on the sloping, stony ground where the brush afforded them cover.

He watched her as she slept. He wished—but there was no hope.

Only they managed to heal what was torn, there was that much.

Morgaine waked him toward dawn, a shadow between him and the day. He heard her voice telling him there was breakfast and he murmured an answer, rolled over and favored an aching arm, holding it across him.

"We should move," she said, "a little ways this morning."

"Oh, Heaven," he moaned, and bowed his head between his knees, arms over his neck.

She did not stay to argue. She went back to sit on her saddle, where she had laid out a cold breakfast on the leather wrappings they used for foodstuffs, knowing matters would go her way.

He followed, and sat down on the grass, and ate in silence no different than other silences.

And did not give way to temper, or venture in headlong.

"*Liyo,*" he said when he was toward finishing: "Listen to me. This enemy of yours—whoever he is. You think he will run. But a man will not run, who thinks himself winning. No one can be that cautious."

She said nothing. It was not a frown on her face, only thought.

"Let them lose us," he said. "Let this Skarrin marshal some defense against us. Let him think he has turned us. A man in power—he will not want to give up what he has. He will go nowhere at all. In the meanwhile we will learn this land, we will go slowly—we will gather strength, rest, find a way to him—am I not right?"

Her lips made a taut line. There was warfare in her eyes, unbelief and consideration. "Possibly. Possibly. But being wrong, Vanye—"

"What will a man do who is cornered? He is far more apt to use the gate at Mante and escape us."

He argued for their lives, for sanity and safety.

And she gathered that *thing* into her lap in silence,

the sword, that weapon which was constantly beside her, day and night, and which gave them no peace.

"*Liyo*, you drive this man and you force this man, and what will he do? You will unseat him: his own vassals will question his power; or you will make him desperate—you always strike too hard, *liyo*,—listen to me: you know no moderation with your enemies. You give them no choices and while they have no warning, that serves you well—but you have no subtlety in the field. You are the kind of lord who loses lives—forgive me." His heart beat hard and he gazed up into her eyes in a dread of the things he had to say with brutal force, that the numbness of recent sleep let him say without stumbling, and the quiet of the dawn let her hear without preventing him. "If it were an army with us I should never question you: if you told me to go against any odds, then, I would do that, and trust there was good cause. But you have no army. You have one man. And he is bound, *liyo*, to cover your back and your side, as long as he can; and he will do that. But he is one man, all the same, and someday, if you keep on as you are, you will lose him, because he will die before he lets you go down first."

The frown had deepened on her face. There was storm in her eyes. "I can guard my own back. I need no fools to kill themselves, plague take you, I have had enough of fools to fling themselves in my way—"

"It is your back I am talking about."

Her breath came hard. His own did. "And I am talking about fools," she said. "Bron's sort. Chei's sort. Arunden, for another." Her enemies saw that look. It had been a long time since she had turned it on him. "Ten thousand men at Irien, who would not hold where I told them to hold, no, they must get to the fore of me, because I am there and their damnable pride makes them do what no lord could order them to do in cold blood, if it means charging a wide open gate—"

"That is what you are doing now. That is what I am objecting to, *liyo*. Do you not see it?"

There was shock in her eyes, and outrage, a shake of her head. "Thee is—"

"I am telling you that you are *wrong*. I do not do that often. And you do not want to hear me because you suppose I do not want the same thing that you want. But that is how much I love you: I do not know enough to understand all the why of the things you do, but I stake my soul that you are right; I have sworn to go on with or without you, *liyo,* and if that is true, then listen to me, will you listen, if you do not think me an utter fool?"

"I am listening," she said in a different and milder voice.

"Be the wind. Do not make our enemy afraid. If he hears reports what happened south of here, he will use his power. He has men to send. He has ten thousand things to try before he is out of resources. He will not run at the first whisper of war. He will attack. And we will be the wind again and go find him in his lair."

"So easily. Did thee ever take Myya?"

Heaven! she has a sharp edge when the swords are out.

"No," he said reasonably, quietly. It is tactic. Lord in Heaven, she knows only the attack, never defense, even with me. "But then, I was one man. They did not take me. And if I had aimed at the Myya-lord's life, I would have taken him, do you doubt it?"

She thought on that point, long and long, with that worried line between her brow.

"Liyo, they are all about us. They are watching the road. All we need do is stay quiet, and I do not think, I cannot believe that the rumor of a rumor will send this qhal-lord running with his tail tucked. No. Being a man used to power, he will likeliest strike first at his own folk, to subdue any disloyalty, and only then think of us; and when he hears we are only two—"

"With a gate-weapon. *That* is what we may well face if he has time to marshal his strength. Whatever he has, he will use."

"He might use it by the time we could get there. We can*not* go there with enough speed. And we would be spent. So let him lay his plans. We can turn them."

She let go her breath, and slid *Changeling* between

her knees, hands on the quillons that were the dragon's arms, resting her head against the hilt.

Very, very long she rested there—thinking, he knew, thinking and thinking.

He rested too, arm on knee and chin on arm, wondering where her thoughts were going, into what nooks that she would report to him, unraveling all his arguments, going far beyond him, telling him new and terrible things.

Then she lifted her head. "Aye," she said. "But it is a fearful risk, Vanye."

All along, he had used argument like weapons in drill—one tactic, the next, the next in despair that any would suffice: only now he heard what she was saying and realized it was agreement.

Then, as always when he had won some lesser point, the doubts came to him. What he truly, at the depth of his heart, yearned for, was for his liege to bring up some miracle, some assurance that she knew precisely how to get into Mante and overcome their enemy.

Knowing that she had no such resource, and that she surrendered her instincts for berserker attack, to his for stealth and stalking, against an enemy of her own kind—

It was as if a weight had come down on him, of the sort that he was not accustomed to bear. And perhaps some of it had left her shoulders. She gazed at him with an expression he could not read, but a less anguished one—perhaps thinking, perhaps planning again, at a range still beyond him.

He earnestly hoped so. For when it came to qhal, he had no idea at all of their limits.

Chapter Twelve

The riders gathered again in a place near the road, and Chei leaned on the saddle of the big roan, weary, and feeling the weight of the mail on his shoulders, in a dizziness in which his very body seemed diminished, the light dimmed, the voices about him become strange, calling him 'my lord' and speaking to him with courtesies. The qhal who served him were not confused. Certainly a few of the humans with him measured the difference in his stature and saw his apparent youth and thought treasonous thoughts, but had they lifted daggers against him, there were enough of his own folk about him to protect him, and there was the captain of Skarrin's warders, who was bound, under present and ironical circumstance, to protect him.

They were a few more than twoscore—of all that company that had left Morund-keep, of the levies; and ten—those men of Skarrin's who had joined them at Tejhos-gate. The rest were dead or scattered or wounded too severely to continue; and it had needed at least half a score men to leave in charge of the wounded, but he had left six and bidden them stay camped where they were for fear the hillmen might hit them on the way back to Morund. That was how desperate things had become.

This open sky is madness, Chei thought. The open blue above them, the land laid open to any witness, shivered through his nerves as if he lay naked to his enemies, though he remembered fighting in such land before, in times that humans had come deep within the plains. Something deep as instinct pulled him in two directions, and feared nameless things.

Most of all, the one he would have turned to for advice was not there, and whenever he turned and looked about him he missed that face, which shifted and changed from silver-haired to red to palest gold like some reflection in troubled water: Pyverrn. Jestryn. Bron. The void ached in him, in a place where the voices could not reach, a point at which all memory found anchor. Qhiverin-Gault-Chei, all alone among the men who followed him, longed for a familiar haven, even if the nature of it confounded itself between stone walls and the closeness of forest—

But his enemy, the enemy which lay hidden somewhere in this place, did not shift like sun on water: of him, of her, of the man he was and the man who pursued, he could not think clearly at all: it was like trying to look at the sun itself, a glare in which no shape was distinguishable.

"The troops from Mante are coming south to meet us," he told his followers, as he paced the red horse along the roadside, where they formed up. "The captain affirms that. We will have reinforcements. And we will not close with our enemy, now we know what we face." The red horse shifted under him and he curbed it, riding it back and forth past his listeners, silver-haired and dark, qhal and human. "But there are other ways. Those of you who have been loyal to me—I will reward after this. Count on it. Those of you who are human I will gift with land. Do you hear me? For those of you who follow me, I will give you the holdings of every man who fled. I will have it known how I pay loyalty—and deserters. We will settle this business, we will settle it on our terms, and give Mante's troops the leavings. Our enemies have gone into the land, that is what they have done; but they do not know their way—and we do. I want this pair. *I want them.* Need I say how much?"

"I have found a place," Vanye said, when they found each other after scouting afoot up and down the area, the gray horse and the white left in hiding the other side of the hill.

"Good," Morgaine said, wiping her brow, "because there is nothing in the other direction."

It was a place they rode to then, where the rains had washed beneath a sandstone cap, and where still a little water ran in a sandy bed, folded on either side by hills and closed round by thorn and a scattered few trees.

And no better place to hide indeed had they found.

It was cold rations and not so much as fire to boil water, but it was rest; it was respite from the pace they had set, and it was a chance for the horses to recover their strength, if it meant walking afield and bringing grass to them to keep them hidden.

So he did, and curried them both till their coats shone, did a bit of work with Siptah's left hind shoe, and afterward lay in the sun and slept, while Morgaine worked at the horses' trail-worn gear. Then it was turn about while she slept, and after that a leisurely supper of cold sausage and cheese and waybread.

It was the last of the cordial they shared, the last sweet taste of arrhendur honey.

They watched the sun go down over the hill in a film of cloud and silken colors, and they sat a while under a golden twilight, leaned shoulder against shoulder and watched the horses drink from the rill and eat the forage he had gotten for them in places he did not think cutting would be evident.

He was content. Morgaine leaned back against the hill and smiled at him in her turn, one of her rare, kindly smiles. The quiet, and the brief, fond glance of her eyes set his heart to racing as if they were both be-spelled. Twilight touched her slanted cheekbones, touched her gray eyes and silver hair and the edges of the mail of her over-sleeves, the black leather, the buckles of her armor, and—like a watchful familiar, the dragon-sword lying beside her against a stone. Its ruby eyes winked red and wicked.

I am here, it said. *I never sleep.*

But it was familiar to him too. Like Morgaine—her

silences, the little shifts of her expression which he could read or thought he read—as now he read something in her level, continual stare which had the silence of the night about it, and the dying light dancing in gray, qhalur eyes and a face every line of which he knew in his sweetest and most terrible dreams.

"How long," she said at last, "does thee think to camp here?"

He frowned as he found himself suddenly back in an argument he had thought he had just won. *"Liyo,* do not think of it. Do not think of when. *Stay camped,* do nothing. Do not move or stir: let the enemy do that, that is my counsel in the matter."

"Until winter sets in?" A frown leapt to her eyes. "It—"

"A few days, for Heaven's own sake. A few days. Five. I do not know."

He had not wanted debate with her. He found his muscles gone tense, his breathing quickened; and she dejectedly flung a pebble into the little rill that ran at their feet.

Fret and fret, she would; she could not stay still, could not delay, could not rest, as if no other thought would stay in her head.

"We cannot wait here for the snows."

"God in Heaven, *listen* to me. Let them move. Let us find out what they will do. That is the purpose of this."

"In the meanwhile—"

"God help us. Tomorrow—tomorrow I will scout out and around."

"We will," she said.

"You can stay in—"

"We can gain a few leagues north. That is all. If the next camp is not so comfortable, then the one after—"

He rested his brow against his joined hands. "Aye."

"Vanye, I take your advice—we go slowly. We let the horses build back their strength. But we dare not be further from that gate than we can reach—whatever the lord in Mante decides to do."

"Let him! Whatever he will do, let him! He will come after us. He will try us. He will not bolt."

"We are risking everything on that. Thee knows."

"Why?" he asked. "Tell me why this lord should leave his people?"

"It is possible that they are *not* his people."

He had thought that he had the shape of things, in this strange war that stretched from land to land, with curving horizons and stars too few or too many and moons that came and went. He tried to make a wise answer to that, so she should not think all her teaching wasted.

"You mean that he might be a human man, in qhalur shape."

"It is the name," she said.

"Skarrin?" It had no qhalur sound. But there were qhal who had uncommon names.

"It is a name in a very old language. I do not know where he should have heard it. Perhaps it is all chance. Languages have coincidence. But this, on a qhal—this name: there are among the gate worlds, a kind older than the qhal. And such of them as survive—are very dangerous."

"What are you saying—older than the qhal? Who is older?"

"Older than the calamity the qhal know. Did I ever say it had only happened but the once?"

He said nothing. He scarcely understood the first calamity, how the qhal had made the gates and made time flow amiss, till Heaven set matters straight again, or as straight as matters could be, where gates remained live and potent, pouring their magics (*their power,* Morgaine insisted, *do not be superstitious*) into worlds where qhal survived.

"Thee does not understand."

He shook his head ruefully. "No."

"I do not know," she said. "Only the name troubles me. A name and not a name. In that language Skarrin means an outsider. A foreigner."

The dark was gathering. The first stars were out. He crossed himself against the omen, whatever it should mean.

"My father," Morgaine said, "was one such."

He looked at her as if some chasm had opened at his feet, and all of it dark. She had named comrades from before his time—from before he or his father before him was ever born.

Of kin she had never spoken. She might have risen out of the elements, out of moonbeams, out of the tales of his people.

I am not qhal, she had said time and again. And at one time: *I am halfling.*

"Are you saying this Skarrin—then—is kin of yours?"

"None, that I know."

"Who *was* your father?"

"An enemy." She cast another pebble into the darkening water, and did not look at him. "In a land before yours. He is dead. Let it rest."

He would not have trod on that ground for any urging.

"He was qhal, to your way of thinking," Morgaine said. "Give it peace. It has no significance here. Anjhurin was his name. You have heard it. Now forget ever you heard it. This Skarrin is no one I know, but my name might warn him, changed as it is."

He took in his breath and let it go again, stripping a bit of grass in his fingers, looking only at that. And for a long time neither of them spoke.

He shrugged. "I will scout out tomorrow," he said, to have the peace back, to ease her mind, however he could. "When I go for forage. There might be something over the hills."

"Aye," she said, and shifted round to lean her shoulder against his back. He sighed at the relief that gave the center of his back, against the armor-weight. "But two of us would—"

"I. Do we need start every bird and rabbit 'twixt us and Mante?" He felt a sense of impending calamity, such that his breath came in with a shiver, and he let it go again. "I will go."

"Afoot?"

"No. I can ride the stream-course. There will be no difficulty." He sighed against her weight on his shoulders, and looked at the sky in which the stars had begun to appear. "We should rest," he said sullenly.

"Is thee angry?"

He drew in his breath, and shifted about to face her. *Aye,* he was about to say. But the sober, gentle look she gave him was rare enough he hesitated to offend it.

She was always and always the same, always devil-driven, always restless, incapable even of reason.

And she had brought them through, always, somehow—was always beforehand, always quicker than her enemies expected, and not *where* they expected.

She might drive a sane man mad.

"Vanye?" she asked.

"What more?" he said shortly.

She was silent then, and sat back with a wounded look that shot through him and muddled all the anger he could muster.

It was not, not, Heaven knew, the face she turned to the world. Only to him. Only to him, in all the world.

He got to his feet and snatched up a wildflower at his other side, knelt and solemnly offered the poor thing to her, all closed up for the night as it was. Bruised, it had a strong grass smell, the smell of spring lilies, that reminded him suddenly of rides on a brown pony, of—Heaven knew—his boyhood.

Her eyes sought up to his. Her mouth curved at the edges, and solemnly she took it, her fingers brushing his hand. "Is this all thee offers?"

"Aye," he said, off his balance in his foolishness: she always had the better of him with words—was not, he suddenly thought, taking it for a jest; or was; he did not know, suddenly; it was like everything between them. He gestured desperately beyond his shoulder. "Or," he said briskly, deliberately perverse, "I might find others, if I walked along the stream there. I might bring you a handful."

Her eyes lightened, went solemn then, and slowly she rose up to her knees and put her arms about his neck, whereat the world went giddy as the smell of flowers.

"Do it tomorrow," she said, a long moment later; and gently she began the buckles of his armor, that she had helped him with a hundred times to different purpose.

Changeling slipped from its place and fell with a rattle as they made themselves a nest there of their cloaks and blankets. She reached out and laid the dragon sword down beside them, the hilt toward her hand, and loosed his hair from the ivory pin.

So he laid his own sword, close by the other side. They never quite forgot. There had been too many ambushes, that they could ever quite forget.

It was up and prepare to move at sunrise, in the dewy chill and the damp; and Vanye shut his eyes, wrapped in his blanket, leaning his back against Morgaine's knee and letting her comb and braid his hair this morning, carefully and at leisure, which a lady might do for her man. He sighed in that quiet, and that contentment.

There was no blight could touch the hour, nothing at all wrong with the world or with anyone in it, and the quick deft touch of Morgaine's fingers near lulled him to sleep again. He shut his eyes till she pushed his head forward to plait the braid, and rested so, head bowed, till she tied it off and brought it through and pinned it in its simple knot at the back of his neck.

So she was done with him. So it was time to think about the day. He leaned his head back against her knees and sighed to a touch of her fingers pulling at a lock by his temple. "Does thee intend to tie this someday? Or go blind by degrees?"

"Do what you like." No blade came on an *uyo's* hair, except for judicious barbering, at his own hand. But his hair was twice hacked and hewn and grown out again, and truth, some of it was often in his eyes. "Cut it," he said, nerving himself. His Kurshin half was aghast. But it was Chya clan which had taken him from his outlawry, it was a Chya he served, it had been a Chya who had proved his true kinsman; and a Chya was what he became, less and less careful of proprieties. He faced about and leaned on one hand, while she took her Honor-blade and cut the straying lock; and cut it again, and cut another.

At that he opened his mouth to protest, then shut his eyes to keep the hair out and bit his lip.

"It was another one."

"Aye," he said. He was determined not to be superstitious; he prepared himself to see her cast the locks away, he would not play the fool with her, not make her think him simple.

But she played him that kind of turn she did so often, and put the locks of hair into his hand as if she had known Kurshin ways.

He scattered them on the moving water, since they had no fire; so any omen was gone, and no one could harm his soul.

And he turned on his knee and settled again on both knees, like a man who would make a request.

"*Liyo*—"

"I have a name."

She had had some lover before him. He knew that now. But into that he did not ever want to ask. Folly to look back, profoundest folly, and against all her counsel—

She had so little she could part with. Least of all her purposes.

"Morgaine," he said, whispered. Her name was illomen. It burned with the legends of kings and sorceries, and too much of death. Morgaine Angharan was the other face, not the one he loved. For the woman he knew, he did not have a name at all. But he tried to fit that one around her, and took both her hands in his as he knelt and she sat on a stone as it were some high queen's throne, under the last few stars. "Listen, my liege—"

"Do not you kneel," she said harshly, and clenched her hands on his. "How often have I told thee?"

"Well, it is my habit." He began to get up; then sank back again, jaw set. "It still is."

"You are a free man."

"Well, then, I do what I please, do I not? And since you are a lord, my lady-liege, and since I am only

dai-uyo at best, I still call you my liege and I still go on
my knees when I see fit, for decency, my liege. And I
ask you—" She started to speak and he pressed her
hands, hard. "While I am gone, stay close, take no
chances, and for the love of Heaven—trust me, however long. If I meet trouble I can wait it out until they
leave. If I have to wonder about your riding into it,
then I have to do something else. So do me the grace
and wait here, and be patient. Then neither of us will
have to worry, is that not reasonable?"

"Aye," she said quietly. "But turn and turn about.
The next one is mine."

"Liyo—"

But he had already lost that argument for the time.
He gathered himself up and dusted off his knees, and
went to saddle Arrhan.

The land was difficult beyond the camp they had
made—little wooded, flatter for a space: he had known
that much when he had chosen the camp they had, a
retreat from the furthermost point he had reached in
his last searching.

Now it was careful riding, by every low spot he
could find that could shelter them as they went, and a
good deal of it east rather than north. It was the
water-courses he had most hope in, and most fear of:
it was water that bound a man to his course in land
like this, water by which their enemies could find
them, nearly as surely as they might have by the Road
itself.

But he spent some time afoot, and finally flat on his
belly on a hill from which he had vantage, scanning
every rabbit-track in the grassland below, every flight
of birds, and listening—listening finally alone, until
the sounds of the land began to speak to him, the
ordinary chirp of insects in the sun, the birds that
ought to sing in the thicket and out on the meadows.

He was alone. There was no one out there: he was
as sure of that as he dared be sure of anything with an
unknown enemy.

Still—he found no sane way to cross that plain,

except to go far to the east and as the stream bore: to cross it even by night, would leave a track plain enough for a child to follow the next day.

That was no good. If they did that, there was no good choice but to pick up speed again, and then they would be no better off than before.

A plague on her haste and her insistence. He lay with his chin on his hand and with the sun on his back overheating the layers of armor, and considered again what his chances were of reporting to her and gaining her agreement, after a day's delay, that the proper course was not northward, but considerably eastward and out of the direct course she wanted to take.

Her anger when it came to her safety was a matter of indifference to him—except that his liege, having gotten a purpose in her mind, was likely to strike out on her own in what direction she chose, leaving him to follow; and that prospect left him contemplating arguments, and reason, and unreason, and the fact that he had no means but force truly to restrain her—and restrain her by that means, he could not, by *ilin*-oath, by *uyin*-oath, by the deeper things between them, not to save either of their lives, so long as she was in her right mind.

And Heaven help them both, she was oftener right even when she was not sane, or at least retrieved her mistakes with more deftness than anyone he knew; and he was still uneasy that he had persuaded her against her instincts. Doubt ate at his gut, a continual moil of anxiety in all this ride out here separate of her, and the only solace in it was the knowledge that she was well-situated, in no likelihood of attracting attention, and in a way to defend herself if trouble happened on her.

It was that things had shifted between them, he told himself; it was the muddle things had gotten to that made him unreasonably anxious. They sinned before Heaven with his oath and hers, and with no priest, and with ten thousand trifling laws he had no regard of— laws it was mad to regard, when there were so many greater and bloody sins on them.

He was half-witted with thinking about her, he had done what he had sworn he would never do and let that thinking come between them in daylight, using that bond to gain his way—he had done one thing after another he had sworn he would not do with her. Decisions that she would make, he had argued to take onto his shoulders when he well knew he was not, of the two of them, the wiser—

If he were back in Myya lands, he thought, with his cousins hunting him, he would lie low for the whole day exactly where he had left Arrhan down under the hill. He would watch everything that moved by day, every hawk that flew, every start of game; and move again only at night. But Morgaine was left worrying back there; and he could never have persuaded her to wait day upon day on him—he could not bear the worry of it himself, to be truthful, if matters were reversed; or keep her still beyond half a day as matters were, unless he could demonstrate some danger to her.

It was a long effort for their enemies to search all the watercourses in the plains.

But long efforts bore fruit, if they had long enough.

And having thought that three times through, he could not rest where he was and he could not risk anything further. He edged down off the height and gathered up Arrhan where he had left her in a brushy hollow; and led her by the dry streambed which had been his route up to this hill.

It merged with yet another narrow water-cut, and took him back into sparsely wooded hills.

Then he mounted up and rode, quietly, back the way he had come, far and far through the hills to the place where the dry bed joined the water.

Beyond that he rode the stream itself for a space, the water only scarcely over Arrhan's hooves, but it served.

It served, certainly, better than the streamside had served another rider.

He saw the mark among bent reeds, the water-filled

impression of a horse's hoof, and searched his mind whether Arrhan had misstepped when he had passed this bank in the morning.

No, he thought, with the blood going colder and colder in him. No. She had not. Not here. They had gone straight along as they went now, making no track at all. He remembered the reeds. He remembered the little shelf of rock where it came down from the hill.

He saw the track merge with the stream further on, a single rider.

Morgaine would not have broken her word to him without reason. He believed that implicitly. She would not have followed, except something had gone very wrong.

There were further marks, down the stream where the water became momentarily and treacherously deeper and a rider had to take to the waterside. He had done so. So had this rider; and one mark showed a shod horse, a shoe of a pattern different than Siptah's and headed the wrong direction.

There was cold dread in him now. He scanned the hills about him.

If he had been in Myya lands again, his Myya cousins looking to have his head on a pike, he would do what he had told Morgaine he would do: he would go to earth and lie close until the hunters had passed and failed to find him for a fortnight or more.

But then he had not had a woman waiting for him, in the direction the rider was going, camped right on the stream-course as if it were some roadside, now the hunters were out. She would not be sitting blind: she would have vantage from higher on the hill—he took that for granted. But there was the horse to worry for—more visible, and tracking the ground despite all they could do to keep cover. If someone rode through, looking with a skilled eye—never grant that every man in Gault's party was a fool, even granted one of them had been careless enough to let his horse misstep in this thread of a stream.

He put Arrhan to more speed. He scanned the hills about him, dreading the sight of riders, finding only, in one place between the hills, a fan of tracks in the grass, as riders had come together and joined forces.

Thereafter tracks met the stream and the bank was well-trampled, the mud churned by the hooves of more than a score of horses.

He followed, trying desperately to recollect every stone and every vantage of the camp they had. It was well enough, he thought: their numbers were only an advantage—they could not go silently, Heaven knew that they were no woodsmen, the way they bunched together; and Morgaine with the least of her weapons could take them, once she had taken some position of defense: the greatest worry she must have was whether her companion was going to come riding in to put himself in danger.

Only—he thought of the pyx he wore against his heart and thought of gate-weapons with a lingering chill—it might not be Gault's folk. It might be something else, out of Mante.

Even if it were not, she would hesitate to use the sword that was her chiefest weapon, for fear of alerting other forces Mante might have sent out southward to find them—

Or through the gate at Tejhos, coming at them from both sides.

Heaven knew what their limit was.

And if one of them had so much as what he carried, it could reshape *Changeling's* gate-force, warp it and draw it in such fashion that *Changeling* became wildly unpredictable, a danger to flesh and substance anywhere between: he had seen one of the *arrhim*, a gate-warder, brave that danger in the arrhend war— and lose—which sight haunted him every time he thought of what he carried.

The gift was for way-finding, was for light in dark places, for startling an ignorant enemy but not as a weapon—never as that, for someone who rode as shieldman to Morgaine Angharan.

He dared not use it now, in any hope of warning her. He had given his sword to Chei and not reclaimed it—not, in all else they had done, turned him out utterly defenseless.

He had no weapon now but his bow.

And Heaven knew how far he was behind.

He listened as he rode the center of the stream, close to their camp. He stopped Arrhan where there was brush enough to hide her, and slid down, and stood for a moment steadying her so that he could hear the least stirring of the wind.

A bird sang, natural, long-running song, but it was not a sound that reassured him. There were the tracks, evident now at this muddy bank, and hours old.

Now it was a hard choice what to do. There was no safe place further than this. He took one risk, and made a faint, careful bird-call: I am here, that said, no more than that.

No answer came to him.

He bit his lip furiously, and put a secure tie on Arrhan, took his bow and quiver and slipped away into the brush, onto the hillside. He was not afraid, not yet. There were too many answers. There was every chance she had heard him and dared not risk an answer.

He went hunter-fashion, stopping often to listen. He found the tracks again where he picked up the stream course; and when he had come within sight of the place where they had camped, beneath the hill, Siptah was gone, and with one glance he was reassured.

Good, he thought, she has taken him, the tack is gone.

But there were marks of the enemy's horses, abundant there, trampling on Siptah's and Arrhan's marks, and no matter the skill of the rider, there was no way not to leave some manner of a trail for a good tracker well sure where that trail began.

She would lead them, that was what she would do. She would lead them around this hill and that until they came straight into one of her ambushes.

But so many riders had gone away from this point, left and right, obliterating any tracks the gray stud might have made, the tracks they could have followed; and left him the necessity to cast about beyond the trampled area—and cast about widely he could not, without risking ambush.

Best, he thought, find out what was still here.

He moved, crouched behind what cover there was, along the flank of the hill, among the rocks, stopping now and again to listen. There was nothing astir but the wind.

Then a bird flew up, taking wing east of his backtrail.

He froze where he was, a long time, shifting only the minuscule degree that kept his legs from cramping.

A bird-call sounded, directly on his track.

He calmly, carefully scanned the hillsides and the points of concealment so far as he could from his own cover, not willing to give way to any feeling, not fear, not self-reproach for anything he might have done and not done: there was only the immediate necessity to get off this hillside and take the enemy, whatever had happened behind him, else he might never find her.

He waited what he judged long enough to make them impatient, then moved, quietly, behind what cover the brush and the rocks afforded, without retracing his steps into what might now be tracking him.

They meant him to go to his horse. They had found Arrhan, that was what had happened, and they were effectively advising him where the ambush was, and where he had to go, if he did not want to flee them afoot.

Where is she? was his constant thought. The whole area had become hostile ground, enemy marks everywhere, his horse discovered, and no sign of Morgaine.

If she had heard the bird-calls, she was at least warned.

He sank down behind a rock to wait a moment, to see what they would do, and there was not a sound, not a stir below.

Not even the wind breathed.

Then a pebble rolled, somewhere on the bare rock around the shoulder of the hill above him. A step whispered across stone and left it again.

Carefully he took three arrows from his quiver and fitted one to the string, braced himself comfortably and waited with the bow unbent, not to cramp his arm, for one quick shot if need be.

The step came closer and the sweat ran on his brow and down his sides, one prickling trail and another.

The sound stopped a moment, then advanced again, a man walking on the rock a moment, then disturbing the brush.

He drew a breath and bent the bow all in one motion.

And held his shot in a further intake of breath as a man in a bright mail shirt saw him and slid down the crumbling hill face. His bow tracked the target.

"Vanye," Chei breathed, landing on two feet in front of him. "For God's sake—I followed you. I *have* been following you. What did you expect when you told me go back? Put that down!"

"Where is she?"

"Gone. Put down the bow. Vanye—for God's sake—I saw them pass; I followed them. There was nothing I could do—"

"Where is she?"

"Northward. That is where they will have taken her."

His heart went to ice. He kept the bow aimed, desperate, and motioned with it. "Clear my path."

"Will you kill me too?" Chei's eyes were wide and outraged. "Is that what you do with your friends?"

"Out of my way."

"Your *friends,* Vanye," Chei repeated, and flattened himself against the rock as he edged past. "Do you know the word? *Vanye!*"

He turned from Chei to the way ahead, to run, remembering even then the whistle he had heard downslope; and saw an archer standing in his path as a weight smashed down between his shoulders and staggered him.

He rolled, straight down the hillside, tucked his shoulder in a painful tangle of armor straps and bow and quiver. His helm came off; he lost the bow; and went up-ended and down again on the grass of the slope.

He came up blind, and ripped his Honor-blade from its sheath, hearing the running steps and the rattle of armor, seeing a haze of figures gathering about him on the hillside, above and below him.

"Take him alive!" someone shouted. "Move!"

He yelled out at them and chose a target and a way out, cut at a qhal who missed his defense, met him with a shock of steel against leather and flesh; but in that stroke his foot skidded on the bloody grass and there was another enemy on him, with more coming. He recovered his balance on both feet and laid about him with a clear-minded choice of threats, finding the rhythm of their attacks and their hesitations for a moment; and then losing it as other attackers swarmed in at another angle.

A man, falling, seized him by the leg. He staggered and others hit him and wrapped a hold about him, inside his guard; and overbalanced him and bore him down in a skidding mass of bodies.

They brought up against a rock together. It jolted the men who held him and he smashed an elbow into one body and a fist into another's head as he struggled free and levered himself toward his feet, staggering against the tilted surface as he tried to clear his knife hand of the dazed man who clung to it.

Steps rushed on him, a shadow loomed out of the sun at his right, and others hit him, carrying him backward against the rock. The point of a sword pressed beneath his chin and forced his head back.

Chei's face cleared out of the haze and the glare, Chei's face with a grin like the wolves themselves, and a half a score of qhalur and human faces behind him.

"Ah," Chei said, "very close, friend. But not good enough."

Chapter Thirteen

They flung him down on the trampled ground of the streamside, and he did not know for a moment where he was, except it was Chei sitting cross-legged on the grass, and Chei's face was a mask behind which lived something altogether foreign.

Chei was dead, as Bron was dead. He knew it now. As many of these men's comrades were dead, several wounded, and he was left alone with them to pay for it. That was the logic he understood. It was not an unreasonable attitude in men or qhal, not unreasonable what they had done in the heat of their anger, with a man who had cost them three dead on the selfsame hillside.

Not unreasonable that Chei should look on him now as he did, coldly—if it were Chei and Chei's reasons. But it was not. He was among men who fed their enemies to beasts.

Morgaine, he thanked Heaven, had ridden clear. She had escaped them, he was sure of it. She had ridden out, she was free out there, and armed with all her weapons.

She might well be anywhere in the country round about. Heaven knew, the same stream that had covered his tracks could cover hers—in the opposite direction, he thought; toward the Road; which their enemies must have thought of, and searched, and failed.

She might have fled toward the north and east as the Road led, thinking to find him by cutting into the country along the way; but that was so remote a chance.

Gone on to the Gate itself . . . that was possible; but he did not think so: she would not ride off and leave him to fall into ambush.

Unless . . . O God, unless she were wounded, and had no choice.

And he did not reckon he would have the truth from these men by asking for it.

"Why are you here?" Chei asked him, as if he had a list of questions in mind and any of them would do. "Where do you come from? Where are you going?"

They had not so much as bound him. It was hard enough to lift his cheek from the mire and regard Chei through whatever was running into his eyes and blurring his vision.

"She has authority to be here," he said, which he reckoned for the truth, and perhaps enough to daunt a qhal.

"Are you full human?"

He nodded and shifted his position, and whatever was dripping, started down his cheek. He dragged his arms under him, and felt, beneath the mail and leather, the pressure of the little box against his heart. They had not discovered it. He prayed Heaven they would not, though they had taken his other weapons, from Honor-blade to boot knife. And the arrhendur sword in Chei's lap he well remembered.

"Is she qhal?"

He had answered that so often he had lied before he realized it, a nod of his head. "Aye."

"Are you her lover?"

He did not believe he had heard that question. He was outraged. Then he knew it was one most dangerous to him. And that Chei in Chei's own mind—had his own opinion. "No," he said. "I am her servant."

"Who gave her that weapon?"

"Its maker. Dead now. In my homeland." His arms trembled under him. It was the cold of the ground and the shock of injury. Perhaps also it was fear. There was enough cause for that. "Long ago—" he began, taking breath against the pain in his gut. "Something happened with the gates. It is still happening—somewhere, she says. Against that, the sword was made. Against that—"

"Bring that thing near a gate, Man, and there will *be* death enough."

He started to agree. Then it came to him that they seemed to know—at what range from a gate the sword was too perilous to use. And that put Morgaine in danger.

"What does she seek in Mante?"

The tremors reached his shoulders, tensed his gut so that the pain went inward, and he wished, for his pride's sake, he could only prevent the shaking from his voice.

"What does she seek in Mante?"

"What she would have sought in Morund," he said, "if we had not had other advice."

Chei? he wondered, gazing into that face. Chei? Is there anything left?

Can you remember, man? Is there anything human?

"What advice would that be?"

"That you were unreasonable. Chei knows." He heaved himself upward another hand's-breadth to ease the pain in his hip, where they had kicked him, and the tendon there was bruised. He determined to sit up and risk a cracked skull from the ones behind him; and discovered that there was no part of him that their kicks or the butts of their lances had not gotten to. It was blood running down his face. It splashed dark onto his leg when he sat up, and he wiped at the cut on his brow with a muddy hand. "My lady's mission here—you very well know."

"Death," Chei said, "ultimate death—for every qhal."

"She intends no harm to you—"

"Death."

It seemed the sum of things. There was no peace, then, once the qhal-lords knew what Morgaine purposed with the gates. He gazed bleakly at Chei, and said nothing.

"Where will your lady have gone?"

"To Mante."

"No," Chei said quietly. "I doubt that she has. I

remember, friend. I remember a night in Arunden's camp—you and she together—do you recollect that?"

He did. There was altogether too much Chei knew; and he despaired now of all the rest.

"I rather imagine," Chei said, "that your lady is somewhere in these hills. I rather imagine that she would have tried to warn you—if she could reach you in time. Failing that—she will follow if we move. If we were foolish enough to kill you, then she might even come looking for revenge—would she not?"

"I do not know," he said. "She might well have ridden for Mante."

"I do not think so," Chei said. "I think she is waiting for dark."

He said nothing. He tensed muscles, testing whether he could rely on his legs if he made a lunge for Chei's throat. To kill this man might at least keep some knowledge out of the hands of the qhal.

It might put some enemy less dangerous in command of this band, at least.

"I think," Chei said, "she will come close to see whether you are alive. Afoot, by stealth. And perhaps for your sake she might come and talk to us a little closer."

"Set me free," Vanye said. "I will find her and give her whatever message you wish. And come back to you."

There was startled laughter.

"I am Kurshin," Vanye said. "I do not break an oath."

Chei regarded him in silence a long time, eyes flickering slowly, curiously, as if he might be reaching deep into something not qhal and not familiar to him. The laughter died away.

"Chei?" Vanye said, ever so quietly, seeking after whatever balance might have shifted.

"Possibly that is so," Chei said then, blinking. "I would not say that it is not. But who knows what you would bring back? No. She will come in for you. All you have to do is cry out—and you can do that with no persuasion, or with whatever persuasion it—"

He sprang, sliding in the mud, for Chei's throat; and everyone moved, Chei scrambling backward, the men around them moving to stop him. Chei fended his first hold off and he grabbed Chei's shirt and drove a hand toward Chei's throat to break it, but hands dragged at him, and the blow lost force as they bore him under a tide of bodies and against the edge of the rock.

There were more blows. He protected himself as he could and the armor saved him some of it. He hoped that he had broken Chei's neck and saved them all from the damage Chei might do—but it was a small hope, dashed when they hauled him up by the hair and Chei looked down at him from the vantage of the rock, smiling a twisted, bloodied smile.

"—with whatever persuasion it takes," Chei said.

"She is not a fool."

"—so she will know you are with us. If she comes in—she will have some care of that fact. Will she not?"

"She is not a fool."

"A fool would kill his hostage. Keep thinking of that."

He made another lunge, while he had the chance. They stopped him. They battered him to the ground and held him there while they worked at his buckles and belts, and when he fought them they put a strap around his neck and cut off his wind.

It was a man of considerable temper, Chei observed, probing with his tongue at the split in his lip: a lunatic temper, a rage that did damage as long as he could free a hand or a knee. But this was the man had wielded the gate-sword. This was the man had taken half his house guard and the most part of the levies.

Another image came to him—a chain was on his leg, and this wild man came riding down on the wolves, leaning from the white horse's saddle to wield his sword like some avenging angel, bloody in the twilight.

This same man, bowing the head to his liege's tempers—defending him with quiet words, glances from

under the brow, measured deference like some high
councillor with a queen—

They had him down, now, having finally discovered
there was no way to deal with him without choking
him senseless. "Do not kill him!" Chei shouted out,
and rose from his seat on the rock and walked the
muddy ground to better vantage over the situation.

They stripped him—he was very pale except his face
and hands, a man who lived his life in armor. Armor
lying beside the little stream—armor lying beside a
river—the same man offering medicines and comfort
to him—

"My lord," someone said, and asked a question.
Chei blinked again, feeling dizzied and strangely ab-
sent from what they did, as if he were only spectator,
not participant.

"Do what you like," he murmured to a question
regarding the prisoner; he did not care to focus on it.
He remembered his anger. And the dead, Jestryn-
Bron. And the sight of his men vanishing into gate-
spawned chaos.

It was the woman he wanted within his reach. It was
the sword, against which there was no power in Mante
could withstand him—the woman with her skills, and
himself with a valued hostage. There was—a thought
so fantastical it dizzied him—power over Mante itself,
a true chance at what they had never dared aim for.

He retired to the rock, sat down, felt its weathered
texture beneath his right hand. He heard commotion
from his men, glanced that way with half attention.
"Let him alone," he said to the man who hovered
near him. "The man will not last till Mante if you go
on, and then what hostage have we against the gate-
weapons? Twilight. Twilight is soon enough."

It was as if the strength the gate had lent him had
begun to dissipate. He heard voices at a distance. He
saw them drag their captive up against one of two
fair-sized trees at the edge of the brush, along the
stream, saw him kick at one of them, and take a blow
in return.

"Stubborn man," he murmured with a pain about

him that might be Jestryn and might be Bron and might be outrage that this man he had trusted had not prevented all the ill that had befallen him.

Or it was pointless melancholy. Sometimes a man newly Changed wept for no cause. Sometimes one grew irrationally angry, at others felt resentments against oneself. It was the scattered memories of the previous tenant, attempting to find place with the new, which had destroyed it.

He had fought this battle before. He knew coldly and calmly what was happening to him, and how to deal with it—how he must to deal with the memories that tried to reorganize themselves, for his heart sped and his body broke out in sweat, and he saw the wolves, the wolves that ep Kantory mustered like demons out of the dark; he heard the breaking of bones and the mutter of wolfish voices as he walked across the trampled ground, to where his men had managed finally to bind the prisoner's hands about the tree.

"Chei—" Vanye said, looking up at him through the blood and the mud. And stirred a memory of a riverbank, and kindness done. It ached. It summoned other memories of the man, other kindnesses, gifts given, defense of him; and murder—Bron's face. "Chei. Sit. Talk with me. I will tell you anything you ask."

Fear touched him. He knew the trap in that. "Ah," he said, and sank down all the same, resting his arms across his knees. "What will you tell me? What have you to trade?"

"What do you want?"

"So you will offer me—what? The lady's fickle favor? I went hunting Gault, *friend*. That is what you left me. And I am so much the wiser for it. I should thank you."

"Chei—"

"I went of my own accord. We discovered things in common. What should I, follow after you till you served me as you served Bron? *I was welcome enough with your enemies.*"

Vanye flinched. But: "Chei," he said reasonably, "Chei—" As if he were talking to a child.

"I will send you to Hell, Vanye. Where you sent Bron."

Vanye's eyes set on his in dismay.

"I say that I was willing. Better to *be* a wolf, than to be the deer. That is what you taught me, *friend*. The boy is older, the *boy* cannot be cozened, the *boy* knows how you lied to him, and how you despised him. Never mind the face, *friend*: I am much, much wiser than the boy you lied to."

"There was no lie. I swear, Chei. On my soul.—*For God's sake, fight him, Chei—Did you never mean to fight him?*"

Chei snatched his knife from its sheath and jerked the man's head back by the braid he wore, held him so, till breath came hard and the muscles that kept the neck from breaking began to weaken. The man's eyes were shut; he made no struggle except the instinctive one, quiet now.

"No more words? No more advice? Are you finished, Man? *Eh?*"

There was no answer.

Chei jerked again and cut across the braid, flung it on the ground.

The man recovered his breath then in a kind of shock, threw his head back with a crack against the tree and looked at him as if he had taken some mortal wound.

It was a man's vanity, in the hills. It was more than that, to this Man. It was a chance stroke, and a satisfaction, that put distress on that sullen face and a crack in that stubborn pride.

Chei sheathed the knife and smiled at human outrage and human frailty and walked away from it.

Afterward, he saw the man with his head bowed, his shorn hair fallen about his face. Perhaps it was the pain of his bruises reached him finally, in the long wait till dark, and his joints stiffened.

But something seemed to have gone from him, all the same.

By sundown he might well be disposed to trade a great deal—to betray his lover, among other things:

the first smell of the iron would come very different to a man already shaken; and that was the beginning of payments . . . his pride, his honor, his lover, his life; and the acquisition of all the weapons the lady held.

Always, Qhiverin insisted, more than one purpose, in any undertaking: it was that sober sense restrained him, where Chei's darkness prevailed: revenge might be better than profit; but profitable revenge was best of all.

And there were those in Mante who would join him, even yet . . . .

Unease suddenly flared in the air, like the opening of a gate. A man of his cried out, and dropped something amid the man's scattered belongings down along the streamside, a mote that shone like a star.

"Do not touch it!" Chei sprang up and strode to the site at the same time as the captain from Mante, and was before him, gathering up that jewel which had fallen before his own man could be a fool and reach for it again—a stone not large enough to harm the bare hand, not here, this far from Mante and Tejhos: but it prickled the hairs at his nape and lit the edges of his fingers in red.

And there was raw fear in the look of the man who had found it.

"My lord," the captain objected. There was fear there, too. Alarm. *That is not for the likes of you,* was what the captain would say if he dared.

But to a lord of Mante, even an exiled one, the captain dared not say that.

Chei stooped and picked up the tiny box which his startled man had dropped amid Vanye's other belongings, and shut the jewel in it. Storm-sense left the air like the lifting of a weight. "I will deliver this," Chei said, staring at the captain. His own voice seemed far away in his ears. He dropped the chain over his head. "Who else should handle it? I still outrank you,— captain."

The captain said nothing, only stood there with a troubled look.

This, a Man had carried. The answering muddle of

thoughts rang like discord, for part of him was human, and part of him despised the breed. That inner noise was the price of immortality. The very old became more and more dilute in humankind: many went mad.

Except the high lord condemned some qhal to bear some favorite of his—damning some rebel against his power, to host a very old and very complex mind, well able to subdue even a qhalur host and sift away all his memories.

From that damnation, at least, his friends at court had saved him, when he had given up Qhiverin's pure blood and Qhiverin's wholly qhalur mind for Gault's, which memories were there too—mostly those which had loved Jestryn when Jestryn was human. And knowledge of the land, and of Gault's allies—and Gault's victims—when Gault was human: but those were fading, as unused memory would.

There were a few things worth saving from that mind, things like the knowledge of Morund's halls and the chance remembrance of sun and a window, a knowledge that, for instance, Ithond's fields produced annually five baskets of grain—some memories so crossed with his own experience at Morund that he was not sure whether they were Gault's recollections or his own.

Gault's war was over. He no longer asserted himself. It was the Chei-self, ironically, which had done it—human and forceful and flowing like water along well-cut channels: young, and uncertain of himself, and willing to take an older memory for the sake of the assurance it offered, whose superstition and doubts scattered and faded in the short shrift the Qhiverin-essence made of it: wrong, wrong, and wrong, the Qhiverin-thoughts said when Chei tried to be afraid of the stone he held. *Let us not be a fool, boy.*

This is power—and the captain has to respect it; and very much wishes he had Mante to consult. And what I can do with it and with what the lady carries, you do not imagine.

"Place your men," he ordered the captain.

"My lord," the man said. Typthyn was his name.

The serpent's man. Skarrin's personal spy.

Chei drew a long breath through his nostrils and looked at the sky, in which the sun had only then passed zenith.

The sun went down over the hill, the shadow came, and they built a fire, careless of the smoke. Vanye watched all this, these slow events within the long misery of frozen joints and swollen fingers. He had not achieved unconsciousness in the afternoon. He had wished to. He wished to now, or soon after they began with him, and he was not sure which would hurt the worse, the burning or the strain any flinching would put on his joints.

He flexed his shoulders such as he could, and moved his legs and arched his spine, slowly, once and twice, to have as much strength in his muscles as he could muster.

In the chance she might come, in the chance his liege, being both wise and clever, might accomplish a miracle, and take this camp, and somehow avoid killing him, remembering—he prayed Heaven—that there was a gate-stone loose and in the hands of an enemy.

But if that miracle happened, and if he survived, then he would have to be able to get on his feet. Then he had to go with her and not slow her down, because there was no doubt there were forces coming south out of Mante, and he must not, somehow must not, hinder her and force her to seek shelter in these too-naked hills, caring for a crippled partner.

A partner fool enough to have brought himself to this.

That was the thing that gnawed at him more than any other—which course he should take, whether he should do everything the enemy wished of him and trust his liege to stay clear-headed; or whether he should refuse for fear she would not, and then be maimed and a burden to her if she did somehow get to him.

Then there was that other thought, coldly reasonable, that love was not enough for her, against what

she served. There had been some man before him.
And she traveled light, and did always the sensible
thing—no need ever fear that she would do something
foolish.

He told himself that: he could do what he liked, cry
out or remain silent, and have the qhal dice him up
piecemeal, and it would do neither harm nor good. He
had been on his own since she rode out of here, and
would be, till the qhal dragged him as far as Mante
and either killed him or, more likely, treated his wounds
and kept him very gently till some qhal claimed him
for his own use.

Or—it was an occasional thought, one he banished
with furious insistence—she might have run straight
into forces sent from Mante, and be pinned down and
unable to come back—or worse; or very much worse.
A harried mind conjured all sorts of nightmares, in the
real and present one of the smell of smoke and the
unpleasant, nervous laughter of men contemplating
another man's slow destruction.

The darkness grew to dusk. The qhal finished their
supper, and talked among themselves.

When Chei came to him, to stand over him in the
shadows and ask him whether he had any inclination
to do what they wanted.

"I will call out to her," Vanye said, not saying what
he would call out, once he should see her. "Only I
doubt she is here to listen. She is well on her way
down the road, that is where she is."

"I doubt that." Chei dropped down to his heels, and
took off the pyx that swung from its chain about his
neck. "Your property."

He said nothing to that baiting.

"So you will call out to her," Chei said. "Do it now.
Ask her to come to the edge of camp—only to talk
with us."

He looked at Chei. Of a sudden his breath seemed
too little to do what Chei asked, the silence of the hills
too great.

"Do it," Chei urged him.

He shaped a cut lip as best he could and whistled, once and piercingly. *"Liyo!"*

And with a thought not sudden, but one that had come to him in the long afternoon: "Morgaine, *Morgaine!* For God's sake hear me! They want to talk with you!"

"That is not enough," Chei said, and opened the box, so that a light shone up on his face from the gate-jewel there. The light glared; flesh crawled. Everything about it was excessive and twisted.

"You have only to feel that thing," Vanye said, "to know there is something wrong in the gate at Mante. Truth, man. I have felt others. I know when one is wrong."

"You—*know.*"

"You have no right one to compare it against. It is wrong. It is pouring force out—" He lost his thought as Chei took the jewel in his fingers and laid it down again in the box, and set the open box on the ground beside him.

"So she will know where you are. Call to her again."

"If she is there, she heard me." He had hope of that small box and its stone. The light that made him visible in the twilight, made Chei a target, if Morgaine were there, if she could be sure enough whether the man kneeling by him was the one she wanted. She might be very accurate—unlike a bowman. Several men might be on their way to the ground before they knew they were under attack.

Or she might, instead, be far on her way to Mante.

"That is not enough," Chei said, and called to the men at the fire in rising. "You can," he said then, looking down, "give her far more reason."

He was not going to put them off, then. He might shout, make a useless appeal: he spared himself that indignity and drew several quick, deep breaths before they got to him.

When the iron touched him he did not even try to hold it back.

It went on, and on. There was laughter. A human

spat in his face, and some thought that amusing. Others, elegant qhal, simply watched.

She has gotten clear, he kept thinking, he insisted to think, like a litany, imagining gray horse, silver-haired rider, far and far across the hills. *She is far too wise for them to catch.*

And that is well. That is very well.

"O God—!"

Then: "M'lord!" someone said sharply, and a hand gripped his hair and a knife pricked his throat.

It is over, he thought.

But something pale appeared and drifted like a cloud in the dark across the stream. He blinked and haze cleared momentarily on a glimmer of silver hair in the dark, black figure in the starlight, the dragon sword, sheathed, set point down in front of her.

"Liyo," he cried from a raw throat. *"Archers!"*

The knife pierced his skin; Chei struck it aside.

"We have a man of yours!" Chei shouted out.

"Liyo, they know—"

A blow smashed into his skull, jolting everything into dark, his sense of place, of whether he had warned her or only meant to—

"Do you want me or do you want to talk?" Morgaine's clear voice rang out of the dark.

Vanye slid his eyes to the open box, the gate-jewel. She could not draw, with that unshielded, without taking him as Bron had gone. He struggled against those who held him, only to bring his legs around, tears of pain running through the sweat on his face.

"Do you want your lover back?" Chei taunted her. "Come in and bargain for him."

Vanye gave a sudden heave, swung his left leg over and brought it down on the lid. The light went out. He was blind.

Then *Changeling's* light flared out, a bar of opal which grew to a white blaze, a shimmering into colors the eye did not want to see. Qhal who had faced that thing before scrambled to escape.

But Chei snatched the box and rolled to cover at Vanye's back, beside the tree.

"I have the stone in my hand," Chei yelled. "Come near my men and I uncover it!"

"Vanye?" her voice rang out. He saw her and all the brush and hill about her lit in *Changeling's* fire. He saw her hesitate, stopped still. But the winds still blew, howling and blowing the grass. No arrow could fly true in that.

"Liyo, he is telling the truth. Do what you have to. They will not keep me in any comfort."

"In perfect comfort," Chei called out, "if you are reasonable."

"What do you want?"

"Liyo, it is Chei!"

There was silence then, and he lay back against the tree, satisfied, then, he had gotten out what would tell her everything. It was all she needed know.

Perhaps there would be a miracle. He thought not. The only thing he hoped now was that she would not try further, understanding now there was no bargain to be made—not with Chei, who knew far too much about her intentions.

"Curse you for that," Chei said at his shoulder, and surprised him into a painful laugh. It was altogether Chei's expression, plaintive and indignant.

"Let me free," he said to Chei. "It is the only bargain you can make. At the least you will have to keep me in better state than this."

"We have him," Chei shouted out into the dark. "Come near us and he will suffer for it, all the way to Mante—he will wear that stone about his neck, lest you have notions otherwise!"

"Let me tell *you,* I will take your men one by one, and you will not kill him—you will not *dare* harm him, else your men die faster, my lord, you will see how fast. And you will not kill him, for your own life's sake, because he is the only thing keeping you alive. Lest you doubt me—"

A man cried out and fell, and Chei whirled half about and clenched his hand on Vanye's shoulder.

"Now what will you do?" Vanye taunted him.

"Damn you—"

Vanye grinned, for all the pain it cost him.

On the slope, *Changeling's* fire went out, leaving them blind to the dark.

And Chei's men murmured in indignation and fear.

They gave him food at the dawn—not much, but a piece of waybread and a kind of porridge that was tolerable to his stomach; they let him eat with his hands free, and drink from the stream and wash, with two score men watching him and most of them close enough to fall on him and weigh him down if nothing else. The humor of it was salve for the pain which rode every breath and slightest movement. He would, he hoped, grow more limber the longer he did move, and he refused to show them the pain that he was in or to ask any consideration they dared refuse. The burns on his chest and stomach bid fair to be the worst, the more so that they intended to set him in armor again—lest, Chei argued loudly with a captain who objected, some accident take him on the road.

Chei prevailed, by shouting, and the forty-odd men watched him sullenly as he pulled on his breeches and his shirt and padding, and the mail, which weight felt ten times what it was wont; but it made his bruised and burned ribs and stomach feel the safer from chance blows. He fumbled about with the straps of the leather, and Chei cursed him, whereat he hurried no more than before, having judged Chei had no wish to try his fortunes and discommode his men before the day was even begun.

Then Chei ordered him tied. He had known that they were going nowhere until they had done it; he had known they would take what revenge they dared in the doing of it, and he resolutely disappointed them by standing quietly and yielding his hands behind him, using his strength only when they put pressure on his arms, intentionally to cause him pain.

And the stone, which had been unshielded the night long, pouring its evil into the air, Chei brought him and hung about his neck as he had said, eye to eye with him for that moment.

"There will be ways," Chei said to him.

"You can save your men, Chei. Give me my horse and let me go. That is all you have to do. You have fifty good years as you are, whether we win or lose. Otherwise you have only a handful of days—if you have that. Do you think you will be the last my lady leaves alive with me?"

There was fear in Chei's eyes. And hate. Chei drew his hand away, and smashed it across his face before he could entirely evade the blow.

There was fear, when he shook the hair back and looked past Chei at his men. There was outright resentment.

"Threats," Chei scoffed, and went to his horse. He waved his hand at the others. "Move! Mount up! We have ground to cover."

There was a small, dull sound. The man holding the red roan for him fell without an outcry, only a puff of foul smoke hanging in the air. The camp broke into chaos, the horse shied. A second man fell, further away.

Chei whirled and flung himself at Vanye, arms about his waist, and came down on top of him with an impact that drove the breath out of him and half stunned him with the blow to the back of his head. He came to himself in pain, being dragged to a sitting position with Chei's arm about him and Chei shouting orders at his men to find Morgaine.

Not likely, he thought. He did not resist being used as a shield. He sat there with his eyes shut and drew small breaths that did not hurt. "If she wants you," he murmured to Chei, "she will surely take you."

There had been forty men and two in their company last night. He had taken account. Losing one last night, two this morning, there were thirty-nine, counting himself.

"Shut up," Chei hissed at him.

He rested, that was all.

When the men, by ones and twos, trailed back from their search of the hillsides, there were thirty-seven, and Chei, standing, shouted furious orders to mount up.

"There are reinforcements coming," the second in command protested, in full hearing of the others. "We should raise a fortification and stay here. You are losing men, Qhiverin, all for your damnable insistence on going ahead with this—"

"Do as I tell you!" Chei shouted at the man. "Get to horse! We are riding out of here!"

The qhalur captain, tall and elegant, bowed his head with ill grace and went for his horse.

To all this Vanye said nothing at all, considering the state of his ribs and his gut. Chei grabbed him by the hair getting him on his feet and even this he bore, that and the hard grip of the men who pushed him at Arrhan. But one of them hit her when she shied from them and at that he resisted, an instant's bracing of muscles before he thought quickly that men of their ilk might as like kill her to spite him. So he struggled to get his foot into the stirrup and let them shove him up onto her back. They tied Arrhan's reins to a sorrel gelding's saddle and she did not like that either, side-stepping and jerking till he tapped her with his heels and spoke to her in the Kurshin tongue, softly, one friend in this situation, where he had as soon not have had her.

The company rode out of the camp and across country, toward the road.

He was not surprised by that. They hoped to deprive Morgaine of cover from which to strike at them. All day they would be thinking of means to save themselves and to have revenge on them both.

Himself, he gave himself up to Arrhan's gait and slept, in what stretches he could, between the pain of burns and stiff muscles and the ache of his shoulders and back, and the peculiar unpleasantness of the unshielded stone which rode close against his throat, as Chei had tied it, a sense of gate-force which reached a mind-numbing pitch and stayed there, never abating.

When Morgaine needed him to do something she would signal him. He had no doubt she would do it in some fashion—perhaps through the stone itself, if it would not likewise advise their enemy.

Beyond that he did not try to think, except where the qhal themselves afforded him something to wonder on. To think what the end of this might be, or to think how he had wandered into this, was too deadly a sink, a place in which he could lose himself. This much he had learned of Morgaine, to deal with the moment and keep his mind flowing with it—like swordplay, like that intricate art in which there was no time to spare for forever.

He waited, that was all.

And by afternoon another man pitched from the saddle.

There were outcries, there was shouting—some men broke and ran and the whole company did, stringing out in disorder.

Two riders veered far off toward the northwest, and kept going.

"They are cowards!" Chei yelled at the rest. "Likeliest they are dead men. Stay with the column."

"Let him go!" one of the qhal shouted back. "Let him *go,* let us ride back to Morund!"

"Silence!" Chei bade him. "Do you think any of us would live out the hour?"

"No one would prevent you," Vanye said. "Go home. It is your high lords who use the gates—this one is spending your lives to no—"

He ducked his head and put his shoulder in the way of Chei's sheathed sword as it came whistling round for him, ducked again from the second blow, and as Arrhan shied, drove his heels in.

The mare jerked and bolted, hitting the reins with all her weight and throwing the other horse into a wild stagger after balance. For a moment he kept her circling and shying up under the impacts of his heels.

Then other riders closed in about him and seized reins and bridles to stop her.

Chei was one. Chei shoved the sheathed sword under his chin when all was done and jerked his head up.

"Tonight," Chei told him. "Tonight."

No one spoke, except Chei bade them put a rope to Arrhan's halter and use that as well as the reins.

They gave him neither food nor water, nor any other consideration for his comfort, so that the ride became one long misery of heat and ache—no rest for him at the times they would stop to rest the horses. They drank at a stream and afforded Arrhan water, but none for him.

It was petty vengeance.

Only once, there was an outcry from the rear of their column, and Chei gave furious orders that sent men thundering back along the road toward a rider that appeared like a ghost and vanished again in the tricks of the rolling land.

He held his breath then. He could not but worry.

But the rider left the road before they came that far.

And within the hour a man pitched dead from the saddle.

"Damn you!" Chei shouted to the hills. "*Damn you!*"

The hills echoed him. That was all.

Vanye did not meet his eyes then. He kept his head bowed amid the murmuring of the others.

They were thirty-three.

Close to him, for some little time, Chei and the captain argued in muted fury, concerning a place for a camp, concerning the hazard of leaving the road for the hills.

"It is him she wants," the captain asserted finally, in hushed violence. "Put a sword in him, take the jewel, and leave him in the road. She will stop for him. No horse for him and a wounded man on her hands—*then* the balance shifts. *Then* we become the hunters. More of this is madness."

It was only too reasonable a course. Vanye listened with a sinking heart, and braced himself to cause them what trouble he could.

But: "No!" Chei said.

"It is your ambition," the captain said. "Your damnable ambition, Qhiverin! No waiting on Mante—no chance of anyone but yourself dealing with it—You will listen to me, or the high lord will when I bear the report to him—"

"You will obey orders, captain, or I will bear reports of my own of your insubordination, of your obstructing me, damn you! I am *my lord*, and Qhiverin is gone, *captain*, with all his disfavor, Gault is dead, what is more, and you do not know me, *captain*, you do not know me in the least and you do not know the enemy you are dealing with and you do not know the weapon you are dealing with. That stone around his neck keeps us alive, captain. Around yours, much as I would like to see it, it would be no more than an encouragement—it cannot take that weapon of hers, need I shout the matter aloud? Whoever holds the stone will go like a leaf in the wind, and that accursed sword will stand fast in this world—*that* is what prevents her, nothing more."

"Her lover bleeding in the dirt will prevent her." The captain ripped his sword from its sheath. "And I will carry the stone, *my lord,* and deliver the stone to Mante, *my lord!*"

Vanye drove his left heel into Arrhan's side and she wheeled, jerking hard at the reins, clear of his reach as Chei's sword came out and rang loud in the turning of that blade, a mirror-bright flash of sun, a wheeling cut and the hiss of other steel drawn, on all sides.

A thunder of hooves and a second man came at him; he drove with his heels and ducked, flat in the saddle, as the stroke grated off his armor, as the man leading his horse swung round and an arc of steel flashed over his head in the other direction, ringing off the rebel's blade close by his ear. Horses shoved and shied and Arrhan struggled in the press: there was nothing he could do but lie flat as he could against Arrhan and the heaving rump of his defender's horse for an instant as the blades rang above him, as blood spattered over him and one or the other fell—

He drove his heels in and fought for balance with an effort that tore muscles in his stomach, with steel still ringing over his head, then let go entirely and landed in a space between the horses, to scramble up again, hands bound, and run.

A shout, a rumbling behind him—riders on either side of him, and a horse shouldered him and sent him rolling; up to his feet again and a second dash for the rocks that he could see—

If Morgaine were near enough, if she could give him cover—

A horse thundered down at him. There was nothing he could do but run, and veer, spinning aside at the last moment as the horse rushed past.

But the second horse he could not evade, and fell, his helm saving his head and rolling free as he hit on his bound arms and struggled after wind and purchase to rise.

A horseman overshadowed him. An extended lance slammed against his armor and pushed him back, the point hovering an unstable distance from the pit of his throat.

He did not know which side had won until Chei's voice bade the rider back away, and men got down to gather up him and his helmet and take him back to his horse.

There were bodies on the road. The captain was one, with his skull split. There were two other qhal who might have been all the captain's and might have been, some of them, Chei's. They left them for the scavengers as they had left the others, and they put him on Arrhan's back again.

He slumped over such as he could to rest then, and to avoid Chei's attention.

There was no more dissent. It was a while more of riding, and very little of speaking at all, until they came into a stony place between two hills, where the Road had cut deep, and where a stream had cut deeper still into the hills beside it.

It was a sheltered place. It was a slit between the rocks where an overhang provided cover against attack, a natural fortification, and when they rode into it, and passed within that shadow, Vanye's heart sank in him as hope had trembled on the edge this last and terrible hour.

They were twenty-six as he counted them again—three dead on the road and four vanished, deserted, he thought, when the fight began to go against them. But the qhal had done this to themselves, and the noise of the fight ought to have reached Morgaine through the hills. There had been a real chance she might have been there when he fled, or after—at the most, that commotion should have drawn her close again, and she might have dealt them damage—might have taken some good position among the rocks and taken out man after man, giving him the chance he needed to run, on foot, if he must—beneath her covering fire.

But she had not been there. There had been nothing at all from her since early afternoon; and Chei had sent men out to hunt her.

She is hurt, he thought. Something has happened to her or she would have come in—she would have come, she would have come—

Now they drew into this place shadowed with premature twilight, close among rocks, where he knew that she could not reach; and that shadow closed over him, his enemies laid hands on him and pulled him off his horse and struck him once in earnest of what else they might do, and for the first time since last night he felt a cold despair.

They bound his feet and let him lie while they had their supper: for him there was not so much as a cup of water, and when in desperation he rolled over to the streamside close by him, they ignored that. It was all they would do for him, until after, that a few of the human servants came and unbound him, and then his hands were so swollen and his arms so lifeless there was little he could do for himself. They gave him leave to relieve himself, that was the sole mercy; and when he turned about again they laid hands on him and bound him and hauled him over to where the qhal-lords sat, the pale and the human-seeming both by the little fire they had made under the overhang; and Chei centermost among them, their faces and their eyes reflecting the white shining of the jewel he wore.

He sank down there on his knees, his head reeling from hunger and exhaustion, and the gate-force humming in his bones. He waited to hear what they would do, and heard the small shifts of the men at his back, the men who gathered close about him, yet more than a score of them.

"Did I make you a promise?" Chei asked him.

"Aye," he murmured, to stay Chei's madness. Aye to anything.

Something has happened to her, he reasoned to himself. *She is not dead, they would have reported that. But hurt, somehow held, pinned down in ambush—O God, or out there, late, perhaps ahead of us, perhaps that is where she is—*

They will want to draw her in, they will want me to draw her—

I must not do that, whatever they do, no outcry this time—

No sound, he told himself over and over, when Chei gave the order that they should take the armor off him.

But: "My lord," one of the qhal said. "No. He is our safety. He is all the safety we have. My lord, we stayed by you—"

Chei said nothing for a long moment. Then: "Do you intend to ride off too?"

There was silence.

"Then go, curse you, go, ride out into the dark and take your chances! Or do what I tell you. Take him!"

The servants hesitated. Of a sudden one of them bolted and ran, and another fled, and the rest after them, afoot, toward the road. One of the qhal gave pursuit.

And fell.

Chei sprang and Vanye rolled and resisted him as best he could, tried to get his legs to bear for a kick, but Chei caught him in his arms and held him fast against him, one arm nigh choking him while shouts and alarm rang about him.

Alive, Vanye thought; and: *"Be careful,"* he shouted out before Chei's fingers pressed at either side of his throat and began to take his consciousness. *"Liyo,—"*

As one and another of the qhal fell and such as were left huddled close within that shelter.

They were six, Vanye saw when the night grew quiet again and consciousness came back to him, as he lay still in Chei's tight grip. Mostly there were bodies strewn out across the open; and one of the qhal by them called a name and crept out to reach a friend, against his lord's advice.

"Get out of here," Vanye said to that man, for a man who would take that risk seemed better to him than the rest of them. "Get on your horse and ride out of here. She will not stop you."

But it was that man who came back and seized him out of Chei's hands and battered and half-choked him before the others pulled him off.

He lay silent after that, dazed and relieved of some of the pain, so close he was to unconsciousness. But the qhal stirred forth, and saddled their horses in the dark, and led them close by the rock where they sheltered, horses enough for them and a relief mount for each, but Arrhan was not among them.

Then they hauled him up and put him ahorse, and they rode breakneck up the narrow way they had gotten into this place.

When day came, there were only the six of them, and himself, and they pushed the horses, changing from one to the other.

But another of them died, at one such change. It was the man, Vanye thought, who had beaten him. He regarded the man in a kind of numbness when he sprawled almost under his horse's hooves, with a black spot on his forehead and a dazed expression on his face. He was not glad of it, except he lifted his eyes toward the low hills and felt as if his liege, unseen, were looking at him this moment.

"It is that cursed stone," one of the qhal said, as others had muttered. "She can *see* it."

"Wrap that cursed thing," Chei said then, and one

of them drew him close and dragged him down off the horse while others got down and lengthened the cord on the stone, and tucked it under his armor at his neck, against his bare skin.

The gate-sense was worse then.

It was worse yet when they had crested a long rise and suddenly found a the land dropping away below them across a wide rolling plain; and the crags which had long hung rootless in morning light, faced them across this gulf.

Then the world reeled about him in a mad confusion of blue sky and golden distances and the crags of yellow rock about them. The horse moved again, and his vision cleared, but there still seemed a distance between him and the world—less of pain, but greater unease, gate-sense that crawled up and down his nerves and prickled the hair on his body.

There, he thought, lifting his face toward the high crags. Mante-gate is up there—

Without question, as he knew the whereabouts of other powers, close by it, like small pools beside an ocean, and that ocean raging with storms and like to swallow up the lives that came near it.

It wanted this stone that he wore, wanted the bearer, wanted all creation, and that was not enough to fill it.

O my God, he thought, my God, if they bring me nearer this thing, if they bring me too close—

He rode, he did not know how. He heard their voices sharp in argument. "You can feel that thing," one said, and he knew what thing they meant: it was all about them, it was in their nerves; it made the horses skittish and fractious.

But it was nothing to them who did not hold it against their bare skin.

No more died—for whatever reason, there were no more ambushes, as they shifted horses and kept a pace that even gray Siptah could not match unaided, in this place where the qhalur road broke down into eroded stone traces, and the riders found a course not straight, but recklessly direct, down toward the valley.

She is left behind, he thought. These crags and this rough land has forced her back to the road and she has fallen behind. They have won, in my case. Somewhere I could have done better than this. Somehow I could have done something better.

It was the first thought he had allowed himself, of might-have and could-have, and of how he had fallen to them and the things they had done, and might do. Well enough, he thought, fool, twice fool—and reviewed every move he had made on that hillside, every sign he might have missed, every chance he had had, until the pain was all that took his mind from his inward misery.

Then: fool, he thought. She has taken the odds down.

It would cost, he thought. Time would cost very dear. And chances were hard come by.

The qhal shared rations at midday. "We had best feed him," one said, "or he will faint." And when Chei consented, one came and fed him a strip of jerky and gave him a drink as they rode, the water splashing down his chin and front and onto the saddle, to dry again in the sun. After that his stomach was queasy, and cramped, and the pounding gait put the taste of blood in his mouth. He wished that he might fall off and simply break his neck and be done, except he was Kurshin, and his body kept the rhythm it had known from childhood, no matter how much he swayed; and the same fool who had fallen into their trap, still thought that there was a hope of delaying them, if he could find the means.

Then he put the matter together and at their next stop, when they were changing horses, as he was about to mount, brought his knee up in his horse's flank and flung himself out of the way as it went hopping and pitching and throwing the horse it was tied to into a wildly swinging panic.

The men grabbed after those and he went for the three a single man was holding, startling those with a wild yell and a shove of his shoulder before someone overhauled him from behind.

He fell, with a man atop him and one of their horses having slipped its bridle and racing off wildly across the road, one of the riders having to free his horse of his relief mount to run it down.

It was a little victory, a little one. The man who had overhauled him dragged him over onto his back and stared at him as though murder was too mild a vengeance.

Vanye brought his knee up with all the strength in him.

Two more of them pinned him to the ground and one of them paid him in kind. After that he lost sense of where he was for the moment, until he felt the weight go off him and heard a shout, and came to with Chei's blade at his throat and a dead man at his side.

And the sound of a rider coming, at full gallop.

Chapter Fourteen

The gray horse became clear, and its rider, and Vanye took in his breath, held as he was against Chei's knee, Chei's sword across his throat. And one of the two qhal with him had taken up his bow, and nocked an arrow.

Vanye swung his leg around in an attempt to strike the bowman. He could not. The blade stung along his neck, taking up what room he had for breathing. "Look out!" he yelled. But Morgaine was drawing to a halt well down the road. She slid down, and started walking, through the tall grass.

The bowman drew back, aiming a high arc for a distance shot.

"You are in her range," Vanye said quietly, and the bowman eased off the draw.

"Fire!" Chei said.

The bowman drew again, with careful aim. And a second time eased off.

"Fire, curse you!"

"The wind is gusting." A third time the bowman lifted the bow and drew. His arm trembled with the strain as he sought an arc and a lull in the wind.

"Wind does not trouble her," Vanye said.

"Wait your target," Chei said then, and the bowman eased off a third time, trembling. Chei relaxed his grip on Vanye's hair, then shifted his hand to his shoulder and pressed gently. "Stay still, man, stay still."

It was worse than the other. His leg began to shake,

at its unnatural angle. He moved it. And Morgaine walked closer still, the bowman's necessary arc continually diminishing.

She reached half-range. The bowman lifted his bow, made a swift draw.

"Haaaaiiii!" Vanye yelled, and Chei jerked his head back. The shaft flew.

Morgaine dropped, and sprang up again, covering ground at a run.

The blade stung, and a slow trickle ran down Vanye's neck. *"I will kill him,"* Chei yelled.

Morgaine stopped. The bowman stopped, a second arrow nocked and drawn.

"Ride off!" Chei shouted at her. "You leave me nothing to lose, woman!"

"I will bargain with you!" Morgaine's voice came faintly on the wind at full shout.

"I will bargain with *you*, woman. Throw down the sword and I will give you both your lives. Or I will cut his throat here and now."

She walked closer, and a second shaft flew, amiss on a gust of wind.

"Curse you," Chei said to the bowman. "Fire!"

The bowman brought up another arrow. But Morgaine had stopped. She lifted her hand, aimed dead at them. "An easy shot for me. Let him free and you are free to ride south. My word on it! Any one of you that wants to live, walk clear."

The bowman lowered his bow; and: "My lord," the qhal on Chei's other side said, and reached, and pressed the blade back from Vanye's throat with his bare hand. "My lord. We are the last. She will kill us. Let him go. We have lost."

There was long silence. Chei's grip faltered on his shoulder and tightened again.

"Let him free!" Morgaine said.

"For a price," Chei said.

"Name it!"

"I will name it later," Chei said. "Do you want him on those terms?"

"Let him go!" Morgaine said. "And I will give you

your lives and your gear—or flay the skin off you if you harm him! Let him go!"

Chei's hand loosed. The sword withdrew and Chei shoved him carefully aside and stood up, a clear target. "Free him," Chei said. "Let him go."

The second man took a knife and cut Vanye's hands free, and with a hand under his arm, helped him to his feet. He was not one of those who had been forward to do him harm—a tall, silver-haired qhal, expressionless even now in this shift of fortunes. His hand was firm and steady, and gently tested his balance before he let him free.

Vanye walked, the whole of the sky seeming for a moment gone to metal and his hands, lifeless and swinging beside him, seeming to belong, like his feet, to some other man. He staggered on a hole in the ground, recovered himself short of a fall, and kept walking, the gusts of wind touching the sweat on his face and stinging in the cuts on his throat.

But the sky went stranger still, peculiarly translucent, and he was on one knee without knowing how he had gotten there, Morgaine rushing up to kneel and seize him by the shoulder.

"I am all right," he said. There was a look of dismay on her face; and rage; and she whirled on one knee and aimed her weapon at their enemies.

"No," he said on a breath, and caught her arm.

She did not fire. He did not know why he had said it, only that it was one more mistake like the rest he had made. He felt the shorn hair blowing about his face and into his eyes, the most visible of the dishonors they had put on him, and her; and that expression of horror was still in her eyes. "I am sorry," he said to her, when he could say anything.

"*Curse* them for this!"

"It was their doing, not mine." He knelt there shifting glances between her and their unmoving enemy, for she had stopped paying them attention. He did not offer the head-to-ground obeisance that might have made some amends for his shame with a Kurshin liege, did not ask for duel with the man who had done this, did not do any of the things that would have driven her to fury with him. *"Liyo,* I am tired, is all."

"I have Arrhan with me. Yonder, beyond the hill." She made a motion of her head. "And all your gear. With her and Siptah to trade about, there was no way they could outrun me." She found the cord that bound the stone about his neck and pulled it from beneath his armor, which itself was great relief. She laid down the black weapon a moment to take her Honor-blade and cut it free. "Where is the case for this thing?"

"Chei has it."

"That is one thing I will get from him.—Is it Gault?"

"Yes." In the tail of his eye, he saw Chei walk toward them. "In Heaven's name, *liyo,* watch them—"

Her gray eyes flicked past his with a killing fury— for them, not for him. He knew then the measure of it, in her red-rimmed and shadowed gaze—the pace she had to have kept, to set ambush after ambush, the strain, constantly to be sure of her targets.

She gathered up her weapon. She rose to her feet, and Vanye levered himself up to stand by her.

"The matter of a price," Chei called out.

"There is no price," Morgaine shouted back, "but your *lives,* my lord, and that is for old grudges, not new ones! You have the casing for the stone. Let it fall. And get out of my sight!"

"The price, my lady!"

Her hand lifted, the weapon aimed. "You go too far with me."

"My enemies—and passage through the gate, for me and mine." Chei strode forward and stopped, hands held wide and empty. "There is no way back for us."

"No way back from *hell,* my lord, and you are treading on the brink. *Vanye* wants your life, I have no least notion why—you can thank him on your knees, before you ride out of here. Now! Drop the case, man!"

Chei's hand moved to his neck. A silver chain glittered in the sun as he lifted it over his head and dropped it.

"On your knees, my lord, and thank him, else I will shoot the legs out from under you."

Chei went down.

"Thank him."

"Liyo," Vanye protested.

"Thank him!"

"I give you my thanks, Nhi Vanye."

Morgaine dropped her hand, and stood staring as Chei got up and went to the roan horse and his remount; and the others, the qhal and the bowman who wore human shape, claimed their own.

"There was one more man—" Vanye recalled with a sudden chill.

"The one who chased the horses?" Morgaine asked. "That one I accounted for." She half-turned and whistled for Siptah. The gray horse threw his head and shook himself and tended in their direction, reins trailing, as they walked toward the place Chei had dropped the casing.

Chei and his men rode off, southward, with no delaying. Vanye knelt, fighting dizziness, and picked up the gray box that Chei had dropped in the trampled grass. Morgaine gave him the stone and its cord and he made a ball of it and put it inside. Its raw power left the air like the feeling after storm, and his hands were shaking as he hung it again about his neck on its proper chain, safe and still.

"What did they do?" she asked fiercely. "What did they do?"

He did not meet her eyes. He gathered up his helm, from where it had fallen. The gray horse came up to them, snorting and throwing his head, and he went and caught the trailing reins and laid his hand on Siptah's neck, for the comfort of a creature who asked no questions. "Nothing, past the time you put a fear in them. Mostly want of food and rest."

"Get up," she said. "I will ride behind. We will find Arrhan and quit this place."

He was glad enough of that. He wiped the hair back from his face, put the helm on, slung the reins over and put his foot in the stirrup with a little effort, with a greater one hauled himself onto Siptah's back and cleared the right stirrup for Morgaine. She climbed up by the cantle and her hand on his leg, and held only to the cantle when they started out, so she knew well enough he was in pain, and did not touch him as they rode. She only gave him directions, and they went over the road and beyond the further hill, where Arrhan placidly cropped the grass with a pair of Chei's strayed horses.

She slid down. He climbed down and went and gave his hands to Arrhan's offered muzzle, endured her head-butting in his sore ribs and leaned himself against her shoulder.

His bow, his quiver, hung on Arrhan's saddle, though different men had stolen them. There was a fine qhalur sword, that one of the lords had worn.

He looked around at Morgaine, at a face as qhal-pale as theirs, and a vengefulness far colder. For a moment she seemed changed far more than Chei.

Then she walked past him to take the rest that she had won, the horses that grazed oblivious to their change of politics. "Remounts," she said, leading them back. "Can thee ride, Nhi Vanye?"

"Aye," he murmured. She was brusque and distant with him, giving him room to recover himself; he inhaled the air of freedom and set his foot in his own stirrup and flung himself up to Arrhan's back, gathering up the sword as the mare began to move. He wanted that in its place at his belt first; even before water, and a little food, and a cool spring to wash in.

Even that impossible gift Morgaine gave him, finding among the hills and the rocks, a place where cold water spilled down between two hills and trees shaded the beginnings of a brook. She reined in there and got down, letting Siptah and the remounts drink; and he slid down, holding to the saddle-ties and the stirrup-leather: he was that undone, now that the fighting was done, and his legs were unsteady when he let go and sank down to drink and wash.

He looked and she was unsaddling the gray stud. "We have pushed the horses further than we ought," she said, which was all she said on the matter.

He lay down on the bank then, sprawled back and let his helmet roll from his head, letting his senses go on the reeling journey they had been trying to take. He felt his arm fall, and heard the horses moving, and thought once in terror that it had been a dream, that in the next moment he would find his brothers' hands on him, or his enemies' faces over him.

But when he slitted his eyes it was Morgaine who sat against the tree, her arms tucked about her knees, the dragon sword close by her side. So he was safe. And he slept.

He waked with the sun fading. For a moment panic jolted him and he could not remember where he was. But he turned his head and saw Morgaine still sitting where she had been, still watching over him. He let go a shaking breath.

She would not have slept while he slept. He saw the exhaustion in her posture, the bruised look about her eyes. *"Liyo,"* he said, and levered himself up on his arm, and up to his knees.

"We have a little time till dark," she said. "If thee can travel at all. Thee should tend those hurts before they go stiff. And if need be, we will spend another day here."

There was fever in her eyes, restraint in her bearing. It was one thing and the other with her, a balance the present direction of which he did not guess at, rage and anxiety in delicate equilibrium.

He felt after the straps of his armor and unbuckled it. "No," he said when she moved to help him. He managed it all himself, glad of the twilight that put a haze between her and the filth and the sores, but while time was that he would have gone out of her witness to bathe, now it seemed a rebuff to her. He only turned his body to hide the worst of it as he slid into the chill water.

Then he ducked his head and shoulders under, holding fast to the rocks on the bank, for he did not swim. Cold numbed the pain. Clean water washed away other memory, and he held there a moment and drifted with

his eyes shut till Morgaine came to the bank with
salves and a blanket and his personal kit, and sternly
bade him get out.

"Thee will put a chill in the wounds," she said, and
was right, he knew. He heaved himself up onto the
dry rock and wrapped himself quickly in the blanket
she flung around him. He made a tent of it to keep the
wind off while he shaved and brushed his teeth, careful around the cuts and the swollen spots, and afterward sat rubbing his hair dry.

She came up behind him and laid her hands on his
shoulders, and took the fold of the blanket and began
to dry his hair herself.

So he knew she forgave him his disgrace. He bowed
his head on his arms and did not flinch when she
combed it with her fingers—only when she put her
arms about his shoulders and rested her head against
him. Then it was hard to get his breath.

"I did not deserve it of them," he said, in his own
defense. "I swear that, *liyo*. Except my falling into
their trap in the first place. For that—I have no excuse
at all."

Her arms tightened. "I tried to come round north
and warn thee. But I came too far. By the time I came
back again it was too late. And thee had come riding
in. Looking for me. True?—True. Is it not?"

"Aye," he murmured, his face afire with shame,
recollecting the well-trampled stream, recollecting every mistaken reasoning. "It might have been you in
their hands. I thought you were, else you would have
been there—"

"To warn thee off. Aye. But I was being a fool,
thinking thee was like to rush into it for fear I had
been a fool; and thee knew *something* was wrong, well
enough, that I was not somewhere about. It was as
much my fault as thine." She moved around where she
could see his face. "We cannot do a thing like this
again. We cannot be lovers and fools. *Trust* me, does
thee hear, and I will trust thee, and we will not give
our enemies the advantage after this."

He pressed his hand over hers, drew it to his lips

and then let go, his eyes shut for a moment. "Will you hear hard truth, *liyo?*"

"Yes."

"You take half my opinion and do half of yours, and whether mine is good or ill I do not know, but half apiece of two good opinions makes one very bad one, to my way of thinking. Hear me out! I beg you." His voice cracked. He steadied it. "If your way is straight down the road, straight we go and I will say no word. My way, to tell the truth, has not fared very well in recent days."

She sat hill-fashion, on her heels, her arms between her knees. "Why, I thought I had done tolerably well by your way in the last few days—I did think I had learned well enough."

"You learned nothing of me—"

"Constantly. Does thee think me that dull, that I learn nothing?"

His heart lifted a little, a very little, not that he counted himself so gullible.

"Does not believe me?" she asked.

"No, *liyo.*" He even managed a smile. "But it is kind."

Her mouth tightened and trembled, not for hurt, it seemed, only of weariness. She put out her hand and touched his face with her fingertips, gently, very gently. "It is true. I did not know what to do. I only thought what thee would do, if it were the other way about."

"I would have gone in straightway like a fool."

She shook her head. "Separately, we are rarely fools. That is what we have to mend." She brushed a lock of hair from his eyes. "Trust *me,* that I will not be. And trust that I trust thee."

He glanced at the dragon sword behind her shoulder, that thing she did not part with even now, that one thing for which she would leave him.

Perhaps she understood the direction of that glance. She settled back on her heels with a bruised and weary gaze into his eyes.

"With my life," he said.

It was not enough to say. He wished he had not had that thought, or given way to it.

I believed you might come, only because we were still far enough from the gate.

Beyond such a point, she had no such loyalties, nor could help herself. He believed that. With the sword, at such a time, she fought for nothing but the geas, —and for her sanity.

At such a time, liyo, you would have taken me with your enemies.

And always that is true.

"Truth, *liyo*, I had no doubt."

She looked so weary, so desperately weary. He rose up on his knees and put his arms about her, her head against his bare shoulder, her slim, armored body making one brief shiver, hard as it was. Her arms went about him.

"We have no choice but move on," she said, her voice gone hoarse. "Chei has gone back toward Tejhos. I do not think he will go all the way south."

"Chei has done murder," he said. "He killed a captain Mante sent by way of Tejhos. The captain's men deserted."

"Was *that* the division." Her shoulders heaved to a sigh, and for a moment her weight rested against him. "None of them escaped. Plague take it—I should have killed him—long since. . . ."

"Chei," he murmured, "went to them . . . willingly," he said. And Mante knows everything he knows by now. I have no doubt they do. There may be more than a few riders out from there."

She nodded against his shoulder. "Aye. I know that."

"And neither of us is fit to ride. What could you do? What could I? Sleep."

She was limp in his arms, and moved her hand then to push away from him, and abandoned the effort, slumping bonelessly into his arms. "Not wise, not wise, of me. I know. We have to move. This place is not safe—'t is not safe at all—"

It was, perhaps, the first time in recent days she had done more than close her eyes.

Chei splashed water over his face and wiped it back over his hair, crouching at the stream. Across from him in the dusk, the remnant the witch had left to him—witch, he insisted to himself, against all the knowledge qhalur rationality could muster. He grew superstitious. He knew that his soul was lost, whatever that was, simply because he did not know how to believe in it any longer; or in witchcraft, except that in the workings of the world there might conceivably *be* prescience, and outsiders might know things he did not understand.

Ichandren had believed in unnatural forces. Bron had never doubted them. The man across the rill of water from him had known them, Rhanin ep Eorund, before he housed a qhalur bowman, and perhaps even yet. They were foreign only to Hesiyyn, the qhal, whose face was a long-eyed, high-boned mask, immune to the worry that creased Rhanin's brow—human expression, woven into the composite like so many subtle things.

Like fear. Like the moil of hate and fear and anger that boiled inside Chei's own self, seductive of both halves: revenge on the strangers; revenge on Mante, which had always been his enemy no less than Chei's; and life, life that might stretch on forever like the life that trailed behind, life that remembered jeweled Mante, and the face of the Overlord which young Chei had never seen, and of kin and friends Gault-Qhiverin had both loved and killed and betrayed for greater good—

Friends and kin the strangers had taken, as they bade fair to take all the world down to dark.

"Go back if you will," he, Chei, Gault, Qhiverin, had said to his last followers, when they had put distance between themselves and their enemies.

Rhanin had only shaken his head. There was nothing for him in Morund, only in Mante, where his kin were, and his wife, and all else Skarrin had reft away from him. The wife he had had, the human one, in the hills—she would run in terror from what Rhanin had become; and break Rhanin's heart, and with it the heart of the qhal inside him. And Chei knew both things.

Hesiyyn had said, with eyes like gray glass: "To live among pigs, my lord? And tend sheep? Or wait Skarrin's justice?"

He did not understand Hesiyyn. Qhiverin when he was fully qhal had never understood him, only that he was the son of two great families both of which disowned him for his gambling, and that he had been under death sentence in Mante, for verses he had written. He had attached himself to Gault and gambled himself into debt even in Morund: that was Hesiyyn.

So they had ridden north again, from the place they had stopped, not having ridden far south at all.

"They cannot outrace us," Chei said, wiping a second palmful of water over his neck. "They will rest. They will seek some place to lie up for a while—but not long. They know they are hunted."

Wounds had stiffened; and Vanye bestirred himself carefully in the dark, while Morgaine slept. He made several flinching tries at getting to his feet then, cursing silently and miserably and discovering each time some new pain that made this and that angle unwise. Finally he clenched his jaw, took in his breath, and made it all in one sudden effort.

"Ah—" she murmured.

"Hush," he said, "sleep. I am only working the stiffness out."

He dressed by starlight, struggled with breeches and bandages and shirt and padding, and last of all the mail, which settled painfully onto strained muscles and shortened his breath. He fastened up the buckles of the leather that covered it, making them as loose as he dared; he fastened on his belts.

Then he walked by starlight to the place she had tethered the horses, and soothed them and made the acquaintance of the two they had from Chei's men, animals by no means to be disparaged, he thought: the Morund folk bred good horses.

Then he gathered up their blankets and bridles and

saddles, the latter with an effort that brought him a cold sweat, but painful as it was, it was good to stretch and move and pleasant to feel some of the stiffness work out of him.

It was even more pleasant to sink down on his heels near Morgaine and whisper: *"Liyo*, we are ready. I have the horses saddled."

"Out on you," she said muzzily, lifting herself on her elbow; and with vexation: "Thee ought not."

"I am well enough." In the tally of the old game, he had scored highly by that; and it was like the stretch of muscles, a homecoming of sorts.

Home, he thought, better than Morij-keep or any hall he had known—home, wherever she was.

She gathered herself up and paused by him, to lay her hand on his shoulder, and when he pressed his atop it, to bend and hug him to her, with desperate strength, while he was too stiff to stand as easily. "A little further before daybreak," she said. "We will gain what we can. Then we will rest as we need to. With the—"

There was a disturbance among the horses, the two geldings and the mare and the stud in proximity ample reason for it, but Morgaine had stopped; and he listened, still and shivering in the strain of night-chill and stiff muscles.

He pressed her hand, hard, and hers closed on his and pushed at him: *I agree. Move. I do not like this.*

He got up then, silently and in one move, for all the pain it cost. He reached Arrhan and quieted her and the remounts as Morgaine took Siptah in charge.

In the starlight, downhill where the stream cut through, a solitary rider appeared, and watered his horse at the lower pool. In a little more, two more riders joined him, and watered theirs, and drank, and rode on across.

Vanye shivered. He could not help it. He bade Arrhan stand quiet with a tug at her head; the others, the remounts, he held close and kept as still as he could, while Morgaine kept Siptah quiet.

They were not Chei's folk, whatever they were. He reckoned them for riders out of Mante, hunting reported invaders—else they would ride the road and go by daylight like honest and innocent travelers.

He moved finally, carefully, and looked at Morgaine. "There will be others," he whispered. "They may search back again along the watercourses."

"Only let us hope they confuse our tracks and their own." She threw Siptah's reins over his neck and rose into the saddle. "Or better yet—Chei's."

He set his own foot into Arrhan's stirrup and heaved upward with an effort that cost pain everywhere.

If they had dared a fire, if they could have sweated the aches out with boiled cloths and herbs, if he could have lain in the sun and baked himself to warmth inside and out, instead of lying cold and rising cold and riding again—but they were too close now, to the gate, and the enemy too aware of their danger.

Turn back, he thought of pleading. Go back into the plains and the hills and let us recover our strength.

But they had come so far. And they had no friends in this land and no refuge, and he did not know whether his instincts were right any longer. He yearned, he yearned with a desperate hope for the gate and a way into some other place than this, another beginning, when this one had gone desperately amiss.

They did not try to make speed by dark, with the ground stony and uneven as it was. They rode down one long sweep of hill, passed between others, and over a brushy shoulder. They kept a pace safe for the horses and quiet as they could manage, under a sky too open for safety.

And once, that Siptah pricked up his ears and Arrhan looked the same direction, off to their left flank, his heart went cold in him. He imagined a whole hostile army somewhere about them—or some single archer, who might be as deadly. "Likely some animal," Morgaine said finally.

And further on, where they stopped to breathe within a stand of scrub: "Time, I think, we gave the horses relief," he said. "But I do not want to stop here."

"Aye," Morgaine said, and slid down, to tie Siptah's

tether to his halter; and to calm the stallion, who took exception to the geldings, flattening his ears and pricking them up again, and swinging between them and Arrhan as Vanye dismounted.

"Hold," Morgaine hissed at the gray, and caught his tether-rope, which usually would stop him; but his head came up and his nostrils flared toward the wind, ears erect.

"Stay," Vanye said quietly, calmly as he could. "There is something there."

The horses were vulnerable. There was no guarantee of cover for them beyond this point. There was no guarantee they were not riding into worse. Siptah threw his head and protested softly, dancing sideways.

"Dawn could see us pinned here," she said. "That is no help."

"Then they have to come to us. *Liyo,* this once—"

"I thought thee had no more advice."

He drew in a sharp breath. Pain stabbed through bruised ribs. *"Liyo,—"*

Brush cracked, somewhere up on the slope.

"I agree with you," he said. "Let us be out of this."

"Go!" she hissed, and it was Siptah she chose to carry her, war-trained and sure, for all the gray was through his first wind.

He took Arrhan on the same reasoning, the horse he knew, the one that answered to heel and knee. He had both the relief mounts in his charge, that jolted the lead against the saddle as they took the next climb over ground studded with rocks, Siptah's tail a-flash before them in the starlight, eclipsed now and again by black brush and trees, the necessary sound of hooffalls and harness and the raking of brush sounding frighteningly loud in the night.

Down the throat of the folded hills, along the track of a minuscule stream, they kept a steady pace, until Morgaine drew in and he stopped, and panting horses bunched together, their breathing and the shift of their feet and creak of harness obscuring what small like sounds might be behind them.

"I do not hear them," he said finally.

"Nor I," Morgaine whispered, and turned Siptah uphill again, a hard climb and a long one with the two led horses tugging at Arrhan's harness.

But when they had come high up on that hill, dawn was seaming the east with a faint glow, and the stars were fading to that black before daylight.

And when they had changed off mounts and ridden the downslope on the two bays, Arrhan and Siptah led behind and too weary to object, the red edge of the sun was rising, offering a dim light, showing the distant crags of Mante's highland upthrust like a snaggled jaw against the sky beyond the hills.

The gelding missed a step and caught himself, and Vanye shifted weight; for a moment the whole of the east seemed to blur and reel, and he caught the saddle-horn, taking in breath in a reflex that hurt. He had bitten through a wound inside his cheek. He did it again, and it was one more misery atop the others.

But Morgaine had drawn up short, and she reached across to him as he caught himself, her horse crowding his amid the scrub and the rocks. "Vanye?"

"I am all right." His pulse raced with a sullen, difficult beat. The sky still spun and he felt a cold fear that he might fail her in the worst way, weighing on her, forcing her to decisions she would not make and tactics she would not use.

But not yet, he thought. Not yet. If threats and blows of his enemies could keep him in the saddle, his own determination could do as much, until the give and flex had worked the stiffness out of him and food and water had taken the dizziness from his skull.

"Beyond this," she said, "no knowing how long the ride. Vanye—we can find a place—That is what we *must* do."

He shook his head, turned the gelding's head for the downslope, and set it moving, too much in misery for courtesy.

An object hissed out of thin air and hit his shoulder like a sling-stone, spun him half-about in the saddle by force and shock: in the next heartbeat the arrow-hiss reached his mind and he knew that he had been hit and that arrows were still flying. His horse plunged in panic and shied back, and he fought it, finding life in the numbed arm, his only thought to get back to cover before Morgaine left it for his sake and tried to cover him. The horse stumbled on the brush, recovered itself, crowding Siptah and Arrhan and snagging the lead-rope as it came up against the others, but it was in cover, behind the rocks. He slid down, stumbled as the horse had on the encumbering brush, and brought up on the downhill slant against a boulder, trying to take his breath as Morgaine slid down and fetched up against the same, firing as she went, as the hillside erupted with ambush, a din of shouts.

"Is thee hurt?" Morgaine asked him. "Vanye, *is thee hurt?*"

The force of the blow had made any feeling uncertain, but the arm worked, and he pushed himself off the rock and struggled back after Arrhan and Siptah, who had wound the tether-ropes into a confusion of frightened geldings and war-trained stallion, in the midst of which was his bow. Arrows landed about him. One, spent, hit Arrhan and shied her off from him, and behind him was Morgaine's voice cursing him and bidding him take cover.

He seized the bow and ripped it loose from its ties on Arrhan's saddle, the same with his quiver; and scrambled for higher vantage, up atop a tumbled several boulders that hemmed the horses in.

The climb took his breath. He gained his knees, blind to anything but the necessity and deaf to anything but the cries of the enemy. He set the bow against the rock and his knee as he knelt, and strung it with an effort that brought sweat to his face.

Then he nocked an arrow and chose his target among those who swarmed up the hill, as if the very rocks and brush had come alive in the murky light.

He counted his shots, knowing the value of his position. He fired, calmly, carefully, with the advantage of height and the surety he was a target if he could not take their bowmen before they came to vantage on him or Morgaine, and they were trying: he picked one off, and selected another shaft, shaking the hair from his eyes and feeling the sweat running on cold skin. He wondered had the arrow pierced his armor after all before it fell away. It had hit enough to cause deep pain, the sort that caused a sweat and the weakness in his limbs and the giddiness that sent the landscape reeling.

But he could still draw. He bent the bow and drew breath and sighted all in one deliberate and enveloping focus, time after time taking targets Morgaine's straight-line fire and lower vantage could not reach, taking the archers foremost, who strove to position themselves and reach him.

But his supply of arrows dwindled.

Chapter Fifteen

The enemy found cover on the rock-studded, scrub-thicketed hill, and targets were fewer. Vanye wiped sweat with the back of his arm, and laid out his last four arrows, with care for their fletchings.

Morgaine left her vantage and climbed to another, a black-clad, white-haired figure in the gathering dawn, whose safety he watched over with an arrow nocked and ready for any move on the slope.

One tried. He quickly lifted the bow and fired, dissuading the archer, but the wind carried the shaft amiss.

Three arrows remaining.

Morgaine reached her perch and sent a few shots to places that provoked shifts in the enemy's positions, and afforded him a target he did not miss.

"We are too close here," Morgaine shouted across at him—meaning what he already understood, that *Changeling* was hazardous in the extreme in this confinement of loose boulders and brush, with the horses herded together in that narrow slot among the rocks and close to panic. "I am going for the horses! Stay where you are and give me cover!"

He drew in his breath and picked up his next to last shaft, his heart trying to come up his throat. He did not like what she proposed, riding out alone, with *Changeling* under Mante's warped touch.

He did not like, either, their chances if the enemy came up on them, and if they waited too late to gain room for the sword; and of the two of them, Morgaine *knew* the weapon. There was nothing to do but hold fast and spend his two remaining arrows to afford her the room she needed.

She edged outward on the rock and onto the slope that would lead her down to the horses.

And an arrow whisked past his position and shattered on the rock a hair's-breadth from her.

He whirled and sought a target among the crags over their heads, desperate. Morgaine's fire glowed red on stone as she fired past him and up at the cliffs.

"Get down!" she cried at him. "Get down!"

"Get to the horses!" he yelled. *"Go!"*

As an arrow hit the rock by his foot.

An arrow flew from another quarter, crosswise streak of black on pale rock, high up the ledges.

Not at them. At the hidden archer. An outcry said that it had hit. Other arrows followed, arcing downslope this time, into enemy positions, starting enemies from cover, as Morgaine turned on her slab of rock and fired again and again at targets suddenly visible.

A dark spot moved in the edge of Vanye's vision: he whirled and fired at a man coming up the throat of their little shelter, near the horses.

That man sprawled backward, his armor of no avail against an arrhendur bow at that range; and screamed as he slid down the slope, while Vanye nocked his last arrow with a deliberate effort at steadiness, as shafts sped unexplained over their heads, as the enemy broke and fled, offering their backs to the arrows and the red glow that flashed on a man and doomed him.

There were, perhaps, two or three who made it off that field. When quiet came the very air seemed numb. He still had the one arrow left. He refused to spend it on a retreating enemy. He slid off his rock and lost his footing in the landing, gathered himself up with his bow in one hand and the last arrow still nocked, and struggled through the brush to the tumbled mass Morgaine was descending.

"My lady Morgaine!" a shout came down from the heights.

He crossed the last distance with a desperate effort,

to steady Morgaine as she jumped the last distance and to thrust her back where there was at least scant cover.

"No gratitude?" The mocking voice drifted down from that place of vantage. "No word of thanks?"

"Chei," Vanye muttered between his teeth, and pressed his body against Morgaine as some large object hurtled off the heights to land close by them, with a sickening impact of bone and flesh.

A helmet rolled and clanged down the rocks. Arrows scattered and rattled; and a qhalur body lay broken on the stone.

He bent the bow, aimed upward, hoping for a target.

"There is my gift," Chei called down to them, never showing himself. "One of Skarrin's pets, none of mine. An appeasement. Do I hear yet thanks?"

"He is mad," Vanye breathed.

"I could kill you both from here," Chei said. "I could have let Skarrin's men kill you. But I do not. I had rather come down to talk. Which shall I?"

"Mad," Vanye said. His arm was shaking as he had it braced. His breath was short. He looked at Morgaine. "There were three of them. I have the one arrow left. I can gather more out there. Cover me."

"Stay!" Morgaine said. "Do not try it."

He lowered the bow and eased the string.

"My lady," Chei's voice drifted down to them. And an arrow struck and shattered in front of them. "Is that earnest enough of good faith? Talk is what I want. On your terms."

"I cannot see the wretch," Morgaine hissed softly, looking upward with the black weapon in hand. "Curse him, he can loft his shots, and I cannot—"

"Let me—"

"We still have another choice."

"Loose rock," Vanye muttered, looking at the set of the boulders *Changeling* might dislodge. "The horses—"

"My lady—" Chei's voice came down. "They have sent a gate-jewel into the field, more than one—Do you want to talk about this?"

"I am listening," Morgaine answered him.

"The while we were on the road the jewel he wore was constantly sending. It could not but draw them. I do not deny—I fought you. But there is no more fighting. If you win, you will destroy the gate at Mante, you will destroy everything, and we die. If Skarrin wins, we die—as rebels. We have few choices left. You want Mante. I want something else. It is alliance I am proposing."

"Alliance," Vanye muttered under his breath.

"Narrow quarters," Morgaine said quietly. "And an unstable gate. And no knowing where our enemies out there have gotten to."

"It is a lie—"

She rested her hand on his shoulder, and looked up at the cliffs. "Come down!" she called to Chei.

"Under truce?" Chei asked.

"As good as your own," Morgaine shouted back. "Do you trust it?"

A pebble dropped and bounded from somewhere above.

"For God's sake, do not trust him."

"I do not. I want him in sight. Remember I have no scruples."

He drew a larger breath. His hands were shaking. From off the rock where the qhal had fallen, blood ran, and dripped.

And from up among the rocks, on the trail they had ridden, the sound of movement.

"There were three," Vanye said again as a rider came down, out of their view behind the hill, hoof-falls echoing among the rocks.

"We do not know how many there are now," Morgaine said. "We have a dead man for proof. Perhaps they would kill their own. Who knows?"

He drew a long, slow breath, resting back against the rock that was no shelter.

"On the other hand," Morgaine said, "Chei has already killed men of Skarrin's. Did you not say? How did that go?"

"Aye." Breath was short. He sent his thoughts back,

to gather everything, putting it in one place. "Typthyn was the name. For the stone. It was the stone the captain wanted. To take it to Mante, he said. And to get clear. But do not believe him for the sake of that. Chei wanted it for himself."

A single rider came into view, on the red roan that had been Gault's, the man a slight, young figure in silver mail.

"The fool," Vanye breathed.

"Foolish or desperate."

"No!" Vanye said. "I believed him a moment too long. He lies—very well."

Her hand clenched on his shoulder, on bruises. "Be patient. We will hear him out. That at least we can afford."

She stood clear to face the rider, who, finding himself in a pocket in the maze of stone, dismounted and leapt up to the flat rock which had been Vanye's post. Vanye took his place at her left shoulder, the bow easy in his hands, aimed at the ground.

But he kept the arrow nocked.

Chei spread wide his hands. "That I have men above me, you can guess. And you have the sword." He walked forward on the slanting surface and dropped lightly off the rock to the ground facing them—spread his hands again, keeping the palms in plain view. "I think the advantage is yours."

"Come no closer," Morgaine said. "For this I have no need of the sword."

Chei stopped instantly. The mockery was gone from his face as she lifted her hand toward him. "My lady—"

"I am not your lady and whatever there is of Chei ep Kantory I should best requite by killing his enemy, *Gault.* I saved you for last, only so *you* might keep the others under your hand. I spared you once on Vanye's word—and because I should have enjoyed it too much—*Do you hear me, Gault?*"

"My men, my lady. Above us."

"We two, lord Gault, are in front of you, and this is the cleanest of my weapons, for which you may thank me. Is there something you want that is worth this?"

"What I always wanted. What I would have freely given, if you had come to Morund. What the boy gave when you befriended him—"

"Lies," Morgaine said sharply.

"Vanye!" Chei said, holding out his hands.

"I had as lief kill you," Vanye said; and bent the bow as Chei took a step closer. *"No farther!"*

Chei fell to his knees, hands outheld. "God help me, I do not know what I am, I cannot sort it out— What else do you leave me?"

"No more lies!"

"Listen to me. I know the way in. Do you want Skarrin? I will give him to you."

"Our guide," Vanye breathed, "to whom we owe so much already."

There was fear on Chei's face now. The eyes flickered desperately, distractedly for a moment, and he moistened his lips before they steadied. "The boy— misled you. I am not that boy. My men have you in sight. Will you throw away your lives—merely to have mine? It seems a poor exchange."

"We can take him with us," Vanye said in the Kurshin tongue. "I will take care of him."

"Skarrin will kill me for what I have done—he will kill all of us. *Listen* to what I am saying. I know how to mislead them. I know the way in. I will give you Skarrin . . . for your promise to take us with you." He rested back on his heels, hands on his knees, and the rising sun shone fair on Chei's curling hair, on Chei's earnest face. "And I will not betray you."

"Why not?" Morgaine asked. "You are betraying Skarrin."

"Because," Chei said with a foreign twist of the mouth, a sullen look up, as he set his hands on hips and sat back. "Skarrin is not a lord I chose, not a lord who chooses *me*, what is more. You are no fool, lady. And I am not. You have knowledge of the gates that I do not have. I made one try. You won. I have spent my life bowing down to a lord who has trod my face into the dust more than once, and the *boy*,— when I will listen to him—" The young features contracted, a kind of grimace. "—the boy remembers you dealt well with him."

Vanye's breath shortened. "Let us get out of here," he said, *"liyo."*

"The boy meant to kill me," Chei said. "He *wanted* to die. He still *wants* revenge. He came to me—to pit himself against me—inside—to drive me mad, if he could." Chei's mouth jerked, neither grimace nor smile, both humorless. "But he has changed his mind about death. It never agreed with him. Or with me. And he has changed his mind about killing you. He thought you would kill him—and me. He was disturbed that you declined. Now he understands more and more what a fool he was, having acquired a man's under-standing, and a warrior's good sense. And what he remembers tells me I am safer right now than I would ever be in Morund."

"He was mistaken now and again. I need no assas-sin at my back."

"You need *me*, my lady. And Skarrin will prove it to you, too late, if you kill me. I know the way into Mante. And you will not find it!"

"I have done harder things."

"I am not a rebel by nature, my lady! Give me a lord I can serve, give me a lord who can win against Skarrin, deal with me as you deal with your own, put me beside you, and you will find I have skill, my lady—in a command twice Morund's size, in any field, I am a man worth having, only so I have a lord more set on winning than on his fears of having me win! I do not rival you. I do not wish to. Only take me and my men and I will tell you how I will prove it: I will swear my allegiance through Vanye, I will put myself under his orders—he is a fair man. I *know* that he is a fair man—"

"But no fool," Vanye said bitterly, down the shaft of the arrow, "besides which, man, I have my own allegiance, which is to my liege, and her safety, and if I have to shoot you where you kneel I will do that before I will let you at her back." The arrow trembled and almost he lost his grip on it, so much the soreness

of his joints and the lightness of his head affected him.
He tightened his fingers, feeling the sweat stinging in
the cut on his brow; and for all his stomach knotted up
in loathing of the choices, it was not for her to do,
after so many other burdens she had. *"Liyo,"* he said,
and lapsed into the Kurshin tongue, looking nowhere
but at the center of Chei's chest. "Let him call the
others down. Let us—as you say—have them in sight.
Let us get down off this hill. And I will deal with
them."

She delayed her answer. The sweat stung his eyes
and ran down his sides, into raw burns; the muscles of
his arm began to tremble dangerously.

She touched his shoulder then. "No," she said; and
the breath went out of him and the world spun so that
he braced his feet as he lowered the bow. "You are
Vanye's," she said to Chei. "What he does short of
killing you I will not prevent." Her hand pressed hard
on Vanye's shoulder. "No," she said in the Kurshin
tongue, "thee cares too much."

He drew a breath and lifted the bow on the draw,
half-blind and choking on the desperation in him. He
fired. But her hand struck his arm up and the arrow
sped past Chei's head to strike a chip from the stone
wall behind him.

Everything froze in its place—Chei in front of him,
white-faced; Morgaine at his side. He trembled in the
aftershock of attempted murder; he felt the weakness
on him with a giddiness that dimmed the light and
made sounds ring in his ears.

"Aye," he said, because something seemed incumbent on him to say then, who had disregarded her
orders. If there was a part of his soul undamned, he
had done it by that act, excepting her forgiveness. He
drew in a breath, straining bruised ribs, vision hazing—
the blows to his head, he thought; the lack of food;
the exertion of the fight. He wanted only to have them
moving again, himself in the saddle with the horse to
carry him. Rest would mend him, a night's sleep—

But, O Heaven, it was not in reach, and Morgaine
listening to this man—

He could not think beyond her, not, in any case, with his head swimming and his thinking and his fears shrunk to the little space between these rocks, and the chance of an enemy which had been all too fortunate in its ambush—

And he must not kill this man. Morgaine forbade it. He had defied her order once. Twice was without excuse.

"Do you swear?" he asked Chei, knowing after he had asked, that oaths meant nothing with this creature.

"I have said," Chei said, and got to his feet. There was darkness in that stare. There was profound apprehension. Then another, more agitated way of speaking: "I swear before God. Is that enough?"

That human expression, that shift of voice, sent a chill through him.

Perhaps it was meant to.

But he let the silence go on a moment, and looked Chei in the eyes, long and steadily, until the air was a good deal colder and Chei surely knew it was not fear held his hand.

Then: "Do not cross me," he said to Chei, "and I will return you nothing of what I owe you. Where is my sword?"

Chei's eyes shifted toward the roan horse.

"I will have it back."

Chei nodded. "Aye."

"Aye—*my lord.*"

"Aye, my lord."

"Call your men down here. They can ride away or they can ride with us, but if one of them missteps, I will lay his head at your feet and lay yours at my lady's. I am nothing you know, whatever you think you gained at Tejhos. I am Nhi, and my clan is not reputed to give second chances."

Perhaps Chei believed him. Chei looked once back at him as he turned to face the cliffs, and once at Morgaine.

Then he shouted up at the height. "They have agreed," he called up the cliffs. "Come down."

Three of them, Vanye kept thinking, and went and

gathered up the arrows that had spilled off the cliff with the dead man—twelve he found with the fletchings and points whole, and put them in his quiver, the while Morgaine kept her eye on matters. His ribs ached.

Three of them, he kept thinking in the throbbing of his hurts and the panicked beating of his heart. *She has gone mad.*

It is this Skarrin—this man she fears. That is what drives her. That is what she wants to know—always, always when she does not know as much as she wishes— she doubts herself—

The Devil rather than honest men, he remembered her saying. *O my liege, you have found him.*

The two from the cliff came riding around the shoulder of the hill as Chei had come, stopped their horses by the red roan; and came to pay their respects to their recent enemy—the bowman and the qhal, the bowman's human face betraying intense worry, the qhal's having no expression at all.

"Rhanin ep Eorund," Chei named them. "And Hesiyyn Aeisyryn, both late of Mante."

"I will give you a simple choice," Vanye said, leaning on his bow, and this time with a quiver half full of arrows. "Ride off now, and go free. Or go with us, do my liege honest service, and I will forget what I owe you. I count that more than fair."

Rhanin nodded, clear of eye and countenance; and had the likeness of truth about him. "Aye," Rhanin said, and let go a long breath, as if he had taken him at his word and had worried, until then.

Hesiyyn lowered his eyes and inclined his head, and looked up with a bland, half-lidded insolence. "Anything you will, lord human."

Vanye stared at him and thought of striking him to the ground. But then it would come to killing—not one but all of them.

The archer had fired on his liege: but in defense of his own lord. While this Hesiyyn, he judged, might do anything and everything for his own sake.

And this, this was the qhal who had intervened to save his life.

"If they ride with us," he said to Chei, disdaining the qhal with a passing glance, "remember I hold you accountable."

And he turned his back on Chei as well, feeling their stares like knives; his heart beat like a hammer in his temples, and his face was hot, the sky like brass. Morgaine said something to him of riding out, that they were well off this hillside. "Aye," he said, and shouldered his bow and his quiver, and went to untangle the horses, which had wound themselves into a predicament, their two with the nervous geldings. Siptah had braced himself, flat-eared, too trail-wise to move, despite Arrhan's lead-rope wound across his rump, and that the blaze-faced gelding had a hind leg in among the rocks, its rump against the wall, one fore-leg crossing its partner's lead.

He cut both free and straightened out the leads, darting an anxious eye to Chei and the rest, but Morgaine was watching them: he saw her. He shoved Siptah with his shoulder to gain room, held Arrhan steady to re-tie the leads, and recalled his sword on Chei's saddle, uphill with the other horses.

He thought of climbing the rocks and making the exchange, but it was a war-horse in question, easier that Chei should deal with it, and he was out of breath and not wanting either the climb or any dealings with weapons at close quarters: bruised ribs and stiff muscles, he thought, leaning on Siptah's side to work past him and lead him out of the confusion.

But when he unstrung his bow to tie it with his gear on Arrhan's saddle, the weakness of his arm and his lack of wind surprised him. He had to make a second pull to slip the string. When he had gotten it tied and set his foot in the stirrup, it more than hurt to pull himself up, it sapped the strength from him and made him sweat and his head reel despite the morning chill.

It is the sun-heat on the metal, he told himself; there is no wind here. Using the bow and pushing the horses about had strained the ribs. *It will pass.*

He sat still, with the sweat running, leaning on the saddlebow, while Morgaine mounted up. *Get us moving,* he thought, feeling the sting of salt in his cuts. There was no wind in this place. He longed to be off this hill, not knowing what they might meet on that slope down there or out in the land: *best hurry before they collect a defense,* he thought; and everything conspired with delays.

"They will go first," Morgaine said, starting out. "I have told them."

"Aye," he murmured. "Let Skarrin's men have *them* for ranging-shots."

"They might have killed us," Morgaine said. "They could have taken the weapons. That much is true."

He thought about that.

"But I do not forget what they did," she said.

"Aye," he said. The hill seemed steeper than he recalled as they struck the open slope—a place littered with dead, thirty, forty or more.

And Chei and his men rode past them, dutifully taking the lead.

"Is thee all right?" Morgaine asked.

"A little faint. I am well enough. It is the heat." He urged Arrhan to a faster pace, and overtook Chei's men.

"Arrows," he said. "All we can gather. We may need them."

"Aye," Rhanin said, and veered off on that chancy slope, at hazard of further attack, from men on the ground, from Heaven knew where on the rocky heights around them.

Rhanin would not, he thought at the back of his mind, come back. The man would take his chance and ride for his own life.

"The sword," he said to Chei.

Chei took it from his saddle and reversed it, passing it over as they rode.

"A good blade," Chei said.

He said nothing. He unhooked his own from Arrhan's saddle and passed it by the hilt.

"Alayyis' sword," Chei murmured.

"My liege did not ask his name," he said harshly, and reined back and hooked the arrhendur blade to his sword-belt, waiting for Morgaine to overtake him.

O God, he thought then, *why did I say that? Why am I always a fool?*

Morgaine overtook him. He murmured an explanation for the bowman's departure, and started up again, riding after the others, a crowded trail avoiding the lumps of bodies which lay like so much refuse on the hillside. He watched carefully such dead as they did pass close at hand, wary of traps. He watched the hills about them, for any flash of armor, any flight of birds or bit of color out of place.

Far across the field, Rhanin searched, dismounted, searched again. Eventually he came riding back, carrying three quivers of arrows. "I would keep one," Rhanin said, offering two as he rode alongside—no grudging look, only an earnest and an anxious one.

"Do that," Vanye said; and the man gave him them, and turned off downslope, to overtake Chei and Hesiyyn.

He hung the two quivers from his saddlebow, and he stared at Rhanin's retreating back with misgivings. They had reached the bottom of the hill, and the last body, which lay face upward. Carrion birds had gathered. He did not look down at it as they rode their slow course past. That man was incontrovertibly dead. The hour was fraught enough with nightmares, and he had had enough of such sights in his life.

But, he thanked Heaven, there were no ambushes.

The hill beyond the next rise gave out onto the flat again, a broad valley; he blinked at the sweat in his eyes and rubbed at them to make the haze go away.

"Vanye?" Morgaine asked, as Siptah's heavy weight brushed his leg.

"Aye?" His head ached where the helm crossed his brow; the sun heated the metal, heated his shoulders beneath the armor and the pain in his ribs made his breath hard to draw.

"Is thee bearing up?"

"Well enough. Would there was more wind."

Chei had drawn rein in front of them, and scanned the ground; and waited for them with the others.

"We should bear south a little," Chei said. "Around the shoulder—" Chei pointed. "Off into the hills. One of them may well have us in sight. But the weapon you used up there—" He gave a small, humorless laugh. "—will have improved my reputation with Mante. At least for veracity. They will be very hesitant to come at us."

"Why south?"

"Because—" Chei said sharply, and pointed out over the plain, below, and to their right, toward the hills. "To reach that, necessitates crossing this, else, and if you have no liking for—"

"Courtesy, man," Vanye muttered, and Chei drew another breath.

"My lady," Chei said quietly, "it is safer. If you will take my advice—lend me the stone a moment and I can send a message that may draw their forces off us."

"Tell me the pattern," Morgaine said.

Chei took up the reins on the roan, that flattened its ears toward Siptah. "Two flashes. A simple report. I can send better than that. I can tell them the enemy has gone up into the hills. In numbers. And if you provoke them to answer you, my lady, and you cannot reply rapidly, they will *know* what you are. I can answer them."

"Do not give it to him," Vanye said, and made no move to hand over the stone.

"No," Morgaine said. "Not here and not now."

"My lady—"

"Can it be—you *have* sent?"

"Aye. From Tejhos."

"And the stone, man!"

"With that," Chei said with a reluctant shrug. "Yes. The first night."

"And *told* them it would stay unshielded. Do not evade me. I am out of patience for guesswork. *What* have you done, what do you suspect, what is out there?"

"They will have known something went amiss from

the time you sealed off the stone," Chei said in a low
voice. "There is rumor Skarrin's gate can tell one
stone from the other, given sure position. I do not
know. I only know there are two more such stones out
there. I saw them, clear as I could see Tejhos."

"In the stone."

"In the stone, my lady. There may be more than
that by now. When yours stopped sending—It is myself they will be hunting, along with you. I am well
known for treason."

"Did you think they would forgive," Vanye asked,
"the small matter of killing your lord's deputy?"

Chei's eyes lifted to his, hard and level. "No. But,
then, if I had won, I would have done what we are
doing now. With your weapons. It is not Mante I
want. It is the gate. . . . With your weapons. I told
you my bargain. And, lady, you have convinced me: I
will not follow a lord in the field who cannot beat me.
I should be a fool, else. You won. So I take your
orders."

There was a moment's silence, only the stamp and
blowing of the horses.

"Let us," Morgaine said to Chei then, "see where
your ability leads us."

And in the Kurshin tongue, when they struck a freer
pace, tending toward the south, into rougher land:

"Do not be concerned for it. I will choose any camp
we make, and he will not lay hands on the stone, to be
telling them anything.—Thee is white, Vanye."

"I am well enough," he said again.

If he confessed otherwise, he thought, she might
take alarm, might seek some place to rest, where they
must not—*must* not go to hiding now, when Mante
knew the vicinity to search, and might throw company
after company into the field. Even *Changeling* had its
limits—

—had them, more and more as they drew near the
aching wound that was Mante.

My fault, he kept thinking. All of this. *O Heaven*,
what are we going to do?

And others, out of the muddle of heat and exhaustion: she has taken them *because* she knows I am near to falling; she needs help; she takes it where she can, against this stranger-lord in Mante—against this Skarrin—needs them in place of me—to guard her back—

O God, that I leave her to these bandits—

It is her own perverse way of managing them, putting them under my hand, forcing the bitter draught down their throats—lest they think they can leave me behind: it is her own stratagem, give them a captain like to spill from his horse, and let them vie for her favor, whereby she keeps Chei at bay, and in hope of succession, and he never dares strike at me, lest he lose what gratitude he might win of her later—If he has not betrayed us outright—if the ambush was not a trick, their own arrangement—

A man learned to think in circles, who companied with Morgaine kri Chya. A man learned craft, who had before thought a sword-edge the straightest way to a target.

She might manage Chei. Surely Rhanin. I should tell her to keep that man.

And: This weakness of mine may pass. It may well pass. She is winning time for me. Gaining ground.

And lastly: Why did she prevent me from Chei? Why strike my hand?

You care too much?

What did she mean by that?

Hills closed about them, brushy ravines and rock and scrub, steep heights on either side. He looked up and behind them, and never was there trace of any watcher.

Except in a fold between two hills, near a stand of scrub, where they came to a stream: there Hesiyyn drew up by the grassy margin and signaled Chei.

They were old tracks. It had surely been yesterday that some rider had paused to water his horse, and ridden along the hillside, in this place of tough, clumped grass which showed very little trace otherwise. The track there went out onto that ground on their own side, not, Vanye reckoned, hard to follow, if one had to wonder where that rider had gone, or if one were interested in finding him.

As it was: "What is this place?" he asked angrily. "A highway their riders use? A known trail?"

"Doubtless," Hesiyyn said, "my lord human. We are all anxious to die."

He sent Hesiyyn a dark look.

"We are no more anxious for a meeting than you are," Chei said. "They are out here, that is all. I told you. Skarrin is no longer taking the matter lightly.—I ask you again, lady, in all earnestness: lend me the stone."

Morgaine leaned her hands against the saddlebow and quickly restrained Siptah from edging toward the roan. It was warfare, now. The red roan's ears were flat, his eyes—red-rimmed, his least lovely feature— constantly one or the other toward the gray stud.

"No," she said shortly, and reining Siptah sharply aside to gain room, dismounted and threw her hand up to shy the roan. "Move him off! We will rest here a little. At least they *have* passed here. And it is at least some cover."

"My lady," Chei said with heavy resentment, and drew the wild-eyed roan aside, along the stream.

So the rest of them. Vanye glared a warning in their direction, threw his leg over the horn and slid down. He dropped Arrhan's reins to let her drink, and let the two horses he led move up to the water, then sank down on his knees and bathed his face and the back of his shorn neck, discovering that insult again, where it had passed in shock when Chei had done it. For this one unjustified thing he was more and more angry, an unreasoning, killing anger, of the sort he had not felt—

—since the day his brother died.

"We will rest here an hour," Morgaine said, sinking down to wash beside him, letting Siptah drink.

"Aye." He dipped up another double handful. It was spring-fed, this stream, and like ice, taking the breath. He stood up with a sudden effort.

The daylight went to gray and to dark.

"Vanye—" Morgaine said.

"Watch them!" he said to her in the Kurshin tongue, and sat down hard where he stood, his balance simply gone, his foot off the edge into the chill water, his wounds jolted so he thought he would not get the next breath at all.

"Vanye!"

"Watch them," he said again, calmly, fighting panic. He drew his foot out of the water. "*Liyo,* I will rest here a little. I am tired. That is all."

He heard her bend near him, felt her shadow take the heat of the sun from his face. He heard footsteps in the grass nearby and that frightened him.

"*Liyo,* do not turn your back on them."

She laid her hand on his brow. "Thee is fevered," she said.

"*Liyo,* in the name of Heaven—"

"We will rest here," she said. The daylight began to come back, but it was still brass and full of illusion, with her as a darkness in the center of it.

"We have no time—"

"Vanye, lie down."

He did as she asked, reckoning if they must stop an hour for his sake, he had as well not waste the time it cost them in argument. He let himself back on the grass and rested his head on his arm, and shut his eyes against the giddiness of the sky. The ground seemed to pitch and spin under him. He had not felt that dizzy when he was riding, and now that he let go it was hard not to lose all his senses. His stomach tried to heave and he refused to let it, refused the panic that lay at the bottom of his thoughts.

A little time, he told himself. They had been pushing too long to keep moving; and a battle and a ride with enemies-turned-comrades did not count for rest. An hour on his back, and he would be good for another ten.

Only, O God, he was weak. And his head spun.

And Morgaine was alone with these men.

She came back to him, knelt down by him, dampened a cloth in the cold stream and laid it on his brow.

"You are watching them," he murmured in his own tongue.

"I am watching them."

"Liyo, kill them."

"Hush, rest."

"Kill them!" He sat up on his elbow and caught the cloth in his hand, the pulse at once hammering in his ears and his gut hurting and his ribs a blinding pain. " 'Man and man,' you said. Then trust me to know. I am telling you these men are after the weapons; they are only waiting to see what more they can find out, whether we have anything else they want—Kill them. And do not give them any warning."

Her hand rested on his chest, pressing him to lie back. He would not yield.

"Listen to me," he said.

"Hush," she said. "Hush. I have an eye to them."

"This is a man who gave Chei to the wolves. This is the guide who lied to us, whose brother I killed. If it is sane inside it is a wonder."

"Lie back. Lie down. Do not make me trouble. Please. *Please,* Vanye."

He let go his breath and let himself back. She wet the cloth again and wrung it out and laid it on his brow. It set him shivering.

"I will ride," he said, "in an hour."

"Only lie here. I will make some tea."

"We cannot be risking a fire—"

She touched his lips with her fingers. "Still, I say. Hush. A little one. Do not fret about it. Be still."

"Willow tea," he murmured, "if you are going to do it anyway. My head aches."

He rested then with his eyes half-open, slitted on Chei and his two men, who sat apart on the stream-bank. He watched Morgaine gather up twigs and grass, and his gut tensed as he saw Chei rise and walk toward her and have words with her.

What they said he could not hear. But Morgaine settled down thereafter and made a fire with that means she could, and Chei and the others began to unsaddle the horses.

He sat up then, and began to get to his feet in dismay, but Morgaine looked at him and lifted her hand in that signal that meant no.

He fell back again, and lay in misery while the pulse beat like a hammer in his temples and the sun glared red behind closed lids.

She brought him tea to drink, infused very strongly with something bitter; and little pellets wrapped in leaves, that were from Shathan, and very precious. He took them and drank the sour-bitter tea, as large mouthfuls as he could bear, simply to get it down, and rested back again.

"I will be all right," he murmured then.

"Thee is not riding in an hour. Or two."

"Dark," he said. "Give me till dark. We can cut closer to the plain at night. Gain back the time."

But he was no better. If anything, he hurt the worse. It is because of lying still, he thought.

Then, clearly and honestly: I am getting worse.

And we are too near the gate.

He rested. It was not sleep that passed the hours into twilight, only a dimness in which Morgaine came and went, and gave him cold water to drink. "I will try," he said, then, "try to ride. Have them put me on my horse. I will stay there."

There was fear in her eyes. It verged on panic. She smoothed the hair back from his face. "We will hold this place," she said.

"With *what?* With *them?* With—" Anger brought a pain to his skull. His eyes watered, blurring the sight of her. "It is foolishness. Foolishness, *liyo*. No more time. Too many of them. When will you sleep? You cannot—cannot depend on me to stay awake. Cannot depend on me."

"I will manage."

"Do not lose for *me!* Do not think of it! Ride out of here!"

"Hush." She touched his face, bent and kissed him, weary, so very weary, her voice. Her hand shook against his cheek. "Forgive me. Trust me. Will you trust me?"

"Aye," he said, or thought he said. She unlaced his collar and took the stone from under his armor; and took it from him.

"Not to him—" he protested.

"No. I will keep it. I will keep it safe."

It was too difficult to hold on. The dark grew too deep, a place unto itself, tangled and mazed. He wanted to come back. He wanted to stay awake to listen to her.

He dreamed of dark, like that between the Gates.

He dreamed of dark, in which she walked away, and he could not so much as tell where she had gone.

Chei rested his head in his hands, weary with his own aches, with the foolishness that would not let the woman see reason.

Will not leave him, the inner voice said, and it echoed a night in Arunden's camp, a doorway—embarrassed youth, rebuffed and dismayed and made lonely all at once, in a child's way; Pyverrn, seeking exile—riding into Morund on a wretched, shaggy horse—*Ho, hello, old friend—Court grew deadly dull without you. . . .*

Thoughts upon thoughts upon thoughts. He rubbed the heels of his hands into his eyes, grimaced with the confusion of images.

"My lord," Rhanin said.

He looked up to see the lady walking toward them—with further delay, he reckoned. She looked distraught, her eyes shadowed and her face showing exhaustion.

She had to sleep. There would come a time she had to sleep. Then there was a reckoning, with the weapons in his hands, and the lady brought to see reason once for all.

He was not prepared to see her hand lift, and the black weapon in it, aimed straight at him. His heart froze in him: *death,* he thought. *Our death, only so a crazed woman dares sleep—*

"My lord Gault," she said quietly, "Qhiverin. Chei. I have a proposition for you."

"My lady?" he asked, carefully.

"I am going to rest. You will tend him, you will do everything you can for him, you will make him fit to ride, my lord; and if he is not better by morning, I will kill you all. If he cries out—*once*—I will shoot one of you at random. Do you have any doubt of that, my lord?"

"He will not *be* fit to ride—the man is fevered—he is out of his head—"

"Do you doubt my word, *my lord?* Do you want an earnest of my intentions?"

"She is mad," Hesiyyn exclaimed.

Chei gathered himself hastily to his feet. "Up," he said, dragging at Hesiyyn, at Rhanin. And cast an anxious glance at Morgaine, whose weapon stayed centered on him, whose eyes were, as Hesiyyn said— mad and beyond all reason.

Chapter Sixteen

"Vanye. *Vanye,*" Morgaine's voice called him gently.

"Aye, *liyo.*" He opened his eyes, trying to bring her face out of the dusk. He could not, quite.

"Vanye, will you trust me?"

"Aye, *liyo.*"

"I am going to go over there and rest, the night. Listen to me. I have not the strength to take care of thee—" Her fingers brushed his cheek. Her voice shook. "Chei will help thee, he will do everything he can for thee—he has agreed, at peril of his life. Does thee understand, Vanye? I do not want thee waking and not knowing where I am. And if he hurts thee I will shoot him. And if thee does not mend I will shoot him. And he knows it."

He blinked at her. When she took that tone it was her intention beyond a doubt, even if it made no sense at all.

"Thee understands?"

"Aye," he said.

The dark swallowed him up a time, and there was movement about him—firelit faces between him and the night sky.

One was Chei's.

He forgot, then, where he was.

"Ah," he cried, and tried desperately to fight them.

"Be still," Chei said, and put his hand over his mouth. "Be still, man. Vanye. Vanye—listen to me."

He recalled then, some insanity that Morgaine was

with him. Or would come. He could not remember which.

"Look." Chei lifted his head, carefully, gently, and showed him a strange sight: showed him Siptah, and at Siptah's feet a stump, or some object, and Morgaine sitting with her hands between her knees. He was afraid, until he saw *Changeling* across her lap.

"You are safe," Chei said. "You are quite safe with us."

"She has promised to shoot one of us." Hesiyyn gently unfastened a buckle at his side as Chei let his head back. "I have no doubt which one of us. My lord Chei is necessary, Rhanin wins everyone, and I am told I make enemies. I pray you know I shall be careful."

He blinked dazedly. He recalled some such thing, mad as it was, and lay still, until they needed to work the mail shirt off. But that they did gently, easing his arms as they worked it free.

It was all one with the dark, the fever, the nightmare that began to become ease of pain. They put warm compresses on his hurts, renewing them constantly; they put hot cloths over him, soaked in herbals; they made him drink something complex and musky, and breathe something that gave his throat ease. He became comfortable, finally.

And slept till Chei roused him and made him drink something else.

"No more," he said.

"Drink this," Chei said fiercely. "Damn you, drink; we will not die for your convenience."

He heard the harshness of panic in that voice. He recalled a nightmare, wherein Morgaine had asked him bear with everything.

He struggled onto his arm, dislodging compresses, to see was she safe and his memory true.

She was there. *Changeling* was still with her. Siptah stood close by her. Her head had fallen forward, her pale hair touched with fire-glow and starlight.

"Drink," Rhanin said.

He trusted them then, and drank, with a clearer

head than he had had. He shivered, and the bruises hurt less. They renewed the compresses out of a pan of hot water, and smothered him in blankets.

Only his chest hurt sharply, where ribs might be cracked. But that, he thought, was bearable, if he were not so drained and weak. The burns hurt far less; the other injuries that had near taken his mind with pain, were so much relieved he seemed to drift in enervated numbness.

The qhal whispered among themselves, urgently, debating something they might give him. Or how much they might give him, to put him on his feet. One said no, there was risk. Another objected he had to ride, and could not else: he would never last in the saddle. And that was Chei and Hesiyyn.

He lay and thought about that. He tested his breathing, how much it hurt; he moved his right leg, to test whether it hurt as it had, and looked at the two who argued.

"Is there something," he asked faintly, in a lull, "will let me ride today?"

He shocked them, perhaps. There was a moment's utter hush.

"Yes," Chei said. "There is something that will. But the end of it is worse than the first. Best you do without it. You will ride. That is what she asked. That is what she will have. We have kept our end of the bargain."

"Do you drink it," he asked, the faintest of whispers, "or swallow it?"

"Not, I say."

"Chei—tell me what it will do."

"It will kill you, that is what it will do. And no."

"It would keep a dead man on his feet," Hesiyyn said. "It would not improve his judgment. And my lord says the truth: it would take a heavy toll."

"Give it to me. To carry. Chei, give it to me and we are quit of a great deal."

Chei gnawed at his lip—young Chei's face, a mature qhal's calculation as he rested with his arm on his knee and his eyes, by firelight, flickering with changes.

"You would take only a taste of it on your tongue," he said. "I will tell you the truth, man, if you use it in extremity—you will not survive it."

He thought about that. He drew breaths against the ache in his ribs, and knew what his sword-arm or his archery was worth at the moment. He thought how far they had yet to go.

"You are not the man I would choose," he said. "But there is a great deal you could learn from my liege. There are more worlds than you know. If you knew more than you did, I think you might understand her more. You would know why she is right. More than I do. Give me this thing and do not tell her. The important thing is that we get there."

Chei looked at him in profound disturbance. His fist clenched and unclenched, of the arm which supported his chin, and his brow was ridged and glistening with sweat. "And you do what—lay this in her lap? Tell her then we tried to kill you?"

"We will have no quarrel, Chei. What do you want? That she stop somewhere further on—for my sake? That is what she *is* doing. Give it to me."

Chei delved into his belongings, and gathered out a packet. "One pellet. One. No more than that. Three and your heart would burst. I am putting it with your belongings. That is all I will do." He busied himself and mixed something with water, and boiled it.

"What is this?" he asked, when Hesiyyn intended he drink it.

"I thought we were allies," Hesiyyn said. "Drink. This is for the fever."

"Also," Hesiyyn said when he had drunk it, "it will make you sleep."

The sun came up, and Morgaine still drowsed, he saw as he lifted his head, with Siptah's tether passed across her shoulder, with the sword in her lap, her back against a rock, and the small black weapon between her knees, in both her hands.

It was Chei whose eyes had shadows. It was Chei

who offered him an overcooked porridge, with a hand that shook with exhaustion.

He took it. He forced it down. It came at too much cost to refuse.

Across the little distance, Siptah jerked his head up and snorted challenge to Rhanin's approach. Morgaine lifted her head abruptly, the weapon in her hand.

But it was a bowl Rhanin brought, offering it to her. Rhanin came no closer, and Morgaine got quickly to her feet, *Changeling* in one hand, the black weapon in the other, and stopped, staring not at Rhanin, but toward him.

He stared back at her, weak as he was, and got up on his arm, feeling the shock of cold air as the blanket fell.

For a long moment she said nothing. Then: "How does thee fare this morning?"

"Much better," he said. "Much better, *liyo.*"

"I had not meant to fall so far asleep—"

He drew a breath, such as yesterday would have cost him pain. It amazed him it did not, overmuch. Only it would be very easy, just now, to weep, and he moved, suddenly, and shoved himself up with a sudden straightening of his arm so that a twinge took his mind off it. He was dizzy then. The whole world swung round.

She came to him and swept *Changeling*, sheathed and crosswise, in curt dismissal of the others, who drew back a few paces. Then she knelt and spared a glance for him.

"I think the porridge is safe," he murmured, "but I would not eat it."

"Has thee?"

"Aye," he said. "It is truly wretched."

She slid the black weapon into place at her belt, touched him with that hand, brushed the hair off his unshaven cheek. She looked tired, tired and mortally worried. "We will ride at night," she said.

"*Liyo*, we cannot wait!"

"Now how are we arguing? I take your advice and you will none of it. We are safe here for the moment. The horses are resting. We can make up the time."

"We cannot make up two days. I can ride." He sat upright and tucked his leg up; and she put her hand onto his knee.

"Thee will lie down, thee will rest, that is what. Thee will not undo everything." She touched his ribs, where Hesiyyn had wound a tight bandage. "Broken, does thee think?"

"No. Sore." He drew a breath, testing it as he had tested it again and again: if he kept his back straight it was much better. "I will manage."

"Vanye." Her hand sought his wrist and closed on it, hard. "Do not give up. Hear me? I will tell thee a thing may comfort thee—"

She hesitated, then. That reticence did not seem to herald anything that should comfort him; and ice settled into his stomach. "What?" he asked. "What would you tell me, *liyo?*"

"Thee knows—how substance goes into a gate—It . . . disarranges itself . . . and some similar arrangement comes together at the other side—"

"You have told me." He did not like to talk of such things. He did not like to think of them oftener than he must—especially now, facing a gate which was not behaving as it should. He wished she would go straight to the point.

"Thee will find—thy hurts—will not trouble thee the other side. Thee will not carry the scars of this beyond it. Thee will mend."

She could lie with such simplicity. Or with webs of truth. Except that it was something kept from him, that he would not like. In such things she would not meet his eyes. It was that simple.

"What are you saying?" he asked.

"I chose a time," she said. "I made a pattern, for thee as for me . . . a rested pattern, a whole pattern, a pattern without flaw. Within its limits—and it has them—it will always restore it. Every gate, on every world—will recognize thee, and always restore it—restore *thee*, as thee was, so far as it has substance to work with. There will be no scars. Nothing to remind thee."

It made no sense for a moment. He put his hand to his ribs, wondering could it mend more than the surface.

Or what other things they had done to him.

"There will always be the weakness in the knee," she said. "That happened before the pattern was made. Would I had done it before that. But there was never the leisure it needed."

"Shathan," he said. "Azeroth-gate."

"Aye. There. The gates will abhor any deviation from that moment. They will restore that moment, so far as they can, always. The thoughts go on. The memories. But the body—will not change."

"Will not *change?* Ever?" A sense of panic took him. He thought that he should be grateful. He thought that it was a kind of gift.

But it was Gate-given. And every Gate-magic was flawed—

"I shall grow older—"

"Never. Not in body."

"O my God," he murmured. For a moment the dizziness was back. Mortality was, reminding him with a sharp pain in his side and a twinge in the hip.

He had always had an image of himself, older, grown to his mature strength—had begun to see it, in breadth of shoulder, strength of arm. A man looked forward to such a thing.

It would never happen. His life was stopped. He thought of the dragon, frozen in snow, in mid-reach.

"My God, my God." He crossed himself, gone cold, inside and out.

"Injuries will never take their toll of thee. Age— will have no power over thee. Thee will grow wiser. But thee will always mend in a gate-passage, always shed the days and years."

"Why such as Chei, then? Why Gault? *Why Thiye, in Heaven's name?*" He wanted to weep. He found himself lost again, lost at this end of his journey as at the beginning. "If it can be done like this, why did they choose to kill—?"

"Because," she said, "they are qhal. And I know things they do not. Call it my father's legacy. And if they should know, Vanye, *that* secret, they would find others, that I will give no one, that are not written on the sword—that I will not *permit* anyone to know and live—" Again her hand brushed his cheek. "Forgive me. I had meant to tell thee—some better time. But best thee know, now—Forgive me. I need thee too much. And the road would grow too lonely."

He took her hand, numb in shock. He pressed it. It was all he could think to do for answer.

"Rest," she said. And rose and walked away from him, stopping for a moment to look at Chei and the rest—at Rhanin, who still had the bowl in his hands, beside the others. "I will make my own breakfast," she said; but to Chei she said nothing. She only looked at him, and then walked on, *Changeling* still in her left hand.

Vanye sat numb and incapable, for the moment, of moving. He trembled, and did not know whether it was outrage or grief, or why, except he had always thought she would betray him in one way, and she had found one he had never anticipated.

You might have ordered me, he raged at her in his mind. *If you were going to do such a thing, liyo, God in Heaven, could you not have bidden me, could you not have laid it on my honor, given me at least the chance to go into it of my own will?*

But he could not say these things. He could not quarrel with her, in front of strangers. Or now, that he was fighting for his composure.

It was his protection she had intended. It was for every good reason. It promised—O Heaven!—

He could not imagine what it promised.

It was, in any case, only the thought of a thought of himself she had stolen. And if she had thought him too foolish to choose for himself, that was so, sometimes. She was often right.

He reached beside him, in the folds of his mail shirt, and felt after a small, paper packet. He found it, and unfolded it, and saw the very tiny beads that lay on the red paper—eight of them.

He folded it up again, dragged his belt over and

tucked the packet into the slit-pocket where he kept small flat things, where, lately, had been a small razor-edged blade. But Chei's men had taken that. He did not, given the circumstances of his losing it, look to have it back again.

He lay back to rest, then, since he had no more likelihood of persuading Morgaine than Chei did. There was justification for the delay: beyond this point, he thought, rested horses and rested men might make the difference, and Chei and his men had gotten little enough sleep last night. If the horses were rested—they might dare the fringe of the plain, and know that they had enough strength to run or to fight.

It was a risk that made his flesh crawl.

"She is staying here," Chei came to him to say, standing over him, a fair-haired shadow against the dawn. Chei was indignant. And came to him for alliance.

He found some small irony in that. "Man," he said quietly, reasonably, "she will be thinking. Go to her. Be patient with her. As thoroughly, as exactly as you can, tell her everything you know about the way ahead: make her maps. Answer her questions. Then go away and let her think. Whatever you have held back—to bargain for your lives—this is the time to throw everything you have into her hands. She will not betray you. You say you will follow her. Prove it."

It was not precisely the truth. But it was as good, he thought, as might save all their lives. Chei clearly doubted it.

But Chei went away then, and presented himself where Morgaine was busy with her gear; and knelt down with his hands on his knees and talked to her and drew on the ground, answering her questions for some little time.

Himself, he scanned the rough hills, the rocks and the scrub which rose like walls about them, watched the flight of a hawk, or something hawklike.

Morgaine was not utterly without calculation, he thought, in choosing this camp. The valley was wide and either end of it was in view. Nowhere were they in easy bowshot of the sides or cover a man could reach without crossing open ground.

Until now Chei and his company, riding ahead of them through the hills, had run the risk of a gate-force ambush, two stones bridging their power from side to side of a narrow pass. Chei had surely known that. And doubtless Morgaine would put him and his company to the fore again when they rode out of this place. Chei would not like that.

But there was small comfort having them *all* riding point, and surely neither of them would do it.

There was better food at noon: Morgaine cooked it. Vanye stirred himself to sit up in the shade, and to put his breeches on and walk about, and to take a little exercise, a little sword-drill to work the legs, and the abused shoulder, which had a great dark bruise working its way out from the arrow-strike.

It would go through several color-changes, he thought, and then thought that it might not, for one reason or the other; and put all of that to the back of his mind with a swing and flourish and extension that worked the ribs as far as he thought safe for the moment. Vanity, he chided himself, taking pleasure in Hesiyyn's respectful look, and was careful to stand very still for a moment after, before he called it enough and walked back to the shade and sat down.

He went through the arrows Rhanin had collected then, and took his harness-knife—the loss of the little razor vexed him—and sighted down the shafts and saw to the fletchings, in both quivers finding only three shafts to fault and mark with a cautioning stain on their gray feathers, and one fletching that wanted repair.

Then he gathered himself up again and went and saw to the horses, running his hands over their legs, looking for strain, looking over their feet, seeing whether there was any shoe needing re-setting. The bending and lifting was hard. And Morgaine was watching him: he felt her stare on his back, and gentled the gray stud with particular care, lulling him with all his skill to keep him from his rougher tricks—"So, so, lad, you have no wish to make me a liar, do you?"

The fine head turned, dark-eyed and thinking; the white-tipped tail lashed and switched with considerable force and he stamped once, thunderously. But: "Hai, hai, hai," Vanye chided him, and he surrendered the ticklish hind foot, with which, he thanked Heaven, there was no problem, nor with the others.

He did all these things. He wanted, looking to certain eventualities, to do them particularly well, and the way he always did.

"Sleep," he bade Morgaine, pausing to wash on his way back to the shade. "Sleep a while."

She looked at him with a worry she did not trouble to hide. He could bear very little of that.

"We have not that far to go," she said, "—Chei swears."

"Perhaps he has even learned to reckon distances."

Her eyes flickered, a grim amusement that went even to a grin and a fond look. "Aye. Perhaps. I do not think I will sleep. Go take what rest you can." She drew the chain of the pyx from over her head. "Here. Best you keep it now."

He closed his fist about it. It was not something he wanted to wear openly.

She sketched rapidly in the dirt at her feet. "This is where we are. Chei says. This is Mante. This is where we will ride. This hill, then skirting the plain and up again. There is a pass. A gatehouse, but not a Gate."

"We are that close."

"Under Skarrin's very eye, if there were a mistake with stone or sword. We will start at sundown. A single night to the pass, if we go direct." She let go her breath. "We will *ask* at his gate."

"Ask!"

"We will not come like enemies. It will be Chei's affair. He says he can pass us through. We will have the greatest difficulty beyond that. So Chei says." She sketched a pocket behind the line that represented the cliffs. *"Neisyrrn Neith*. Death's Gate. A well of stone, very wide. There are gate-stones within it—here, and here, and here."

He sank down on his heels and onto his knees. His breath grew short.

"Chei swears," Morgaine said, "there is—no other way in. In all their wars, in all their internal wars—no enemy can come at them, except by the highlands. And that, they rule utterly. *Those* lords are loyal."

"God save us." He drew breath after breath. *"Liyo,* —turn back. Turn back, give this more time. We can find a way—"

"Those lords are loyal, Vanye. And the south cannot stand against them. I have thought of it. I have thought of pulling back to Morund and trying to take the south—but it could not hold. This whole southern region is a sink, Mante's midden-heap—it is where they send their exiles. It is where they breed their human replacements." She went on drawing. "Herot, Sethys, Stiyesse, Itheithe, Nenais—I forget the other names. Here, here, here—this is a vast land. And I do not doubt this Skarrin set the World-gate purposely on Morund. Perpetually on Morund, in the case any intruder, any rebel, any rival—should attempt him. Here, below these cliffs, this rift in the world—lie Men; and his exiles. Here above, across all this continent—lie the qhalur lands. There is irony in this. We knew our young guide was abysmally incapable of reckoning a day's ride—"

"Or lied to us."

"—had never traveled much in all his life, except the hills, except forest trails and winding roads. Straight distances bewildered him. He lived his life in so small a place. And he did not know anything beyond it. The distance between Morund and Herot, is less than he thought. Sethys and Stiyesse abut against marsh he did not know existed. These are little places. These are holds humans once had. Qhal have moved in, those exiled, those out of favor—like Qhiverin, who became Gault. The south has no resource against the north, not if the north realized its danger. And by now, since Tejhos—Skarrin does, though Chei does swear—for what it is worth—that he did not tell Skarrin our purpose here. That is the only grace we may have, if we can believe it."

He leaned his hands on his knees and bowed his head a moment. "We *should* have gone to Morund, the way you wanted to. We would have learned this. We could have dealt with whatever we found there— what*ever* we found there. This is my fault, *liyo*, it is *all* my—"

"It was my decision. It was *my* judgment. Do not be so cursed free with blame. It is still my decision, and all of this may be wrong. Chei has the notion we can come close before they will take alarm."

"With *our* horses—"

"Or his. That roan of his is no unremarkable beast, in itself. No, they will surely know us: they will have gotten the description from their watchers afield. It is a question of keeping them uncertain what we intend." She looked at the ground in front of her and seemed lost for a moment. "Chei says if they have thrown no great number of men into the field since yesterday, they are taking a cautious path. He talked at some length of his own difficulties with his Overlord— he was high-born, was a member of a martial order that lost its influence at court: disastrously for him, though more so for others. Connections saved his life and sent him to Morund, to redeem himself, if ever he could—The arrangement by which human lords were permitted to rule in the south was collapsing, on evidence of human Gault's complicity with the rebels in Mante—*that* was how they lured the original Gault into their trap: and sentenced him and Qhiverin to one conjoined existence—on that point Qhiverin's friends intervened virtually to kidnap Gault from his jailers and coerce the gate-wardens to join them, to forestall enemies who would have preferred not to have Qhiverin at Morund."

"Where he served their interests well enough—"

"So he has done. So he fully intended to come home, someday. Except—as thee says, possibly we could have persuaded him to go against his lord from

the beginning. He says so. Certainly he is quick enough
to commit treason. I do not know. At least—he has
had some little credit with Skarrin for setting affairs in
the south in order, if, as he says, they do not take that
for too *much* success, and if his connections in Mante
have not lost all influence. That we have arrived in the
south without a force about us—that they have lost
contact with him, whom they do not trust, under uncertain circumstances, after he has faithfully sent them
a report from Tejhos and seemed, there, under the
witness of the wardens there, to be fighting us—all of
this, he thinks, might create some debate among
Skarrin's advisers. The question is whether we should
attempt stealth—or bewilder them further. Recall that
there is one way in, that we must pass within *that,* that
thing they call *Seiyyin Neith,* the Gate of Exiles, and
within this league-wide pit of stone, that they call
Death's-gate—they can kill us with a thought. As you
did say: a man who thinks he is winning—will not
flee."

"No, he will send us straightway to Hell, *liyo,* and
we will hardly see it coming!"

"Chei will get us to Exile's Gate. There is where
they will be vulnerable."

"God in Heaven, are we leaning on this man's word?"

She lifted her eyes to him. "This man—wants to
live. So do the men with him. Did I not say I trusted
him more than honest men? They *have* no cause, no
cause for which they would give up their lives. Skarrin
cannot promise them anything they would believe.
Not as deeply as they have tangled themselves. They
know that."

For a moment he truly could not breathe. His eyes
went involuntarily to see where Chei and the others
were, but they were not in earshot, even for Hesiyyn's
qhalur hearing, and it was the Kurshin tongue they
spoke.

"The sword—" he said. "If we use it at this Gate of
Exiles—will be very near those standing stones."

"The sword is unstable. Like the gate. We cannot
predict. There is no way to predict—what will happen."

"Aye," he said, and wiped at the sweat which gathered on his lip, and wiped his hands on his knees.

She scratched through the map once, twice. "Go, rest, take whatever sleep thee can. Thee will need it."

He went back and lay down again, staring at the sky through the branches, counting leaves, that being better than other thoughts that pressed on him. He put the stone about his neck, and lay with his hand closed about the pyx to shield it, to be certain of its safety.

And when the sun started below the hill he rose up and dressed methodically, laced up the padding tight and worked the mail shirt on: that was worst. Morgaine came to help him with it; and with the buckles beneath the arm.

"I will saddle up," she said. "No arguments from thee. Hear?"

"Aye," he said, though it fretted him. "Pull it tight, *liyo*. It can take another notch there."

"Thee has to get on the horse."

"I have to stay there," he said.

To that she said nothing. She only tightened the strap.

They mounted up while there was still a little light beyond the hills. It was Hesiyyn who rode farthest point, Hesiyyn with his brown cloak about him, his pale hair loose about his shoulders, his weapons all covered. His horse was a fine blood bay with no white markings.

It was Hesiyyn's own reasoning that he should ride foremost, to forestall any ambushes: "It is likely the only company in which I shall ever find myself the most respectable."

With which the qhal-lordling put his horse well out to the fore, passing out of sight around the bending of the stream, while Chei and Rhanin went a distance behind. "Come," Morgaine said, and chose her own distance from that pair—herself cloaked in black; and Vanye swept his own cloak about him when he had gotten up, and threw up the hood over the white-scarfed helm.

Ambush was possible. Hesiyyn might betray them, signaling to some band out from Mante. Everything, henceforward, was possible—

Even that they should come to the verge of the starlit plain unmolested—a last hillside, a trail down a steep, rocky slope, on which Hesiyyn sat waiting for them, resting his horse, spinning and spinning a curious object on the surface of the slab of rock on which he sat.

"The lots come up three, three, and three: are you superstitious?"

"Curse your humor," Chei said, reining back his horse from the descent.

They changed about with the remounts, one to the three qhal, the blaze-faced bay going turn and turn with Siptah and Arrhan: and again Hesiyyn went to the lead, but not so far separated from them now.

Down and down to the plain, a difficult slope, a long and miserable jolting. *Hang on,* Vanye told himself, cursing every step the bay made under him. Sweat broke out, wind-chilled on his face. He clenched the saddlehorn and thought of the red packet in his belt-pocket.

Not yet, he thought. Not for this. To every jolt and every uneven spot: not for this, not for this—

Across the plain, the mountains—not the peaks of a range like the Cedur Maje of his homeland, but a wall of rock which giants might have built, as if the world had broken, and that were the breaking-point, under a sky so brilliant with stars and moon it all but cast a shadow.

"They are not preventing us this far," he said to Morgaine.

He wished in one part of his reeling mind that the enemy would turn up, now, quickly, before they were committed to this—that somehow something would happen to send them on some other and better course.

But there was no sign of it.

They came down onto the plain at last, a gradual flattening of the course they rode. Vanye turned as best he could and looked back at the track they had made as they entered the grassy flat, a trail too cursed clear under the heavens. "As well blaze a trail," he muttered. If there had been the choice of skirting the hills instead of taking Chei's proposed course across the plain, it was rapidly diminishing.

They drew their company together now, Hesiyyn riding with them as they struck out straight across.

And the cliffs which had been clear from the hillside showed only as a rim against the horizon.

Then was easier riding. Then he finally seized hold of his right leg by the boot-top and hauled it with difficulty over the saddlehorn, wrapped his arms about his suffering ribs and with a look at Morgaine that assured him she knew he was going to rest for a while, bowed his head, leaned back against the cantle and gave himself over to the bay's steady pace in a sickly exhaustion.

He roused himself only when they paused to trade mounts about. "No need," Morgaine said, sliding down from Arrhan's back. "That horse is fit enough to go on carrying you, and I will take Siptah: I weigh less."

He was grateful. He took the medicines she carried for him, washed them down with a drink from her flask, and sat there ahorse while others stretched their legs. It was not sleep, that state of numbness he achieved. It was not precisely awareness either. He knew that they mounted up again; he knew that they moved, he trusted that Morgaine watched the land around them.

No other did he trust . . . except he reasoned if betrayal was what Chei and his men intended, it did not encompass losing their own lives, not lives so long and so dearly held; and that meant some warning to them.

Some warning was all his liege needed. And half-asleep and miserable as he was, he continually rode between her and them: it was a well-trained horse, if rough-gaited, and Siptah, he thanked Heaven, tolerated it going close by him.

He did truly sleep for a while. He jerked his head

up with the thought that he was falling, caught his balance, and saw the cliffs no nearer.

Or they were vaster than the eye wanted to see. His leg had gone numb. He hauled it back over, and his eyes watered as the muscles extended. Everything hurt.

And the riding went on and on, while a few clouds drifted across the stars and passed, and a wind rose and rippled through the endless grass.

Another change of horses. This time he did dismount, and walked a little, as far as privacy to relieve himself, discovering that he could, which did for one long misery; and saw to Arrhan's girth and the bay's.

But facing the necessity to haul himself up again, he stood there holding the saddlehorn and trying, with several deep breaths, to gather the wind and the courage to make that pull.

"Vanye!" Morgaine said, just as he had found it. He stopped, unnerved, with a jolt that brought tears to his eyes; and: "Chei," she said, "one of you give him a hand up."

"My lady," Chei said. And came and offered his hands for a stirrup.

Shame stung him. But he set his foot in Chei's linked hands and let Chei heave him up like some pregnant woman.

"For a like favor," Chei said to him.

He recalled it. And flinching from Chei's hand on his knee, he backed Arrhan out of his reach.

The cliffs cut off the sky before them, against the dimming stars, and they had left a trail a child could follow, the swath of passage in tall grass. The horses caught mouthfuls now and again: there was no time to give them more than that.

Morgaine rode the bay now; it was Siptah due the rest. And the sky above the eastern hills was showing no stars: the sun was coming.

We are beyond recall now. That was the thought that kept gnawing at him. *Wise or not, we are beyond any change of mind.*

God save us.

* * *

By sunlight, at the lagging pace of weary horses, the rock face in front of them rose and filled all their view—a plain of dry grass, a wall of living stone, so abrupt and so tall it defied the eye's logic.

It had one gap, shadow-blued within the yellow stone, in noon sunlight, and closing it—the gatehouse that Chei had named to them. *Seiyyin Neith*.

Doors—the size of which a Kurshin eye refused to understand, until a hawk flew near them, a mote against their height.

Exile's Gate.

Chei turned the roan back a half-circle as they rode, reined in alongside and lifted a hand toward it. "There," he said, "there, you see what we propose to assault. That is merely the nethermost skirt of Mante." He leaned on his saddlebow and gave a twitch of his shoulders, a shiver. "A man forgets it, whose eyes are used to Morund's size. And the boy, my friends, . . . is terrified."

He gave a flick of the reins and sent his horse thundering on ahead to join his men.

Chapter Seventeen

Another space of riding. This time it had measure, that vision of the towering cliffs which rose steadily before them. Vanye looked up at the doors, whose valves were iron, whose surface held twelve bronze panels each, of figures far more than life-size, the actions of which he could not at first understand, until he saw the detail. They were scenes of execution, and torment.

"Can such things open?" he wondered aloud, and his voice was less steady than he wished. He expected some sally-port: he looked for it among the panels, and saw no joint.

"Oh, indeed," Chei said, "when Mante wishes to diminish its vassals—and its exiles. They do open."

"Mante has a taste for excess," Morgaine said.

"They want a man to remember," Hesiyyn said, "the difficulty of return."

Vanye looked at Rhanin, who rode alone ahead of them, weary man riding one exhausted horse, leading another, dwarfed by the scenes of brutal cruelty looming over them.

He felt something move in him then, toward all of these his enemies, a pang that went to the heart.

He saw not Seiyyin Neith, of a sudden, but a steep road down from gray stone walls, and on it, beneath those walls which had seemed so high and dreadful, a grief-stricken boy in a white-scarfed helm, with exile in front of him.

This at least they had in common. And they were

brave men who did not flinch now, in the face of this thing.

This barrier, Mante reared in the name of justice. This was the face it turned to its damned and its servants. This was what the power of the world held as honorable dealings with its own subjects—men hanged, and gutted and burned alive, and what other things, higher up the doors, he had no wish to see.

He drew a copper-edged breath and leaned on the saddle, a shift of weight that sent a wearying, monotonous pain through his sides and his gut, a cursed, always-present misery. He was not certain there was life left in his legs. He had found a few positions that hurt less, and kept shifting between them. But the approach to this place meant different necessities, meant—Heaven knew what. If they must fight here, he could do that, he thought, as long as they stayed mounted.

"How is thee faring?" Morgaine asked him.

"I will manage," he said.

She looked at him, long, as they rode. "On thy oath, Nhi Vanye."

That shook him. He was much too close to judgment to trifle with damnation. It was unfairly she dealt with him—but she had no conscience in such matters, he had long known it.

"Vanye, does thee leave me to guess?"

"I will stay ahorse," he said, half the truth. "I can defend myself." But he could imagine her relying on him in some rush to cover, or doing something foolish to rescue him if he should fall. He sweated, feeling a coldness in the pit of his stomach. He had not used the qhalur medicines. He abhorred such things. More, he did not think they could deal with a numbness that had his right leg all but useless, prickling like needles all up the inside. "It is walking I am not sure of. But my head is clear."

She said nothing then. She was thinking, he decided—thinking through things he did not know, thinking what to do, how far to believe him, and what of her plans she must now change—all these things, because he had been a fool and brought them to this pass, and now began to be a burden on her.

I shall not be, he would have protested. But he already was. And knew it.

He let Arrhan fall a little back then—the horses fretted and snorted, having the scent of strangeness in the wind, the prospect of a fight—always, always, the prospect of war wherever they came to habitations of any kind. The qhal cared little what he did. And Morgaine had her eyes set on the thing in front of them.

He slipped the red paper from its place and carefully, with fingers which trembled, managed to get one of the tiny pellets beneath a fingernail, and then, losing his resolve and his trust of the gift, dislodged it and let it roll back into the paper. He folded it up again, and put it back.

Fool, he thought again. Coward.

But he knew that *he* would take care for her. He was not sure what the stuff in the red paper cared for. And there was too much and too delicate hazard to deal with, which needed clear wits and good judgment.

He gained leverage as he could, took his weight mostly on his arms, hands on the saddlebow, and let the pain run as it would, while he made the right leg move, and bend, and the feeling come back in tingling misery. Sweat fell from his face and spattered his hands, white-knuckled on the horn.

He watched Chei ride up to the very doors, draw the red roan alongside that door-rim and pound with a frail human fist against that towering mass of metal, which hardly resounded to his blows.

"I am Chei ep Kantory," he shouted, in a voice that seemed far too small. "I am Chei lord of Morund, Warden of the South! I have brought visitors to the Overlord! Open the doors!"

They will not, Vanye thought then. It seemed too improbable that anyone inside could even hear them. He looked up dizzily toward the masonry that supported the great doors, expecting there, if they had any answer, the small black figures of archers, and arrows to come down on them like sleet. Forewarning was all the grace he sought of this place—*time,* for Morgaine to draw the sword, with all the risk *that* was, this close to the gate.

But metal boomed and clanked and hinges groaned with a sound that hurt the ears and shied the horses: Arrhan came up on her hind legs and down again, braced in an instant's confusion. He caught his balance, steadied her, colliding with the panicked bay at lead, at Siptah's left.

The iron doors groaned and squealed outward, opening on a shadowed hall of scale to match them, pillars greater in girth than all but the greatest trees of Shathan.

He slipped the ring that held his sword at his back, and let it fall ready to his side.

"Not yet," Morgaine said, as Chei and his companions started forward and rode into that hall. She began to ride after, calmly, slowly as the men in front of them.

He touched Arrhan with his heels and curbed the mare's nervousness with a pat on her sweating neck. His hand was shaking.

Reason enough, he thought, as he passed between the doors that towered either side of him, greater than Ra-Morij's very walls. He could not see what images were on the inside: he dared not take his eyes from where they were going, into an aisle of vast pillars wanly lit with shafts of sunlight from above.

There was a second set of doors before them, far down that forest of stone.

They were closed.

Did we expect more? he asked himself, and breathed the air of the shadow that fell on them, a dank chill the worse after the noon warmth outside. He heard the clank that heralded the sealing of the doors behind them, and steadied Arrhan, who shied and danced under him. The blaze-faced bay jerked and jolted at lead, fighting it. Shod hooves clattered and echoed on pavings, under the machine-noise of iron and chain and ratchets.

And the ribbon of daylight which lay wide about

them, narrowed and vanished with the meeting and sealing of the doors at their backs.

The horses settled, slowly, in a profound silence.

Footsteps sounded within the forest of pillars. A qhal in black armor, his silver hair loose around his shoulders, walked out into their path, into a shaft of light.

It was not the only footfall in the place. But the pillars hid what else moved about them.

"My lord Warden," Chei said, as the roan fought the rein.

"South-warden?" Seiyyin's Warden asked. He was not young nor old. The face might have been carved of bone, the eyes of cold glass.

"Yes, my lord," Chei answered him—youth's form and youth's face; but that was not what sat his horse facing this grim lord. "I was Qhiverin Asfelles."

"With?"

"Rhanin ep Eorund, once Taullyn Daras, and Hesiyyn Aeisyryn, under my orders, in the performance of my office, with persons traveling under my seal. We are escorting this lady and her companion to Mante."

The lord Warden's eyes traveled past the others to Vanye and to Morgaine, and lingered, unreadable and cold. "These are the Outsiders."

"They are, my lord. I urge you speak civilly to them. It was a mistake they ever came through Morundgate, and due to their falling in with humans, and due to lies humans have told them, there have been costly misunderstandings. This lady is a warden herself, and she is not well-pleased with the things she has met on her way."

Wise man, Vanye thought, light-headed with the pounding of his heart. *Chei, get my lady through this and I will be your debtor, I swear it.*

And, O Heaven, the Warden's cold eyes shifted toward them with the least small fracture in his command of the affair.

Not a stupid man either. Nor one incapable of shifting footing. "Where are you warden, lady?"

Morgaine rode a little forward; Vanye moved instantly to stay beside her.

"Where I am warden," Morgaine said, "and more than warden—is something between your Overlord and myself. But I thank you, my lord, if I am about to meet more courtesy than has been my experience on this journey. It will do a great deal to mend matters."

For a long moment the Warden was silent. Then: "We will advise the authorities in Mante," the Warden said.

"I would suggest—my lord—you advise Skarrin himself, and do not waste my time with 'authorities' and deputies. He is the one who *can* say yes or no, he is the one to whom your 'authorities' have to appeal if they are not utter fools, and I assure you, lord Warden, he will be better pleased if you do *not* bring my affairs to him through a succession of subordinates, not all of whom *need* to know my name or my business, for your *safety*, my lord Warden."

It was very still in the vast hall.

Then: "I pray you," the Warden said, "leave your horses to my deputies and accept my hospitality. Advise me of whatever complaints you have, with names where you may know them. Our lord will see justice done."

A cold crept through the sudden warmth, a sense of meshes closing. "It is a trap," Vanye murmured in his own tongue. "*Liyo*, I beg you, no."

"My lord Warden," Morgaine said gravely, gently, "I should fear then—for your own well-being. I am not a comfortable guest. The Warden of Morund and his men are in my custody, as I think your lord will sanction when he hears what I have to say. The South-warden has come into more knowledge of my business than your lord may like, as it is. *And* he has created difficulties for me. I have promised him if he makes amends and if his lord will release him, I will take him and his men with me, and save their lives. But I am *not* disposed to leave this world with an entourage of half your lord's councillors and his wardens. I advise you in all earnestness, my lord of Seiyyin Neith: my affairs are secret, and I have told you enough already to put you at some risk. Do as I tell you. Send this message directly to your lord: Morgaine Anjhuran is here to see him, under circumstances you may explain to him."

"Anj—"

Morgaine spelled it. "Be precise. Be very precise, my lord. Do you understand? Your safety and his are in question."

"I—have no direct contact with the high lord. I can gain it. It will take time. I beg you—step down, rest your horses, let us offer you food and drink—"

"We will wait here."

"A drink, at least—"

"We have our own supplies, my lord. We trust your hospitality includes haste."

"My lady." The Warden looked profoundly offended, and worried. "It will be some little time. I beg you understand. Stand down and rest. Take it or no, my people will offer you what hospitality we have. Your leave, my lady."

He inclined his head and walked away into the shadows.

They were alone then, and not alone, in this chill place where the smallest move echoed, and the stamp of an iron-shod hoof rang like doom.

"We have disquieted him," Morgaine said quietly, in her most obscure Kurshin accents. "That may be good or ill. Vanye—give me the stone."

He gave it. His heart hammered against his ribs.

"Come," she said, and sent Siptah suddenly forward, down the vacant aisle, toward the sealed doors.

There were running footsteps beyond the columns behind him, a quick spurt that died away in the direction the Warden had gone.

Someone had sped to advise him.

And Morgaine veered off into shadow, the other side of a vast column three quarters of the way down the long aisle, drew in and wheeled Siptah about as Vanye arrived, as Chei and Hesiyyn and Rhanin clattered in close behind him.

"What are you doing?" Chei asked, a young voice, which rose incongruously in pitch.

Light flared, white and terrible as she opened the case of the gate-jewel. It touched columns, faces, the wild eyes of the shying horses—and damped as suddenly as she closed her hand about it, veiling it in flesh, awful as it was.

"Give it to me!" Vanye exclaimed, knowing the feel of it, imagining the pain of handling it this close to Mante. But she held it fast, letting a little of its flickering light escape to strike the stone pillar beside them.

"Watch the surrounds!" she ordered. "Chei—what is our host saying?"

There was no word for a moment, in which Vanye loosed his bow from his shoulder, set its heel in his stirrup and strung it in the strength fear lent.

"He is reporting our presence—our breach of his orders—" Chei said.

"To whom?"

"To whoever is watching—I do not know—I do not know who that would be.—He reports himself in danger. He is going to open the doors. He hopes we will leave—"

"—into their reach," Morgaine said. There was pain in her voice. "Has he sent what I bade him?"

"No—or we have not seen it—"

"Take it. *Do* it."

"Send *what?* Who *are* you, that he should know you—curse you, woman, have you lied to me?"

"Believe everything you heard me tell the Warden— *Send* the cursed message, man, send it exactly as I gave it and keep sending till we have answer, or take your chances with the lord Warden's archers! Or with that thing outside! Make your choice!"

Chei reached. For a second the stone flared bright between them, blinding, light glistening on Morgaine's pale face, on his, which grimaced as he took it, and the red roan and the gray horse shied apart, both fighting the rein.

Engines began to clank and chain to rattle at the other entrance. A seam of daylight lanced through the hall, blinding bright. The horses sidestepped and fretted, more and more panicked, doubtful between the gate-force in the air, and the racket and that view of escape.

"It is more powerful than his," Chei said between his teeth. He used the shuttering of the lid to send, less sure in his use of it than the dimmer, rapid flickers of the Warden's sending, which came through as weak pulses in his intervals. "We are drowning his sending—Rhanin! are the warders moving?"

"No, my lord," the bowman said.

"If the gate at Mante should open," Hesiyyn said, "my lord, and you are holding that thing—"

"Send and wait for an answer," Morgaine bade Chei harshly. "Again and again—the same message. Watch around us! They have only to get one gate-jewel positioned—"

"My lady!" a voice called down the aisles. "My lady, cease! You are free to go!"

"Ignore it," Morgaine said under her breath. "I take it that the lord Warden is lying."

"He is lying," Chei said, reading the silence of the stone in the intervals. "He has never reached—*Ah!*"

Opal shimmer flared, rapid pulses. Chei cupped his hand about it, and the muscles of his face tensed with pain. "Skarrin," he said hoarsely. "Skarrin himself—has just discovered treachery—has bidden silence. He—knows your presence. And your name. He—tells the Warden—let us pass—not to—oppose us.—He asks who wields this st-stone, my lady."

"Answer him. Tell him it is ours. And we have come to talk with him."

It needed a moment. Chei's face stood out in taut-jawed relief in the flashes, that came brighter from the stone, brighter than the glare from the open door.

Then: "He will hear us," Chei said, hoarsely. And shut the case, letting his arm fall. "He forbids—more use of the stone."

Morgaine was silent a moment. It was an affront she was paid, by Skarrin's order. She reined close and recovered the pyx.

"He bids us," Chei said, "come to Mante."

"On his mercy," Vanye murmured. "Among the stones out there."

"It is Shein's enemies," Chei said in a ragged voice. "*My* enemies—in court—who killed all my Society. They have made a fatal mistake, thinking this was my doing— that you were my prisoners. They thought to kill us three—that is what they are about; and gain credit for it—like the lord Warden. Only he had to ask his masters what to do. And now his own head will be on the block. They will disavow him, or try to. They will not attack us. Not now."

"They could only lose by it," Hesiyyn said. "Either the Overlord will destroy us out there—or you have favor with him. In either case, lady, we are in *Skarrin's* hand, for good or ill."

"We came," Morgaine said, "knowing there was no other way in."

She turned Siptah's head toward the light, and rode in the shadow toward the doors.

Vanye put his heels to Arrhan, and sent her forward, jolting hard at the horse at lead. Cut it free, he thought, laying a hand on his Honor-blade, and then thought again—seeing the expanse before them, and the ride there was yet to make as they passed the second set of doors: distant cliffs in a glare of sun— distant and with the threat of the standing stones to dominate all this plain of patchy grass and sere dust, this well of stone open to the sky; and heat that hit like a hammer-blow after the coolth of the building.

For a moment Vanye felt the giddiness—for a moment Arrhan ran uncertainly, waiting direction, until he took the reins in and swung alongside Morgaine. Chei and the others overtook them on the left. He bore over again, to have it clear to them how close they dared come to Morgaine's side.

"Let be," Morgaine said, "let be— If Skarrin will kill us he will do so." She looked behind her, turning in the saddle. "No one is following us, that is sure. If he is in control of the gate—"

"He is always in control of the gate," Chei said in a

faint voice. "There are men in Mante counting the hours of their lives now, and others hastening to desert them. That is the way one lives in Mante. That is the *law* in Mante."

Chei's face was pale. In Hesiyyn was no vestige of humor.

Rhanin said: "We have kin who have managed to survive in Mante. And whether they will survive this day, we do not know."

Morgaine made them no answer. Possibly she did not even hear them. She set Siptah to an even, ground-devouring run, which the most of their horses were taxed to maintain. She gazed ahead of them, where their course lay—no road to follow, except the aisle of standing stones that paced widely separated toward the cliffs—marker-stones only, carriers of the gate-force, not the deadly ones, not the ones which, at his whim, the lord of Mante might use against them.

Those stones stood—Vanye could see one in the distance—far taller, and over against the cliffs that formed this well of stone.

The way of exiles. Death-gate. Mante's enemies who breached Seiyyin Neith found themselves here, in a plain utterly dominated by those three stones.

So Mante's exiles rode to their dismissal from Seiyyin Neith, during all the crossing of the plain knowing that that ride was on sufferance, that they lived or died as Mante and Skarrin pleased.

Like crossing the very palm of God, he thought; and went cold at the blasphemy, while the sun heated the armor and the sweat ran on him and the pounding of the horse's gait drove knives into his gut.

The stones measured the course: a hundred fifty and two. Chei knew their number. They all knew. It was the number of lords admitted to council. They stood for silent accusers to the damned; eyeless, watched them; mouthless, cursed them—stood waiting, finally, to welcome the exile home, who wished once to see Mante, and surrender body or life, as the high lords pleased.

A man had to think of such things, somberly, as surely Hesiyyn and Rhanin thought of them; and thought of kindred and friends, who by now might know that their kinsman had made the choice to return.

And their enemies would know—as they would know the lady had gained Skarrin's ear, and quickly after, as the lord Warden sent all he dared send—that the South-warden had been taken for a playing piece in this game.

There would be those rushing to exert influence where they could, to save what they could.

Blood—would flow; might be flowing even now, of remotest and humblest connections Shein Society might have had, from the moment certain powers in Mante knew that Qhiverin Asfelles was returning. But all his dead company was avenged, as he had said—a revenge as perfect as he could have contrived, his enemies done to death by their own power to rule the doings at court.

There were the few lords who had supported Shein, whose mark Qhiverin's natural body had worn tattooed above the heart, whose sole survivor he was. But the high lords had their bodyguards and their own sources of rumors, and if they were taken by surprise, they were fools—the more so if his messengers had gotten to them from Morund-gate and Tejhos.

He had done well, he thought. Live or die—he had done well, and he aimed for the unthinkable.

But there was still within him a small bewildered voice, of a boy further and further from home and missing one who should have ridden with him—

Well, lad, he told it sorrowfully, *so do I. Pyverrn should have seen this day, damn us all. He would have laughed to think of the lord Warden back there, scrambling to save his neck.*

The boy did not understand what he saw, except that they rode through the region of a gate which could drink them down at any moment, at the Overlord's pleasure, and that the lady had a name that she trusted Skarrin knew.

The boy feared now, that the lady he had once followed and the man who had betrayed him—had lied to him from the beginning.

So do I fear it, he told the boy. *But we have no choice, do we?*

Never speak to it—the wisdom ran, advising against such accommodation.

But it did not go away. It was there. It watched everything, it wanted to learn of him—

Most of all it wanted not to die.

You gave me to the wolves, the boy wept. *You killed my lord.*

So I did. You were trying to kill me, *at the time. As for Ichandren—I tried to spare him. It was Arunden stirred that pot—for Arunden's gain. Now Arunden is raven-bait. Stop sniveling, boy. It is death we both face. The world is like that. And better the company around us than some I have known. Gault was a liar and Ichandren a conniver and Arunden a bloody-handed traitor. Wake up and see, boy. Wake up and know the world you were born to, Mante's refuse-heap. . . .*

More of sun and heat, of glare on dusty ground, and a cloud which rose behind and around them, a long effort for weary horses, jolting which brought the taste of blood.

The longer they delayed in this place, Vanye thought, the longer the lord in Mante had to hear other advice, change his mind, come to other conclusions—or some other power snatch its opportunity and bring the power of the World-gate at Mante to bear on the standing stones of Neisyrrn Neith.

Then the last thing they might know would be a sudden rending of the sky and ground, and the howl of winds fleeing into that rift, taking them with it—aware of their deaths, Heaven knew how long or how keenly.

That thought kept him in the saddle, though it was hard to breathe. He coughed, and wiped his mouth, and saw blood smearing the dust on his hand.

A cold feeling came on him then, a chill dizziness as if truth had been waiting for him to find it, before it sprang on him and shook him and all but took his wits away.

O Heaven, not here, not now, not yet, not in this place.

He spat blood, wiped his stubbled mouth, and wiped the hand on his dusty breeches. Morgaine was ahead of him. She had not seen. He measured the distance yet to go—they had come halfway, now, halfway along the aisle of stones that led to Mante, and that far again was all he might be able to do—

—at least not slow her in this place. At least cross this plain and know that she had gotten safely to its far side, where she had a chance: to draw *Changeling* here was impossible, for loosed within a gate, it would take the very world asunder.

It was too cursed late for Chei's medicines, not by the tightness in his chest, by the lack of breath; but he found the folded paper, a red haze in the dust and the darkness that threatened his vision. He pinched up what he hoped for one pellet in his fingers, but he thought was more than that—he was not sure. He almost dropped it entirely, and put the medicine into his mouth and held it through a cough that brought up more blood. He swallowed, wiped his mouth with a bright smear of scarlet across the back of his hand; and hung on and waited for the strength he hoped would come to him.

It did come. He was aware of his heart pounding, of his vision dark-edged, of a cessation of the pain, at least—but he could not get his breath. He felt his balance going, and was aware of Morgaine looking back and reining around. The strength left in a rush of heat and cold, and he knew in one terrible moment he was leaving the saddle, the ground coming up at him—

He hit, and twisted sideways, stunned, in a second impact, lost in dust and pain that lanced through the drug-haze, skull shaken, spine rattled, limbs twisted, pain like a dull knife driven through his side.

Through the dust, Morgaine's dark figure, running toward him, sliding down to her knees.

"Vanye!"

The others had stopped. Chei—behind her, on the red roan, Rhanin and Hesiyyn like ghosts in the dust.

He tried to get up, knowing it was necessary, and the pain was in abeyance for the moment. He tried to get his arm under him.

And heard the wind howl, saw Morgaine whirl and rise and reach for *Changeling's* hilt as the sky tore in two above them, showing the dark beyond, her hair and cloak streaming, dust pouring skyward like water pouring over a brink.

The world ripped. And there was only the cold and the dark between.

*

—He saw her hand on the hilt, that would bring the Gate in upon itself.

"No," he cried to her, because they were still alive, and the time was not yet—

*

The rift came full circle, and blue swallowed up the black, leaving only a rush of wind and chill.

Then he lay on his back on stone, and rolled onto his arm, to see Morgaine with the sword half-drawn, the blade shimmering crystal, its runes running with opal fires.

She slammed it home again, seeing him, and he got to his knees, dazed, disentangled himself of his bow that had come awry of his shoulder and shed it. He saw Siptah and Arrhan riderless and confused, Chei and the others fighting for control of their frightened mounts—standing stones all about them, stones like a forest of such slabs, all about the walled court of blond stone in which they had suddenly found themselves.

There was no pain. There was no ache anywhere about the bandages bound too tightly about his ribs, no hindrance in his limbs. He might have come from a morning's easy ride.

Gate-passage. The gate had flung them here, unscathed and whole except the dust and the dirt that turned Morgaine's dark armor pale and made her face a porcelain mask.

God in Heaven, he thought, remembering the fall,

then, and the blood in his mouth; and then thought it might be blasphemous to thank Heaven for qhalur gifts. He had no idea. He only knew he could stand, and Morgaine was throwing an arm about him and embracing him, the dragon-sword in her other hand, the scarred and battered longbow in his. "We are alive," she said, and said something else urgently in a tongue he could not understand, telling him, he reckoned in his dazed state, that they were none of them dead, that they were somewhere of Skarrin's choosing—

She held him tight. He held to her as if he were drowning, and then remembered there were enemies. He scanned round about the stones which rose in a five-fold stagger between them and the walls; and looked up, at the rim of the masonry walls against the cloudless sky.

There was no one, no one but Chei and Rhanin and Hesiyyn, on horses exhausted and head-hanging, themselves hardly fit to climb from their saddles and stand.

But they, themselves—and the white horse and the gray—

"There *is* sorcery," Vanye murmured, misgiving of everything, most of all his memory, which insisted there should be pain, and broken bones, and not this unnatural strength, recovered flesh, that made the buckles and bandaging all too tight. He trembled, and wished he could shake everything from his head and begin again. "Mother of God, there *is*—you cannot tell me else—"

She wiped the corner of his mouth, with fingers that came away, shaking, with blood and dirt. Tears marred the dusty mask of her face. She pressed her lips tight, held him by the arm and looked up and about the slow circuit of the walls, seeking who had done this to them.

Then to Chei, in anger: "Is *this*—ordinary, Skarrin dropping his guests into this place? Is *this* the way to Mante you simply neglected to tell us?"

"I do not know." It was bewilderment. It was utter consternation. "No. Not—for what I know."

There was fear—in Chei's look, in Rhanin's—even in cold Hesiyyn's eyes. It was fear directed toward them both, for the healing the gates had done for them, and the horses they rode, and not for themselves.

"None of us know," Rhanin said, a faint voice. "Never—never that I have known of—"

"*Skarrin!*" Morgaine shouted to the walls and the sky.

"He has spared us," Vanye said. "*Liyo,* he has *spared* us—"

She turned a look on him—not the face he loved, but a qhalur mask in white dust, tear-streaked and implacable in purpose. "Do not believe it."

On the one side, Chei and his companions, who knew something had been done with gates such as ought not to have happened, within the laws they knew—

On the other, Morgaine—

I know things they do not. Call it my father's legacy. And if they should know, Vanye, that secret, they would find others, that I will give no one, that are not written on the sword—that I will not permit anyone to know and live—

She hooked *Changeling* to her belt. She walked a few steps and recovered his helm from the ground and threw it to him. He caught it. The wind blew at his hair, still shorn. His armor was filthy with dust and blood. Why this should be, and other things mended, he did not understand.

He did not hope to. Nor wish to. He put the helm on, slung the bow to his shoulder, and followed her across the courtyard to the horses.

She stopped there. From that angle, among the standing stones, an open gateway was visible in the masonry wall.

Chapter Eighteen

There was no sound in the high-walled courtyard, save their own movements and those of the horses. There was nothing above them but the sky.

And the open gateway, among the standing stones.

Morgaine took Siptah in hand to look him over and Vanye looked over the exhausted bay and gathered up Arrhan's reins, as Chei and his two comrades led their exhausted horses toward them, slow clatter of iron on stone.

"There is the way out," Morgaine said. "Such as our host gives us. Do you have any reckoning where we are?"

"Neneinn," Hesiyyn said quietly. "That is where we would be, I am relatively certain of it. The citadel itself. But no one sees the inside of that, except the Overlord's own guards. And they rarely come and go in the city."

"The Gate itself?"

Hesiyyn looked about him, at the sky, the walls; and pointed off to the right of the open gateway. "There, by my guess. The gate is close—very close to Neneinn, at the crest of the same hill. That weapon of yours—I should hesitate to use anywhere about these premises."

Morgaine was silent a moment, looking at Hesiyyn. The tall qhal-lord wore an unwontedly anxious expression.

"Where is your loyalty?" she asked him.

"Assuredly not in Neneinn," Hesiyyn answered in a

faint voice. "I am under banishment. Skarrin dislikes
my poetry."

"None of us has any loyalty here," Chei said. "I
assure you. Nor prospects."

There was nothing of arrogance in them. Their courage seemed frayed, their strength flagging in the face
of their own unnatural vitality—men hollow-cheeked,
eyes red-rimmed with exhaustion, their horses dull-
coated and ill-fed beneath the dust that coated all of
them. They did not ask what had happened, or why,
or, indeed, venture any question at all.

"Then tell Skarrin nothing," Morgaine said shortly,
and turned and hooked Siptah's left stirrup to the
horn. She let out the girth no small bit, at which the
warhorse grunted and sighed.

Arrhan needed the same. Vanye saw to it, hung his
bow from Arrhan's saddlehorn and let out first Arrhan's
girth and then the straps of his own body-armor, that
were tight to the point of misery; but the bandages
and the padding he could not reach, and he drew a
breath and strained at them, trying to stretch against
what would bind his draw and his sword arm.

Even in blackest sorcery, he thought, gathering his
gear about him, there were cursedly maddening short-
comings.

Morgaine flung the stirrup down and gathered up
Siptah's reins, looking back toward Chei and the rest.
"I will warn you," she said, "You may be safer here.
Death—may be safer than where we go. Choose for
yourselves."

Chei looked astonished. It was young Chei's expression. The frown which followed was Gault's. Or
Qhiverin's. "You jest, lady."

"No," she said. "I do not." And led Siptah among
the tall stones, toward the open gateway.

Vanye led Arrhan after her, the blaze-faced bay
following perforce, with lagging, wearied steps.

The others came behind him, then, a clatter of
iron-shod hooves on stone.

He had as lief not have them at his back. He recollected the medicine Chei had given him, and what it

had done to him when at last he had had to rely on
it—

—Chei had warned him, he recollected. To do justice to the man, Chei had warned him clearly.

Chei had given it to him after that warning, of
course—in hope, perhaps, of *not* having him between
them and Morgaine—in any sense. And if he had used
it before that, Heaven knew what would have been
the outcome.

He kept constantly between Morgaine and the qhal,
now, on the winding track among the stones, pale gold
of standing stones and of pavings and masonry—and
of more sunlit paving visible through the gateway.

Another trap, he thought.

But the gateway opened out into yet another such
courtyard, this one with a single standing stone in its
center . . . a flat, paved courtyard, the end of which a
building closed, jumbled planes of wall and tower, and
at the sides—

A sheer drop: and buildings upon buildings, upon
buildings and buildings, pale gold stone, red roofs, as
far as the eye could see.

He stopped in his tracks and stared—only stared,
senses confounded, when he was mountain-born and
used to heights and perspectives.

But not to men and the works of men so vast they
spread like a blanket about the hill and across the
plain—to the verge of the cliffs that dropped away into
the circular abyss of Neisyrrn Neith, and along and
away till the roofs lost themselves in haze and distance.

Morgaine had stopped. So had the others.

"Mante," Chei said softly. So a man might speak of
Heaven and Hell in one.

The others said nothing at all.

And Vanye could not forbear looking at it, though
he tangled his fingers in Arrhan's coarse mane and
feared irrationally that the sight might drive the horses
mad, and bring them too near the edge, however far
away they stood.

Morgaine led Siptah further. It was the sound of the
gray's steps that woke him from trance, and brought

him after her, resolutely, as she walked toward the open doorway at the end of the courtyard.

The others followed, at distance.

This door—had little sunlight about it. This one let into the very heart of the fortress, by a long narrow aisle, shadowed by columns.

They had seen such before, of many kinds. Such buildings were always near the World-gates. They held the machines to command and direct the forces.

It was what they had come to find; and Morgaine would go in. He had no doubt of it. He saw her lay her hand on the sword-hilt.

"Liyo." He searched after the chain of the stone he wore about his neck, drew it from his collar and over his head as he led Arrhan quickly to overtake her. It was a weak thing—stronger by far than the Warden's mote or many another sending-stone in this land, he suspected, but not *Changeling's* match. It was useless to him, a means to sudden death, if he matched it against anything of *Changeling's* power.

Or against the gate Hesiyyn swore must lie close hereabouts.

"He knows you have a gate-weapon," he said. *"Take* it. It is larger than the ones they use. It may be he will mistake this for it."

She understood him then. And refused it with a shake of her head. "The sword," she said in his language. "I cannot wield both. And no—he will not."

"The sword is too dangerous," he whispered hoarsely, and started at a movement in the corner of his vision, in the deep shadow within the narrow aisle ahead—a qhalur man, alone, nor very old.

Some high servant, he thought, the while his heart skipped a beat and his hand went for his sword-hilt; and then he thought otherwise, seeing the eldritch figure drifted, mirage-like, and was only an image.

It spoke. It spoke words he could not understand, but he knew, whatever they were, that they were not meant for him, or for Chei, or any of them other than Morgaine. He heard Morgaine answer in that tongue, and saw the man's figure grow dimmer as it retreated down that aisle.

She walked forward.

Vanye caught at her arm, the barest touch, before she reached that threshold. She looked at him. That was all; and she turned and hit Siptah a resounding blow on the rump.

The Baien gray sprang through the door, hooves echoing on stone, off high walls, and stopped inside, unscathed.

She went, then, through the doorway, in a single step and a second one which cleared a path for him to follow. He did so, in a motion so quick he did not think of it: he was there, Arrhan was behind him, and he whipped the arrhendur blade from its sheath, for what it was worth against this illusion and the more substantial things it might call down on them.

A question then, from the man of light and shadow. The voice echoed about them, rang off the walls of this long, narrow passage.

"He does not understand you," Morgaine said.

"He is human," the image said then. "I have read everything—in the gate-field. I know what you carry. Yes. How could I fail to remark—a thing like that forming in the patterns? I read his suffering. I intervened, against my habit, to save him. I trusted there *was* a pattern—if you valued him. And I was not mistaken."

"I thank you for that," Morgaine said.

"I wished to please you,—who come wandering the worlds. Anjhurin's daughter. It is likely that we are kin—remote as that kinship may be. How does Anjhurin fare?"

"He is dead," Morgaine said shortly.

"Ah." The regret seemed genuine. The image murmured something in the other language.

"Perhaps," Morgaine said, "he was weary of living. He said as much."

Again it spoke.

"No," Morgaine said. And to another query: "No." And: "I travel, my lord."

A harder voice then.

"For my companion's sake," she said. "Speak so he can understand." And after another such: "Because he understands it and because I wish it." And again: "That may be. I would be glad of it." She lapsed for a moment into the other tongue. Then, gently: "It has been a long time, my lord, since I have spoken the language. It has been a long time—since I have had the occasion."

"You bring me felons and rebels." The mouth of the image quirked upward slightly at the corners. "As well as this human warrior. You have turned my court upside down, lifted every rotten log and sent the vermin scurrying forth—from Morund-gate to the highest houses in Mante. What shall I do for you in return?"

"Why, give me the three rebels in question," Morgaine said, "and the pleasure of your company, and in due time, the freedom of your gate. I am a wanderer. I seek no domain of my own."

"Nor to share one?"

She laughed. "We do not *share* a world. My father taught me that much. I will find a place. Or do you give this one up, my lord of shadows, and come wander the worlds with us."

"With a rebel, a killer, a doggerel poet and a human lordling?" Skarrin laughed in his own turn. "Come ahead into my courtyards, my lady of light. Wash off the dust. Take my hospitality." The drifting face became melancholy, even wistful. "Go with you. That is a thought. That is indeed a thought. You will sit with me, my lady, and tell me where you have traveled and the things you have seen—convince me there is something different than one finds . . . *everywhere*. . . ."

The image faded.

The voice drifted into silence, leaving the stillness of the tomb behind it.

Old, Vanye thought with a chill, *old—more than a Man can reckon.*

And he found himself staring into Morgaine's eyes, lost, beyond understanding what she did or what she meant to do any longer, and with the least and dreadful fear—that she had found something in common with this lord who contemned everything he ruled, who despised the qhal, who themselves used human folk for cattle—

She had had to defend her companying with a human man. He had sensed that. He imagined the questions which had gone by him, and fitted her answers to them, his liege, his lover . . . defiant, in the beginning—toward a man of her own kind, who could speak with her, trade words with her in a language she had never taught him, quickly and unexpectedly draw the sort of laugh and light answer from her such as had taken him—oh, so long to win.

"We will do as he asks," Morgaine said.

"Aye," he said. He was too far into strange territory to say anything more. He did not even agree for loyalty or love or out of common sense. He was only lost, on ground which continually shifted and threatened to shift again. They stood in a foreign lord's elegant forecourt with three confused horses in their charge, and three men awaiting their fate outside who were, surely, no less bewildered.

Then: *a clear target,* he thought, like a shock of cold water.

How else do we come at him—except she draw him out?

And how can she persuade him?

"Call Chei and the rest," she bade him in the Kurshin tongue. "Quickly."

He left Arrhan to stand and went back to the sunlight. "My lord," he said to Chei at the doorway, and lowered his voice. He was determined to observe courtesy with the man and forestall argument. "We are going ahead. We do not know into what. Be aware: the Overlord brought up the matter of your exile. My lady claimed you for her own and Skarrin gave you to her. So if you have any scruples, I think you are honorably quit of debts to him, but I do not know what favor this wins of him if things go amiss."

Chei looked at him and gnawed at his lip. It was young Chei's expression for the instant. It was doubt;

and then amusement. "I was quit of debts to him when he failed to kill me," Chei-Qhiverin said. "That was *his* mistake."

Chei led his horse forward. Hesiyyn and Rhanin followed, Rhanin with his bow strung and slung over his shoulder. Vanye cleared the doorway, gathered up Arrhan's reins, and led the white mare up alongside Siptah as Morgaine began that course Skarrin chose for them.

Ambush was in his thoughts, constantly. But Morgaine went, with *Changeling* slung at her hip, and walked the long court in which the horses' pacing made a forlorn and lonely sound.

"Games," she said to the air. "I do not like games, my lord Skarrin."

At the end a door whisked open, in that way which doors could move, in such places of gate-force—on a sunlit court.

Vanye cut the lead next the bay's bridle and sent it ambling past them with one slap and another on its dusty rump. It came to no grief in the doorway. And they came through into afternoon sunlight, into a stable court clean and well-supplied with straw and haystack, rows of stables, with well and stone trough. The bay went straightway to the water, and Siptah and Arrhan flared their nostrils and pricked up their ears and approached the trough with keen interest.

"Hospitality," Vanye muttered, for the first time beginning to wonder was there good will in this beckoning of doors and corridors and ghosts. "Dare we trust it?"

"He needs no ambush," Morgaine said, and bent and washed her hands and her face, and let the water wash black, clean trails over her dusty armor. She drank from the demon-mouth that poured fresh water continually into the trough.

He took the chance for himself, doused face and hands in cool water, wiped his hair back from his eyes, washed and drank as Chei and the others arrived.

There was no one to threaten them. There was not a horse other than theirs in all the stable-court. There was no servant and no groom to serve them. Vanye stood, with the wind chilling the water on his face, scanning the walls around them, looking for some sign of life and seeing nothing but bare stone.

"Ghosts," he said aloud. "And of them this Skarrin seems chief."

"More than ghosts," Morgaine whispered in the Kurshin tongue, and caught his shoulder and leaned close to him. "We may be overheard. I do not know how many languages he may have known or where he may have traveled."

His heart leapt in him and fell again. "Even Kursh?"

"There are tracks among the Gates: thee knows. No knowing which path he has come to arrive here. There are a handful of the old blood, in all the worlds gates reach. They have no congress with one another. They are too proud. Each settles to a world—for a while—using a knowledge of the gates the qhal do not have— They *rule*. There is no likelihood that they will fail to rule. They direct affairs, they make changes at their pleasure. And inevitably they grow bored—and they move on, through time or space or both. Some are older than the calamity, older than the one before it. My father claimed to be."

"What 'one before it', what—"

"—And some are born into *this* age—of one whose life has stretched across ages. Some are born of events which cannot be duplicated, events on which vast changes depend—Some lives, in that way, anchor time itself. So the lords assure themselves of continuance—in more than one way. Such am I—but not what my father planned. *I* exist. Therefore other things do not. Therefore *he* does not."

"I do not understand. You have left me." He felt a shiver despite the sun. "What shall we do?"

"I shall court this man," she hissed softly. "By any means, Vanye, *any* means, and thee must not object, does thee understand that?"

"Let us take the sword, let us go through this place until we find him—" He felt cold to the heart now. "That is the only sense."

"He will not be there. He can retreat *within* the gate. He can leave us here. Has thee forgotten?"

"You cannot fight him hand to hand, *liyo*, in the name of Heaven, you cannot think of—"

"I will do what I have to do. I tell thee now: do not attempt *anything* with this man. I beg thee. I do not want help in this. Or hindrance. Thee says thee is still *ilin*. Nothing have I asked of thee by that oath—in very long. *This* I ask. For my sake. For thine."

"*Tell* me what we shall do!"

"On thy oath. Nothing. *I* will do it."

"And I tell you—if you hang my soul and my salvation on it—I will throw them away, if it comes to harm—"

"Thee will take the sword if it comes to that. Thee will bear it. Thee will trust Chei and the rest if it comes to that. All these things—I ask thee, as thee loves me,—do. Does thee love me? Does thee understand what I ask?"

It reached him, then, the thing that she *was* asking of him, and the sense of it. It shook the breath from him for a moment. It was not the sort of thing a man wanted to agree to, who loved a woman. It was harder than dying for her, to agree to leave her to die.

"That much," he said, because anything less was betrayal, "yes, I understand. On my oath, I will." He looked up uncomfortably at their comrades, who did not understand what passed—their comrades, who expected, perhaps, betrayal prepared for themselves, in this exchange in another language.

"We will go on," Morgaine said to them, and drew Siptah away from the water.

"*Where* do we go?" Chei asked.

"Did I promise I knew?" Morgaine answered, and led the gray horse on, through the stable-court, down the empty rows.

"It makes no sense," Hesiyyn said. "There should be servants—there should be attendants. *Where* are the people?"

"Heaven knows," Chei answered him, and found no

incongruity in saying so. There was an angry young man in the center of his being, as lost as he was, in this place which had dominated both their lives and ruined their separate families—and which proved, after all, only hollow and full of echoes. "People come here," he said, half to the lady, who seemed some old acquaintance of Skarrin's. "People serve the Overlord. What has become of them?"

She offered them no answer.

"Perhaps he is holding them elsewhere," Hesiyyn said under his breath, and with an anxious look toward Chei.

Death, the lady had said; and in this court which should, at least, have horses, have some evidence of occupancy and life—Chei found a scattering of memory which was human and adult and frightened—

Gault had been imprisoned here, had been hailed up from the outskirts of this fortress by his kidnappers, to the gate above these walls. *Gault* remembered. And there had been others in that dark hour, there had been servants, there had been abundant life in this court, torchlit and echoing with confused shouts as Qhiverin's friends dragged him struggling and resisting toward the hell above these walls.

"Even the horses," Chei-Gault-Qhiverin said aloud, finding a shiver down his spine and a terrible feeling of things gone amiss in this daylit, sterile vacancy, "even the horses—No." He quickened his pace, tugging at the weary roan he led, and caught Vanye's arm. "There were people here. Now even the horses are gone. *Something* is direly wrong here. It is a trap. Make the lady listen."

Vanye had rescued his arm at once. There was on his sullen face, a quick suspicion and a dark threat. The shorn hair blew across his eyes and reminded them both of things past, of miscalculations and mistakes disastrously multiplied. A muscle clenched in his jaw.

But if there was at the moment a voice of caution and reason in their company it was this Man, Chei believed it: the boy's experience told him so and

Qhiverin's instincts went to him, puzzling even himself—except it was everywhere consonant with what the boy knew: a man absolute in duty, absolute enough and sane enough to lay aside everything that did not pertain to the immediate problem.

Trust him to listen, was the boy's advice. *Nothing further.*

And Qhiverin, within himself: *Boy, if the one thing, with what lies between us, then anything; and you have been a mortal fool.*

"It is for all our sakes," he said. "I swear to you, Nhi Vanye. We are walking into a trap. Every step of this is a trap. He has vacated the place. Even the horses. Even the horses. I do not know where."

"The gate," Vanye said, looking down the little distance Chei's slighter form needed.

"To Tejhos?" Chei asked. "—Or elsewhere?"

Vanye cast a look toward Morgaine, whose face was stern and pale and set on the way before them, which led toward yet another gate in this maze.

"Anything is possible," he said.

A man who is winning, he had said to Morgaine again and again, will not flee.

But the man of that face and that voice which had spoken to them—

—Go *with* you, it had said.

Convince me there is something different than one finds . . . everywhere. . . .

Older than the calamity, Morgaine had said of Skarrin.

And: *Not of human measure, not predictable by human intentions,* his own experience told him.

Deeper and deeper into this snare Morgaine went, leading the rest of them in what haste they dared—

Lest Skarrin strand them here, lest he go before them and seal the gate and leave them imprisoned here forevermore.

He did not question now. He understood the things that she had attempted to tell him throughout their journey—and he had overwhelmed her arguments, delayed her with his foolishness, his well-meant advice and his hopes and, Heaven forgive, his desire of her, which had stolen her good judgment and thrown his to the winds.

But for me, he kept thinking, the while he walked beside her: but for me she would have ridden straight to him and stayed him from this; but for me she would have gone straightway to Morund and enlisted qhalur aid and learned more at the start than ever young Chei could have taught us.

And perhaps Chei would be alive, himself, and Gault would be Gault, and their ally.

"Tell her," Chei hissed at him.

"She has always understood," he said to Chei and his murderer, "better than I. Better than any of us. She gave you the chance to turn back. It is not too late to take it."

The gate before them was open. He was not in the least surprised at that. And this one let into the building itself, into a shadowed hall which might hold more than ghosts—but he began to doubt that there need be guards or soldiery, nor any hand but Skarrin's own, which held the gate-force. He kept beside Morgaine as far as that doorway, and suddenly sent Arrhan through ahead of them, expecting no harm.

The arrhendur mare came to none, only stopped, confused, her feet striking echoes from polished pavement, in a hall supported by columns much lest vast than those of Neisyrrn Neith, but vast for all that, shaped of green stone and black.

A table was set there, set with pitchers and platters bearing fruit and bread and what else his eye did not trouble to see.

Skarrin's ghost hung before them, welcomed them, smiled at them with all beneficence and no little amusement.

"My guests," he said; then, and with less mockery: "My lady Morgaine Anjhuran, my youngest cousin— sit, take your ease. You can trust my table. Surely you know that. And you might indeed leave the horses outside my hall."

"My lord Skarrin," Morgaine said, "forgive me. I have known so many and so bizarre things in my travels—I have found folk do things for remarkable reasons, some only because they can, some only for sport—I do not know you, my lord. So I keep my horse and my arms—and my servants. My father's friends may, for all I know, be no less mad than some others I have met on the way."

The drifting image laughed, a soft sound, like the hissing of wind in grass. "And thus you decline my hospitality?"

"I do not sit at table with shadows, my lord. Our mistrust is mutual—else you would not hesitate to come and meet me face to face—if you can."

"My lady of outlaws and rebels—should I trust myself to your companions, when they think so ill of me?"

Morgaine laughed, let fall Siptah's reins, and walked over to the table, to pull out a chair and sit down. She picked up a pitcher and poured a cup of red wine.

Vanye let Arrhan stand alone too, and went and stood at the side of her chair as she lifted it and sipped it in courtesy to their shadowy host.

Whereupon Skarrin laughed softly, and drifted amid their table, severed at the waist. "You are trusting."

"No, my lord of Mante. Only interested. I knew when I heard your name from young Chei—who is host to my lord of Morund—what you *might* be. I took your gatewardens' behavior for yours—to our mutual discomfiture. No one saw fit to apprise me of the truth—in which I do fault you, my lord of Mante. So much could have been saved, of affairs in the south, if I had known. Now I leave you a humankind in war and disorder—an inconvenience, at the least, for which I do apologize."

"There are other lands. The world is wide. I weary of Mante."

"I took this for the greatest of your cities. Are there others? Truly, this one is a wonder to see."

"Ah, there are hundreds. Everywhere—there are cities, as unvarying as the worlds. Everywhere is boredom, my lady of light, until you came—traveling, as you say. With a human servant, no less—what is his name?"

"Nhi Vanye i Chya. Nhi Vanye, if you please."

"My lord," Vanye said. To say something seemed incumbent on him, when the image turned its cold eyes in his direction and the face seemed to gaze straight at him. He was in danger. He knew beyond a doubt that he was in peril of his life, only for being human, and for standing where he stood, and for more than that: it was the look a man gave a man where a woman was in question—and blood was.

The glass-gray stare passed from him and turned slowly to the others, and back again to Morgaine.

"Why have you come?"

"Why should I not?" Morgaine said. "I take my father's lesson, who found one world and a succession of worlds—far too small for him. *That* was Anjhurin." She leaned back, posing the chair on its rearmost legs, and stared up at the image. "From all you say, you have arrived at the same place as he—you have wielded power over world and world and world—am I right? And you have found this world much the same as the last."

"And the one before," Skarrin said. "And before that. You are young."

"As you see me."

"Very young," Skarrin said softly, this young man with gray, gentle eyes.

"You knew Anjhurin," Morgaine said.

"A very, very long time ago." The image became merely a face, drifting in the shadow, a handsome face, with Morgaine's own look, so like her among qhal it might have been a brother. "Anjhurin dead! Worlds should shake."

"They have," Morgaine said softly. "And things *change*, my lord of dust and stability. You do not love your life. Come risk it with me. Come join me."

"To what purpose?"

"The changing of worlds, my lord, change that sweeps through space and time."

"Even this, I have seen. I have ties in many ages, many worlds. I will survive even the next calamity. What new can you offer me?"

"Have you *risked* that hope, elder cousin? It is risk makes immortality bearable—to know that personal calamity is possible, oh, very possible, and tranquility, what time it exists, is precious. Anjhurin is dead. Does that not tell you that fatality is possible? Come with me. There are worlds full of chances."

"Full of cattle. Full of same choices and same tragedies and same small hearts and smaller minds which lead to them. Full of stale poets who think their ideas are a towering novelty in the cosmos. Full of rebels who think they can change worlds for the better and murderers who see no further than the selfish moment. Mostly, full of cattle, content with their mouthful of grass and their little herd and endless procreation of other cattle. And we are finite, calamity endlessly regenerate, disaster in a bubble. One day it will burst of sheer tedium. And the universe will never notice."

"No," Morgaine said, and reached and took Vanye by the arm, drawing him to the table edge. "I have news to give you, my lord. *Qhal* reached outside. They stole *his* ancestors in real-space, and his cousins voyage there, *not* with the gates, *not* within them so far as they know—"

"It will not save them."

"No. But they are widening the bubble, my lord who sees no change. They are involving all who meet them—and all who meet their allies. Do you see, my lord of shadows? There *is* chance and change. *His* kind—humankind—have realized the trap. They have refused it. More, they have set out to prick the bubble themselves."

There was long silence.

"It would doom them," Skarrin said.

"Perhaps. *Their* threads reach far beyond their own world, but they were not that deeply entangled."

"If they have taken it on themselves to do this, by that very act they are entangled."

"And they know *other* races who know others still."

Vanye listened through that silence, his heart beating harder and harder. Morgaine's light hand upon his elbow held him fast, by oath and by the surety that somewhere in this exchange he had become all humanity, and that existence was the prize of this struggle—*What must I do, what must I say, what is she telling him—of threads and bubbles?*

This man can kill us all. He has stripped this house of its servants, its goods, its cattle. He has destroyed them or he has sent them through the gate before him—and means to follow.

—Humankind—has refused the trap.

What is she telling him?

"Change," Morgaine said, "is very possible. That is the work I do."

"And *this*—for heir," Skarrin said. "This for companion. His get—for inheritors."

"Come with me," Morgaine said, "down the thread that leads to infinity. Or bind yourself more and more irrevocably to the one you have followed thus far. Eventually change *may* become impossible. But you will not find it inside the patterns; you find it linked to these—to qhal, and to humankind. And to *me,* lord Skarrin, and to those with me."

"So I should serve your purposes."

"Follow your own. Did I ever say I wished to share more than a road and the pleasure of your company? We will bid one another farewell—in time, in time I cannot predict, my lord Skarrin, nor can you. That is *chance,* my lord Skarrin. Have you grown too attached to this age and to what is? Have you found your own end of time, and are you content with solitude among your subjects—or do I tempt you?"

"You tempt me."

"We have a horse to spare." She held Vanye's arm the tighter, and laughed softly. "What want you, an entourage, a clutter of servants, lord Skarrin? I have my few, who will serve you the same as me. A horse, a bedroll, and the sky overhead—your bones are still young, and your heart is not that cold. Come and learn what a younger generation has learned."

The image smiled, slowly and fondly. "Was Anjhurin—fate's way of creating you—who see no wider than that?"

"Perhaps that is all there is worthwhile, my lord kinsman. *Freedom.*"

"Freedom! Oh, young cousin, lady, you mistake the roof for the sky. We are prisoners, all. *Inside* the bubble we work what we will and we shift and change. The gates end and the gates begin. And all the hope you bring me is that the contagion is spreading and the bubble widens. Is *that* cause to hope? I think not. In the wide universe we are still without significance."

"You are melancholy, my lord of shadows."

"I am a god. The cattle have made me so." There came laughter, soft and terrible. "Tell me, is that not cause for melancholy?"

"They name me Death. Is it not reasonable that I am the youngest of us, and the most cheerful?" Again she laughed, and stood and leaned against Vanye's shoulder, clasping his arm. "Few of humankind love me. But, lord of shadows, I shall live longest, and so will those who ride with me. It is helpers I seek. Come ride the wave with me, down to the last shore. Or do you want eternity in Mante, with shapes of your own devising, in a world of your own making? Another stone palace and more worshippers? Come, let us see if we can shake the worlds."

The image faded abruptly to dark. The hall was very still, except the random shift of a horse's foot, which rang like doom on the pavings.

"What are you saying?" Chei asked, suddenly breaking that peace. "What *are* you, what are you talking about—waves and shores? Who *are* you?"

"I have said," Morgaine said quietly, and her hand never left Vanye's shoulder, a calming touch. If it had not been there he would have reached for a weapon for comfort. It was; and he felt himself numb like a bird in the eye of the serpent—not afraid, not capable, he thought, of fear at all any longer. He knew her lies, even when they were told with the truth. Even when they were entirely the truth. He trusted. That was all there was left to do.

"Perhaps you can flee," Morgaine said to the others. "It seems likely. I do not think he will trouble himself with you."

Rhanin edged away. And stopped, as if he did not know what to do, or as if he had expected the others would, or as if he had had second thoughts. He only stood there.

Then distantly, softly echoing, came footsteps in the corridors.

This time, Vanye thought, it was substance which came to them; it was substance which appeared in the shadows of the corridor which let into this hall.

It was Skarrin himself who walked out into the light which was always available in such places, that power drawn of gate-force, come full in the room.

"My lady of mysteries," Skarrin said, halted there in that entry. "Am I in truth welcome?"

"Oh, indeed," Morgaine said in a still, hushed voice. "Good day to you, shadow-lord." She walked a few paces closer, and stopped, and Vanye stood with a shiver running through his limbs, a twitch that was the impulse to follow her, stay with her instantly; but that was a fool's move, to show hostility to this lord, and useless. He watched Morgaine stop and stand, hands on hips, head tilted cheerfully. "You are smaller than I thought."

For the least instant he frowned, then laughed in offended surprise. "We are well-matched." His gaze swept the room. "And this, the company you ask me to keep. You—Man. Come here."

Vanye's heart turned over. He measured the separation between him and Morgaine and between him and Skarrin with a nervous sweep of his eye, and used that small chance to bring himself even with Morgaine.

"I take my lady's orders," he said as mildly as he could, while his heart beat in panic.

"Defiance from a human?"

"From *me*," Morgaine said, and walked a little forward, to stop again with hand on hip. "Not that I am discourteous, my lord, but I do not lend my servants; I will reckon you have your own, and I will trust there are loyal folk among them. Or has this kingship of yours gotten too old and the intrigues too many? Or have you ceased to care? My folk will serve you. Bring your own servants—I care not, only so they are strong enough to last the course and honest enough to guard our backs. Let us set the gate and quit this tedious place. Keep to my path a while. I shall at very least value your company—and your advice. I am, after all, youngest. You can teach me—very much. And I can teach *you,* lord of dusty Mante—that there are new things under new suns. *I* am sufficient guarantee of that."

"You are arrogant."

"So I am told." She walked two paces forward and stood wide-legged. "I am terminus. And perhaps I am inception. Time will prove that. My origin is very recent as you measure time. I have never existed until now."

"As you dream—you have not existed."

"I am *Anjhurin's* daughter, Anjhurin who claimed to have seen the calamity. Think of *that,* my lord. And my mother came down a thread he had never known, that one which leads to stars outside, my lord. By seizing *that* he hoped to widen his power. But causality doomed him. He used force. She despised him. So, my lord, did I. And I destroyed him."

"You."

"With a will, my lord. All of Anjhurin's causality rests in *me.* That is my weight in the web of time—the youngest and the oldest of us, in one, and *I* reach outside. In me, every causality meets."

Skarrin backed a pace.

She lifted her hand so naturally and so quickly the red fire had touched the lord before Vanye could both realize the weapon was in her hand and draw in his breath.

"I cannot *die*—!" Skarrin cried; as a second time the red light touched him, from Morgaine's hand, amid the forehead: he fell with a horrified expression.

Die . . . die . . . die . . . the walls and the vaulted
ceiling gave back. They echoed the heavy fall of
Skarrin's body, and the nervous shifting of the horses.

Vanye caught his breath, shaken in every bone, not
believing it had been so sudden or so without warning.

And knowing then by the dread in Morgaine's face
as she turned that it was not over. It was far from
over. It was wizardry they fought, whatever Morgaine
named it; wizardry that could knit bone and heal flesh
and put blood back in veins—and his liege's face was
pale and desperate. "Follow me!" she cried, and ran
toward the dark of the corridor.

Chapter Nineteen

Vanye ran, sword in hand, abandoning everything to Chei and his comrades—ran with a desperate burst of speed to close the gap between himself and Morgaine as she headed alone toward the corridor inward.

He heard someone behind him then, and spun to a halt and saw Chei and the other two coming. "Watch the horses!" he shouted at them, not wanting them at his liege's back, not wanting the horses unguarded either.

Then he raced after Morgaine, reaching the corner an instant after her—the corridor ahead filled at short range with a double rank of drawn bows and loosed arrows.

He hit her from behind in utter panic—that quickly the arrows flew and he fell to the floor atop her, did not think, except they were both like to die here, did not know what he did, except that the enemy had to nock their next arrows and he was already rolling toward them, onto his feet and toward them with a Kurshin yell—"Haaaaaiiiiiiii——Haiii!"—hurtling for the flank of their double line with sword swinging even while they were thinking some of them to shoot him and some nearest him to parry him with bowstaves and daggers.

The curved blade swept along the parry of a bowstaff and, skidding off it, came around into an unprotected arm and neck, and he laid about him left and right and round about without time to see where attack was coming from until it came within his circle, and then he killed it, with sword in his right hand and then Honor-blade in the left, for what came at him too close.

A blade scored his armor at his back; he gained room with the Honor-blade, and followed with a sword-stroke. A bow whistled round toward his head; he ducked under it, stabbed under a rash fool's chin, as some fallen enemy groped after a hold about his knees, raking the heavy leather and braces of his breeches and boots with a dagger stroke. He sprang aside from that, used his bow-arm bracer to counter a descending blade on one hand, clove a man's face horribly in a slash to the right and brought the blade back to deal with the return stroke on the left.

That enemy fell arrowshot through the neck, and he did not know where it had come from, except he saw the flash of red on a man's armor that meant Morgaine's weapon, and there were fewer and fewer enemies. He gasped for air and struck out, turning, sliding off a blade with his curved one to deal a man a blow that staggered him—hard effort then on the desperate one after, and on the parry he swept around to save his own skull. Steel rang on steel, bound and slipped as he made his sweep the faster, out of breath now, sight hazed and sweat streaming, on a carnage widening by the instant, red fire taking man after man. One man fled him; red flashed on his armor and he fell, screaming, on a heap of his comrades.

Others tried to surrender. Fire cut them down as they were halfway to their knees, and fire swept the wounded on the ground. *"Liyo!"* Vanye cried in consternation—but it was done, there were none alive as he staggered clear of the bodies and hit the wall with his back, gasping after air and gazing in horror on the slaughter.

Chei pulled his sword from a body and Hesiyyn and Rhanin stood back as Morgaine recovered herself, there at the edge of the carnage, the black weapon in her hand. *She will kill them too*, Vanye thought on the instant. There was no reason and no mercy on Morgaine's face.

Then she caught her breath and ran for the unde-fended door, opened it with quick passes of her hand on the studs which marked its center.

It gave back on hall and hall and hall brightly lighted, leading toward other doors.

"Hold here!" she cried. "All of you, hold the doors! Vanye—stay with them! Do not count Skarrin dead!"

She ran, before he could muster protest; and he thought then and knew he was guard of those who guarded them—to ward their retreat when it would surely be in haste.

"One of you," he shouted at Chei, "get down to the end of the hall and guard the horses!"

"Curse you, we are not your servants!"

"Dead men *have* no precedence! We are all in this, and likely to be stranded if we have no horses!"

"Rhanin!" Chei shouted, and Rhanin tucked his bow in hand and ran, vaulting dead men as he went.

That was the only one of them presently with other than a sword and dagger. Vanye longed for his own good bow, which he had left with Arrhan, and took a dead man's in its place, gathered up a quiver of arrows and slung it to his shoulder.

One arrow to the string, two others in his bow-hand. He tested the draw, and moved down to the intersection of the halls to set his shoulders against the wall where he had vantage of the right-hand corridor, while Chei took up a bow as well, and a quiver; and by the way he handled it, at least one part of him was no stranger to the weapon.

Morgaine's footfalls had died away in distance, within the farthest doorway, and he pressed his shoulders against the wall and watched, arms both at ease and ready on the instant, if there were any movement down the lighted corridor.

Such places he knew. There would be machines. There would be traps and such things as Morgaine dealt with better than ever he could in that room where she had gone, to deal with whatever Skarrin had done to the machines that controlled the gates. But he trembled as in winter cold, the reaction of muscles into which the bandages cut, and the fight which still had him drenched with sweat, and cooling now in the chill of Skarrin's keep. He blinked at the film on his eyes, shook his hair aside as it straggled into his face, his heart pounding in his chest with a kind of terror he had seldom felt in his life.

Qhalur enemies, he knew. Chei and Hesiyyn across the corridor from him made him anxious, no more than that. But this—

This man who knew the gates well enough to frighten Morgaine herself, whose mastery of them excelled hers—

What manner of enemy could die that death and not die, struck through the skull and through the heart?

Except there be witchcraft and sorcery which Morgaine denied existed.

But I am skilled in both. What matter it invokes no devils? I have met devils left and right in her service, and slain no few, except this last, that says he cannot die—

O Heaven, could we come so far and across so many years and fall to this, this creature, at the height of the sky, while so many men are surely going about their business in the town below, in all ignorance what passes here—if they are there—if the whole of that great city has not gone like the servants.

God deliver us. I do not know what more to do than stand here and guard her back.

Chei shivered, against the wall, looking toward that portion of hallway which was his to guard. Exhaustion ached in his knees and his gut and trembled in his hands. And the lady—

The lady had not killed them. That much they knew of her. Nothing more, that the boy had believed of her. *Nothing* more, except she was perilous as ever Skarrin was—more than perilous: murderous and hellbent and—which she had said—more than a match for any gate-warden.

Skarrin's match—that was very clear. Of Skarrin's disposition: that remained to be seen.

Across the hall, Hesiyyn, warding the other direction; and at the opposite corner, Vanye; and the slow minutes passed, while something happened in that room down the hall—the master boards for the gates of all the world: *that* was what Morgaine Anjhuran had her hand to, who had *defeated* Skarrin—that was the fact which could hardly take hold in a shaken mind: Skarrin, who had ruled in Mante from time out of mind, Skarrin, ever-young and ruling through proxies, but cruel beyond measure when some rebellion came nigh him—

Skarrin, around whom conspiracies and plots continually moved, like a play acted for his amusement—

Gone—in a lightning-stroke, the simple act of a woman who had not come to parley at all.

And at whose actions with the gate, in that room—sent the lights brightening and dimming as if all Neneinn were wounded.

"What is she doing?" Chei asked furiously. "What does she think to do?"

"What needs no hearers," Vanye returned shortly across span of the hall which divided them. "Trust her. If she wished you dead you would be dead with the rest."

"I have no doubt," Hesiyyn said, and tightened a buckle of his armor—wan and exhausted, Hesiyyn, as all of them, shadow-eyed and dusty. He took up his sword again from between his knees. "But whatever she is, she has done fairly by us, and that hound Skarrin is dead or dead as fire can make him." He made a kind of salute with the blade. "There is all I need know."

It was a desperate man, Hesiyyn who had no choices; and himself—himself with so much good and ill mixed in him of his varied lives that he could not see the world, either, in dark or light. And Nhi Vanye, who knew, with more confidence than either of them, where his loyalty belonged.

It was irony, Chei thought, with pain in his heart, that he, Qhiverin, found more and more reason to like this man, while the boy—the youth forgave him, *him*, Gault-Qhiverin, because of old betrayals and loss of

kin and things in which they fit together like blade and
sheath—never mind that some of those griefs had been
at Qhiverin's hand, Qhiverin's fault, in the bloody
deeds incumbent on a warden of the warlike South—
Qhiverin could find sympathy, Qhiverin could embrace and comfort Chei in his desolation. There *was*
no more war between them, except the boy would not
forgive, would not listen, would not reason—

—for too much self-blame lay within it.

Here is insanity, Chei thought in a heart-weary panic.
Peace, boy, or we both go under.

And the boy, who did not want to die: *He will kill
us if he can—finally, when we have done all they want,
one or the other of them will kill us. Knowledge was all
they ever wanted.*

Then they made a poor bargain, did they not? He wiped
tears from his eyes. *Boy, we will guard his back. You
are a fool, is all—a great fool. And would you had
never made him my enemy. Your brother would have
had more sense. It was yourself coming up on the
man's sword-side, it was Bron drove his horse between
to shy you off. That is the truth I remember.*

Liar!

*And your Gault, boy—your Gault the hero was a
traitor the same as Arunden. He would have sold you
all for his peace. Have you never known that? He
betrayed Ichandren before I did. I took him, yonder,
on that hill, because I had no choice. But ah, boy, he
was a scoundrel. Scoundrel and fool. What a legacy
you give me.*

What a cursed great—

Light and sound came from the room at the end of
the hall, where the lady had gone, a high thin moan
which no living throat could make, and a deep roaring
like thunder sustained.

"What is she *doing?*" Hesiyyn asked hoarsely, leaning against his wall. "Lord human—"

"I do not know," Vanye said, biting his lip, and
looked toward the door which lay open at the end,

where red light flashed, and the wailing grew. "Hold our retreat open!"

He ran. He trusted the men for what they might be worth and raced down the slick stone hall at all the speed he could manage, down the hall and through the gaping doors and into such a place as he had seen more than once in his travels—where light dyed everything the color of blood, and inhuman voices wailed and thundered and shrieked from overhead and all about.

"Liyo!" he shouted into that overpowering racket. *"Liyo!—"*

She turned, red-dyed with the light from silver hair to metal of her black armor, with the light flaring about her and behind her as the boards blinked alarm.

"He is not dead," she cried. "Vanye, he has stored his essence inside the gate—he is still alive, for the next poor soul that ventures that gate."

He tried to understand that. He stood there staring at her and thought it through twice and three times.

"For us," she shouted. "He has trapped us and I cannot dislodge him!—That is the wrongness we have felt in the gates—he has kept his pattern there continually, kept it bound to him, day and night—He will *take* the next living man that enters the World-gate! He will go through, he will be free, there is no way we can stop him!" She came to him and caught at his arm, turning him for the door, not running, but walking quickly, by which and by the flashing of the lights at their back and the uncomfortable prickling in the air, he knew that the gate of Mante was set on its own destruction, on some near time which—he hoped to Heaven—she had chosen. "He had a snare set that would have sealed the gate once he was free. I broke that lock easily enough. I set it to a new time, a few hours hence. I dare not leave it longer. There is too much knowledge in this place,—and the chance of someone re-opening it, except I build destruction into its pathways—that, I dare not risk."

It was old Kurshin she spoke, awkward in the things for which the qhalur language had ready words, which conjured the inner workings of the gates and the things she had showed him, how to redirect the power like damming one stream and opening another, to flood throughout the channels and destroy the means to reactivate it.

"I have set it to destroy the core-tap," she said in the qhalur tongue, meaning the line of power which ran from the earth's deep heart.

And everything round about it. Such a thing, she had told him—might cause havoc with a world, involving gate-force and the power in the earth itself. *I do not know what happens thereafter,* she had said. *No one comes through such a gate again— or any of the gates linked with it. It is no good thing for the world. And I would not willingly do it. Time itself closes in on a gate once it is shut. Ordinarily, time itself will destroy one as thoroughly in a few years without touching the core, and there is no need for such a catastrophe. And I do as little as I dare.*

He thought on the city spread about the hill of Neneinn, the countless lives, the city on the brink of a well only gate-force or cataclysm could have shaped; and his gut and his knees went to water.

It was a death-sentence. That was the wailing, that he had never heard, the threat to life all about this world's gates—Morund and Tejhos and Mante and wherever else gates had their veins of power sunk into this world's heart.

"How much time do we have?" he asked.

"Three hours," she said, qhalur-reckoning. He measured it against the daylight and the sun, Kurshin-fashion, and there was ice about his heart. "I dared not give it more time," she said. "This is a qhalur city. And there is the warden down at Seiyyin Neith, *if* he is still there and not fled with the rest—"

"One of his guards might solve matters for us," he said, reckoning—O Heaven, what was he become—to think cold-bloodedly where they should get a victim?

"We cannot know it if they do. Do not speak of it to our comrades. Does thee hear?"

He saw Chei and Hesiyyn waiting for them in at the intersection of the corridors, saw their anxious faces.

"Does thee hear?"

"Aye," he said, clutching the remnants of his soul to him; and no likelihood that fate would offer better.

Like the men who had surrendered; like the forty on the road; like the city spread below them, doomed with the gate, men and women and babes in cradle—

For the sake of all the worlds, she told him. *All* the worlds was too large a thing for a man's heart to understand, when it was the one under his feet and the lives around him and the murder and the choices were his.

Not tell them—not offer even the chance to choose or to fight—

"Come," she said to Chei and Hesiyyn, gathering them up as they strode along toward the hall where they had left the horses and where Rhanin stood guard. "We are bound for the gate. Hurry. There is not that much time. I have set it to seal behind us and there will be no following after us."

They did not question. They kept pace with weapons still in their hands, and Chei whistled to Rhanin and called to him as they came into the hall.

"We are bound for the gate," Chei told Rhanin as the archer lowered his bow and met them there, where he had herded the horses into a corner of the hall. "Quickly. Come, man. The lady is keeping her promises."

But from Rhanin there was no such eagerness. "My lord Chei," he said. "My lady—I have a wife—"

O Heaven, Vanye thought.

"—I beg your leave," Rhanin said. "Let me go bring her."

Chei looked to Morgaine.

"No," Morgaine said. "There is no time. That gate will *seal,* and there will be no more passages; and if we do not get there in time, there will be none for us."

"How long?" Chei asked.

"An hour," Morgaine said. "Perhaps. Skarrin has done damage I cannot correct. We have no *time,* man,

and your lord has need of you and I do—where we go
is no place for a hallbred woman. A hard trail and a
long one in sun and storm and lightning; and war,
man, that I can promise you. Come with your lord,
and hurry about it."

"I cannot." There was torment in Rhanin's brown
eyes. "Lord Chei—I cannot leave her."

He turned and went to the horses. Morgaine lifted
the black weapon in threat. "Stop!" she cried; and:
"My lady!" Chei exclaimed.

Rhanin stopped, but he did not turn. After a few
heartbeats he started walking again.

Morgaine let fall her hand. She stood in silence as
Rhanin mounted up. "Fare well," she said quietly
then. "Fare well, Rhanin."

Rhanin cut the tether of the remount he led, gave it
to Hesiyyn, and saluted his lord and the rest of them,
before he swung up to the saddle and rode, black
shadow against the light, for the stable-court and the
city below.

"Mount up!" Morgaine bade them.

Vanye swallowed against the knot in his throat and
went first for Siptah's reins, to bring the gray horse to
his liege while the others sought their own. He held
her stirrup for her. He did not look in her eyes. She
did not, for all he knew, try to meet his.

She said no word at all, nor quarreled with him that
he did her these courtesies.

He must, he thought. He had no words to tell her
he was with her.

He felt the shorn hair about face and neck, and it
seemed apt, of a sudden, the felon's mark, the mark
of an honorless man, penance for Mante, for Rhanin
and his wife, for lies and for murder yet to do.

Honest men, Morgaine had said, must fight us. Brave
men must.

"We have to *find* the way out in this warren,"
Morgaine said shortly. "And hope the stable court
leads to some road up the hill—"

"No need to search for it," Chei said, drawing his
horse alongside in the hall. "There is a way from the

stable court. *Gault's* memory is clear enough on that. I came up from the city—but Gault was here. Follow me."

It was leftward Chei led, beyond the fountain. The blaze-faced bay lipped up some meager spillage of grain on the dirt by the stables nearby: "I will get him," Vanye said, distractedly—to leave the poor brave beast to Mante's fate seemed impossible to him, was, at least, one death he could prevent. He rode wide of the group, leaned from his saddle and snagged the reins that had fallen as the animal lowered his head. It did not want to come. It jolted his arm, then surrendered, of habit, perhaps, and followed.

He overtook the others before they had gotten to the stable-gate, never having taken his eyes off them, and Morgaine acknowledged the rescue with a worried frown, a flicker of the eyes which understood him entirely, as Chei got down from his horse and pushed at the latch. "Let it free outside," she said. "It will balk at the gate. We cannot afford difficulties."

It was true. He knew that it was. He held onto the reins as the stable-gate swung wide on a long colonnade, and Chei mounted up again. He drew the horse along with them as they rode that long course to a second gate, the latch of which was high enough for Chei to trip from horseback; and that gate opened out on a road and a barren hill, where standing stones made an aisle leading upward.

"At least the saddle," he said, then, outside; and slid down while the whole company waited, and hastily loosed the bay's girth and tumbled the saddle off; unbuckled the bridle and threw it away, and sent the confused horse off with a hard slap on the rump. He did the same for the horse Hesiyyn led, then, and sent it off after its fellow.

He came close to tears, then. He turned and flung himself to the saddle, and swallowed down that impulse.

Fool, he told himself, to weep for a pair of horses, when there is so much else we do. It belongs to this world, that is all.

And there may indeed be trouble—at the Gate.

O *God,* are we right? If only I knew that we were right.

He kept close at Morgaine's side as they struck out up the road which wound about the rocky hill, Chei and Hesiyyn close on his left.

"A great many horses," Hesiyyn said, of the trampled ground ahead of them, of the sparse brush about them, that was broken and trodden down.

"Everyone in Neneinn," Chei said.

But not, Vanye thought, heart-heavy, *not enough for all of Mante. There is no escape for them.*

He thought that if he turned, high as they climbed now, he could truly see a wondrous sight, a vantage over all Mante, over Neisyrrn Neith and Seiyyin Neith and perhaps the plains and the hills beyond, to all the distance a clear day would afford them.

But the sight of him would haunt him. *I do not look back,* Morgaine was wont to say; and he clung to that wisdom now: once through the world on a single track, a single purpose, without touching more lives than they must.

Too much knowledge here: he understood that. It had been unconscionable hazard to have left his own cousin near a faded gate, except there were warders to prevent him coming near it until it was dead beyond recall.

Here—there were no warders they could trust: a corrupt gate-warden and a twisted gate, and all too many who would rush to enliven the gate and seize power for themselves—not Skarrin's measure, it was sure, but equally deadly, in the affairs of worlds and stars and suns which Morgaine understood, and which he did not.

Now he wept over two doomed horses, and longed with all his heart for enemies.

But none presented themselves, and the storm-sense grew in the air, making the hair prickle. Arrhan side-stepped and worked at the bit, so ready to run she hardly seemed to walk on the earth; and the rest of the horses rolled their eyes and threw their heads, snorting their dislike of the place.

Skarrin's presence—a man warded from assassination and accidents because he had stored—whatever of him mattered, in such fashion that the ordinary traffic of the gates would deliver him a host virtually instantly, were it ever needed: different than qhalur knowledge, Morgaine had said.

Different—root and branch.

My father's legacy, Morgaine had said.

And called Skarrin kinsman—whatever Skarrin's true name was.

Or hers.

The great Gate came slowly from the unfolding of the hill, the screening of the standing stones—a towering arch of stone, within which the blue sky shimmered like fever-vision. Hesiyyn's horse fought the bit wild-eyed, and the red roan Chei rode threw his head and fretted in distress; but Siptah went with his ears laid flat and pricked up by turns, trying to get rein to go, knowing where he was bound, what he must do, and all too anxious to make that jump, till Morgaine reined him down and patted his shoulder.

Closer and closer then, at a careful pace. There were no enemies at hand. They were alone at the height, on this Road which led to a place where the very air had sound and substance; and smaller sounds, those of hoof and harness, lost themselves.

"You can see the city," Hesiyyn said, looking over his shoulder.

"Goodbye to it," Chei said and seemed lost already in the Gate's spell.

They had reached the last of the road. After this it was the barren, rocky slope leading to the Gate itself, tracked and scarred with hundreds of feet, with the hooves of horses, the wheels of wagons; and here Morgaine drew rein.

"Go through," she bade Chei and Hesiyyn with a wave of her arm. "I have yet something to see to from this side. I will overtake you, have no fear of it."

Chei drew up on his reins and used his heels, for the

red roan fought to turn away, and Hesiyyn circled his horse to distract it from full flight.

"Rhanin," Chei said.

"The gate will give no warning when it seals. There is no time! If he comes, he comes. We cannot wait for him. Go through!"

Chei reined hard over and about again, holding the roan as it fought to get the bit. There was a frown on his face. He looked at Vanye then, full at him, and Vanye held his breath as Chei turned the horse yet again.

And back again, hard-reining it. This time as he came about, it was a wary look, a more and more misgiving look.

"Like the horses, is it? Send us through—*first?*"

"That you go at all is my lady's gift!" Vanye shouted at him. Gate-force oppressed the air, like impending storm. Hair crackled and metal stung when the hand brushed it, as he felt after his sword-hilt. "Go through!"

Chei's hand went to his own hilt; and in the same instant he cast a sudden and wide-eyed look toward Morgaine, toward a threat far more substantial than steel.

"My lord," Hesiyyn said anxiously, fighting his horse steady. "My lord, likely it is safe. The lady has—"

"—set the gate herself," Chei said; and looked her direction; and Vanye's, slowly, with a hard hand on the reins. "Is that it? Is it a trap, eh?"

"She set no trap," Vanye said.

"No?" There was long silence. "Then it is his you suspect. Is it not? *Is it not?*"

Vanye said nothing at all. He could think of nothing to say.

"Oh, my friend," Chei said quietly. "What are you prepared to do? Threaten us with death—to make us risk that?"

"Death is not a risk here," Morgaine said. "It is a certainty. *There,* in the gate, is the only doubt. Take it."

"Or you will kill us. What good are we then?" Again Chei turned the horse about, and drew it in with a hard hand. "How will you know? How will you ever know that it is safe?"

"The risk is to one," Morgaine said. "That is the truth. And it will not be myself; and it will not be Vanye. I promise you that." She lifted her hand. *"This* need not kill."

Chei stared at her, very long. Then he looked, slowly, toward Vanye.

"Forgive her," Vanye said. "She has no choice."

"Not forgive *you?"*

"She has no choice. I have. And for her sake—I cannot take it. I cannot even offer you fair fight."

"It is not any grudge. Is it?"

"No, my lord. Not in this. Skarrin is waiting—within the gate. We could not dislodge him. That is the truth. That is the trap. One of us—will host our enemy."

Chei laughed—laughed, shortly and silently; and laughed a second time, reining the red horse about yet again. "He would. He would, the bastard. *That* was what he meant."

"That was what he meant."

A third laugh, shortest of all. "The boy urges me there is a logic in this. He has had his revenge. He confuses me. He urges me—we are best suited to this fight. It is his revenge on me. Or mine on him. *Damn you to hell, boy!* Damn you and all your choices! —Hesiyyn." He took up on the reins, turning aside. "Hesiyyn!"

"No, my lord!" Hesiyyn cried, and rode his horse across Chei's path.

"I will race you for it," Chei said, and cracked the rein ends down on the roan and drove with his heels. The red horse went, as Hesiyyn fought the bay about and into a run. "Let *him* choose!"

The gate took them. One—and the other. Hesiyyn did not slow at all.

Vanye shut his eyes, and rested so, a long, long moment, till he heard Morgaine ride up beside him, until living warmth brushed against him. He looked then, at the vacant gate that loomed above them, with blue sky shimmering again where dark had showed for an instant.

"It is safe now," she said, and reached and rested her hand on his arm.

"It was Chei and Qhiverin," he said then. He was trembling, as if the gate-cold had gotten to his bones. "Skarrin—is their enemy. And Hesiyyn's. But Chei is overmatched. Both of them—are overmatched."

"Skarrin has had only one body," Morgaine said.

He looked toward her then.

"Chei was right," Morgaine said, "altogether right. They are peculiarly apt for that fight. And Skarrin is their enemy." Her fingers tightened. "We have given them such as we could. It is all the charity we have. Nhi Vanye—"

There were tears in her voice finally. He was glad of that. Her burden was absolute, and older; and that she still could weep—gave him hope for himself, in such a time, after so many journeys.

He took her hand in his and held it till the horses moved apart, fingertip parting from fingertip. Siptah was bound for the gate. Arrhan followed, of her own accord.

Gray horse and white. Dark rider and light. There was no knowing where they were bound, except they went together.

DAW

SCIENCE FICTION MASTERWORKS FROM
THE INCOMPARABLE
C.J. CHERRYH